THE CHRONICLES
OF
SIR JOAN
And her friend Michelle

BY
DANIEL COTTLE

To Paul —
who might recognize
some of these places —

Dedicated to my students past and present, who gave me their encouragement and inspiration for this book.

Special thanks to **the real Michelle** who gave me inspiration for the character and was an invaluable help in the formation of this book, to my 2016-2017 Fifth Grade Students who gave unselfishly of their time to proofread and provide input on this book, and for all others who gave of their time and interest.

Published by Old Lee Music LLC
3509 Queen Anne Drive
Fairfax, Virginia 22030

First Edition
d

The match begins. Her opponent walks to the box, taking his place at his end of the track. Joan goes to her own spot but it is these first steps that begin to unnerve her opponent, for in his eyes they are like those of a stalking panther before the kill. The ten thousand hours of practice are first revealed, the repetition almost past memory, as Joan smiles, nods or shakes hands, and with a snap of her head closes her face guard. The opponent can no longer see through the mesh but he knows the eyes are brave and confident.

He begins his attack like he always has, and since she has seen and mapped his every move like a chess master seeing eight, ten moves ahead, his attack fails and the tip of her foil is on his chest. One-zero. By now he is angry and attacks again, but she already knows how he thinks and it's like he announced it to her out loud so that one minute later it's all over at five-zero. How does it feel to compete against someone who dematerializes long enough to score her point and then stands there smiling?

Now it's your turn, and she's as cool as a cucumber while the sweat is already starting to trickle down your back. You glance over at your friends and they're not even watching you, they're watching her, and you realize it's because they can see the future. That future, well, it ain't got you in it, brother, except maybe a certificate of participation saying you just showed up, instead of a trophy earned after practicing three hours a day for two years.

In two minutes – or less if you were dumb enough to be in a hurry - it's five-zero, she lifts her visor and shakes your hand. For the first time you realize the eyes are beautiful and intelligent, but a moment later she nods and takes one step and suddenly she's the panther after the kill. Eventually you realize that lots of others have also provided food for this panther, and in a while you will get to watch her next opponent get devoured.

In the wee hours of the night ahead, the vanquished are asleep and dreaming. In the imaginations of anyone who ever put on fencing gear, they see themselves wielding a real sword and wearing real armor while vanquishing a fierce opponent. But for many of those dreamers that opponent is a girl, her face framed by black hair, those beautiful eyes looking for a place to skewer you.

Chapter One
Beginnings

Joan

It's not every day you read about a high school girl who was in a real sword fight with her principal, but things didn't always go the way I planned. Lots of things happened that I wasn't expecting. Some are good, like meeting Michelle and finding out I had a best friend, or meeting Dwight's grandpa for the first time and learning that I'm alive because of him. Or bad, like kissing Mama good bye for what is supposed to be a three-day trip and finding out two days later that she's dead. Somewhere, there has to be a reason for all these things happening.

We were a happy family, Mama and Papa and me. Papa is a professor of Archaeology, and Mama is ...was... a lady he met in France. They met while Papa was working on an archaeological dig and Mama was home from her University in Paris. They hit it off right away, got married, and I was born in Mama's village of Domremy la Pucelle nine and a half months later. During most of the year we lived in the United States, but every summer we went back to France to stay with Grandmother Jeanne.

I spoke French with Grandmother and everyone else in the village, but when Papa was at home Mama spoke to me only in English. Papa could speak French perfectly well but they both wanted me to grow up knowing both languages. I can switch back and forth between French and English with no problem, but some people say that now and then I speak English with a touch of a French accent, or vice versa. Since Papa always joined us in August, by the time we were on our way back to the US I had learned how to speak English again.

When I was three I started going to a summer preschool in Domremy and although I could sit and listen and play with the other kids I was still shy. For

2

When I was three I started going to a summer preschool in Domremy and although I could sit and listen and play with the other kids I was still shy. For some of the kids, there were a few tears at first but that made everybody freak out. I sure didn't want that attention, so I learned that if I smiled and shook my head yes or no, people would smile back at me and leave me alone.

One day I was at school after having slept fourteen hours the night before, so I was completely awake when everybody was supposed to lie down for a nap. They got out a bunch of little cots, turned down the lights, and put on some quiet music so that before long everybody was asleep. Except for me, that is. Instead of making me sleepy, the music was annoying and I was lying there wide awake.

My cot was all in a corner behind a low bookshelf, and I saw that if I moved about six inches further back nobody could see what I was doing.

After I moved, I saw a big plastic box on the bottom shelf. Legos! Their color in the dim light reminded me of the church across the street from Grandmother's house, so I made a private work area for myself and got started. With some experimenting, I figured out that they stuck together different ways, and if you added more it made something bigger, and my little corner was becoming a church like Grandmother's. Before long, there were four walls, a bell tower, and the big front door where Father Andre would greet us after Mass and pat me on the head before I went home to take a nap. Just thinking about a nap made me yawn, so I curled up around that little church and fell fast asleep.

"Jeannette?" a gentle voice said from somewhere above me, and I knew it was Mama and opened my eyes. I felt something under my hand and realized I was still hugging the church, so I slowly untangled myself and sat up.

"Bonjour, Mama," I said, rubbing my eyes. Madame Jobert was standing with Mama and giving me the strangest look. I was still not completely awake but something didn't feel right, so I looked down at the church and back up at Mama. I guess these things were special and I didn't ask permission or anything. Oops. "I'm sorry, Mama."

"No, no, Jeannette, you have done nothing wrong," said Mama in the special way she had, so I relaxed. "Where did you find the little church?"

"I made it," I said, and pointed to the box still half full of Legos.

"The church," Mama replied softly. "It's...exact. The proportions, the windows, the doors – everything. Jeanette – I want to speak with Madame Jobert for a moment. Don't worry, you are not in any trouble, not at all." It was great that Mama said that to make sure that I didn't have to worry. They brought a laptop computer back over to the corner and looked up a picture of the church, then down at my Lego church on the floor, then back at the screen while they gently moved my church around so they could see the sides.

"How did you make it?" Mama asked.

I shrugged. "I had a picture in my head, so I put together Legos until it looked the same."

Mama smiled at me, but it was different now. It was loving of course, and cheerful, yes, but something else was in it, something brand new. When we left school that day for the walk home, we did not turn left by the bakery where we usually did but kept on down the road toward the river.

"Mama, this is the wrong way," I said hesitantly.

"We are going a different way today," she said, "somewhere special. Is that all right?"

No kid could ever turn down an invitation like that, usually because there is something that tastes good at the end of it. The path led past the end of the road and down a gentle slope to the river where there were lots of places to picnic or go fishing. The grass was long and soft, and as we walked down the path grasshoppers, dragonflies and a few quail were startled and whirred away. There was a pasture with cows grazing, and soon the path led to a space under a huge old tree with thousands of long, slender branches that drooped all the way to the ground. It was cool and quiet, a natural canopy overhead tinted with pale yellow and green as the sun filtered through.

Mama studied the tree for a moment, then reached up and gently broke off two of the long branches, stripped off the leaves and taking hold of the thicker end waved each of them tentatively up and down. Free of their leaves they made a swishing sound through the air, able to move much faster now. She pinched both to the same length, swished them once more, and beckoned me over to her side.

"We are going to start special lessons today," she said, and I could tell from the serious sound in her voice that I needed to listen and not just go somewhere and play.

"Lessons in…what, Mama?" I looked around. "Where are the books?"

Mama laughed. "There are many, many lessons that are not in books, Jeannette," she replied, using her special name for when she was very happy. She took one of the sticks and handed it to me. "Take this branch in your hand and hold it very still. I want you to do exactly as I say, and sometimes exactly as I do. Right now, I want you to find a good place to sit and watch. "

My life changed a lot after we started practicing every day, and I still laugh when I hear kids complaining about having an hour or two of homework. That first day Mama and I practiced for two hours, then the next week it was three hours every day including Saturdays and Sundays. During each practice, she was teaching me a sword dance where we moved up, down, right, left, legs and arms moving according to a specific pattern. Before long Mama and I could do it side by side and it was like I was the little mirror to her big mirror.

Some people say it's crazy to spend that much time with a little kid since they can't pay attention very long, but I don't ever remember being bored. Sure, I got tired and grouchy now and then, but it was also fun and interesting and most important it was time for Mama and me. I now know that it's only through practice that you get better at something, and when you steadily get better at something, you start to internalize it, and once you internalize it, you have it forever. If you keep practicing, that is.

If you have this mental picture of an adorable little girl with a fencing foil in her hand, then you have another thing coming. Not that I wasn't an adorable little girl, but it's difficult to reconcile being an adorable little girl and having such a bad temper. There was so much to learn, from hand and arm and wrist and foot positions to practices without any weapon in my hand at all, and it was all hard and complicated.

One time I kept getting touches from Mama's foil and the more it happened the madder I got. I was about to lose my temper when Mama seemed to trip, I lunged forward, and in a moment found myself flat on my face. Mama bent down and helped me to my feet, and I stood there feeling like an idiot.

"Why are you angry?" she asked.

"Because you're getting all the touches," I answered.

"And did it help to be angry?"

"No, it didn't."

"Jeannette, you thought I made a mistake so for one quick second you didn't watch me but bored right in and did exactly what I wanted you to do. You need to remember that a great fencer will beat her opponent far more with her mind than with her weapon. There will always be those who are bigger than you, faster than you and assume they have more tricks up their sleeves than you do. That is their greatest weakness, for then they will be arrogant and sure they will win, and it only follows that they will then become careless. If you learn to read your opponent, to get into his mind, you will wait for when the arrogance takes over and that is when you win."

"How do I learn that?" I said and felt even more stupid for having asked the question because I already knew the answer. "Lesson number one," I said before Mama could continue, "don't ask a question when you already know the answer."

Mama laughed. "Touché, Jeannette. Now I will teach you exactly what we did together."

That was a great lesson and it is amazing how true it has been over the years. I get into my gear at a tournament and there is my opponent who looks at me . and says to himself, I am bigger, I am faster, I am stronger than you and anyway you are only a girl, so prepare to lose. I smile back, only my eyes are zeroed in on his every move. If they are normal they're not paying attention so it's a total surprise when it's all over in two minutes.

I was five when we moved to Williamsburg and all I remember is a lot of packing, a long trip, and then finally getting to our new house. Mama and I kept up our fencing practices, and it got easier and easier for me until it was a regular part of our daily routine. Sometimes Papa would sit with a glass of wine after he came home from work and watch us, laughing when he knew I was getting mad and clenching my fists to calm down like Mama taught me.

When I was seven I finally got to be in my first tournament, but instead of hanging around with the other kids Mama insisted that I get out my notebook and take notes as I watched the matches of everyone I was going to face. By the end of the day, my notebook got to be half full of observations, everybody had his or her own page, and on the way home Mama and I would discuss what I wrote. After some practice, I could watch how an opponent moved and file that away in my head. I lost some matches at first, but as I learned how to observe my opponents I started to win.

By the time I turned twelve, I was going to three or four events every month and had won enough to qualify for the State Tournament. Since the Tournament was the first Sunday afternoon in December, I'd been practicing extra hard that fall and was all excited to go. We went ahead and registered, but the Monday before the tournament Mama found out she had to go to Paris for some emergency. Before she left, we checked out the calendar together and saw that with luck she would be back by Saturday, so until then I would make sure to practice on my own.

I worked hard for three days and on Friday evening I got my gear all set so I would be ready to go when Mama got back. As I was saying goodnight to Papa, the front doorbell rang and Papa went to answer it, except it wasn't Mama because I heard Papa talking to somebody with a deep voice. I saw two men in dark blue suits talking quietly to Papa, who was standing frozen by the door.

"Papa?" I said from the top of the stairs.

He turned to face me and his cheeks were wet, and I collapsed right there on the top step like I was hit in the stomach.

And that's all I have to say about that right now.

Chapter Two
Moving and Friendship
Joan

We adjusted the best way we could, and every day the school bus dropped me off at the University so I could go up and wait in Papa's office. He has a big, old overstuffed leather chair that I adore, and if it's been an especially long day I would snuggle in and fall asleep. Sometimes we ate at home when I would make a few things that Mama taught me, but since it was always real lonely we went out to eat the rest of the time.

We decided to skip Christmas that year by going somewhere out of town, and for some reason, Papa picked New Orleans. It wasn't cold and I could use my French lots of places, and we also spent two whole days visiting a college over in East Texas where they wanted to meet with Papa about something. When we got back home, however, the house was so quiet that we dropped off our suitcases and went out.

Even though we ate in restaurants all the time, we didn't talk much, and especially we didn't talk about what happened...especially since I never did find out. There wasn't a funeral or visitors, or...anything. One day she was there, then...she wasn't. It was as if a door closed over the whole thing. Since I also saw how Papa hardly ever smiled anymore, I made it my job to do whatever I could to keep his spirits up. As time passed, I pushed it all to the back of my mind as best I could, and never asked what happened.

The rest of the school year passed uneventfully. After school was out I hung out in Papa's office and did a lot of reading while Papa taught Summer School. By the end of July, I began to suspect something was up when I saw that some of his bookshelves had been cleared off. After he finished teaching for the day Papa and I got into his car as usual, but when he drove right past our street I knew for sure that something was up. In our family, we would always go out to dinner when there was something for all of us to discuss so that by the time we got home whatever it was had been settled one way or another. He picked our favorite seafood restaurant and insisted on waiting until the actual dinner plates were put on the table before he would tell me what was going on. The restaurant was crowded that evening, which made talking a lot easier because we were surrounded by other people. I treated myself and ordered crab cakes, and Papa ordered a steak, something I had never seen him do before.

"So?" I asked, taking my first forkful and looking at him hopefully.

"Smithfield," he said. "Smithfield College. I've been offered Archaeology Department Chair. Full Professor."

Papa had been wanting something like this his whole life, so this was great news for him and something we could both celebrate. I gave him a huge hug and sat back down all excited.

"There's something else," he said. "You're going to Smithfield High School," and gave me that quiet expectant look that he always did when there was something special.

Wait a minute! "You said...*High School?* Like in High School, ninth to twelfth grade and all of that?" In case this sounds like a strange question, I'd like to remind you that I had just finished seventh grade and my thirteenth birthday was in two days.

"Yes, high school. You know your grades are good enough, you finished Algebra last year, you write as well as most adults, and you are bilingual so taking a language isn't a problem."

High school? Even though this hit me like a ton of bricks, I could tell Papa was waiting to see what I would say. We're in this together, I thought, and I've had tougher challenges than this one.

"Okay," I said. "I'm in. When do we move?"

"The day after tomorrow," he replied. "Seven o'clock in the morning."

Here's your hat, and what's your hurry? As it turned out I'd remember this conversation for a long time, especially my thinking that 'I've had tougher challenges than this one'. That would come back to haunt me with a vengeance.

Well, it's about time I get my own words in here, but I shouldn't complain. This book is mostly about Joan anyway, at least the first part, and she's lived in France and everything. Me, I have always lived in the United States although I've been to China about six times.

I'm thirteen years old, tall like a lot of other girls my age, and I have long black hair. I don't wear glasses, I read all the time, and I like to write which is one reason Joan is letting me do this in addition to the fact we are best friends. We have everything in common, Joan and I, like...we're both thirteen-year-old girls and new students beginning ninth grade, both of us have parents who are college professors, we both play instruments - so you see, and we have a LOT in common. What's more, she's extremely athletic, I'm...not, she speaks French and I speak Mandarin Chinese...

Okay, okay, we don't have *everything* in common, but we both like to talk and write and explore new things. Both of us also read all the time, and since it's not only dystopian novels but history and science and politics and everything we always have lots to talk about. Most importantly, Joan and I trust each other and together have been through some things you wouldn't believe.

I was born in Cambridge, Massachusetts, where Mom and Dad were both in graduate school at Harvard. They were both born in China and didn't meet and fall for each other until they got to University. Their families were nervous at first, but since they were both smart and getting Ph.D.'s as well as in love, they worked it all out and got married. After Mom graduated they moved to New York City where she worked at the UN as a translator while Papa did some research at Columbia University, and that's when I showed up. We lived in New York while I grew up, Mom walking me to school, translating for the day, and then taking me to the park on our way home. After a few years, my little brother came along, so along with everything else I am also a big sister. We speak Mandarin at home and I go to Chinese school on Sunday morning so there's my week.

When I'm at home I usually practice the piano or read, but one of my favorite activities is writing. It was something of a problem in elementary school when the teacher would ask for a story and I would stay up past midnight and turn in fourteen pages the next morning. I love to put together brand new stories, and when Joan first talked to me about this book I absolutely jumped at the chance.

But even though I love school it hasn't always loved me back. My teachers were great, most of them anyway, but there always seemed to be at least one kid in each class who gave me a hard time. I tried not to react every time something happened, but there were too many times I was thankful that the day was over.

And then it all changed. One day Mom came home and told me we were going to move, and I admit I was nervous about it. As a matter of fact, "YOU'VE GOT TO BE KIDDING ME!" was a more accurate way to describe how I felt. New York was home to me and I couldn't imagine living anywhere else. I sulked a lot while I was pretending to pack, but I also got to thinking. Yes, we lived in New York, but no, school wasn't great, I didn't have any good friends and I knew I missed that. It was a great opportunity since Mom was going to be a professor in the Modern Languages department and Dad was going to teach Asian History, but I still worried about it.

I finally figured out it was going to be okay after I heard that nobody could be a good writer unless they had experienced a real challenge. Heck, even though kids at school bugged me sometimes, my biggest real challenge was where to pile the books I was reading and on the challenge scale of one to ten, this was about a 1.0001. Since I was determined to be a writer, it looked like Fate had dropped this giant opportunity right in front of me and I'd be an idiot not to take it. Besides, Mom had already packed my laptop so if I was going to see it again I'd better hop in the taxi and I mean right now, young lady, the plane leaves in two hours. We arrived at the New Orleans airport and right away I could tell we weren't in Kansas anymore. Smithfield College sent a van for us and it was an interesting trip driving past swamps and more swamps and then it got hotter and this is ridiculous, why don't we please turn around the van and go back home? I woke up after we got to Smithfield and Mom was shaking my shoulder, so I looked out the window and there's our new house, our own house! It had a huge yard with beautiful big old trees and flower beds and looked enormous.

But for about one minute I missed our old place. Back in New York, we had a tiny apartment on the 43rd floor, my single bed almost fit into the closet they called a bedroom, and only one of us had to sit on the kitchen counter when we ate meals. In our new house, the kitchen was half the size of Grand Central Station and my bedroom was as big as our whole New York apartment. After the moving vans arrived the next day and moved in our things…well, let's say there was LOTS of room left, so for the next two weeks we made a bunch of visits to Ikea and flea markets and antique shops, and the house slowly started to fill up with furniture. For the first time in my life, I had enough bookshelf space, I had a great big desk for my computer and things I was working on, my clothes fit into a nice old antique dresser, and I could even put posters and things on the wall. It was great, and I started to spend each afternoon there getting things organized or relaxing. That's where I was a few days later, lying on the bed and reading when Mom came into the room.

"School registration today," she said. "Ten minutes."

Chapter Three
A New Best Friend
Joan

Me? High school? I only just turned thirteen, for crying out loud. What am I going to do? Everybody will be bigger than me and...well, they're going to be bigger than me.

We were going over to the school and register, and that morning at breakfast Papa could tell what I was thinking and told me not to worry. "Besides, you'll have a new friend at the high school," Papa said cryptically.

I turned and stared. "You pick now to tell me this?"

For the first time in weeks he grinned, and that made me feel so good I would have given anything to keep it going. He used to smile all the time and I missed that like I missed Mama, and the hundreds of things that people do that you don't notice or miss until they're gone. That started it, and I couldn't help it and a tear squeezed out of the corner of my eye, I couldn't turn quickly enough to hide it and Papa saw, and his grin vanished. I took two steps forward and hugged him, and he hugged me back, and after a minute I made coffee, pouring a cup for each of us.

"I was asking around at the University and found out that there are two new faculty members who have a daughter your age," Papa said, sipping his coffee. "I found out that she is also going to attend Smithfield High School, so I made a point of having lunch with them at the new faculty orientation and we actually hit it off. Dr. Marc Han will be teaching Asian History and Dr. Jin Han will teach Languages and Political Science."

"What about this daughter of theirs?" I asked.

"Her name is Michelle, she's very smart, and unlike someone I could mention she's also wasn't happy about moving or going to a new school."

"I didn't exactly say I wasn't happy..."

"AND from what they told me it sounds like she's a bit offbeat. She is also thirteen, her mind is very quick and she likes to tell puns and jokes like you. She also apparently had a bad experience at her last school so they are anxious for her to have a fresh start."

The old tired look had crept back into his eyes and I knew that one of the reasons he told me this was that he had the same worries about me. It was all set: I was going to go to Smithfield High School, get a new start as a freshman instead of going to eighth grade, and have a ready-made friend to hang out with. If I did my best, Papa would have one big thing less to worry about.

The high school was at the end of a long, curving driveway on top of a hill. Schools in this part of the country seem to have all the land in the world, and this one had so much grass I almost expected to see buffalo grazing out front. There was a covered entryway with parking nearby, and as we drove past it looking for a visitor's spot I saw the biggest pickup truck I had ever seen in my life. It was RED, it was BIG, and it shouted out that it was the biggest and reddest truck in the whole world, and don't you forget it! I felt sorry for our poor little 1996 Toyota Corolla as we drove past.

"So, that's the Principal?" said Papa, turning off the engine and pointing to the huge sign displayed prominently in front of the truck's parking space.

> **RESERVED PARKING**
> **MR. TODD ONLY**
> **ALL OTHERS TOWED**

"Well, it's not exactly the principal," I said. "But it's probably his truck." Papa looked at me. "Look on my works, ye Mighty, and despair."

I looked at him and when I said "that's a real cheerful thought for my first day," he threw back his head and laughed. If this is what it took for him to cheer up, I would gladly enter a new school every day of the week and twice on Sundays.

The office was down the hallway from the front door and past the longest trophy case I had ever seen. There were trophies going back at least thirty years for about every conceivable sport you could imagine. There were a few tiny ones only a foot or two high, but the center of each section had at least one gigantic trophy that reached within an inch of the blazing case lights in the ceiling. Everything was polished, even the old ones, and it made for a nice effect if being blinded is your thing. Papa had gone into the office ahead of me when a great big friendly looking student in a football jersey walked up and saw where I was looking.

"Impressive, huh?" he said proudly.

I nodded. "I don't think you have my sport here."

"What sport would that be?"

"Fencing."

"You mean swords and stuff?" he replied, sounding excited. "That's cool!"

I shook my head. "They're called foils, not swords. So, no fencing team, I guess."

"You could still try out for volleyball or something," he said, sounding hopeful. "They need new talent for the team."

"Maybe," I replied, trying to stay friendly, "but I'll probably have too much homework."

"Well, maybe you'll work something out," he said wistfully. He seemed like a good guy and I found myself not wanting to disappoint anybody on my very first day.

"I'll think about it," I said, reaching out my hand. "Nice to meet you..."

"Jimmy," he replied, shaking it. "Nice to meet you...."

"I'm Joan," I replied.

As he walked on down the hall, it occurred to me that I needed to start meeting some new people, but something also told me that the word about the new kid who does fencing would get around the school without any extra help from me.

Papa was already at the front counter filling out my paperwork, where a lady with a badge saying MISS ROSE was patiently checking off items one by one as she created my official school persona. Once you are safely inside the school computer you get to officially exist, but not one second before.

"Go sit over there," said Rose as soon as she saw me, "and Mrs. T will be with you in a few minutes to give you your schedule. It will take about half an hour to wrap up everything."

Papa signed one last paper and looked at me. "You got the rest of this, squirt?"

"Ten-four," I replied.

Miss Rose looked up, dismayed. "But you will need to sign her course forms, Mister..."

"Darcy," he said. "And as it happens, I already did. As far as her courses go, Joan is a smart girl and I will support whatever she selects."

We had worked out all of this before and it felt perfectly normal for me to take over and do the rest of this on my own. I glanced at my watch. "I'll give you a call when I'm all wrapped up here."

Papa nodded. "Sounds like a plan," he said, and almost leaned forward to give me a quick kiss on the check like he usually did, but for some reason, he aimed for my forehead like he used to when I was little. "Au revoir," he said and headed for the door.

Miss Rose stood there looking dismayed while I smiled and waited. This was not normal procedure for this office, but Papa could be real convincing when he put his mind to it, so she finally sighed and gestured at the row of chairs over against the wall.

"You can wait over there until Mrs. T is ready for you," she said, so I picked up the pile of stuff she pushed across the counter and took a seat. Not being a dentist's office there were no ten-year-old magazines, but there was a copy of last year's Smithfield Yearbook so I satisfied myself with that.

About half a minute later the door opened, a girl came in and walked directly over to the counter, and to my surprise, Rose didn't react at all. The girl stood there waiting. And waiting. And waiting.

Finally, after about a minute she asked: "Is..."

"Not yet, Michelle," Miss Rose interrupted, and pointed over in my general direction. "Go take a seat over there next to Joan and you'll see Mrs. T in a few minutes." The tone was more of a command than a suggestion, so Michelle walked over and sank into the chair next to me.

"Hi Michelle," I said in a friendly voice. "You are THE Michelle, aren't you?"

She gave me a slightly quizzical look that was quickly replaced by one of recognition. "And you are...THE Joan, aren't you?"

I nodded. "Absolutely."

She nodded slowly. "Dad told me there would be one other college brat here, so I guess...you're it. Or we're them."

I nodded very slowly and solemnly. "Yep, we're them."

12

"I guess we are," she replied, every more slowly and seriously.

"Them, that is," I replied even more slowly. "We."

"We arrrre," said Michelle, surreptitiously glancing up to where Miss Rose was starting to get visibly agitated. I knew I was being tested to see how long we could keep this up, and I could already hear pencils tapping behind the room divider.

"Theeeeemmmmmmm...." I said slowly, which I guess finally pushed Rose over the edge. She slammed down her pencil, gave both of us a dirty look, and announced "MRS. T WILL SEE BOTH OF YOU NOW DOWN THE HALL FIRST DOOR ON THE RIGHT!"

Abruptly the big blue door behind her desk crashed open and a voice thundered "WHAT THE BLUE BLAZES IS ALL THE YELLING ABOUT?"

Apparently used to this, Miss Rose said in a sickly, sweet voice, "I was sending these students down to Mrs. T's office, Mr. Todd."

A tall, florid man with an unpleasant expression came out of the office and glared at us. Seeing that we were only students, he turned down his voice but he was still giving us a dirty look.

"You best get a move on, young ladies," he barked. "And don't be messing with Miss Rose here." At that, he disappeared back inside the office, slamming the door behind him, Miss Rose jerked her head in the direction of the hallway, Michelle grabbed my arm, and we were on our way out of there.

We were already halfway down the hallway when Michelle stopped and let go of my arm. I could see her face was flushed and I couldn't quite tell if she was nervous, angry, scared, or maybe all three at the same time.

"Didn't that bother you?" she asked. "The principal yelling at us like that?"

"Sure, it bothered me," I replied. "But some people are like that."

"He's the Principal for crying out loud," said Michelle angrily, stomping her foot. "He's supposed to be an example of the right way to act, not like what we just saw."

"I guess we're not in Kansas anymore," I replied, looking her right in the eye.

"Got a bucket of water?" she said, looking right back.

I've known a lot of people who never did get my jokes, but I have never met anyone who got them as quickly as Michelle. I knew that if we didn't get moving both of us would have lost it right there in the hallway, so we stifled our laughter and went down to a door with a sign that said "Counselor's Office."

"I hear she's one of the few humans in this school," said Michelle.

"Glad to hear that."

We jumped, and inside the office, a very small woman with short hair was getting a big kick out of listening to us. All three of us started to laugh, and I saw that this lady was a much better representative of the school than the ogre who greeted us a few minutes before.

"Come on inside, girls," said Mrs. T. "Have a seat and take a load off."

It was a small office with a big desk loaded to the top with folders, a computer shoved off to one side, a bookshelf behind the desk that stretched up to the ceiling, a big spider plant hanging in front of the window with shoots trailing all the way to the floor, a nice looking hooked rug on the floor, and two of the most comfortable chairs I've ever sat in. Mrs. T went back to her desk and pulled two folders out of a pile, plopping them onto the space in front of her. She flipped one open, glanced up at us for a second, and continued reading, flipping through pages back and forth, and finally going back to the first page again. Finally, she looked up at Michelle, who smiled back nervously.

"Do you know what courses you are going to take?"

Michelle nodded. "English, History, Spanish, PreCalculus, Biology, PE, and Band. That's what I planned on, anyhow."

Mrs. T nodded. "Well, we'll be able to work with you on most of those. Sorry to report we don't have Band anymore since the program got cut last spring. As for the rest, we're in good shape, and it so happens that you two are both in all advanced classes." She pulled two more folders from another pile, nimbly yanked one paper from each one and handed them to us. "Look and tell me what you think."

Each of us had some courses that were different but were going to be together in Home Room, Honors English 9-12 whatever that was, History, Biology, and PE so there was going to be plenty of time for us to get to know each other. I already liked what I'd seen of Michelle so far and hoped she felt the same about me.

"No change about Band?" Michelle asked hopefully. "I was *really* looking forward to it."

Mrs. T shook her head. "Sorry, Michelle, that's a done deal. But as far as your Honors English 9-12 goes, that is our most advanced class. It's the only section in the whole schedule, Mrs. Coates has been teaching it for years, never repeats what she teaches, and believe you me, she will work you till your fingers ache."

Michelle and I looked at each other, grinned, and nodded. "Sounds great!"

It was like we had given Mrs. T. a surprise birthday present. "That's the attitude we need more of around here, at least as far as academics is concerned."

I had one surprise on my own schedule, something I hoped wasn't a typo. "I never knew high schools had five years of French," I said.

"We didn't have before this fall," said Mrs. T. "Seems like you're in luck." She handed me an official looking sheet of paper with a big blue seal of the US State Department. It informed everyone officially that under the auspices of the United States VF exchange program, Miss Catharine Renoir had been appointed to be a French Language Teacher at Smithfield High School.

"We did have a few students taking French before, but that got cut a few years back. Now from out of nowhere, here comes one heck of a new teacher and it doesn't cost the school anything. I met her yesterday and she's a real peach. What's more, she'll be the ticket for you, young lady."

She looked over at Michelle. "I'd like to finish up some of Joan's paperwork, Michelle, so would you excuse us?" Michelle looked surprised, but took the hint and stood up as Mrs. T opened the door. "You have a seat out here, and Joan will be with you in a minute."

Oh brother, here comes the big speech. Poor little orphan girl needs special session about how to handle grief and loss. Been there, done that, over and out. I started to say "you don't have to do anything special..." but Mrs. T gave me a look that said, Hi Joan, sit down, close your mouth for a change, and listen. "Your Papa and I talked for a while last evening, Joan. He's been worried about you and wanted to make sure things were covered for you here at school. He has a LOT of confidence in you, but he also said that lately, you don't speak up much."

I hated it when people were being nice to me on purpose, but I had to admit that Mrs. T was being different than people usually were and that maybe the whole moving thing was harder for me than I would admit. I looked up and smiled somewhat, knowing it was hard letting down my defenses but something also told me Mrs. T knew that already. "Thanks...I'll work on that," I said.

She looked me right in the eyes. "Are we OK? You and me?"

"Yes Ma'am," I replied, and reached out to shake her hand.

"One piece of advice," she said, "two....three, actually. First, you get to be friends with Michelle out there. You two have a lot in common and it's a real stroke of luck that you are both new students at the same time and in the same grade. It does seem like you're both special in lots of ways, so you'll each have a buddy and can watch each other's backs."

"Second, you keep your eyes open and stay away from the Principal's office except for I can't wait emergencies, and that's only when you can't find me. Lots of different reasons for that, but you'll find those out once you're here for a while."

"Third, you two call or visit me anytime you need to. Doesn't have to be in school. She looked more serious, and her voice lowered a bit. "Most of the other college faculty kids go to a private school in town, so you two are the first ones we've had here in a while. Don't let that go to your heads, because if I see bad grades from either of you, well, use your imagination."

"Fourth, use your ears a lot more than your words. Listen, pay attention, and put two and two together before something comes up behind you and bites you in the rear end."

"I thought you said three things," I remarked, helpfully.

She looked at me over the top of her glasses and shook her head. "Bye, Joan."

In the waiting room Michelle was talking to a quiet looking boy sitting in one of the chairs, but when she saw me coming she stood up and grabbed her own backpack from the floor.

"Nice to meet you, Ryan. See you around!" said Michelle.

Ryan smiled back shyly. "See you later."

There was a side door that led directly into the hallway, and in a moment, it closed behind us.

Good to have those two, thought Mrs. T, but I will need to keep an eye on them. Right now they're fish out of water and this school is different from anything they ever experienced before.

15

There was a gentle knock on the door and after a cheerful "Come in!" Ryan entered. "What can I do for you today, Ryan?" she said, "other than give you a big hug and ask you how your summer was." Mrs. T. stood up and the hug was given and received, but she could tell there was something on his mind.

"Where is Mr. Landry?" he asked nervously. "I've come to the school every day this week and he's not around anywhere. The band room is locked up and I tried to look through the window but it's dark and I can't see anything."

"Whoa, Ryan," she said patiently. "Where were you all summer?"

"At home with Mama and Daddy, but we went to Grandpa's house a lot."

"Well, I'm sorry to tell you that Mr. Landry isn't at school anymore, Ryan. He retired and moved to Florida."

"Who's the new band teacher?"

Mrs. T turned her head and bit her lip. "Ryan, you know the band was getting smaller all of the time, like basketball and the other sports teams."

"So you mean...."

"There's no band anymore. Not like before there isn't."

Mrs. T cared for her students like nobody's business and knew that Ryan had more challenges than any normal person should ever have to deal with. Ever since the accident, his main reason for coming to school every morning had been to play in the band, especially since Mr. Landry had taken him under his wing and taught him to play an instrument.

"Ryan, some folks in the school wanted it that way, and that's all there is to it. All the schedules are changed and the band students are in other classes now. There is something else you might like, though. Mrs. Coates, bless her heart, is going to have a class last period two days a week, and even though the name isn't exactly band that's what it's going to be. It's a Pep band. That's a special band that plays for football games, basketball games, anything they want. The class only meets on Tuesday and Thursday but it's still a band and the only one we've got."

"Can I be in it?"

He was looking more hopeful already, and I thanked God and Mrs. Coates for their generosity. Lord, this boy needs music like a fish needs water.

"Of course, Ryan. I'll go ahead and change your schedule right now." She popped up his schedule on the computer and it was done in a minute. She handed a copy to him and he held like it was made of spun glass. "Now Ryan, you do a good job for Mrs. Coates and I'm sure she'll keep you busy. I'm counting on you, now."

He reached out and gave her another hug. "I'll do a good job, Mrs. T. I'll show you I can."

Chapter Four
Revelations
Michelle

There are times in history when two people first come into contact and history changes. Lewis meets Clark, Washington meets Lafayette, Watson meets Crick,

16

all great examples of 1+1=3 because two heads are better than one. If Joan heard me say this, she would immediately add "Yeah, Right. Caesar and Brutus. Napoleon and Russia. Cherry vanilla ice cream and spaghetti sauce," all things that made no sense but indicated other unique friendships like ours, all except maybe Caesar and Brutus who had their own relationship issues.

When Joan and I finally left Mrs. T's office we agreed that we should find someplace to eat lunch together. Since we both brought sack lunches we looked around the school for someplace to sit and as luck would have it the band room door was open. We poked our heads in, flicked on the lights, and found a lot of clutter but also a table with a few chairs that were just right.

After we got settled the first thing we saw that it was a band room without a band, and in fact without anything musical except a long line of huge trash cans with all sorts of musical stuff piled inside. It was a shock because both of us had been at schools with big music programs, and the band room was always a central gathering place for all the nerdy kids. Here, it was like the husk of something that had died but hadn't been buried yet.

In the meantime, we were both hungry and this was the first quiet place we had found. There was just enough light making its way through the grimy windows that we could eat, and it also was muted enough to hide the dirt and clutter. I got out a few boxes of some yummy leftovers from last night, making Joan look wistful, especially since all she had was a PBJ on white bread. Seeing her look, I got out a third container and another pair of bamboo chopsticks.

"I keep this for emergencies," I said.

Without hesitation, Joan picked up the chopsticks, reached into the container and got a few pieces into her mouth without dropping anything.

"Tofu Hunan style," I said. "Snow peas and bok choy, a pinch of ginger and soya."

"You're a great cook," she said.

"Thanks," I replied. "Love to teach you sometime if you want."

"I'm interested in almost everything," she replied, but for the moment was interested mostly in eating.

"Me too," I said and got down to the bottom of the box. Closing the lid, I put the container back into my lunch box and took out another with something that looked more familiar to her. "Want an egg roll?"

The room had been used so heavily there were deep scratches in the floor, the ceiling tile was starting to crack, and some of the instrument cabinets on the walls had doors that didn't fit properly anymore. The walls were all covered with wood paneling and the floor was shaped like an old Greek theater, with semicircular levels down to the floor. We wandered around the room and it was sad. The remains of a few old metal and fiberglass Sousaphones leaned against one corner, and one wall had been covered with picture frames with nothing left but faded, empty rectangles from where they had been taken down.

"What happened here?" I asked softly. "It's almost like you can hear the music that must have soaked into the walls."

"Remember what Mrs. T said about the band being cut last spring?" said Joan.

17

"Why, for heaven's sake?" I answered, gesturing angrily around the room. "I mean, since when do they 'drop' band?"

"Maybe the director retired or something?" she asked.

"So why didn't they hire a new one?" I retorted, flopping down into my chair. "I mean, I've played clarinet since fifth grade and was looking forward to this. I'm not exactly athletic material as you see, so band was going to be my..."

Suddenly we heard voices outside, including one that we had heard turned up to full volume in the main office.

"Oh crap," I whispered. "We're probably not supposed to be in here."

Joan

If there's anything that Mama taught me, it was not to get caught sitting still in a potential emergency, so I yanked Michelle by the hand and we dove into the one instrument closet that still had a working door. There was lots of room inside although it smelled like old musty instrument cases, and we managed to pull the door closed just in time.

"How long this place been empty?" said a man's voice.

"Since the end of school last year," came a reply in the same voice we had heard at the office. "Teacher retired and here we are. The place always did look like a dump."

"That don't matter," said the first man, the footsteps squeaking as he was apparently walking down the risers. A foot stamped solidly. "Solid floor under all of this, so there'll be lots of room when we tear all this wood out."

"When can you start?" asked Mr. Todd, still sounding like he was near our door.

"In a few days if everything's worked out," the man said. "I still need to know why we're doing this in case anybody asks. Like, why there's no band anymore."

"Now don't you go bringing that up like there's something you've got to do about it," said Mr. Todd, the laughter replaced by something menacing. It didn't help we were in this totally dark closet.

"Don't go getting on your high horse," he said. "I've heard from the parents of some of the kids who used to be in the band, and they aren't happy about the whole program getting scrapped."

"That's all under control," said Mr. Todd. "Just tell them the director 'retired', remember?"

The man laughed. "Ain't exactly what I heard, but it's your picnic."

"Okay, he had some encouragement. That good enough for you?"

"Listen, I don't want to be working in here and have somebody come in and turn this whole thing upside down. I got to know, then maybe I can back you up on this thing. Neither of us needs this getting out into the open."

"Okay – he was told that there was some money missing after the annual Band cookie sale and that if he quietly retired nobody would press charges."

"And he swallowed that?"

18

Mr. Todd laughed. "Listen, the guy was already five years over retirement age so I made it easier for him, that's all." Todd's expression changed and the chill came back into the room. "So now you know. You ready to go or not?" "Ready to start next week."

"All right. Stop by the office on your way out and pick up the contract. It's all signed and ready to go."

All at once Michelle grabbed me by the arm and I could tell that she was tensed up and squirming around. I did my best to hold her down but it was like she was having trouble breathing or something, but then I heard the faintest sound of her iPhone ringing from her pocket. She was using her hand to push against the phone pocket as hard as she could, masking the sound enough that it couldn't be heard more than a few inches away. Outside we heard the band room door creak open, pause, and slam closed.

Michelle

After the coast was clear I pushed the closet door open and we stepped back into the room. We were both a sight, and it was real obvious that nobody had cleaned those closets for a long time. Joan started to laugh, when suddenly I went into a sneezing fit that seemed to last forever, and so loud I was real thankful that the band room was soundproofed.

"I think we'll talk about this sometime later," I whispered.

"By the way, are you going to check your phone?" Joan asked.

"Oh shoot," I said and flicked it on. "My Mom is at the office waiting for me to go and get all those shots we need before they let us start school. I'd better go."

Joan looked right at me and for a moment she let down that bravado stance of hers and let me see the real warmth beneath. "I think I'm going to like being friends with you," she said.

I tried to match her tone, trying not to get all emotional. "Me too." I carefully cracked the door and looked down the hallway both directions. Nobody in sight. I took off down the hallway and only looked back a second to wave.

Chapter Five
Christine

No matter how many times people offered, Christine would never let anyone drive her home after practice. She had a whole list of excuses: daily practice, errands to do, meeting with a teacher, so after a while, they took the hint and didn't ask anymore. It was just as well because she simply didn't want any of them to see where she lived. Most of her friends came from families with big houses, lots of food in the refrigerator, and big screen TV's in all the rooms. It hurt when they asked her over and she felt she had to turn down their invitations since she could never ask them over to her own house.

When her Daddy first walked out on the family, Christine's Mama had gone through a whole series of jobs that lasted a month here, six weeks there, always starting with high hopes that this one would last but sooner or later ending as the factory or store or restaurant closed, sometimes without any notice and sometimes without the last paycheck she was owed. Then, out of the blue, the miracle happened – the job at Smithfield College, the one that she had hoped and dreamed and studied for, the one that should last for a long time and finally give them decent insurance. She had even talked about taking some of the courses that College employees could take for free, but the time simply hadn't worked out since Christine's practices always lasted until after the time the little ones got home from school.

Christine wasn't a particularly religious person but one thing was sure: each morning when she got up she thanked God she at least had a talent that could take her out of this. Since volleyball and basketball were the two lucky aces up her sleeve, her team had a good shot at taking the State Championship in one or both of her sports. Then with luck, there would be recruiters watching and the scholarship offers would start coming in.

The kitchen started to fill with the aroma of frying eggs and the cornmeal mush that Mama liked so much. There had been bacon every day up until last weekend, but since it was one of the most expensive things in the store Mama simply took it off the menu. There was a sound of water running and a few seconds later the kitchen door opened. Christine put on her brightest smile, the coffee cup already filled and on the table, and with a grateful smile Mama sat down and took a sip in a way that spoke volumes. Tired already, yes. Long day ahead, yes. Still employed, Thank God. Worried, always. Can't pay attention to that now, Christine thought as she went over to the stove and started to fill a plate.

"Not too much, Sweetie," said Mama. "I'm not very hungry this morning." Sometimes this was true but today there wasn't the usual confidence in her voice. A long time ago Christine had thought this was lying, but as she grew older and understood more about the reality of their family life she grew to understand why Mama did it this way. Funny, but sports had also helped her understand this better, like when you are down 74-36 the last quarter and you still fight until the buzzer.

"Don't worry, Mama, there's plenty this morning," said Christine. She worked four hours every evening stocking shelves at the Piggly Wiggly, with the bonus that she was also able to bring home some outdated food before it got thrown away. For a while, Mama had resisted but it came in so handy she didn't press very hard.

It was heartbreaking to see Mama eat so slowly, but the coffee was ready and it had recently become the most natural thing for Christine to also pour a cup for herself, the two of them sharing a few last minutes of quiet time together as the heat and caffeine poured some of its own energy into each of them.

Christine finished her coffee and went back into the bedroom to get dressed as quietly as she could, but the twins had already smelled breakfast and were getting themselves ready. "Great job, guys," she said in her best Team Captain voice that her sisters loved, to which they gave their favorite answer.

20

"Aye Aye, Captain!" and giggled. Well, great day so far, Christine thought. She took advantage of the early hour to run all the way to school before there was much traffic, not that there had been since the factory closed. It was always cooler and she had the whole road to herself most of the time, and being in such good condition already it gave her more peace and quiet as well as a time to think about the day ahead. Practice had already been going on for three weeks and the team was shaping up well, but last year's graduating seniors were going to be missed. Volleyball had started to go down in popularity and it was harder and harder to get good athletes to go out for the team, even those who were still going to play basketball in the winter. It was also getting harder to wind herself up in the morning since she'd started working but given their financial situation, quitting wasn't an option.

As she rounded the corner onto Smith Road and saw the early lights of the High School ahead, Christine started to time herself, the distance being just over a mile. The summer had been a hot and humid one but last night things had cooled down and it was a real pleasure to be out running. A few cars passed and honked their horns in a friendly way, everyone knowing better than to offer her a ride this time of day. The third car she recognized as Jimmy's, her buddy since Elementary school. He had been nice enough the night before to give her a ride to work, and he had mentioned something about meeting a freshman girl who was also a swordfighter.

"It's called fencing," said Christine dryly.

"Yeah, that's right," he'd replied. "You know, she seemed real athletic,"

Christine laughed. "You would notice that. Think she'd like to go out for volleyball?"

"You know, I asked her," Jimmy replied thoughtfully. "She didn't say yes but she didn't say no, either. You could probably look her up and see how good she might be. New kids are always looking for things to join. Helps them fit in."

"What does she look like?"

"Well...not all that tall, real dark straight hair, brown eyes, young looking..."

"Oh, come on. Unlike you, I don't want to date her. I want to know how she moves. You know, how she would handle herself on the volleyball court."

"It was weird – she looked really fast on her feet. You know, moving smooth and coordinated like a dancer."

Great reflexes, quick to move, and...strong legs? If there was anything that killed volleyball players it was when their legs cramped up. Control that and you've got yourself championship potential. Yes, this kid is worth looking into.

As Christine trotted through the gym door she checked her watch and yes, the cooler weather helped get her time down to six and a half minutes. For a change, she wasn't particularly tired after her run, and as she came inside she saw Lisa, Terri, Bobbi, and Stephanie practicing two on a side. Normally she would run out and get into the rotation but the idea of this new kid thing had sparked her interest. With only six in the rotation, the team needed all the help they could get.

"Huddle up, people," she called, and the girls obediently formed a circle around her.

"Aye Aye, Captain!" they all said in unison, a routine left over from childhood where they would all get together and watch the show. At first, it sounded dumb but after the fans started to join in they all got a kick out of it.

"Hey, people. As you know we lost a few players last year..."

"No kidding," Bobbi said under her breath.

"...and anybody who finds out about any possible new recruits is supposed to tell me. So, anybody hear anything?"

The room got quiet, the girls looking at each other, but apparently, nobody had any new ideas. Well, now is the time, Christine thought. "Jimmy told me about a brand-new kid. Her name is Joan...something, I don't know what. Anyhow, Jimmy said he met her when she was coming in to pick up her schedule, and she told him that she does fencing."

Lisa laughed. "Fencing, huh? My Daddy could use her on the ranch. We got a whole lot of fencing that needs...."

"Not cattle fencing, you idiot, fencing like with swords and stuff. Anyhow, I've seen a few fencing matches on the Olympics and you would not believe how fast those people move. We have plenty of height on this team with Lisa, Bobbi and me, but we are going up against other teams with twelve to fifteen players. You play too many minutes you get tired, you get tired you start to miss, you miss too often you lose the game and that's all there is to it. If we get at least a few more people who are fast on their feet, who can recover spikes and give the front line a good set up, there's nobody in the state who can beat us."

If last summer was any indication the team looked terrific this year. Christine was sure they could make it all the way to the State tournament, but we are sure going to be in for a long season. The more game time each of us has, the more tired we get. The more tired we get, the sooner one of us gets injured. And if Christine got injured or worse, badly injured, then no scholarship.

"Lisa – I want you to actually find this Joan kid, and make sure you know where I can meet her so I can talk to her myself." She turned to the rest of the team. "And anyone else bumps into her, SEE ME at lunch time. Got it?"

"Aye Aye, Captain," they replied in unison, and the bell rang.

Chapter Six
New Beginnings

Joan

I took the bus on the first day of school and followed the river of kids down the sidewalk and into the front door. As I pushed my way through the crowd I recognized Jimmy but he didn't see me and I didn't see Michelle anywhere either. We had talked since our lunch in the band room, but that was three days ago, so I was looking forward to getting together with her. I made my way down the hallway toward the room marked COATES and Michelle ran up.

She was all wound up and I could see right away she was as relieved to find me as I was to find her. Mrs. Coates was in the hallway speaking with some other teacher, and since we were early we found seats at the furthest corner from the door. As the other students came in they all saw someone they knew and sat down in little clusters that gradually filled the remaining seats. Now and then someone half turned to glance in our direction but when stared back, they turned around and laughed.

When Mrs. Coates entered, the class quieted down as she picked up a clipboard and started to take attendance. When she called my name, I said "here", and thirty-five people turned to look at me.

Lisa, who was sitting in the back, punched Jimmy hard in the shoulder to get his attention. Startled, he half jerked upright in his seat.

"What was that for?" he whispered.

"IS THAT HER?" Lisa replied in a stage whisper, pointing to the front of the room.

Jimmy turned, saw where Lisa pointed and nodded his head.

When she finished, Mrs. Coates put down the clipboard and leaned against her desk.

"All right, everybody. This will be home room, the first place you come in the morning and the last place you come before leaving school in the afternoon. When I am not teaching home room I am teaching English, so one way or another I will see all of you every day."

"If you have any problems, come to me. If you have any questions, come to me and if I don't have the answer it probably can't be answered anyway. If you're late I will count you tardy and if you miss homeroom I will count you absent and if you miss too many classes they will make you take the whole year over again. Neither of us wants that, so make sure you get here every day."

The bell for first period rang about one second later but everyone stayed frozen at their seats until Mrs. Coates gave us a wink and said "Class dismissed." The class emptied out in about five seconds but Michelle and I were here for first period, too. I needed to do something so I grabbed the desk in the front row, wrenched it back into line, and moved my way down the line and in a minute Michelle and I had the whole room back into shape. You could have knocked over Mrs. Coates with a feather the way she looked at us, and in its small way it reminded me of that look Mama gave me under that willow tree so many years ago when I did something right and it made someone feel better.

"Thank you, girls," she said quietly.

It was obvious from the first minute of English class that Mrs. Coates was a complete pro, loved teaching, and that it was worth our time to be in her class. To our surprise, there were only eleven of us, all sharing the fact that we liked to read - and argue, as it turned out.

In fact, arguing was our very first activity. We counted off 1-2-1-2, sat on opposite sides of the classroom, and Mrs. Coates wrote SHOULD 16-YEAR-OLDS HAVE THE VOTE? on the blackboard. She pointed to me (I was a ONE) and said "Your side is for the law", then pointed at Michelle (who was a

23

TWO) and said, "Your side is against the law." She then stepped back and said, "Okay, you have ten minutes to figure out your arguments. Pick one person to write them down." A few of us sat there not knowing what to do next but a few of the kids who had been in the class before cranked our chairs around and we started to put together some ideas.

By the time the bell rang we were ranting and up and down and arguing inside our group and outside our group so that the time went faster than for any class I had ever taken before. As we filed out into the hallway, Michelle punched me playfully in the arm. "This is going to be fun," she said. "See you at lunch."

A few minutes later Lisa found Christine on her way to second period. "She's in my homeroom," Lisa said excitedly. The two girls walked down the hallway together, headed for the Language department at the other end of the school.

"What does she look like?" asked Christine.

"Well, a lot shorter than me, maybe up to my chin, straight black hair cut to her shoulders, a real intense look," said Lisa. "Muscular in a girl way."

"That's just what Jimmy told me," said Christine, "like a dancer or something. Now where is she going to be last period?"

Lisa stopped smiling. "You mean I..."

"Look, if she's in Mrs. Coates' homeroom class then Mrs. Coates will have her schedule, especially since she's a freshman. Just ask her."

Chapter Seven
Miss Renoir

Catharine Renoir stood near the door and waited for the first-period students to arrive. Since her arrival in Smithfield only three weeks before, there had been so much to learn about the American school system that there had been little time for anything else. As she had already done a hundred times before, she scanned her classroom to make sure that everything was in place. It had not been her original goal to become a teacher, but one does not turn down the opportunity for which she had been preparing for more than four years.

It had been a shock at first, the hectic pace, the immediate descent into first names, and of course the food – or most of it – but overall there were many redeeming factors. Most people were genuinely friendly and she recognized their pride in hospitality. Everybody in this part of the country had been pioneers or refugees at some point, so one did not necessarily have to be part of an established aristocracy to be accepted. She had some freedom in her teaching, and since the program that brought her to America also paid her salary and she was the only French teacher in the school, she could teach students at whatever level they understood whether there were one or twenty students in her class.

When the bell sounded and the cacophony of an American High School filled the halls, Miss Renoir was ready. She stood at the door and greeted the students as they came in – all four of them. The hall emptied, the bell rang, and within a few seconds everything was finally quiet. One last look, one last little prayer under her breath, and she turned to face her first class.

24

To her surprise all four students were sitting in the very last chairs in the very last row, as far away from the front of the room as it was possible to get and still be inside the room. The group was busy in its own little whispered conversation, so she stepped briskly over to the group and held up a copy of her class list.

"Attendance please."

"Robert."

"Here."

"Gerald."

"Here."

"Lisa."

"Here."

"Christine."

"Here."

Good, she thought, one hundred percent and the class is only four, and all of them have names as French as any in Paris.

The class period was a mad dash of students running around the room, looking for and copying down French word cards that Miss Renoir had posted. Easy finds were quickly exhausted as the students had to use their imaginations for where to look next. Since she had included words like Ceiling and Behind, putting cards on the Ceiling and Behind the door, it was, to say the least, something of a challenge. After a few minutes, the students designated Lisa to be the scribe and things started to work more smoothly. To add drama Miss Renoir breathlessly announced every now and then how much time was left.

"Oh no, only seven minutes left, oh, sorry, that's seventeen minutes," and so on until she was counting down the final seconds.

"Time!" and as if on cue the hallway bell rang. "How many, Lisa?"

Lisa counted quickly. "Sixty-three!"

"Magnifique! Remember, the first thirty words will be on your quiz at the end of the week. Au revoir!"

As Gerald was leaving, he turned to her and grinned. "I think I am going to like this class."

"Merci, Gerald. Now study!"

Well, they appear to be normal children so with some work we will all be in good shape. I must also remember that although I will do my best, they are not the main reason why I am here. That one is coming in about two minutes. I reviewed the dossier again last night and nothing remains until we finally meet.

"Can you believe that class?" asked Lisa as they went down the hallway.

"What's the problem?" said Christine. "Seems like a good teacher."

"That's not what I'm...*that's her!*" Lisa pointed down the hallway where Joan was headed in their direction. "That's Joan!"

Christine patted Lisa on the shoulder. "Let me do the talking," she said, then turned and smiled. "Hey, Joan!"

Joan, anxious to get to her class but surprised to hear her name, turned to face the girl walking toward her.

"Hi. I'm Christine Cooper, captain of the SHS volleyball team, and I've heard a lot of good things about you."

"Like what?" Joan responded, looking at her watch impatiently.

"That you are a fencer and all. That must be interesting."

"Uh...yes, I fence. I guess Jimmy told you."

Christine nodded. "Since you came so highly recommended, we'd like to invite..."

Joan interrupted. "Sorry Christine, but maybe we can talk later. I don't want to be late for class on my first day. Thanks for asking." The bell rang again and Joan stepped into the classroom, closing the door behind her.

The hallway was quiet as Christine and Lisa walked together, already five minutes late to their next class, and Lisa knew better than to say anything. Well, Lisa thought, I found Joan like she asked and Christine had gotten to talk with her. Lisa couldn't figure out how Joan could turn down an invitation. She had dreamed of being a volleyball player since third grade and it had been the greatest day of her life when she went to open tryouts and made Varsity. Here was this kid Joan, a freshman, being offered a spot on the team just for showing up, and then turning it down? Go figure.

If Christine wanted Joan for the team, then Lisa was going to have to make sure that Joan accepted whether she wanted to or not. Like Lisa's Dad always said, there are three ways: your way, my way, and the Hard way. Looks like Joan picked the Hard way.

French 5

The language department was in the oldest part of the school with old fashioned single light bulbs in the ceiling, green ceramic tile walls, and the oldest linoleum Joan had ever seen, so it was not until she was inside the classroom that she saw Miss Renoir. It was both the resemblance and the differences that made her catch her breath. Miss Renoir and Mama could have been cousins, each with the same straight black hair, same level intelligent expression, and the same unconscious grace of movement. There was also the same aura of assured self-confidence, and within moments Joan felt absolutely at home.

"Bonjour, Jeannette," said Miss Renoir.

"Bonjour," replied Joan.

There was a pair of chairs in front that had been set up a few minutes before, and Joan did not sit down until Miss Renoir indicated which chair to use. From the beginning, they spoke entirely in French. They quickly established that yes, Joan's French was excellent, grammatical, and without an accent, but her vocabulary was a bit limited from being immersed in English for most of the last eighteen months. There was no question, however, that Joan belonged in a highly-advanced French class, and Miss Renoir surprised her by saying they would be spending only part of their time studying French.

26

"What else will we do?" asked Joan, perplexed.

"Read," replied Miss Renoir. "And write, and speak together, and translate. We will read the great works written in the world's most beautiful language, study the history of France and its people, and much more. Your vocabulary will expand enormously as we encounter new and different words, and in addition to literature we may spend a week cooking, or studying a map, or even sport."

This sounds wonderful, thought Joan, and this must have shown on her face as Miss Renoir's face softened a bit to reveal a warm, friendly smile.

"Now we must begin." She stepped over to her desk and removed a small pile of books from one corner, delivering them to Joan. "This is for the first month or so, Jeanette. Do you recognize the titles?"

Joan looked at the books, each in what looked like a leather binding. Les Miserables was a real brick, but the second was hardly a pamphlet, and Joan saw that it was of all things an official tourist guide to...Las Vegas?

Miss Renoir chuckled out loud at the surprise on Joan's face. "The first is to read, and the second is to...translate?" asked Joan.

"Fantastique," said Miss Renoir, the first compliment of the day. "For tomorrow read until page 100 and be prepared to discuss characters and their development. Think of it as if I were a detective and the people in the book are members of a street gang that you must describe to me. Not only their names, but how they think, how they will react, and their strengths and weaknesses. For the pamphlet, by next Monday a complete translation in colloquial French. Do you have any questions?"

"Je comprendes," replied Joan. "Ten four."

Miss Renoir looked puzzled. "Ten...four?"

Gotcha, thought Joan. "It is a familiar colloquial expression in American English, meaning 'I understand and will do.'"

How appropriate, thought Miss Renoir, especially today. They read together for the rest of the class, and when the bell rang Joan got to her feet but did not move to leave the classroom. Miss Renoir started to speak but suddenly Joan came over and gave her a hug, then disappeared out the door.

Michelle

Since Joan and I had every class together for the rest of the day, we had agreed that whoever got to the cafeteria first would find a table and do her best to reserve an empty seat. Since the weather was good enough for the seniors to eat outside, the cafeteria was half empty. I found an empty table, draped my backpack over the back of a chair, and looked around for Joan. This was the first regular school I had attended and the sheer number of kids was intimidating. Like Joan, I was only thirteen years old and tall and skinny, but at least tall was normal around here for ninth graders so I didn't exactly stick out like a sore thumb.

Except for being Chinese, that is. Everywhere I looked the other Chinese students weren't there in droves, and in fact were conspicuous by being absent.

27

Not that it bothered me because I wasn't going to be elected President of the Chinese Students Association or anything, but to tell the truth I didn't like being the 'only' of anything.

There is an insulation that comes with being the only one of something. I grew up being almost an only kid until my little brother came along and I was finally allowed to breathe as Mom and Dad shifted their laser beams from me to him. It also helped that I was curious about everything and had almost as many books in my own bedroom as Dad had in his office. Since I had learned how to argue so well, by the time I was eleven they were both convinced I was well on the way to being a great lawyer.

I'm rambling, I guess, but Joan finally came in, pushed her way through the chairs and people and like me draped her backpack over the chair. By this time the lunch line had thinned out so we both went up and grabbed our trays. Right in front of me Joan got three little dishes of vegetables and two fruits along with a bottle of water. The way it looked didn't exactly at first ring any appetite bells with me but I also hadn't eaten since six thirty and it did smell good and was laid out there in front of me waiting and it was now almost Noon so I grabbed two hamburgers and an apple, beat Joan to the cashier, and was at the table with half of it gone by the time she sat down next to me.

She looked at me funny as she rather daintily took a bite out of a celery stick. "Is ze meal to Madame's liking?" she asked with a fake sounding French accent.

One of the cool things about being bilingual is that you can say something terrible and if you have a nice smile and a gentle voice people will smile back at you. Using my nicest voice, I said something evil to Joan in Mandarin, she gave me a knowing smile and answered me back in French, and that's how we went through the rest of her lunch. Since then we have tried to remember exactly what we said to each other, but it probably went something like this:

Joan: I sincerely hope you are enjoying that disgusting slop.
Michelle: Your lunch looks like it was turned down by a rabid hyena.
Joan: Oh it is so kind of you, you half brained Yak herder.
Michelle: It's so wonderful that you look like a vulture with dandruff.

"Well, how was your morning?" asked Joan, suddenly breaking back into English.

It took me a moment to think of an answer that didn't have any insults in it. "Not too bad so far. Math was good. Challenging for a change."

Joan nodded. "That's great. Look what I have for homework," she said and showed me the book that she got from French class.

I took the book wonderingly. "She gave you THIS copy to read, not some dumpy old paperback?" It was leather and actually smelled like a book. It was great having that in common with Joan since we both lived in houses where there were too many books for the shelves and people didn't complain if you were reading all the time.

Joan nodded. "One hundred pages by tomorrow," she said.

I also had some homework for tomorrow, only a couple workbook pages that were all review anyway - but a hundred pages was serious business. "Well, good luck with that."

"Should be fun," Joan said, meaning it.

We finished our lunches and grabbed our backpacks as the bell rang. Since we had the rest of our classes together, we went out the cafeteria door and as soon as we entered the hallway we heard the voice - HIS voice, and it didn't sound happy. There was a big foyer outside the cafeteria with four hallways leading into it, each divided by a double door marked Enter and Exit with a pillar in the middle, and Mr. Todd was yelling at any student who dared to go through the wrong doorway.

"HEY, OPEN YOUR EYES AND READ THE SIGN. ENTER, ENTER, ENTER!" and he would grab their backpacks, yank them backward and shove them through the correct doorway. The whole area got real quiet, everybody slowed down, and the river of students visibly parted so that everyone was entering and leaving at the very far side of each doorway, scraping the door jamb to keep as far away from Mr. Todd as possible. Like salmon entering a flume, Joan and I joined the ENTER line and had gotten to the door when he blocked the doorway right in front of us.

"YOU THE NEW FRENCH KID?" he asked Joan or rather shouted in her face.

Joan looked him right in the eye and said, "Huh?"

The temperature in the foyer dropped forty degrees in about a quarter of a second, the hallway grew completely silent, three or four students behind me muttered "Uh-oh" and at least eight made the sign of the cross. Everyone was watching, everyone was holding their breaths, and you could hear a pin drop. Ding.

Joan stared him straight in the eye and for some reason, her reaction seemed to make him uneasy. For someone so used to making everyone petrified, he didn't seem to know what to do next.

"I said, are you the new kid, the French kid?" he asked more quietly.

Joan looked perplexed, and then a huge smile blossomed on her face. "Oh, Monsieur, yez, yez, I be za new French keed. Zis school iz, how they say, so very wonderful to be here. Excuse moi, we be late for ze next class. Au revoir!" and walked right through the EXIT door.

This loosened up what was left of the crowd that had backed up in the foyer, and soon it was flowing again, including me. After I made it through the doorway, I looked back and saw to my relief he was still there, shouting at some other poor kid who had dared to go through the wrong door. Joan had slowed down to let me catch up and in a second we were back together.

"Are you totally out of your mind?" I asked.

"He should have better manners," she replied.

I grabbed her shoulder. "You're my buddy but it would be much nicer if you don't go out of your way to paint a target on your own back."

"Michelle, I will always have your back, no matter what - but in this school, everybody has a target on their backs, if not from him then from someone else."

"What do we do about it?"

"We don't go after people," she said, "and we don't let others go after people either."

"But isn't that dangerous?" I asked.

Joan nodded. "That's the whole point. There are a lot of people who can't defend themselves. That means it's our job to watch out for them, so we can look at ourselves in the mirror every morning."

Chapter Eight
Danger Signals
Michelle

For all her empathy, Joan never could understand why so many people had trouble finding their way around places or took so long to do it. With her leading the way, we found the gym and got changed into the fashion statement they called gym clothes.

"You look absolutely stunning," I said. "Wherever did you find that ensemble?"

As we filed into the gym Joan was figuring out something appropriately cutting to say when the teacher came in and turned her attention to the class, a whistle ready in her left hand.

"Good afternoon, girls. My name is Miss Anita. After we take attendance we're going to do some tests to see what you're able to do." She motioned to where Lisa stood off to the side, balancing a volleyball on her left index finger. "Lisa here is going to serve up a few shots to each of you, and for your part, you're supposed to try and get it back over the net. Nothing complicated. Any questions?"

I looked around, always nervous that I was supposed to be doing something, but to my relief, nobody else moved. In case you hadn't figured it out by now, PE was not my favorite subject.

"Okay, everybody get into line over here," Miss Anita said, pointing to a long red line on the side of the court as Lisa moved to the back corner, the ball ready in her hand.

"Number one!" and the first girl left the line and went to the center of the empty side. Lisa tossed up the ball and gave it a tap that sent it over the net and just to the left of where the girl was standing. She moved under it, locked her hands together, and easily popped it back over the net where Lisa caught it. It went like that for the next eight people and then it was my turn. I walked out to the center of the court and waited, feeling somewhat uneasy.

"Number ten," said Miss Anita, and Lisa tossed up the ball and this time it was way over her head. When it had reached its peak Lisa jumped straight up and hammered it with her right hand, sending it flying over the net, clearing it by at least two millimeters, and heading straight for...MY FACE, with enough time for me to jump out of the way.

30

"You missed," I said, and the whole group got quiet. Lisa stopped, looked me right in the eye the way a diamond cutter looks at an uncut diamond looking for a place to split it in two, then went back to her spot. The next twelve girls were given the easy treatment and then it was Joan's turn.

Joan is extremely athletic, but it's all under the surface. What's more, I could tell that even though we weren't standing in line together she didn't like what Lisa had done. When her number was called, she walked to the center of the court, faced Lisa, and stared at her for about ten seconds. It reminded me of a documentary about snakes, and was exactly the way a rattlesnake looked at an unsuspecting mouse quietly eating a sunflower seed.

To our surprise, Lisa gave the ball the same gentle tap over the net that she had to the first girl, Joan moved effortlessly to return it and it popped over the net landing about twelve feet to Lisa's left. Lisa recovered the ball and was headed back to her corner when Joan spoke up.

"That the best you can do?" Joan asked.

Lisa skidded to a stop and the whole gym got quiet. Lisa smiled back at Joan, and her look had a lot in common with that snake I was talking about, except this time the snake was mad but not wanting to show it. "Sure," she said. The teacher looked at the clock on the wall, then turned back to Lisa and nodded.

One, two, three steps and Lisa was back in position. Joan went back to the middle of the court and stood there watching like before, except she was a tiny bit raised up on the balls of her feet, her arms six inches out from her sides. Lisa tossed up the ball and when it came down to about seven feet she jumped straight up and hammered it with her right hand, sending it flying over the net, clearing it by at least two millimeters, but about five feet off to where Joan...

...had been, but Joan wasn't there anymore, she was right in front of Lisa and the ball bounced off Joan's left hand at a thirty-degree angle and ricocheted to the floor well inside the line on Lisa's side.

The teacher checked her roster. "Good return, Joan."

"It was okay," said Joan, and got back into line, except the others in line weren't looking at Joan, they were looking at Lisa, and then almost as one they turned and looked over at Joan. One of them came over and whispered in her ear.

"Watch yourself," she said in a low voice, then patted Joan once on the shoulder. "Great shot."

Joan nodded, the teacher blew the whistle, and we all jogged for the locker room.

Ten minutes later Lisa was walking across the student parking lot to her car, the other girls calling Hi or see you tomorrow, everyone happy to have one day off practice.

"Did you..." Christine started to say as Lisa clicked the door locks open.

"Yep," answered Lisa as she got into the driver's seat, started the car, and swung out into the long exit line that went with driving to school. She was silent the whole way out of the parking lot and halfway into town, Christine patiently waiting, knowing it was unusual for Lisa to be quiet at any time let alone for this long and with the two of them together.

"Tell me," said Christine.

Abruptly Lisa pounded the steering wheel three times, the last so hard the car jiggled. *"We need Joan,"* she said. *"You would not believe what she did, for that matter, I still don't believe what she did!"* Lisa was so excited her voice trembled. "That little punk, that incredible little punk aced me, and ALL ALONE!!!" She turned to Christine, her face shining. "If we get her on our team, it's not only the State Championship, it's....it's...I don't know what. Is there something bigger than State Champion?"

"The Olympics," answered Christine blandly.

"We got to get this kid," said Lisa. "Whatever it takes."

"Let's hope that she makes up her mind to join," said Christine.

Or else, Lisa thought but knew better than to say it out loud.

When they got a block away from her house, Christine said a quick goodbye to Lisa, and a minute later was walking into the kitchen where her Mama was putting away the rest of the dishes.

"I could have helped you with that," Christine said as she slumped into a chair.

"It's okay, honey, the twins helped me and you still haven't had your dinner." She reached into the bowl on the table and in a moment the room was filled with the familiar aroma of spaghetti. Usually Christine's favorite, she didn't have much appetite but for Mama's sake she managed to eat about half. Since she had to be at work no later than 7:15 she got dressed quickly and was out the door fifteen minutes later.

Mr. Jones had been nice enough to give her the extra hours she asked for, so it would not be a good idea to be late. She had been up since 5:30 that morning, gone through a whole day of school, and with tonight's shift she would now have two days this week with less than five hours of sleep. There were games on Thursday and Saturday, each one after at least three hours at the store, before she could finally enjoy the once-a-week privilege on Sunday morning of sleeping in until 8:00.

Chapter Nine
Toussaint's

Joan

That afternoon the bus door opened and I stepped onto the sidewalk next to the Smithfield College Humanities building. There was something about a college campus that was totally familiar, having spent much of my life in and around them, and this one was particularly attractive. Perched on the top of the only real hill in town, it always caught the best views morning and evening as well as any stray breeze that happened along that way. As hot as it had been at school it was much cooler up here, helped by the enormous old live oaks and cottonwoods that shaded almost every inch of sidewalk.

I ran up the steps, heaved open the old oak door, and squeezed through. On either side of the foyer, a wide staircase led upwards, the steps still labeled UP and DOWN as they were when first built a hundred years before. Papa's office was on the second floor and I could still hear his voice in the lecture hall as I walked down the hallway. I opened the door and the light was off but enough light still filtered in that I could see that for once his big leather chair was empty, another sign that he had remembered our plans for the evening. I eased myself into it with the familiarity of putting on an old comfortable sweater, the leather feeling cool and smooth as it always did. I had been in this chair so many times it wasn't funny, first as a baby being held by Papa or Mama, then being able to sit by myself with my legs sticking straight out, my arms barely reaching the big armrests.

There were always a lot of books lying around and they were as disorganized as always, old leather-covered volumes piled helter-skelter with ragged looking pamphlets, various complete sets appearing in bits and pieces wherever he had found an empty space. Not that his mind was that way, not at all: he had great recall and could quote long passages verbatim...which was the problem. He could remember things, lots of things in fact, that were once silly and happy memories and that now reminded him of Mama and all that we had lost when she died.

Students were now moving in the hallway outside, and the door opened as Papa breezed inside, talking with Fred, his graduate assistant. Papa dropped his pile of class materials expertly onto the already precarious pile on the desk and gave me a quick wink before turning back to Fred.

"You're headed in the right direction, Fred. Your theory is on the right track, and should yield some interesting results if you don't get bogged down in too much detail."

Fred brightened. "You think..."

"Yes, that it has possibilities for some meaningful research, and we have some artifacts that should support your contention. It will also be a real help when we go back to the dig next summer" Papa replied. "Now Joan and I have a dinner date, so we will see you at eight o'clock sharp tomorrow in the museum."

"Hi Fred," I said as perkily as I could.

Fred was apparently startled by this but quickly recovered. "Hiya Joan. How was school today?" He turned back to Papa. "First day, right?"

Papa turned back to face me again, apparently having forgotten until now. "That's right. How was it?"

"It was good, thanks," I said, as much to get Fred on his way out of the office as to get us on our way to dinner.

After Fred left Papa sat on the corner of his desk the way he always did when I was in his chair.

"So how was it?" he asked.

"Not bad," I answered. "It was...an experience. How about over supper?"

He smiled back. "That's not only a good idea, I have a surprise for you."

That was always a good way to get my attention. "What is it?"

He smiled even more and shook his head. "How about over supper?"

Fifteen minutes later we were in a part of town I hadn't seen before, behind the high school and at the bottom of a long hill closer to the river, where we could start to hear the evening frog music, especially strong this time of the evening as the day was starting to cool off. Except for the crunch of tires on the gravel parking lot the only other sound was the cheerful racket that comes from a popular restaurant on a busy evening

"How did you find this place?" I asked.

"Well, you can be sure it doesn't show up on any Google search," replied Papa as we reached the steps leading inside. "There's a great old Cajun guy in our department named Antoine who has lived around here his whole life, and when we were talking yesterday he recommended it to us."

"Looks great, Papa," I said, my appetite already growing as we went inside.

It was cheerful, loud, and as French as any place I'd ever seen this side of the Atlantic. Not French in name, but French in the general feel of the restaurant, a place to eat and talk and drink and argue and laugh and sing, and when the music got going to dance till you dropped. Each table had a basket of baguettes in the center, a crock of the greatest butter I had ever tasted, a carafe of mineral water, and all of it sitting on a starched, checkered tablecloth. There was also a dance floor made from enormous wide cypress boards polished by feet, scrubbing, and a few thousand coats of floor wax.

The restaurant was busy that evening, and a tiny stage occupied one corner where a cheerful little man was perched on a stool playing the accordion and singing in a cracked voice. There were old folks who looked like they had eaten dinner here every night for years, a few courting couples, and two or three huge round tables with big extended families, the little kids eating, playing, or trying to dance to the music. The Maitre'd found us a table for two and we soaked up the atmosphere until our waiter found us.

He was a tall, thin high school student wearing an apron, a familiar face, and a tired expression so without further ado Papa ordered food for both of us, and then out of sheer habit a bottle of wine. He had done this when he was out with Mama but never with me, and I realized that he had done it out of pure reflex. I told him I needed to use the bathroom, and on my way, I took the waiter aside and changed the order from a bottle to a glass.

"Don't worry, Jeannette," he said. "Got you covered."

"How do you know my name?" I asked.

"Like I said, got you covered. I'm Antoine and Fred's my brother. The man who works at the college, old Antoine, is our Grandfather and this whole evening is prearranged."

"Prearranged?"

"Listen to me, Joan. Your Dad is the best thing to come along to that college since they invented sliced bread. He's smart, he's funny, and what's more important he treated Grandpa like a real human being. He invited Grandpa into his office, opened a bottle of Cognac, and then swapped stories for more than two hours. What goes around comes around, and we are going to give you two the best dinner you've ever had, so go back to your table, sit down, and have a good time!"

When I got back to the table the glass had arrived, and Papa did my chair for me like he used to do for Mama. I sat down with my most dazzling smile and exquisite manners, thanked Papa in my most excellent French, daintily touched the napkin to my lips, and tore off a hunk of the baguette that had been making my mouth water ever since we walked in the door. It was delicious, still hot in the center and with that ideal degree of flakiness that comes from being only a few minutes out of the oven.

Our dinner arrived after the right amount of time for us to work up a good appetite. It was a simple meal, two large bowls steaming hot with little bubbles still popping on the top from being ladled.

Papa closed his eyes and ever so gently breathed in the aroma, his expression worshipful. I watched, mesmerized, and after a few seconds he looked at me, picked his spoon, and held it out questioningly. I nodded, very slowly. He dipped the tip of the spoon into the soup and broke the surface enough to release more of that incredible aroma. He lifted the spoon, savored it for a moment, and ever so slowly put it into his mouth. He pursed his lips as he swallowed, turned back to me with this dreamy expression and said: "Dig in, Squirt."

He hadn't called me Squirt for a long time. Since...well, you know. It was without question the best soup I have ever heard of, read about, or seen, bar none. The only ingredients were goat's milk, wild woods mushrooms, white wine, fresh cut basil, crayfish, new potatoes, leeks, melted Brie, salt, fresh ground black pepper, and pure magic.

"So how was your day?" asked Papa about halfway down the bowl.

"Good, actually. I had four classes with Michelle, we ate lunch together, and I have a reasonable amount of homework, part of which I finished in your office," I answered before digging back into the bowl.

Two minutes passed.

"How was your day, Papa?" I asked, now about three-fourths finished.

"Great," he replied. "Classes are the right size. Students – most of them anyway – are interested in the topic. Fred's a very smart guy and going to be a big help, especially when we go back to Domremy next summer. I have all the materials I need and I get to teach in a nice big old fashioned lecture hall...with guess what?"

"Real blackboards?" like I didn't already know the answer.

"You're no fun," he said and took another sip.

We finished our meal in the classic way of wiping our bowls with fresh baguette not to leave even the smallest drop of that unbelievable soup, and after they whisked away the bowls Antoine brought something I had never seen before called Chess Pie. There was an older man along with Antoine, wiping his hands on his apron and beaming as Antoine introduced us. Papa stood up, and the older man said welcome and hugged Papa in the old way that you would have sworn they were old Army buddies at their fortieth Unit reunion. The man grabbed a spoon and clinked against Papa's glass, at which the noise settled down.

"My friends, I want to welcome our new friends Professor Paul Darcy and his daughter Jeannette to our community. May they always find a warm welcome, a helping hand, and enough gumbo to keep the wolf from the door."

Papa responded in a French dialect with something I couldn't quite understand right away. It turns out it was an old Cajun expression that meant "Thank you, God, for putting the Cajuns and the crawfish on the same Earth." That brought a big cheer and a general raising of glasses. It was wonderful seeing such friendly people with a peppering here and there of "Sante" from those who spoke or at least remembered a few words of French. There were some fishermen at the bar by this time, and over on one side in on the corner of the stage there was someone who smiled back at me when I caught her eye. In a moment, I was beside her table.

"Great soup," I said, motioning to the bowl. Duh.

"Magnifique," Miss Renoir replied, her eyes smiling as she motioned for me to sit. Now that I was at the table, everything I was going to say evaporated out of my brain. I felt a hand on my shoulder, knowing it was Papa saving me from looking like a complete idiot. Or so I thought.

"Perhaps you could introduce me?" It still amazed me that he knew exactly what's in my mind when I hadn't said a word. Maybe he read my body language or something, but he always knew the right thing to say. It also helped that he's the complete gentleman and of course he will ask for an introduction.

I stood up. "Papa, I would like to introduce my new French teacher Mademoiselle Renoir. Mademoiselle Renoir, this is my Papa." Nice, simple, basic, and brainless, but accurate at least. Papa continued being the complete gentleman, except that he switched into French and I realized that I was speaking in English, so my brainlessness came full circle.

I am a moderately religious person, or at least had been a regular at Mass up until…you know, but not lately. However, someone up there took pity on me because at that moment the accordion player started up and in about two heartbeats the dance floor was full. The music was infectious and I was over my embarrassment enough to be moving with the beat, but I looked at Papa and suddenly had an idea. Here's my gentleman Papa being introduced to a nice French lady who's alone in this restaurant, and dance music has started so there's only one gentlemanly thing to do. Yes, my brain was back in gear so I announced "be back in a minute" and took off back to the server's station.

"What are you nervous about?" Antoine asked.

"I am not nervous," I answered, but not convincingly.

He nodded. "Yeah, sure. You know, she's a real nice lady and even speaks our dialect. It's great to have a customer like that." He indicated across the floor to where instead of dancing Papa had sat down at Miss Renoir's table. "I think you are finished, Jeannette."

"Finished with what?" I said, half listening but staring across the room.

"Your bathroom break, dummy. Now shoo!" he said and gently pushed me out into the open. I made my way back to the table where I stood behind Papa and put my hand on his shoulder.

"It's wonderful that she will finally be challenged," Papa was saying. If you don't understand this, then imagine this: you are 13 years old and in a class where you are required to sit for ninety minutes a day copying out nice round block letters on paper where it's two inches between the horizontal lines.

"It has been a pleasure to meet you, Professor," Miss Renoir said, giving me a wink. She stood up and shook Papa's hand firmly, then turned to me. "Until tomorrow, Jeannette. Bonsoir."

Papa made a bow, and as we headed back to our own table I could tell he was waiting to ask me something but wasn't going to do it inside the restaurant. As we left we could see a tiny Renault turning in front of us, Miss Renoir at the wheel, and as she made the turn she gave us a smile and a wave. I waved back, Papa popped the locks on our car, and I got inside.

"A very nice lady," he said as we started out the driveway to the main road. "And very good for you, too, I dare say."

"Yes," I answered. A lot had happened today and even though I knew I had at least an extra hour of homework after we got home, I needed to talk. Papa was nonjudgmental and patient and everything but he had his own problems and I didn't want to be the one to add to them, but he could tell something was up.

"What's up?" he said ever so gently.

"Stuff," I answered. "Everything."

He waited.

"I got bullied today. At least Michelle did."

"And?"

"I think I stopped it. At least for a while, anyhow – but now I have a target on my back."

"Why?"

"Because they want me to join their stupid volleyball team, that's why. Supposedly they don't have enough people for their team so they think I'm the answer. Like I told them, I don't want to play but it seems they can't take no for an answer."

He was quiet for a minute, negotiating the gravel roads a lot more slowly than the way he usually drove in town. Toussaint's was a great restaurant but it sure was out in the middle of nowhere. We finally turned from gravel onto the regular pavement and he sped up.

"Why is their volleyball team stupid?" Papa asked. "It obviously means a lot to them."

This was not what I was expecting him to say. I thought he'd say something gentle and understanding like, 'Of course you don't have to join their stupid volleyball team' but instead he comes up with this.

"Before you say the first thing that comes into your head, think about what I said, and why I said it. A lot of people make the mistake of not seeing what other people value, and not giving them credit for what they find important. That's not right and it's not fair, so give me an answer after you've thought it through."

"It's...not stupid. You're right, it is what they value and I guess it feels good for them to be good at it."

"You know what that's like. So?"

"I guess if they want me so badly, they must see me as the answer to their problem."

"What's wrong with that?"

"Because I don't want to be on any volleyball team or any other team. I want to start fencing again." It was out of my mouth before I realized it. I missed fencing. A lot. A whole lot, in fact, and hadn't wanted to admit how much it reminded me of Mama.

He wasn't surprised. "I think I saw that coming," he said, and darn it, he started to get that little smile again. I was good and sad now, and enjoying it, and was determined I was not going to feel better, and the fact that he was smiling was not helping, and - oh shoot, now I'm smiling too..

"While I was talking to Miss Renoir the subject of your fencing came up. She was very interested."

"What do you mean by 'interested'?" I asked.

He burst out laughing, shaking his head. "Squirt, you sure could become a good trial lawyer. That is exactly what I would have said at your age, and you know what, you're right. You should know what I meant." By now we were on our street and turning into our own driveway, and after we parked he switched off the car and faced me.

"What it means is that Miss Renoir was a member of France's 2004 Olympic fencing team. She retired from the sport to become a teacher and as you know she happens to be teaching at Smithfield High School, where, as I recall, you are a student in her French 5 class. Try real hard to put two and two together."

"She actually wants to do this? To teach me?"

"After one class, she already thinks very highly of you," said Papa. "Yes, she is interested in teaching fencing again, but only if you are her pupil. Does that sound 'interested' enough for you?"

"I'll have to think about it," I said and put on a serious face. But only for a few seconds.

Chapter Ten
Football Night
Michelle

In some parts of the US, there are traditions forever associated with certain days of the week. Sunday morning church, Saturday Fish Fry, Friday Happy Hour, all represent times of the week when people leave work behind and gather together to enjoy each other's company.

Friday night for much of the country was football night, when the townspeople gathered at one stadium or another and cheered on the local team. From tiny towns in West Texas where they played five-man football, to cities where crime increased on Friday nights because everyone was at the game, the ritual continued. Nearly everybody in town was involved. There were players on the field, cheerleaders on the sidelines, the band sweating in their uniforms, more parents in the stands with their noisemakers and seat pillows, and students to yell and chase and flirt and hang out and occasionally actually cheer on the team. After the game was over, pizza shops would crank on until the small hours of the morning, and fast food restaurants would be packed with kids eating, laughing, hanging out, and jostling to park next to one special car.

Smithfield had its own Friday Nights, starting a hundred years ago, with a few students playing a rather genteel form of rugby in a cow pasture, and evolving into a perennial State Champion that other towns envied. Coach Reed had kept his program both clean and on top for almost twenty years, but the whole program had almost come crashing down the year before with Brian Granger's injury and Coach Reed's going to prison.

There had been an official inquest since Brian had been hurt so badly, but Todd's testimony and Brian's blood work settled it. There was a news conference where Todd made an emotional speech about how much the football program meant to the community, and after he got everybody in tears he made a direct plea to the State Athletic commission to forego suspending the school from league play. It didn't hurt that Todd's old fraternity buddy was on the commission, and it was by that one vote that football was kept alive at Smithfield.

Joan

Ever since our talk about my starting up fencing again, Papa was getting more interested in what I was doing at school, and to my surprise, he was pleased that I agreed to be in the pep band.

"It will help you make friends, for one thing. I know it sounds like a broken record, but it is good for you to do something for the school."

When he put it that way it made more sense, I guess, since it was true and our family rule was to always do your part. Even more importantly, it was my chance to do something for Mrs. Coates. She was a genuinely nice person, and both Michelle and I could always count on her for a hall pass or a quiet place to come in and sit.

I polished up my Saxophone, bought a few new reeds, and even practiced for an hour or so to start getting my chops back. Michelle and I worked it out so that Papa would drive us to and from the game, so when Friday evening rolled around Papa dropped us off at Smith Field and said he would be back to pick us up at 10:30.

We made our way through the crowd to gate three where Mrs. Coates told us to go, and the ticket taker saw our instrument cases and waved us through. Smith Field is quite a unique stadium and one of the best playing fields I have ever seen. About a half mile away from the High School, it is actually a converted ravine that still has a stream running through it on one side. The sides of the ravine were smoothed out years ago, and instead of having a stadium pushing straight up in the air you have a stadium that nestles into the ravine like a smaller mixing bowl fits perfectly into a larger mixing bowl. Instead of the entrance to the stands being at ground level. The main entrance to Smith Field is at the top, with thirty rows of seats going down until you get to the field at the bottom. It also meant that on game nights the ravine concentrates the noise so that cheering turns into a wall of sound inside the stadium.

Michelle and I entered this maelstrom and made our way to where the rest of the pep band was sitting. After getting settled, we looked across the field to see that the other team had brought a band so enormous that they filled half of the visitor's seats. In contrast, we had an enormous group consisting of one trumpet, two trombones, Michelle's clarinet, my saxophone, and one bass drum. With all of that, we would be lucky if we could be heard by the football team twenty feet in front of us.

Mrs. Coates was grateful and thanked Michelle and me for coming, and since the two of us increased the size of the band by 35 percent I guess we knew why. Since this was our first game a few of the other members had tried to give us some advice, but what they described seemed so exaggerated that neither of us took it very seriously. Now that we were inside the belly of the beast, however, a lot more of what they had said made sense. I could talk to Michelle, and she could talk to me, but unless we shouted we couldn't hear each other unless we were six inches apart.

Mrs. Coates waved her arms and the others stood up, so we did too while a few of the cheerleaders dragged some giant horseshoe shaped thing onto the field with a big piece of flimsy paper on it, a giant S painted in the middle.

"What's the most important rule at a game, Ryan?" yelled Mrs. Coates.

"The most important rule is to play LOUD," Ryan yelled back.

"And don't stop, no matter what happens," yelled Lenny, the trumpet player, at which the others looked meaningfully at each other and nodded. The two trombone players Dwight and George both reached into their pockets, took out little orange earplugs, and stuck one into each ear.

"Here they come!"

There was a signal from down on the field, and Mrs. Coates' downbeat started us playing the Fight Song. It was probably the best I had ever done sight-reading a piece of music, but I will never know for sure since I couldn't hear myself play. The roar that enveloped the field reminded me of something out of Jurassic Park, and I am not talking about the poor Triceratops with his giant pile of poop. I am talking about the T-Rex when he is right on top of the car with those two kids inside, trying to get them to move so he opens his mouth and roars directly into their faces. It was a roar that had its own personality, address, and fan club, and if it were anywhere else except here at a football game I would have started to run.

"Great job, Ryan," said Mrs. Coates, and all the other band members started clapping, with Ryan grinning like we were the nicest people in the whole world.

As for Mrs. Coates, I guess she could at least tell we were playing and that we looked like we knew what we were doing, because there was no way in the world she could have heard a single note. George's Dad delivered a big bag of hot dogs and a cold drink for everybody, and after the Star-Spangled Banner was over I settled back to eat and watch and take it easy for a while. Little did I know.

An hour later the first half was finally over, and everyone in our group drooped in utter exhaustion, lips numb and fingers sore from constant playing. I never knew that I could grow to hate any particular song, but since it was the custom – and our job – to play the Official Smithfield High School Fight Song every time there was a home team touchdown, or even a first down, up went Mrs. Coates' arms and off we went again. Since it was now halftime the other band was on the field making a giant lawn mower and we had at least fifteen minutes of our own.

"Hey guys - we're going to get some popcorn," asked George. "You guys want to come?"

It's always a surefire method to get Michelle moving by mentioning food, so with Ryan bringing up the rear we made our way down the steps and onto the running track that circled the football field. During football games, it also served as a combination food court/shopping mall, and fans could visit the Pizza stand, the Hot Dog stand, the Lerch's Donut wagon, the Football Parents team souvenir shop, the Kettle Corn stand, and of course the restrooms. I had promised myself not to drink much when I was not sure of restroom facilities, and the look of the massive line stretching from the lady's room affirmed the wisdom of this plan.

The twins were talkative, friendly, and especially nice to us, and surprisingly they did not only talk about sports.

"Ever meet anybody named Dwight before?" asked Dwight.

It turned out that his Grandpa fought in France during World War II and had been something of a hero. "Daddy heard so many stories when he was growing up that it seemed natural to name us after Generals, I guess, "said George. "I guess maybe he hoped it would rub off on us someday but it hasn't yet."

"I'd like to meet this Grandpa of yours," I said, meaning it. Domremy was occupied from 1941 to 1944 and more than once the Germans took people off the streets and shot them as hostages. Since the Americans liberated the village in August 1944, anybody who fought for France was a hero in my book.

"Sure," he replied, sounding genuinely pleased. "Any time."

The popcorn stand was still open with only a few people standing in line, and as we waited I saw one student in a wheelchair who glanced over at us like we were talking too much. I was sure I'd seen him before, and although I usually didn't talk about people I was genuinely curious.

"Dwight - who is that over there, in the wheelchair? I remember seeing him around school once or twice."

"That's Brian. He used to be the best football player we ever had at this school and even made the Varsity team as a freshman. But a year ago, at the Garland game, the biggest game of the year, something happened. Something bad."

"What was that? What happened?"

"He got injured," Dwight replied, his voice getting softer. "He made a phenomenal touchdown run at the end of the first half, and we thought for sure with him playing, we had the whole game wrapped up. Then, in the first play of the second half a whole bunch of Garland players creamed him. Weren't sure at first he was even going to live, spinal cord damage and all, and they even got a helicopter to take him to the hospital."

"You saw it happen, didn't you?" I asked quietly.

Dwight nodded.

"That's quite a thing to remember," I said.

"The injury wasn't all, unfortunately," replied Dwight. "There's more that came out afterward, a lot more, that he'd been on drugs or something and was half out of it before that game even started. It got worse, lots worse."

Chapter Eleven
Brian

Friday nights in the fall always meant football to me ever since I was old enough to go a few hours without taking a nap, and with the enthusiasm in our family, it was natural for me to want to play myself. I started with peewee football when I was five and worked all the way to being a first-string by the time I was in eighth grade. This is one of the reasons it hurt so much sitting there in a wheelchair instead of being out on the field helping our team win.

Not that I hadn't been injured before, or seen injuries happen. There was a time during 5th grade when I got hit right in the nose by a football being passed less than ten feet away and the blood squirted into my eyes, but I intercepted the darn thing and ran it in for a touchdown. During the first play of my first eighth-grade game I was playing defensive guard and my buddy Robb was playing defensive tackle, and on the first play, there was a CRACK! and Robb looked down to see the end of his arm bone sticking out. The game resumed after the ambulance left and I was so mad I sacked the other team's quarterback five times. We won that game 54-0.

Mr. Todd came to our house after that game, and after Mom and Dad sent me to bed they talked for a long time. Even though I was exhausted I managed to sneak out of my room and lie down on the hallway carpet so I could listen to the conversation downstairs. Everybody had their voices turned way down after Mama shushed them a few times, so it was hard to make out exactly what they were saying, but I did hear the word State Championship and Scholarship and All-State and other incredible words being tossed around. After a while, I snuck back into bed and lay there dreaming for a while.

Problem was, by the end of eighth grade, I still hadn't grown very much. I was in great shape and muscular but I still weighed only 125 pounds and that wasn't going to cut it. That summer I tried out and easily made the Junior Varsity team, but what I actually wanted was to be a Varsity player.

The second week in August I went to the locker room after an extra workout and saw that someone had been in my locker. There was a small box sitting inside labeled "Mineral Supplement" with a yellow sticker like you get from the doctor with a three boxes checked off. There was a long list of vitamins, minerals, and something called trace elements in it, and that it was "guaranteed to rejuvenate dormant growth processes." Since there was nothing I wanted more than to be big enough to make Varsity, I popped it open and chugged the whole thing right down. My stomach took it OK and it even made me feel full, but I also had a burning sensation in my throat and nose like I had taken cough syrup. That night I slept like a baby and woke up the next morning full of energy and so hungry I could eat a horse and a real big one at that.

By the end of October, I had gained twenty pounds, my legs were solid muscle, I could bench press 210 pounds, and although I was no taller I was nobody to mess with on the football field. Mama was going to start buying new shirts for me, but since I started wearing my football jerseys to school every day it put an end to that problem for a while.

It wasn't without its problems, though. Sometimes I would get double vision about half an hour after the morning bottle and I had to make sure I didn't drink one before a game, but if I gave the morning bottle the whole day to work I could still have an energy boost by game time. This worked out great, and whenever the supply got low another full box appeared all by itself. After a few weeks, I found that if I had one more bottle right after school on Friday, I would be all set by game time that evening.

I got my promotion up to the Varsity team and did so well that I started to see some serious game time. By the afternoon of the big Garland game in November, I had already finished two bottles that day and during the pep talk before the game, I couldn't keep still. Mr. Todd had been talking about how we were going to run them off the field and told me he was expecting great things that evening. Coach Reed said he wanted to talk to me before the game started, but when I got there Mr. Todd was with him.

"There's a scout from Texas A&M up there in the stands," said Coach Reed.

"Never too early, is it, Brian?" said Mr. Todd, but Coach Reed didn't look happy about it.

"You do your job tonight, Brian, and don't try to be a hero," Coach Reed said. "We are eight and zero for the season, and Garland is two and six. We don't need a miracle for this game, just solid football without anything fancy."

Given the way my head was feeling it sounded right but I wasn't used to anyone telling me to take it easy. Garland had always been our biggest rival and everybody I knew was in the stands tonight. As we went down the tunnel toward the field it got louder and louder until we exploded onto the field, and you could feel the ground shaking with all that energy.

We got the first touchdown two minutes into the game, and our kickoff team went out and Garland ran it back to the 40. I put on my helmet and started to go out with the others when I heard Coach Reed yell at me to get back on the bench. I stopped dead in my tracks and half turned around, not believing what I was hearing. Coach Reed looked right at me and pointed at the bench like he does when he means business. I wasn't the only one wondering what the heck was going on but one look from Coach Reed and I sat down. That's the way it was the whole first half, me sitting there and Coach Reed putting in second stringers and our team getting run all over the field about half the time, and by the time the second quarter ended Garland was ahead 31-16. Jimmy had done a great job kicking for two twice in a row, but seeing that Garland had the ball for two-thirds of the first half he didn't get many chances.

Coach Reed had an ironclad rule that nobody but nobody who isn't either an official or a doctor gets anywhere near his players during a game, but that day he had to order Mr. Todd off the field three times whenever he came storming out of his box seat and onto the field.

"You get him into the game," hissed Mr. Todd.

"This is my team and I say I won't," replied Coach Reed. "There's something not right about him tonight, and I am not going to take any chances." He pointed back at me. "That boy is potentially the best player we have and we don't need him in this game tonight."

Mr. Todd shook his head. "You still want to have a job this time tomorrow?"

Coach Reed stood and stared at him. "You wouldn't," he said.

You know, I didn't think about this at the time especially since Coach Reed was three games shy of the being the winningest Coach in State History, but he was also three years past mandatory retirement age and there was no way he would ever get back into a school, especially since his heart attack last spring. As far as I was concerned, all I wanted was to get out there on the field and show those college scouts what I could do. The referee blew the whistle to end the timeout, Coach Reed traded another look with Mr. Todd and turned to me.

"Number 67 in for 24," he said. I shoved on my helmet and ran out onto the field, the crowd getting to its feet and going crazy. Being in football made me understand why Rock Stars and Movie Stars will sometimes do anything to stay in front of crowds for as long as they can. There's something about that sound, when thousands of people yelling all about you that makes you think you're immortal.

We went into the first play and I got the handoff, charging my way through two different Garland players and knocking them aside like bowling pins. The field was clear in front of me and I ran like an express train fifty-five yards down the field with Garland players getting further and further behind me, and before I knew it I was across the goal line, spiking the ball and soaking up the delicious roar of the crowd. Jimmy ran it in for the extra two points and the score was 24 for us and Garland one touchdown away at 31, and by this time the crowd yelling so loud I thought the stadium might collapse. The gun cracked to end the first half and we were off down the steps and back into the locker room with everybody slapping Jimmy and me on the back.

Coach Reed always had this thing about halftime being the time you recharge your batteries. I swabbed off my face and neck the way I always did and noticed right away that I was dog tired which didn't make any sense seeing that I was only on one play the entire first half. When I went to my locker, staring me right in the face was another little bottle of the Mineral Supplement, and without another thought, I popped it open and swallowed it in one gulp. That made it a total of three I'd had that day, but in a few seconds, I felt that old familiar warmth start to kick in and ten minutes later I led the team back down the corridor and up the steps back onto the field.

We kicked off to Garland the second half, they fumbled the return, and we recovered the ball at the thirty-five-yard line. By now I was revved up like a Formula One car and nothing could have kept me from going onto the field. We got into the huddle and halfway through his instructions Jimmy stopped short and stared at me.

"You feeling okay, Brian? You don't look too good."

I had no idea what he was talking about. I was fired up and pumped up and about every other up and waiting for a chance to go out and eat some Garland players for a snack. I wanted to win, sure, but I usually remembered that the guys on the other team were guys like me and I wanted to beat 'em, sure, but not destroy them. That was not on my mind this evening and especially not here on the field before this play.

"I'm fine, Jimmy," I said, and tried to slow myself down.

Jimmy took one more look and said, "34, Brian up the middle on 82." We slapped hands TEAM and got into our positions.

Garland had made some changes, too, because when we got into line they had five players all lined up on my side of the quarterback, all of them glaring at me like I had a bull's-eye painted on my helmet. When I got into position I started to feel light headed and then...

"82!" Everything slowed down, the ball was in my hands and I couldn't remember what I was supposed to do next, and the last thing I remember was the faces of those five Garland players.

The Garland game was on the evening of November 9th and it wasn't until the 16th that I finally woke up. They had stopped the game and didn't dare move me until the paramedics came, and after one look they called for the Medivac helicopter which ended up landing right in the middle of the field.

It was traumatic spinal cord injury, "affecting the area between T2 and T3 with highly localized neurological trauma affecting the voluntary motor functions below." If that sounds fancy, it's because I heard that phrase repeated to every doctor and medical student who came to see me. The other part was "Exacerbated by the presence of methyl stenbolone which has contributed to significant muscular hypertrophy. However, MPTP is additionally present. Prognosis uncertain." If you are wondering what all of that means, well, the upshot was that I had a bad spinal injury that left me paralyzed from the mid-chest down, and probably would never walk again.

Seeing that I was...had been a football star, I was expecting maybe there would be a whole lot of flowers or cards or at least something cheerful in that hospital room, but there was only one little vase of flowers from Mama that she kept replacing every day she came to visit me. One day when they were sitting there and nobody was saying anything, I'd finally had enough. "Whatever it is, spill it," I said.

"What do you mean, Brian?" said Papa.

"Whatever it is that nobody is telling me. For example, why are you two the only ones coming to see me? Where's Jimmy, where's the team, and especially where's Coach Reed?"

The room stayed real quiet for a minute, but Mama was always the one to tell the truth first.

"Coach Reed is gone, Brian."

"What do you mean, gone?"

"Gone meaning he's in jail, Brian," said Papa angrily. "He pled guilty and he's up at Central."

I wasn't hearing this, I just wasn't. "Central? Central what? Pled guilty to what?"

"Central State Prison. Guilty to supplying you with those drugs, Brian. For doing this to you!"

"What do you mean, doing this to me? WHAT DRUGS?"

"Those darn drugs that Coach Reed gave you, Brian," said Papa, almost shouting. "Remember those little bottles of 'Mineral Supplement?' Well, they were all made in Mexico real nice and illegal, and they found six boxes of it locked in his office closet. Inside each bottle was something called methyl-something or other, a steroid that's supposed to build up your muscles, but this one is so dangerous they won't even let it into the country." Papa was walking around the room now, the way he did when he was getting more riled up. "They got a tip, and when they opened the closet in his office Coach Reed stood there staring at those bottles and mumbling about he should never have sent you in on that last play. The prosecutor offered him a deal and they shipped him off to prison the next day."

Chapter Twelve
October

Joan

The first month of school had come and gone, and everything was going more or less okay. I'd talked with Miss Renoir about fencing, and we agreed we would let me get settled in and start the beginning of October. Michelle and I saw each other for three classes every day and were lucky enough to have lunch together, so it was great touching base during the day when each of us had something to share.

We had something else in common, too. In case you hadn't figured it out by now, Michelle is *smart*. When that happens at a school like this, you need to play it down or you're going to get yourself in trouble. I can take it or leave it as far as raising my hand to answer questions in class, but unfortunately, Michelle is not built that way and in some of her classes she already had been marked by the teacher as a completely reliable person to call on.

Unfortunately, both Michelle and I still had to put up with an occasional snide remark, our books accidentally being shoved off a table, or being bumped hard in the hallway. I could take care of myself, but it bothered me that the volleyball players had apparently gotten it into their heads that picking on Michelle would supposedly make me agree to be on their team. I had so far avoided telling anyone else about it, but the way things were going it was only a matter of time until one of them would go too far.

Miss Renoir's class was the high point of my day, even though I had more homework from French 5 than all my other classes put together. There was always a long list of questions I brought with me each morning as I worked my way through Les Miserables. Since so much of the vocabulary was new and interesting, I even found myself using some of the new words in my conversations with Papa and Miss Renoir.

At the end of French class on October first Miss Renoir closed Madame Bovary without giving me a new assignment for the next day. "Are you ready, Jeanne?" she asked. "If so, we will add fencing to our daily routine beginning tomorrow. I have spoken with Coach Anita and she has given us permission to use the basketball court outside."

I had never fenced anywhere except in a studio, and doing it outside at school in front of...well, everybody, seemed too different. "Won't that be...well, weird?" I said, and immediately realized I struck a nerve.

"Why do you use that word, 'weird'? What does it mean, exactly?"

The more I thought about it the less definite it seemed, and every direction my mind took for a definition always ended up sounding stupid. "Weird means...unusual."

"When you go into the woods and see a new and rare bird, you say it is weird?"

"No...but..." She didn't let me finish.

"I hear you use this word for only one reason: that you have heard others use it and you are too lazy to find a word with the correct meaning." By now she was quite passionate, and I saw her take a breath before continuing. "Jeanne, language is beautiful and cutting and emotional and technical and everything you want it to be, but only if you think before speaking. The world is full of intelligent people, but many do not think before they speak and their intelligence is dismissed. That is NOT to be what happens to you!"

Hearing the passion in her voice, I knew truly for the first time how much she cared about me, and it made me resolve to follow her advice the best I could. When I begin to get emotional, I become one of those people whose expression speaks the truth, and right away I saw her face soften as she saw that I truly understood what she was saying.

"Bien, Jeannette," she said and gave me a quick hug before locking at her watch. "I will see you on the court immediately after school, dressed for our practice. Agreed?"

"Oui."

"Very well. Au revoir."

I was there exactly on time, rather self-consciously wearing my gym clothes. The court was in a back corner of the oldest part of the school, and except for a few crows perched on the roof we were alone. The pavement was so old it was cracked and the two basketball hoops needed a coat of paint, but it was very private. Two blue chairs sat on one end, along with a box that I recognized as a foil case.

"Go over there, please." She pointed to a spot on the court about three feet in front of the basket. I did as she said, realizing that I was getting excited. One of the great things about having an eccentric teacher is that you never quite know what is going to happen next. She unlocked the case, withdrew a gleaming foil and handed it to me.

"Show me what you can do," she said, picking up one of the chairs and placing it on the foul line "That chair is your opponent. Surround it with steel, but do not touch. Do you understand?"

"Oui." It felt strange to be holding a foil without wearing any gear, and at the school of all places, but it also gave me a feeling of lightness and release. I took it properly in my hand, testing its weight, its supple feeling in my hand and wrist, finding the balance that Mama had always made me practice so endlessly...

"Are you ready?"

I nodded and imperceptibly curled my toes, rising a centimeter.

"Allez!"

My heavens this feels great...

Miss Renoir

It is a wonderful thing to watch Jeanne prepare for fencing. I have only seen it in those who began at an early age, but once you grow to be one with the blade it becomes an extension of yourself. Her expression changed and with it the entire way she carried herself. Her senses were totally concentrated as she unconsciously demonstrating dozens upon dozens of variations and surrounded the chair with a shimmering steel shell. A regular fencing match is over in a few moments but today she seemed able to keep going forever, until...Thwack!

"Touché," I said. "The chair has won."

She saw the hint of a smile on my face, grinned back at me, bowed to the chair, flipped it around and sat in it, flushed and happy.

"This is the best blade I have ever held in my life," she said, turning it lovingly in her hand, feeling its heft and exquisite balance.

"Perhaps you may earn it someday," I replied quietly. "Now we will begin our first lesson."

Chapter Thirteen
Real Friends
Brian

After my injury, I was in traction for two weeks to give my spine the best possible chance to get itself back into position, the parts that worked anyway, and it was the hardest two weeks of my life. They put you into this bed where they strap you up and then attach cables and weights and springs every which way hoping to get the pressure off from where the nerves were damaged. Everybody was relieved that my arms were okay, but the first time I tried moving my legs I near fainted from the pain. The crazy thing is they said that was good, too, because when the pain was there the nerves were working. Tell me about it.

But because the nerves worked it didn't mean that they all worked right, and when they hauled me out of that bed and into the wheelchair I wasn't about to rent the Church basement for a celebration. I went home two days later and found Mom and Dad had turned the TV room into a downstairs bedroom. They had renovated the bathroom with a giant shower stall and even had a waterproof wheelchair so I could sit right in there and wash myself, not exactly a fan of the idea that someone else was going to do it for me.

My arms were already strong and it was no great trick to learn how to drive the wheelchair. Since Smithfield was also flat as a board, I was also able to go almost anywhere and to zip along as fast as I wanted. I went back to school one month to the day after the accident, and since I didn't say much everybody thought I was doing fine.

Except I wasn't. I was mad, madder than I had ever been in my life, and I aimed all of it at myself. Stupid, stupid me, who wanted a shortcut to success when more patience and hard work would have gotten me there. I was especially mad at whoever came up with the Mineral Supplement that pushed everything over the edge. Right after the accident the police came up came up with the idea that it was all because of Coach Reed, but I didn't believe for a second that he had anything to do with it. Someone else had been putting those bottles into my locker, and whoever did it was still out there.

I went through the motions every day, doing my homework, watching a lot of TV, and turning into a slob. I had spent my whole life planning to be a Smithfield High School Football Player, and when that was over for good I didn't find another door open and waiting. Daddy saw this and between him and Mama they came up with a plan to get me out of the house and keep me out of trouble. They got one of those special vans with a wheelchair lift, so they picked me up every day after school and started taking me to the ACE Security store where I got a job working at a computer doing all the ordering and stuff. Cousin Fred owns the store and his son Louis had gone off to college, so I at least didn't push anybody out of a job.

I had been typing since elementary school and on the first day, they got me started by entering a big pile of invoices. If you've ever watched people do online accounting then you know it's not the same as brain surgery, so there I am after an hour and the whole pile finished as nice as you please. Now there's nothing left for me to do and two more hours left for me not to do it in. I have no idea why it took Cousin Louis three hours to do this but it did get me to thinking: here I am on my first day and it took me all of ten minutes to figure out how to do this job.

So, either I'm smart, or I'm just plain lucky that this computer stuff is so easy. With what happened to me I don't think I'll put a checkmark in the just plain lucky column, not yet anyway, so that means smart is the one that's left. But if I'm so smart, then what was I doing taking that Mineral Supplement? Either there are a lot of different ways to be smart or lucky, or there's good and bad smart like good and bad lucky. It's hard to figure out.

So here I am in my usual spot at the third football game of the season and I'm hungry as a horse. Papa had picked me up from work and driven me straight to the field, so I missed supper without thinking about it. The first half went by quickly the way it always did, we were ahead 64-0, and I was feeling like total crap except there's no way for me to get home until the game is over. A couple different people came up to talk to me, but I didn't answer other than to say "Okay" to their questions.

It's easier than you think to be alone in a stadium full of people, especially if you make sure to be unpleasant. I could have made a sign that said something like

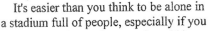

But I didn't think about it so I had to keep saying it out loud. Right on schedule at halftime here comes Dwight and George and Ryan on their way over to the Kettle Corn stand and they've got those same two girls with them as before. Dwight comes over to say Hi and I say Hi back but nothing else, and when he asks me how I am I say Fine and nothing else, and when he starts to say something more I want to tell him to get lost except I look away and don't say anything.

Dwight takes the hint and so does George and Ryan and they head back over to the stands but a minute later I feel a tap on my shoulder and here's one of those girls again. She's tall and has long hair and looks Chinese or something, but I can also tell that now she's ticked off too by the way she is standing there all wound up. I'm expecting her to start yelling at me about the way I talked to George, but she says something else instead that catches me completely by surprise.

"You hungry?" she says, standing there with one hand on her hip.

"No," I answer.

"Liar," she answers back and keeps looking at me. Apparently, she has a lot more patience than me because five minutes later she's still standing there and I still haven't said anything. I finally turn and look at her, and instead of being mad she's barely holding in her laughter.

"Why are you still here?" I said, growling at her but that isn't working and despite myself, I can't seem to stay mad. I thought I was stubborn but it looks like she's a real piece of work in that department.

"Because I've been watching you for almost two hours and since you haven't had anything to eat or drink, I brought you something," she says, and reaches into her backpack and pulls out a box of what looks like Chinese food.

Thank you, God, are the first words in my mind, but what comes out is a strangled "Got a fork?" and one appears magically in her hand.

"Say please first," she says in a real hokey little girl voice but thinks better of it when she sees my look and hands it to me. I open the box and it's not Chinese but spaghetti with meatballs and there's even an extra packet of Parmesan cheese and yes, it's been thirteen hours since I had anything to eat and before you know it the box is empty. I've had spaghetti before and since, but I swear that was the best I ever ate. You know, since I was both hungry and feeling sorry for myself at the same time, I guess it took more energy to do both at once.

"Thanks...what's your name?" I finally asked, or did after a huge burp.

"Michelle," she answered, then got back into that hand-on-my-hip-pay-attention-to-me-or-else pose. "You still hungry?"

"You sound just like my Mom," I said.

"Good," she answers, "but answer my question before you tell me about your family."

"You sure are pushy," I answer.

"You betcha," she says. "So I guess you still are hungry." She reached into her backpack again and pulled out another box that looked like the first one.

"More Chinese?" I ask. "As a matter of fact, yes for this one, although 'more' is a bit inaccurate." She opens the box and this one had deep fried shrimp inside, except there were tiny pieces of pepper cooked into the breading along with shreds of coconut and something else I couldn't tell but didn't get a chance to because these were also gone in about two minutes. I look up at her while I was chewing.

"Deep fried shrimp with pepper, cocoanut and Hoisin sauce," she said.

"Tastes like Cajun," I answer.

"Chinese Cajun. I got the peppers at the Piggly Wiggly." Michelle sat down right there on the grass and said, "So tell me about what you are going to do about this wheelchair."

For almost a year people had been smiling at me all sad looking and asking me how I felt and telling me they were sure hoping I would feel better and slobbering feeling sorry for me but not saying so, and you have no idea how tiring that gets unless you have ever been the one sitting in a wheelchair looking back. Here I've known Michelle for a whole ten minutes and she's the first one to cut to the chase and ask about what I'm going to do with myself. I start to tell her about how I got injured but she cuts me off short.

"I don't want to know how you got into this chair. That's in the past and unless you are still doing whatever it was that put you here, it's not important anymore. What I want to know is what you are going to do so this chair of yours doesn't hold you back. People get hurt all the time and sometimes they get into one of these things and it just takes over. It stops being a way to get places and starts defining who you are."

52

She was looking right at me and it was weird how passionate she was getting. Mom says that sometimes I need hit over the head to get my brain in gear, and this time it started up without the thump she would sometimes give me to emphasize her point. Then it dawned on me: this isn't about me it's about her, dummy, but since she isn't in a chair herself it must be...

"So, who in your family is in one of these things?" I asked. Bingo, the man wins a cigar.

"My cousin Paul," she said. "Big college athlete, but he had a swimming accident and it broke something in his back, like you. He dropped out of college and was moping around for almost three years before he finally pulled himself together."

"And..."

"Now he's the owner of a big software company out in California and you'd never guess what he specializes in," she said with a grin. "No, not special software for people in wheelchairs – he writes spacecraft simulation software for the Air Force. Can't walk down a flight of steps but he sure can pilot a rocket all the way into orbit. Seen him do it, too – in the simulator, that is."

"So, your point is, that I can be like your cousin, right?" I asked, but I was in for a surprise.

"No, you're not smart enough," she replied, and gave me that look again.

I laughed so hard I was afraid I was going to lose either the spaghetti or shrimp or both, but I didn't care. It was so darn refreshing to be talking to her because everybody – and I mean everybody – had been feeling sorry for me. Maybe, just maybe, she was the one person who would be straight with me.

"Can I ask you something, Michelle?"

"Sure."

"I have a part time job doing computer work for my cousin and it's supposed to be this big complicated thing that would take me months to learn. You know what? It only took me about fifteen minutes to figure out, and now whenever I go to work scheduled for three hours I'm done in fifteen minutes with all that extra time left over. Got any ideas?"

"If you get the work done right do they care what you do with the rest of your time?" she asked.

"Guess not. I've been there for nine months and they said it's the first time ever that they haven't had something sent back, so that must count for something. Business has been great lately so there are a lot of new installations every week..."

"Installations of what?" she asked. "You haven't told me what they sell."

"The company is called Ace Security. They sell computer security systems, and..."

"And you are wondering what to do with your extra time?" she exclaimed. "Sitting there in a business that...do you have ANY idea how great that is?" She was so excited she started pacing around in circles. "There's a computerized security system at Smith College where my dad works, and your company must have installed it because there's a big ACE Security sign on the server. It's connected to absolutely everything on campus, and not only burglar alarms. They control all the internet traffic in and out, the remote A/V equipment, entrance gates, you name it. If you like what you are doing and you have that much time, I'll bet they would give anything to have a family member with the expertise to design and set up those systems. Got to. There's always a big shortage of people who can do that!"

"I'll make you a bet. You promise to ask your cousin if you can learn how to set up the servers, and if he turns you down I'll make shrimp for you every school day for a month. What do you say?"

"How about Spaghetti?" I asked.

I had Mom take me in on Saturday morning to talk with Cousin Gerald and sure enough, not only was Michelle right but he practically sat down and cried. Apparently, he had to turn down some sizable contracts because they simply didn't have enough systems engineers, so that same day he gave me a system to take home and learn with. It might sound like bragging but I stayed up late learning how it all went together and six weeks later we shipped the first server that I had set up by myself. The customer was happy, Cousin Gerald was happy and I even got a nice bonus. Mom and Dad were both ecstatic and surprised, and me? Well, we invited Michelle over for dinner and had the best spaghetti ever. By the way, she brought it with her – but I did the dishes.

Chapter Fourteen
For the Love of Volleyball
Lisa

When I was in Middle School I sometimes talked to other girls who had been on the volleyball team during high school, and they would always tell me about how much fun it was to be on the team, hanging out with the other girls, practicing hard, and riding to and from games on a school bus. Once I was on the team, I found out they're right about the fun and the friendships, but since we have such a small team parents drive us to our games. It's still a lot of fun to go to the away games, except for the fact that we can't talk about anything without some of the grownups listening in.

We had a great record of 11-2 overall and 9-0 in our conference, but there were still some tough opponents ahead of us. We did have another record that none of us wanted to talk about, the record of having the smallest varsity volleyball team in the school's history. We were down to seven players, which meant that during an average game we rotated out exactly once during the game. If we had tough competition, we were sometimes never rotated out at all. All of us were wringing wet and exhausted by the end of every game, especially if it went past fifteen points like it did more and more often. Christine kept playing as hard as always, and it was heartbreaking to see how much it took out of her.

Some of us kept working on getting Joan to join us, and even Christine was getting hotter under the collar to see Joan walking around the school not part of our team. We also noticed how Joan was always hanging out with that other new girl, Michelle, which is how I came up with the idea. There's an old country saying: to catch the cow, lasso the calf. Michelle wasn't exactly a calf but if we put pressure on her maybe Joan will want to make that pressure disappear.

The Challenge

Ever since she was a toddler Joan had a temper. Even now there were moments during fencing practice when a certain move went screwy or wasn't getting any better and every time this happened she could still feel the water start to boil inside her.

One day when she was eight Joan got so frustrated that she started to shout and stamp around, so her Mama stepped up to her, smiled, and suddenly pushed her flat on her back. Joan was so surprised that her anger evaporated, and her Mama stood there looking down with that wonderful, annoying smile of hers.

"Did I take you by surprise?" she asked.

Joan nodded, still in shock from what happened.

"Would I usually be able to do that?"

Joan shook her head.

"So why was I able to do it now?"

Joan started to say the first thing that came to her mind but seeing Mama's look, she took a deep breath and settled back for a moment before answering.

"Because I was not thinking."

"What got you here on the ground?"

"I did. I mean my attitude did."

"Very good. And what was on your mind?"

"I was getting angry about not getting the footwork right."

"And if that were to happen in an actual fight?"

"My opponent would defeat me."

Mama had taught her long before that there is a very big difference between an opponent and an enemy. An enemy was someone, or something, very special and never, ever to be taken lightly.

"No Joan, you would defeat yourself. Sometimes anger can give you an edge against an opponent for it adds passion to your cause, but it is very, very dangerous to do so without thinking. It is especially dangerous to become angry when that is exactly what your enemy wants you to do. You need to be two or three or a hundred steps ahead of your opponent, and that cannot happen when your anger controls you."

For Joan, the memory of that lesson had come in particularly handy the past few weeks, getting to know the school and figuring out her place within it. Unfortunately, there had been some harassment, too, unpleasant things from people who knew nothing about her, and despite her resolve, it had started to get under her skin.

Christine

One Friday in PE we were having Volleyball practice on one side of the gym while the PE classes were on the other side. They were doing relays today, running from one side of the gym to the other, touching the wall on one side to rebound and race back to touch the hand of the next person in line.

That day we had split up into Blue and Gold teams, and when the first scrimmage was finished we huddled up to figure out what to do next. The team was especially wound up after thirty solid minutes of play and as usual, I was looking for something to fire them up for the rest of practice. When I saw Joan and Michelle standing on the out of bounds line on the other side of the gym, some of the fatigue vanished and some of my anger returned. Here we were, working ourselves ragged for this team and the potentially best player in the school won't come to her senses and join.

I glanced over at Lisa, who saw where I was looking. "Spike practice?" she asked in a low voice.

I nodded. "Set 'em up."

We went to our positions, and Tiffany set up a perfect ball to Lisa, who jumped straight up and hit the ball perfectly, sending it rocketing toward the other side of the gym where it passed exactly between the two girls.

"Sorry," said Lisa in the sweetest voice she could muster, and the rest of us snickered but not too loudly as Coach Anita was both watching and listening. Michelle backed several feet out of the way, but Joan turned and glared at her for a second.

This was not the way this was supposed to happen, I thought. She's supposed to get real startled and then do something like move to the other side of the gym, especially since Lisa is the one who spiked it. It looked like we were going to try something more drastic, so I turned to Tiffany and said: "Set me up this time."

Tiffany sent another perfect lob a bit more to the right, where I could hit the sweet spot. There was a hard smack! as my hand hit the ball, and another smack a half second later as the spiked shot struck Michelle right between the shoulders, sending her sprawling and almost hitting her head against the wall. Almost before I could take a breath Joan was right in front of me on the other side of the net.

"Want to pick on someone your own size?" said Joan, staring me straight in the eyes even though I'm at least six inches taller than she is, and the gym got quiet like someone had flipped a switch.

Coach Anita who appeared as if by magic and grabbed me by the arm. "Now hold it you two..."

"Joan challenged me," I said. "Nothing..."

Joan spoke up in a calm, controlled, and icy voice that carried over the whole gym. "What I said was, do you want to pick on someone your own size?"

It was Anita's policy to let students figure out a way to settle disputes on their own, and when it involved athletes not by fighting but a head-to-head fair competition between the two challengers in front of witnesses. It was crude but a lot more productive than pistols at twenty paces, and sometimes after the challenge the two challengers even became friends.

"Unless you want me to take this to the office, you two have something to settle, you do it right here," said Anita.

"Okay by me," Joan said.

"Suits me fine," I said.

"Since you say that I challenged you," said Joan, "you will have the choice of weapons. Or in this case, games," still smiling that icy smile and staring me right in the eye.

Deep down inside something was talking to me, pleading, begging even, saying don't do this, you will regret it! For me to turn down this challenge in front of my team and the whole crowd in the gym, well, that was not going to happen.

"Spikes. First to make two points?" I said.

Joan nodded. "Done. Set 'em up, as you say. You start." The door to the gym slammed as someone ran out into the hallway, and in the distance, I could hear them excitedly calling others to come to the gym. Even before Coach Anita had cleared off the volleyball court the door was open again, with dozens of kids pushing their way in and climbing up into the stands. She even had to blow her whistle five times before everyone got seated and things quieted down.

"You two, come up here," said Coach Anita. We stood there, me on one side and Joan on the other, and Joan still had this quiet, weird smile while she just looked at me.

"Ground rules: set up and then the spike. Any ball inbounds is a point for either person. If the server scores the point, they go again. If the receiver scores a point, they serve the next ball. Score a point, you go again until out of bounds or a valid return. First to two points is the winner."

$\mathcal{M}ichelle$

Joan talked to me about this later, and I still wouldn't have believed it if I hadn't been there. Joan stood quietly, the same calm smile on her face, her arms crossed, watching Christine, her eyes analyzing and cataloging the way she moved, the way she reacted, which side she favored. Her Mama always told her to use her eyes and her brain and time to see what makes your opponent tick and if you pay attention they will give away all the information you will ever need to vanquish them.

"Well, Michelle, Christine's left eye is dominant," Joan told me. "She swipes her right hand down and across instead of down and out, and she gets off balance if the ball is about five feet or more directly over her head. She also thinks that little dance of hers gives her an advantage but it puts extra strain on her right ankle that was already tired." How she ever figured that out from fifteen seconds of observation I will never know, but it was one of the most impressive things I had ever heard of, especially with what happened next.

"Christine, who is your set up?" asked Coach Anita.

"Tiffany," she replied.

"Joan, who is your set up?" asked Anita.

"I will do my own setup," replied Joan. She pointed to a spot about six feet away. "To keep it fair I will toss it into the air starting at that spot. That OK?"

The sheer audacity of the suggestion shocked Coach Anita, but she couldn't see anything problem except that it put Joan at a clear disadvantage. If Joan even got a chance to spike, Christine would know exactly where the spike was coming from, whereas Joan would have to move to wherever Christine happened to aim it, which amounted to the whole thirty feet of the receiving side.

"Are you sure about this?" she asked quietly, and Joan nodded.

Something else was going on here, Anita thought, right under the radar, and with all her years of experience, she had a sneaky feeling that the unexpected was going to happen. What's more, Christine didn't have a clue.

Anita turned toward Christine. "You agree to that, Christine? Joan will do her own setup?"

You've got to be kidding me, Christine thought, but it's her funeral. "Agreed."

"Just a second," said Joan. "Like a duel, this contest of ours is supposed to solve something, right?" It was surprising for Coach Anita to hear the confidence and authority in Joan's voice, seemingly impossible for a girl only thirteen years old, and yet the tone already started to affect the kids sitting in the stands who were now breathlessly waiting to see what would happen next.

"As a matter of fact, that's right," replied Coach Anita. "What do you propose?"

"Christine wins, I stay out of her way and apologize to her in front of the whole gym. If I win, she promises to leave me and my friends alone." Joan had made a slight adjustment to her voice, adding extra force so that it echoed throughout the gym. The crowd now looked at Christine, and Joan stood with her arms crossed, waiting.

"If you win, I apologize like you said," said Christine. "But if I win, you agree to join the Volleyball team for the rest of the season."

"Agreed," said Joan.

"Call the toss," said Coach Anita, taking out a coin.

"Christine may go first," said Joan, who turned her back on the net, walked back five paces, and stood quietly, her arms now uncrossed. "Give me thirty seconds to warm up." Joan closed her eyes, entering that special place where her senses became completely concentrated. She balanced herself on her toes, closing her eyes for a moment, and her breathing became very even and soft. Her arm rose, holding an invisible stick, and one, two, three, four, one, two, three, four, she traced an invisible pattern in the air up, down, right, left, almost dancing, forward, backward, left, right, the pattern seemingly aimed at someone in front, then back again, and then to the right, and back again, and like it always did the image of Mama and that very first day under the tree appeared in her head, her breathing returned to normal, and she opened her eyes.

"Ready," she said.

Even though Coach Anita had never tired of using the old saw "you could have heard a pin drop," she had only experienced it once or twice in her life. The whole gym was completely quiet, the spectators mesmerized at what was happening in front of them. Many years before Anita went to go to the Los Angeles Olympics and there was a tiny member of the Japanese karate team who did a warmup that looked something like this. Ten minutes later he had demolished his opponent with about as much effort as it took to sit down and open a book.

"Set 'em up," said Coach Anita, stepping back to the sidelines.

Joan stood in the center of her side, her smile gone, mouth slightly open, arms crossed at her side and slightly raised up on her toes, while Christine was still bouncing, oblivious to the change in mood there in the gym. This is not a volleyball shoot out, Anita thought, this is a tiger looking at a particularly appetizing baby gazelle.

Tiffany sent the ball to right over Christine's head, and at the right moment she leaped up, her arm extended, and smacked the ball in a perfect spike aimed directly at Joan's head. Still watching her opponent, Joan moved two inches to the left, the ball whistling past her ear and hitting the floor behind her right inside the line.

"Point Christine," said Coach Anita, and there were some cheers from the stands. Someone lobbed the ball back to Tiffany and Christine returned to her spot.

"Set 'em up," said Christine.

Tiffany, good old reliable Tiffany sent the ball to right over Christine's head like she had done a thousand times before, and Christine leapt up, her arm extended and smacked the ball in another perfect spike aimed directly at Joan's head...except Joan wasn't in that spot anymore, Joan was now eighteen inches in front of her, in a fluid jump even higher than Christine's, and instead of rocketing to the ground the ball thudded against Joan's outstretched hand and deflected perfectly downward, all the force of Christine's spike sending it rocketing to the ground on her own side, not Joan's.

"Point Joan," said Coach Anita. One person in the stands started to clap and half a second later another four or five joined in, and in a second everybody in the stands started clapping.

The ball in her hand, Joan stepped over to the spot she had indicated and stood there quietly, Christine bouncing and seething on the other side of the net opposite where Joan had said she was going to do the setup for herself. Three or four seconds passed.

"Go ahead, Joan," said Coach Anita.

"I am waiting for my honorable opponent to get ready," Joan said quietly, but loudly enough for the entire gym to hear.

"I'm ready," said Christine.

Joan put the ball into her left hand and tossed it in an arc exactly above the spot she said, Christine on her feet and right arm extended - but Joan had unexpectedly moved one foot further down the net and simply tapped the ball

59

with her left hand, sending it about two inches over Christine's left shoulder and bouncing on the floor.

"Point Joan," said Coach Anita, who then came forward and put her hand on Christine's shoulder. "Come up to the net."

Christine shook her head, glancing back at the stands. "Not in front of everybody."

"No, Christine, a deal is a deal," Anita said sternly. "You have something to say, and you are going to say it or you're on probation. Players on my teams keep their word. It's not all about winning, and it's not all about you."

Joan was standing and watching all of this, and despite herself, she felt a deep sadness. This girl in front of her was not an enemy but a kid like herself, but so fragile she had to put on this big show and make a splash in front of her friends to get even the tiniest bit of affirmation. Joan knew that behind most of the high school so-called popularity is a huge ocean of loneliness and a desperate hunger to belong.

"You don't have to apologize, Christine," said Joan quietly. "Just have your people leave my friends alone."

"What's this, Joan? What about leaving you alone?" asked Coach Anita.

"I can take care of myself," Joan replied. "But I have to do this for the other kids."

"What other kids?" asked Christine. "What do you mean by that?"

"Who's going to be picked on next? There are other kids at this school who can't protect themselves and need to be left in peace," Joan replied, looking right at Christine. "Everybody deserves that."

Inside Christine, the built-up anger and the humiliation of losing in front of everybody just evaporated. A memory came back, a painful memory from many years ago, that still woke her up once in a while.

When Christine was five years old they didn't have much money at home because Papa had lost his job and Mama was out working at people's houses cleaning and taking care of their kids. Her older sister Catharine did her best to take care of things while Mama was gone, but it was always a lot of work. Papa didn't bring home any money and he was likely to be home on those evenings when Mama wouldn't get back from work until the next morning.

One night he came home after having too much to drink, and after he stumbled in the front door Catharine shushed him real gently and asked him to leave his shoes at the door. He took them off, but in cleaning up the floor Christine had missed picking up one of her jacks and Papa took one step forward and stepped right down onto it. He had a real abrupt temper and let out a bellow, and then shouted right in Christine's face.

"Who left that on the floor?"

Before Christine could say anything, Catharine spoke right up.

"I did, Papa. I'm sorr.."

Catharine never got to finish that sentence because Papa slapped her so hard it knocked her to the floor before he stumbled up the stairs and into bed. It was

60

lucky he didn't hit any harder but it was still a minute or two before Catharine picked herself off the floor, the imprint of a hand still livid on her cheek.

Christine ran up to her, tears streaming down her face. "I'm sorry, Catharine, I thought I got them all. Listen, I'll go upstairs and tell Papa I left it,"

Catharine took Christine's shoulder and looked her straight in the eye. "No, pumpkin, you aren't going to do any such thing. It's all right, I'm not actually hurt this time."

"But why didn't you tell Papa it was me?"

"Sometimes you have to protect those who can't help themselves."

Christine looked at Joan, her anger gone and leaving her so, so tired. "I'll see you're left alone. Both of you. I promise," she whispered.

Joan hadn't expected this but it came as a shock to see the real pain in Christine's eyes, and something more – a note of desperation. There is something else going on here, Joan thought, and despite herself, she reached out and patted Christine on the shoulder. "Never you mind," she said, turned, and walked over to where Michelle waited by the door.

In five minutes the gym was empty, the kids on their way home, the odd bits of trash, discarded papers, and lost textbooks all gathered into neat piles at the bottom of the bleachers. It was sometimes one of Anita's favorite times of the day, the gymnasium now a big quiet room with a nice little echo in it where she sometimes hummed or sang to herself, getting a kick out of her voice echoing through the room.

While she worked, she couldn't help thinking about what she had witnessed. Coach Anita had never heard any student talk like this before. Something deep inside told her that Joan was different, that she wasn't going to be a volleyball player, and that was OK. Joan didn't have the need that Christine did for the cheers, her name echoing through the PA system, and at the end holding up a trophy and getting her picture in the papers.

The Smithfield High School trophy case had at one point been so full that they had to remove a whole bunch of trophies and put them into boxes down in the furnace room. Once upon a time every one of those trophies represented a season and a bunch of kids and pictures in the papers, but after a time the kids grew up, the trophies got all tarnished, and the newspapers got recycled. What they remembered was each other, the friendships, those few special games, and eventually the ones who had passed on.

Before she turned out the lights Coach Anita made a promise to herself. I'm going to take a real interest in Joan, not to be on the volleyball team but to make sure she is left alone by those who would give her a hard time. For Coach Anita knew there were some in this school who knew how to apply pressure when they wanted something, and woe betide those who gave No for an answer.

Chapter Fifteen
Todd

There were two times every day when Todd felt good - when he got into his truck for the ride to work, and when he finally left the building at the end of the day and saw his truck sitting there in the principal's parking space, dwarfing every other car in the parking lot. Problem was, he had been the acting principal for two years and hated every minute of it. He had always thought being a principal was sitting in a big office all the time, having two or three secretaries to boss around, and walking through the hallways with a walkie-talkie.

His Uncle Joe had been principal when Todd was a student, and Todd was amazed how everyone looked up to him. He was out of his office roaming the hallways a lot of the time, and knew every kid by name along with their parents and brothers and sisters too. If a teacher was sick he would step in and run the class for a few periods with no problem, so the staff loved him and there was almost never a teaching vacancy. When he was in the hallways there was always a group of kids walking with him, talking up a storm, laughing, or sitting in groups and talking. There had even been some talk of renaming the school Martin High School after Uncle Joe, but after a speech in which he thanked everybody for the compliment and talked about the value of tradition he had the whole room in tears and the idea was put quietly away.

When Superintendent High died unexpectedly, the school board promptly appointed Uncle Joe to be Superintendent in his place. Wouldn't you know it, he kept the Superintendent's office right there in the high school, adding it to everything else he had done as a Principal and doing the same thing every day that he did before, the same groups of kids still following him around. For a while it drove Aunt Gladys crazy, but since he took care of the Superintendent's job by 9:30 every morning, things stayed the same.

It all started when Todd was in his final semester of college and Uncle Joe took him out to dinner.

"Todd, I'm in this superintendent thing right now and it's gotten a bit much·to do both jobs, so we need a new Principal. A member of this family has been the principal at one time or another for the past seventy-five years, so now it's going to be your turn."

"But Uncle Joe, I just started my student teaching, and..."

"Let me finish! You would be the acting principal, not the principal. Seems there's a loophole in State Regulations where the Superintendent can put anybody into any position for a one-year appointment, and renew it as many times as he wants. All you need is three years and a few more courses and you'll have the job for real."

It was such a radical idea that Todd had to stop and think about it. If Uncle Joe was Superintendent, it was Todd's fastest and easiest way to move straight to the top of the ladder. Once he got there, it was only a matter of time until Uncle Joe retired or died and left the top spot open, so the trick was to make the first jump and then to make sure that Uncle Joe's last official act as Superintendent was to put Todd into that position. Since Uncle Joe was pushing seventy years old it would be about any time now, and since eight of the past nine Principals became Superintendent the way looked clear for Todd to do the same. Even better, he'd be out of the classroom for good.

"I'll do it, Uncle Joe," said Todd.

"Atta boy. I'll get the paperwork moving and you can start bringing your stuff into the office."

All that was two years ago, two years of being the acting principal, cramming all those classes into two semesters and finally getting his state administrator's license. Then a week ago, there was an email announcing a special 9:00 board meeting, so about 8:58 Todd strolled down the hallway to the Superintendent's office.

"Is he in?"

"Go right on in, "answered Aunt Gladys, "Everyone else is there."

Everyone else? What – WHO everyone else? Opening the door, Todd saw Uncle Joe at the end of the table as usual, and sitting to his right was Phyllis Donner, the Middle School principal, who smiled at Todd about the way an alligator smiles at a wounded carp.

"Have a seat, Todd," said Uncle Joe.

Todd sat down at Uncle Joe's left, directly across the table from Phyllis, and the temperature in the room dropped about twenty degrees.

"Now, I have asked you two here to let you know that I am planning to retire at the end of this school year. Doc says I need to slow down, and I've been in this game long enough to know that I don't look forward to coming to work the way I used to. Still get a kick out of seeing kids and walking these hallways, but things have changed and it's time to get new blood into this office."

In spite of himself, Todd smiled. Here comes the big announcement.

"Both of you have been working real hard, so deciding which one of you deserves this job isn't the easy job you might think. Superintending is a different game, a lot more to do with public relations and getting out to meet people, and not like a Principal's job at all. Both of you are well qualified so I'm confident that the next Superintendent is right here in this room. The only question is, which of you is it?"

"Aren't you forgetting something, Joe?" asked Phyllis.

"What's that?"

"Well – to be a full principal, the law requires three years' experience." She smiled over at Todd who wanted to go over and punch her in the nose. "Todd has one more year to finish."

"That third year already started," replied Todd. "Besides – what exactly is mandatory retirement age? I do believe that Phyllis is…is it sixty-six now?"

It was his first real mistake but as usual, it was out of his mouth before he knew it.

Uncle Joe looked at Todd real sharp. "Never stopped me," he said ominously and sat back in his chair. "We'll meet again at the end of the first term to see how things are going."

Chapter Sixteen
Board Meeting

The Smithfield school board met four times a year whether they needed to or not. For some reason that went back before anybody could remember, they met in a room on the back of the stage with no windows and only two doors, one leading to the stage itself and one directly into the Principal's office.

During his time as Principal, Uncle Joe had used the room for his more private meetings with parents. He also found the rather dank atmosphere perfect for having those heart-to-heart discussions that are sometimes necessary with students. There were a long, heavy table and a big credenza with ceiling high storage cabinets at one end of the room. Hanging on the wall directly over the Superintendent's chair was a solid oak plaque with two crossed swords, the official symbol for the school's Mascot, the Smithfield Cavaliers. There was a framed photograph of each Superintendent since 1932, and all the photos were labeled with the same last name.

This evening's board meeting had two invited guests waiting outside on the back of the stage where the custodian had left the same blue plastic chairs used in most of the classrooms. On one side of the doorway sat Middle School Principal Phyllis Donner, her briefcase neatly on the floor, phone in her hand endlessly scrolling through emails. On the other side sat Todd, a manila folder on his lap, and nothing else to occupy him except his usual feeling of intense annoyance. The door clicked open and Aunt Gladys emerged. "Please come in, Phyllis," she said as an announcement, even though Todd was the only other person waiting. Phyllis stood, slipped the phone smoothly into her briefcase, and went into the room.

When the contractor had started work on the new training room, Todd inserted a line item into the work order labeled "A/V and Security Renovation as directed - $6000". The money had been used to purchase Ethernet security camera systems for the main entrances to the school, and Todd had simply taken one, installed it himself into the frame holding Uncle Joe's photograph, then added it to the list of cameras that could be controlled by the primary server. Now when he wanted to know what the board was doing, all he had to do was bring up the security system on his desktop computer, find the correct line item in the list of security cameras, and the whole meeting was in front of him. As a matter of fact, this meeting was being streamed to a file on his own laptop, so there weren't going to be any secrets he wouldn't know about.

There was a click and the door opened as Phyllis shook hands with the Board members one at a time. Gladys held the door as Phyllis walked out and across the stage without a backward glance at Todd, but if he could read anything by her walk she was happy about something. He stood up and went inside.

"Have a seat, Todd," said the older Mr. Kershaw, sitting in his usual place at the head of the table. "Let the secretary call the roll."

Gladys took her clipboard in her hand and checked off down the list.

"Mr. Kershaw Senior. Mr. Kershaw Junior. Mr. Augustin. Mr. Austin. Mr. Joseph Martin."

Mr. Kershaw nodded. "The minutes will indicate all board members and superintendent present. The notes will also show Todd Martin in attendance before the board."

"So noted," replied Gladys. "Mr. Augustin has the floor."

The old man was dressed in a suit that had become a bit too big for him but was as spiffy and neat as when he had bought it thirty years before. The owner of the biggest ranch in the county, he or one of his family had been on the school board since there was a school board, and Todd could claim kinship to him through at least four different cousins who had married into the Augustin family over the years. He had also gone to grade school with Uncle Joe, and in an area of the country where connections mattered, he was a safe vote. He cleared his throat, looked at Todd with a benign expression, and smiled.

"Well Todd, it's a pleasure to have you before us tonight with your application for the Principal position..." He stopped as Gladys grasped his arm and whispered into his ear. He straightened back up. "Excuse me, your application for the Superintendent's position. Our present superintendent Mr. Joseph Martin has announced his retirement effective next summer, and has recommended to the board that we consider your application."

Keeping his composure was not one of Todd's strengths, but he managed to nod politely.

"We have reviewed the present status of both of your schools, and have developed some criteria for each of you. Your success in meeting those criteria will play a part in our decision." He nodded to Uncle Joe, who had been silent up to this time.

"This town of ours has always taken a lot of pride in high school sports but there hasn't been a whole lot to cheer about lately. Winning teams mean happy people, and people who are happy with their school don't put up a fuss when we ask for more money, pure and simple."

Uncle Joe glanced around the table and Todd saw everyone nodding in agreement except the two Kershaws, who were silently shaking their heads.

"Bring us two championships and improve your test scores and, well, you can write your own ticket." At that, both Kershaws turned and looked straight at Todd, and each nodded once.

"Any questions?" said Mr. Augustine.

"What's the deadline?" asked Todd.

"April 15th, right after State Tournament Finals and Third Quarter test results," said Uncle Joe. "They are both due the same day." He turned and nodded at Gladys, who was obviously cued.

65

"That's all, Todd," she said, getting up and opening the door onto the stage. "We'll be in touch."

"I'm telling you, Joe, I don't like this but I went along with you. He may have been acting principal these past two years, but it doesn't mean he can cut it as Superintendent," said Mr. Kershaw with a surprising amount of energy. "I know there's been a Martin in the Superintendent's chair since 1932 but that shouldn't make it automatic. Phyllis is far more experienced."

"We went over and over this," said Mr. Augustine impatiently. "Phyllis has zero sports experience and can't tell a touchdown from a field goal. If we don't produce some winning teams we're going to have a whole lot of transfers over to Garland, and then we might as well throw up our hands and close this district permanently. Last year this state had twenty-three high schools that consolidated, and when you drive through those towns on a Friday night it's like they went out and rolled up the sidewalks. Closed stores - some of 'em with smashed out windows, houses sitting vacant." He looked from face to face. "And I for one do not intend to see us end up like that."

"Well, there's a fire lit under him now so we all have six months," said Mr. Kershaw junior. "Next time we meet in January we'll have to see how things are going."

Five minutes later the Board room was empty except for Uncle Joe, who had moved back into the seat at the end of the table. There was a knock at the door into the Principal's office, at which Joe walked over and opened it.

"Come on in, Todd," he said, "and shut the door. What I'm going to tell you does not leave this room. Ever, do you understand?"

"Yes, sir," said Todd.

"You are skating on mighty thin ice right now with some of those people and I didn't get you this chance to watch you let it go. I know you are spending a lot of time coming up with extras like that new training room, but it isn't enough and you know it. Time was that we'd have a hundred boys show up for football tryouts, but now we're lucky if we get twenty-five. Same with Volleyball: this year's team has exactly seven players when we used to have fifteen. Small teams give you leaders but it also means injuries and some of them bad ones like with football last year. Families in this town still have the drive and pride to want to be winners. Got to make kids want to be on the team."

Todd was about to reply when Uncle Joe put his head down for a second and rubbed his face distractedly then looked back at Todd. "Like with Volleyball. Small teams give you leaders but then kids get hurt like in football, but we've got to make kids want to be on our teams. Got to," and Uncle Joe started rubbing his face again.

Something's going on here, and he... repeated himself almost word for word and has no idea that happened. An idea popped into Todd's head. Show you sympathize with him and you might find out what it is.

"I can help, Uncle Joe," said Todd, reaching out and patting Uncle Joe's arm where it rested heavily on the table. "Family is family like you always say." Uncle Joe looked up at him and there was a tear running down his cheek. Aha, thought Todd.

"Like I said, this does not leave this room," said Uncle Joe. "I have...I mean I have been to see Dr. Tremont but I told you that before. Haven't been feeling like myself since last May, but they did those tests and now I know. Seems like I'm in the early stages of Alzheimer's, or have been, for almost six months. Tests from last May and tests from last week, well it doesn't look too good, but I can do most things as good as ever and will not step out of this job until I see another Martin in it. I know what they said about Phyllis, but you're the one to make this school like it was twenty years ago. Here's what we're going to do. I'm still the Superintendent and everybody will see it that way, but if you're serious about wanting this job...."

"I am," replied Todd, hard pressed to keep from shouting it.

"...well, you're going to have to get some on the job experience. You're going to be the acting superintendent, too, but only you and I know about it. You willing to do that?"

For the first time in months Todd got into his truck, started it up, and turned the radio up full blast. A piece of cake, with Uncle Joe putting the keys to the kingdom right into my hand as neat as you please. It looked like there would be at least two or three State Championships this year, and according to the State Capitol sportswriters they were a shoo-in for girls' basketball. As for the end of year tests – well, that part was going to be a lot easier than anybody thought. Funny thing was, he wouldn't even have to get the teachers involved. A couple quiet hours with an eraser and the tests would all come out the way he wanted.

Last year's football team had been on the way to a championship until Brian had that accident, and Todd never did figure exactly what happened that day. Todd had used that same Mineral Supplement himself since College, bringing it up from Mexico every few months or so. He had known anxious Brian was to make First Team, so it had been a worthwhile experiment to slip a box into his locker. Brian was going along with the program, getting bigger and tougher each game until Coach Reed got stubborn.

It was only by some very quick last minute thinking at the Garland game last fall that he was still sitting here today. He didn't expect Brian to live, which would have made some things a whole lot simpler, but when the kid survived a hit that would have crippled an elephant Todd had to move into high gear and cover his tracks. It was sheer luck that he had enough time to get the remaining three boxes of Mineral Supplement out of his office and into Coach Reed's closet, taking care to bury an empty at the bottom of the waste basket in the football locker room. It had been icing on the cake that he'd managed to plant the rumor Coach Reed was drugging his own players.

Chapter Seventeen
Progress

Joan

Football season was almost over and only one more game left, the big one against Garland. I never thought I would enjoy going to football games but it's been fun and I will miss it a lot when it's over for the year. It will also be a relief, though, since I have started fencing again and it feels great to have that back in my life. It is taking some time for me to get used to the way Miss Renoir does things, but she's as strict as Mama ever was and I'm learning a lot. My muscles and reaction time had softened over time but since Mama started me when I was three most of it is still there, locked up in my bones and muscles.

Once our lessons started in earnest we had a routine between Miss Renoir, Papa, and me, that had me take my lesson at the tennis court and then Miss Renoir and I would drive out to Toussaint's to have supper with Papa. Since Miss Renoir would not take any money for the lessons Papa insisted that we at least buy her dinner, and she didn't put up too much of a fight. There were a lot of great things about Toussaint's but one of them was their weekly special which they never advertised ahead of time because they didn't know what it was going to be until the day they made it. The determining factor was simply whatever was catching in the Gulf or out in the bayou. We'd had everything from alligator to rock lobster, all of it fantastic.

It had been a great lesson that day and Miss Renoir ended the lesson early. "I am very pleased, Jeannette," she said, "and to tell the truth I am hungry. Pack up and let's be on our way." I hadn't had anything since lunch at 11:15 so I was more than ready and got into the car before she did.

"The first match is in six days," I said, checking the calendar on my phone as we drove. "I'm excited about it but..." I hated to admit being nervous, and it didn't happen too often that I was, but it had been a long time since I had faced any opponent not my teacher.

Papa had already gotten a table when we walked in the door at Toussaint's, and he stood up and held Miss Renoir's chair for her like he always did. He was beaming at us after we sat down and I suspected he had some good news that he was waiting to share. It didn't take long.

"Great news," he said, which was a great way to get our attention. "Some of the artifacts from the dig at Domremy are going to the National Gallery of Art for a special exhibition, and..."

"You're invited?" I finished, breathless, and he nodded. "When?" I asked, already making plans, but he was a step ahead of me and the news was not what I wanted to hear.

"Next weekend," he replied, "the 9th until the 11th," and we understood at once what he was getting at.

"Friday's the last football game," I said.

"And Saturday's your first tournament, Jeannette," she said.

"That's a lot to miss," Papa said.

I looked at Miss Renoir and she looked right back at me, not saying anything. I then looked at Papa and he was looking back at me the same way, and of course he read my mind and beat me to it.

"I had lunch with Professor Han today and when he congratulated me, he mentioned something about Michelle had been asking for a time that you two..."

"...could have a sleepover..." I interjected.

"...and made an offer that you could..."

"...stay with them for a few days." It sounded like fun and it sounded...well, scary too. I hadn't stayed away from Papa for a single day since Mama died, and suddenly it didn't sound like so much fun. But this time it wasn't about fun, it was about Papa's accomplishment, and as much as I wanted to go with him I was...well, I was getting used to living here, too.

Papa reached out and patted my hand. "Like I said, it's your decision, Squirt." There it was, and I knew I had already decided to stay home.

"This is a big break for you, Papa," I said, "and a new start for me, too. You promise to call me every day and we'll update each other. You'll be back before we know it." I looked hard into his eyes. "You be careful, okay?"

On Thursday afternoon, I got out of the car carrying my sleeping bag, backpack and fencing foil, lugged them up the steps to Michelle's room, and plopped them all into the corner she had prepared for me. The University Van delivered Papa to the airport while I was at school, so there we were with a whole long weekend ahead of us.

Michelle had a very cool room, a lot like mine except for the fact that it was neat, neat, neat, and mine was slightly reminiscent of the aftermath of a not very powerful tornado. There was a bed like I had, a closet like I had, and shelf after shelf of books, not exactly like I had since I had books in French and Michelle had books in Chinese, but we were otherwise even in that department. There was a desktop computer with a big monitor, a nifty little laser printer, and an office style chair that she could sit in and spin which happened to be exactly what she was doing right now when she stopped and looked at me.

"Hungry?" she asked, and when I nodded she opened one of the desk drawers and took out a package of what looked like Oreos except the label was in Chinese. She opened it and reached it out to me, I took one, and a quarter second after biting into it I realized I had found the holy grail of snack foods. I must have rolled my eyes or something because she was spinning in the chair again and trying hard not to laugh. "You can keep the bag, but..."

"Don't ruin your appetite," we finished in unison, at which moment a call came from downstairs and we hightailed it down to the dining room.

Mrs. Dr. Han sat at one end of the table, Mr. Dr. Han sat at the other end of the table, Michelle and I sat on one side of the table, and her little brother Kevin sat on the opposite side staring at me. There were three large bowls of food on the table which I guess were Chinese and had something inside that smelled so good that I closed my eyes to inhale that incredible aroma.

"We are very glad to have you with us, Joan," said Mr. Dr. Han. "This is a good chance for us to get to know you better."

"Thank you, Dr. Han," I responded, showing my best manners, but I wasn't exactly thinking about manners right now since I was waiting for...as I matter of fact, I wasn't sure what was going to come next. I had never been in a Chinese household before and had some idea that there were special customs involving sitting and eating I had never heard about.

Thus, my surprise when Mrs. Dr. Han reached out for my hand on one side and Kevin's hand on the other, and Michelle reached out for my other hand on one side and her Dad's hand on the other. When Kevin completed the circle Mr. Dr. Han bowed his head and said grace, short but sweet, the only difference being words, and...it was the first time I had prayed before food since...before, and the old habit kicked in and I said grace too, but in French without realizing it. I let go to genuflect at the end which made Kevin's eyes get big, so I took a second and explained it to him.

"I'm Catholic and it's what we do when we finish grace," I said, short and sweet. He seemed to accept that but his mind was already on the food. He brightened up considerably when Mrs. Dr. Han opened the lid of the first bowl but looked betrayed when she gave me the first helping.

"Mange, S'il Vous plait," she said to me as she turned to fill Kevin's plate, to which I automatically answered "Merci," and dug in...or at least was going to but there wasn't a fork to be found, only two beautiful jet-black wooden chopsticks. I started to pick them up when I felt a nudge from Michelle.

"Fork?" she asked in a stage whisper. "I can get you..."

I shook my head. "Let me learn," I answered. "Never know when I'm going to be eating Chinese food."

That did it. Michelle burst out laughing much to the horror of her parents, but when I also laughed Kevin joined in and then Mr. and Mrs. Doctor completed the picture. They say that laughter helps the appetite, which must be true because by the time dinner was over there wasn't a scrap of food left in those bowls. The laughter also turned on the conversational faucet and everybody at the table was either asking me questions about France or fencing or how I liked school or what I thought of politics. Michelle had told her Mom I had finished Les Miserables so Mrs. Dr. Han and I discussed that for a few minutes in French which at first surprised me until I remembered she had been a UN translator. I switched back to English and started asking her all about the UN and New York. Michelle joined in on that and even Kevin managed to put in two cents worth when he didn't have his head buried in his fourth helping of that incredible dinner.

As we finished Michelle started to stack the plates but Mrs. Dr. Han spoke right up.

"Homework!" and looked down at Kevin. "Kevin will finish the dishes tonight."

70

It was like Michelle won the lottery and Kevin got coal in his stocking at the exact same time. I think if I had not been there Michelle would have whooped for joy but tonight she was being nicer and helped Kevin carry the dishes to the kitchen.

We worked out a system in her room where Michelle sat at her desk while I lay on my back holding Roman de la Rose poised in the air over my head. After a few minutes, she looked down at me nervously.

"You comfortable like that?" she asked.

"Totally," I answered.

"You want to change places?" she asked.

"Nope," I answered.

Thirty seconds of silence.

"You sure?" she asked.

"Yep," I answered.

A half an hour later I am fifty pages further along, having to search my memory or my digital dictionary for some words, the archaic French cool and romantic sounding, and the poetry so old and formal. French poetry has a magic for me, the same way a lullaby does – in other words, I can only take so much until I start to yawn. The only way I can dig myself out of that rut is to do something else like Algebra 2 problems or Chemistry equations, but I am in a fencing tournament in two days and need to do at least thirty minutes of practice.

"Got my half hour of fencing drills to do," I told Michelle. "Out in the driveway okay?"

"Uh…sure, no problem," she answered, again nervously looking back at the computer. "Is it okay…"

"Of course, it's okay if you stay here," I said as I pick up my face guard and foil. "I'll be fine unless you have wild animals around here or something."

"Only college students," she said and pointed at my foil. "But you have a sword, after all. Should be enough to keep them at bay."

"I'll call you if I need any help."

It was getting colder so there was almost no daylight left by the time I got started. The light over the garage door went on automatically as I found my spot and started my stretching exercises. They've helped me a lot in times like this when I've been sitting or staying still, and after a few minutes, the blood was flowing and both my fingers and toes tingled. Behind me, there was the sound of a window being raised and I turned to see Mr. Dr. Han leaning on the windowsill.

"Okay if I watch?" he asked.

I smiled, grateful for the company. "Sure it is. Thanks!" I started the next part of the routine, the descendant of my first practice under the willow tree all those years ago. I heard the window close and I thought he was getting cold, but ten seconds later he opened the door beside the garage and came out onto the driveway.

"Pardon me, Joan, but when I was watching you right now...something you were doing was very, very familiar to me. Would you mind starting over, not everything but only what you have been doing the last few minutes?"

"Sure," I answered, and moving more toward the center of the circle the light made on the driveway, I started over.

"Where did you learn that?" he asked when I finished, excitement in his voice.

"From Mama."

"Where did she learn it from?" he asked again, starting to pace back and forth the way people sometimes do when they are making a connection.

"My Grandmother."

"When did she learn it?" he asked, still excited.

"I...probably about 1945 or so," I replied. "The only time Mama ever talked about it was to say that it was traditional, which coming from Mama meant hundreds of years old."

Mr. Dr. Han nodded and walked out into the light. "Joan – I want you to watch what I do very, very carefully. Pay attention to what I do and especially how I do it. Don't say anything and don't interrupt, it won't take long. Michelle tells me you are a very good observer."

"Sure," I said and settled down to watch.

He turned so that I was now directly to his right, positioned his feet, and took a long, deep breath. He then started what looked like very slow ballet practice, but with his arms straight or curving at specific angles, very deliberate and accurate steps and turning....and then it hit me. This is exactly like Mama's routine, but much slower and without the sword.

He stopped. "Do you see it?" he said excitedly.

"Absolutely!" I replied.

"You say your Mama learned from her mother, and then from her mother, going way back? Right?" he asked.

I nodded.

He clapped his hands and it was like I gave him a winning lottery ticket. "What I was doing is called Tai Chi, not the Martial Arts kind but very similar and very rare. It is meant to give you mind-body connection. It is very, very old – more than one thousand years. This version is something that has not come out of China, not even after Mao. It is a very local thing. There must have been some long-ago connection between your family and someone from China."

"Would you like to record it?" I asked.

"I have something better," he replied. "Can we try it at the same time?"

We took up our positions about twelve feet from each other, making sure he was well out of sword range and started. It took a minute or two to match each other's pace but since we were both watching each other we had it down. It flowed like everything else Mama taught me, and in another minute we were finished. Applause came from above us, and I looked up to see Michelle at one window and her Mom at another, laughing and clapping and Mr. Dr. Han was so happy he started clapping too.

72

Fifteen minutes later I was showered and curled up in my sleeping bag on Michelle's bedroom floor where a futon had been put down. The room was quiet except for Michelle's snor...er, breathing, and a beautiful big moon showed enough light that the walls were visible. My mind was full of a lot of things, especially since Papa had called to check in, and as the day started to catch up with me I couldn't help but have the image of Michelle and her family all at the dinner table together, Mr. Dr. at one end and Mrs. Dr. at the other. All that business about a possible connection with the warmup routine and an ancient Chinese martial art was very cool and all, but ever since they first started to talk about it I was a million miles away, remembering Mama, Domremy, and my first lesson under the old willow tree.

We had left my preschool and were on the path that led past the end of the road and down a gentle slope to the Meuse River. There were lots of places to picnic or go fishing, or even swimming for the brave few who could stand the cold water. The grass was long and soft, and grasshoppers, dragonflies, and a few quail startled out of the grass and whirred away. Soon we were on the path and Mama headed toward a huge old tree with thousands of small branches dropping down toward the ground, even brushing it in some places. It was cool under the tree, a natural canopy overhead tinted with pale yellow and green as the sun filtered through.

Mama studied the tree for a moment, then reached up and gently broke two of the long branches from the tree. With a single motion, she stripped off the leaves and taking hold of the thicker end waved them tentatively up and down. Free of their leaves they made a swishing sound through the air, moving much faster now. Mama looked thoughtful for a moment, studying them further, then pinched both to the same length and snapped off the thinner end. She swished them once more and beckoned me over to her side.

"Jeanette, we are going to start our special lessons today," she said, and I could tell from the serious sound in her voice that I needed to listen.

"Lessons in…what, Mama?" I asked. "There are no books here."

Mama smiled, but strangely did not laugh. "There are many, many lessons you will never find in books, Jeannette," she replied, using the special name for when she was very happy. She took one of the sticks and handed it to me. "Take this in your hand, and hold it very still right now. We are going to start now and I want you to do exactly as I say, and sometimes exactly as I do. Right now, I want you to find a good place to sit and watch what I do. "

After I sat down she took the other stick in her hand, and it was weird and wonderful to see how easily she held it, and it was not like anything else I had ever seen. This was not a broom, or a spoon where it was swished back and forth in the kitchen but a magic wand instead, seemingly an extension of her arm and even more graceful than the ballet dancers I had seen once on television. She balanced herself on her toes, closing her eyes for a moment, and her breathing became very even and soft. Her arm rose, holding the stick, and one, two, three, four, one, two, three, four, she traced an invisible pattern in the air up, down, right, left, her feet tracing almost a dance in the grass, forward, backward, left, right, the pattern seemingly aimed at someone in front, then back again, and then to the right, and back again, and then to the left, and back again, and little by little getting faster and faster until the stick was a blur and my eyes could not follow or predict where she would go next. It was beautiful and mesmerizing at the same time, and I almost dared not blink for fear of missing even a tiny part of it. There was a lifting, and an aching pause, and then it began again, left, right, forward, backward, up, down, but this time getting slower and slower until each motion was the most exquisite, tragic dance all winding backward until it reached back where it all began. When it all stopped, I looked up at Mama and to my surprise realized that she had her eyes closed the whole time. She stood motionless except for her breathing, faster now, and then letting out a long, continuous breath she opened her eyes and looked right at me.

"What did I do, Jeannette? Think a moment before you answer me."

I knew this was a test of some kind. It sometimes annoyed teachers because I never answered right away, and they had to learn that it took me a second to answer.

"You did the same thing over and over, Mama, but it got faster and faster and then you slowed it down."

She nodded in approval. "And what about when I slowed it down – what else happened?"

I was about to say "you stopped" but that was too easy an answer, and Mama almost never asked easy questions. I never knew exactly when it started but it seemed to me afterward that I could record movies in my head and play them back in slow motion. The demonstration Mama had done was starting to be cemented into my own mind and later my own body that day – and it was the pattern that made it easier to remember. I knew the answer, at least I thought I did.

"You did it backward, Mama."

"What do you mean, Jeannette?"

"Like when you count 1, 2, 3, Mama – the things you did started out 1, 2, 3, and then that all changed to backward like you were going 3, 2, 1."

Mama knelt on the grass and reached out for me, and I can still feel her hug in that beautiful place on that special day. "Fantastique, mon Cher," she said, then looked straight into my eyes. "And now you will learn."

"Today?"

She shook her head. "No, Jeannette, you will not learn it today, but you will begin to learn it today. If you work hard it will become a part of you and you will be able to find it all in you at any moment without calling it first. It will come to you by itself."

Chapter Eighteen
Tournaments
I. Volleyball

The Volleyball team had arrived at their hotel about eight o'clock the previous evening, with enough time for a quick snack and then off to bed. Coach Anita had been strict about lights out, which she enforced by getting two connecting rooms and leaving the connecting door wide open. She had developed that special ability to fall asleep wherever and whenever she wanted, and waking up as easily, so it was no big deal to keep everybody nice and cozy where they belonged. She had also gotten a hotel twelve miles outside of town, so there was no added distraction of another team or some rowdy fans roving the halls at night looking for adventure. The only hometown parents she had seen were the players' own families since everyone else was staying home for the big football game which was going to start exactly one hour later than the Volleyball final.

At the gym late the next afternoon, Coach Anita was gratified that her girls were more focused than she had seen them all season. They had already demolished their first opponent 15-6, so they were psyched for the final game that would put them on top. Lisa had accounted for three goals during the first game, but Christine…well, Christine had been incredible, scoring nine goals including five in a row. She was more focused than ever and had developed the ability to turn a teammate's mistake into a shared joke that segued into a quick technique lesson. Now when the team shouted "Aye Aye, Captain!" it was happy and enthusiastic.

At the final game, it was sad to see how few of the hometown crowd were in the seats behind them, but if it all came together they would be 20-4 for the season, the best in school history. There were at least some College recruiters out there, so with luck, a few of them would notice Christine.

The girls were grouped around the Smartphone that Coach Anita had allowed Christine to carry this one time, to read the texts that their friends back in Smithfield were sending.

"BREAK A LEG HA HA GOOD LUCK GIRLS JIMMY" read Christine.

"How does he have any time to send a text?" asked Bobbi.

"Football game doesn't start for an hour," says Lisa. "What's the next one?" Christine scrolled and touched the screen. "BEST OF LUCK TEAM".

"Who's it from?" asked Stephanie impatiently. "It's so, like, you know, original."

"Don't knock it," says Christine, but with a grin. "It says 'Joe's Barber Shop'."

"Yeah, like they rented a bus so they could all come down here," said Lisa sarcastically.

"BON CHANCE MON AMIS" read Christine.

"Like that's any real mystery," said Lisa somewhat kinder than Christine expected, at which Christine turned and lightly punched her friend on the shoulder.

"You're learning," she said cheerfully.

"What's that all about?" asked Tiffany.

"It's from Joan," answered Lisa defensively. "Yes, that Joan, and I'm not going to hear any of you say anything against her or you'll regret it. Understand?"

"Okay, okay, I only asked what it's about," said Tiffany. "Why the big change?"

Lisa got all quiet, but Christine figured they ought to know the truth.

"Well, Lisa and I are taking First Year French and not doing all that well," said Christine.

"To put it mildly," said Lisa under her breath.

Christine glared, but only for a second. "All right, we were both flunking. In case you didn't know, having an F in a class means you lose your sports eligibility. No passing French, no Volleyball team - then from out of the blue Joan offers to help us. For free. At my house."

"After all that stuff you and Lisa pulled?" asked Tiffany.

"Yeah, even after all that stuff," said Lisa. "She's such a good tutor both Christine and I brought our grade up to a B if you can believe that. Joan has spoken both French and English since she was born so she taught us some good rules..."

"Joan could talk when she was BORN?" exclaimed Stephanie, barely managing to dodge one more punch from Lisa.

Coach Anita came up and Christine slid the phone back into the bag with her other gear.

"Anything special?" Coach Anita asked.

"Lots of Luck from Jimmy, Joe's Barber Shop, and Joan," replied Christine, a hint of disappointment in her voice. "Nobody else. Guess that tells us where we stand."

"You stand right here with the rest of us," said Lisa emphatically. "One more game and we're champions, and we couldn't have gotten here without you."

During warm-ups, it soon became apparent that the Austin East team had never played anyone quite like Smithfield before, and their well-choreographed routine started to fall apart. They had never seen anybody popping the ball like Smithfield, to the point that it became impossible to follow. What was worse, the tiny contingent in the Smithfield stands had started up the Sponge Bob theme song, and to their consternation, it spread like an infection. People all over the gym joined in, including some of the Austin East supporters.

Smithfield finally finished with a shout of "Aye Aye, Captain!" and the teams took their places. As the game got going, it became painfully obvious it was going to be short and sweet, and if Christine had any worries their leap to a 4-0 lead in the first two minutes put her mind at rest.

Fifteen minutes later it was all over, and they were lined up getting their pictures taken with the Championship Trophy. Pictures over, the tournament officials were hustling them to get off the court so the next game could get started. The last thing the girls wanted to do was to watch another game, so Mrs. Coates herded everyone into the school van for the trip home. Since the team was so small there was plenty of room for everybody, and the gentle rocking of the van soon combined with the cumulative fatigue from two games so that everybody was asleep

Except for Christine, that is, sitting behind Mrs. Coates and cradling the trophy in her arms. Surprisingly she wasn't sleepy, and it didn't take much thinking about the season to put some things into perspective. Despite that season's rough start what with practices, homework, and working at the Piggly Wiggly, it had all gotten a lot easier about the fifth week right after the shootout with Joan. Those few words "never you mind" had taken the sting out of the shame Christine felt about the whole bullying thing, and then with Joan's help with the French tutoring – in a way this trophy was hers as much as theirs.

About three weeks before, she and Lisa had finished a session with Joan that Miss Renoir had set up in her classroom. Lisa's dad had arrived early so for a few minutes it was only Christine and Joan waiting by the front door. By now, the lessons had erased their previous tensions and both girls were surprised to find they could actually talk together. They weren't exactly friends yet but that was coming, Christine at least was sure. About Joan, she couldn't tell, which reminded Christine of something that Lisa had said about Joan.

"Can I ask you a question," Christine asked. "Nothing personal or anything."

"Sure," Joan replied, "make it personal if you want."

"Well, maybe it's personal. Back a while we had that...thing in the gym? Well, I've...always wondered something about that day. Two things, in fact. First, right at the beginning, you didn't even try to return my first shot. You were standing there and watching me like I was weird looking or something. Were you trying to psych me out by doing that?"

77

Joan laughed. "Is that what it looked like?" Christine nodded. "Well, I guess I've never seen myself doing that before. No, I'm not trying to psych you out, but you're right, I was watching you."

"Why?"

"Because that way I learned what you were going to do and how you were going to do it. I watch for three things: first, where you are looking. Second, how you move your legs and body around, how you move forward and turn and bend and that stuff. Third, how you move your arms and hands in relation to the rest of it. It... tells me how you move and all I have to do is take advantage of that."

Christine had never heard of this before and started to replay the spike contest play by play. Joan had missed the first one – or let it go by on purpose, she now realized. One, two, she beat me two straight...but how...and it hit her. "You aimed for my blind spot."

Joan nodded. "It was real obvious. You're tall and strong and have a strong right-hand dominance to the point that it doesn't get in the way when you are a couple yards from someone, but if they get inside that distance it's like your left side can't react fast enough, or maybe you can't see the same way. Everybody has one eye that's stronger than the other."

"How do you adjust for that?"

"In fencing, you have to force yourself to practice on your own blind side so you start to see better. My Mama made me practice both right and left handed and it helped. A lot." She looked at Christine, who saw the same open-mouthed concentration Joan had at the shootout. "Like I see you right now, the way you are seated here, the way you hold yourself. I'll bet you go down steps left foot first. Am I right?"

Christine had thought a lot about what Joan said, and when she got home that evening she started to develop a routine, and at their next practice, the team had its first left-right handed back and forth exercise. It had taken all of her willpower to keep from yelling at the team as they started to complain about it being too hard, or too complicated, but in their next game Bobbi had four saves all while using her left hand. For her part, Christine played closer to the net on purpose and started watching the other team the way that Joan had described. During the first timeout, she clicked off what she had observed to her teammates, and when the game resumed it was almost as if an entirely new team of mind readers had taken the floor. It wasn't a hundred percent, but what was expected to be a close game ended with Smithfield 15, Natchez 8, a victory that clinched Smithfield for the finals. Yes, we owe Joan a lot.

"Game's on, Girls," called Mrs. Coates from the front seat, and after a few buzzes and snorts from the speakers the Smithfield-Garland game came on the car radio.

II. Football

If Joan had thought the previous games that year had been crazy, they hadn't prepared her for the insanity that greeted her when she and Michelle got out of the car for the Garland game. As they made their way to the "officials" entrance they spotted Brian in his wheelchair checking passes. Joan noticed that he was a lot more cheerful than the first time they had met two months before.

"Can you believe this crowd?" he shouted as they passed through the gate. "This is always a big game but there's never been a Regional championship riding on it. I've been here for two hours already and I don't know where they're putting everybody."

Joan tapped her pass, still on the chain around her neck. "Glad we got these."

"Mrs. Coates takes care of her family," said Brian. "Always has and always will."

"Want something to drink or eat?" Michelle asked, or rather shouted in a nice way. Brian shook his head, reaching around to pat the full pack hanging from the back of his wheelchair.

"Got my provisions right here," he shouted back but quickly added "But I'd love some kettle corn if you can get through the line. Don't worry about it until after the first quarter." Michelle visibly brightened at the request and Joan knew she would be absent for most of the second quarter.

Twenty minutes later they had finally scrambled into their reserved seats, normally a one minute walk from where they had left Brian. Three seats away Dwight and George waved hello, any talking a hopeless proposition. It was then that Michelle noticed Ryan was missing and waved her hand back and forth to get Dwight's attention.

"Where's Ryan?" she shouted, but Dwight gave her a perplexed look. Michelle then stood up and pretended to beat an invisible bass drum. Dwight pointed down to the field where Ryan was standing next to the biggest bass drum she had ever seen. When the roar had finally dwindled from rocket launch level to Niagara Falls level, Joan leaned over and half shouted directly into Michelle's ear. "Think we'll hear him up here?"

Michelle shook her head and shouted back. "Not sure he'll hear himself!"

When the pregame scoreboard finally rolled down to 0:00 the U.S. Marine color guard started off toward the center of the field. The silence was so abrupt that some doves circling in panic overhead actually landed in the field and were fluttering away as the Marines marched past. In a minute the flag started to go up the flagpole, and the Garland band struck up the Star-Spangled Banner.

The fact that the Garland Band had more than two hundred members and the Smithfield Band had six wasn't lost on anybody, so instead of a strained rivalry, it was more like a Big Brother relationship. The Smithfield Band was always invited to share in the hot dogs, soft drinks, popcorn, candy bars, barbecue sandwiches, watermelon, or (believe it or not) corn on the cob that the visiting Band Boosters provided.

The food was on Michelle's mind when the Star-Spangled Banner ended, her mind stuck on the garbled speaker sounding like "The Home of the Gravy," but that was quickly forgotten as Mrs. Coates put up her arms to start the Smithfield Fight Song. The band had actually heard their own fight song for the first time the previous week during practice in Mrs. Coates' room, even though they had played it at least two hundred times that season. When you pit six high school musicians against 7300 screaming fans, it isn't the trumpets you hear.

But they did hear Ryan, and in fact, Michelle wondered if they could hear Ryan in New Orleans two hundred miles away, which was apparently where Mrs. Coates had found that enormous drum. A minute later she was sure when the paper covering the back shredded to reveal an enormous smiling alligator, and the crowd got to its feet and cheered until the PA came on to announce the beginning of the game. The players finished their warmups, the captains flipped the coins, the benches filled up, and for the last time that evening the crowd got quiet up to the point of kickoff, which is to say the sound was like a jet on the runway prior to takeoff.

Billy Landrieu was receiving for Smithfield and started forward with an easy lope like he had done a hundred times before that season, but instead of heading for the goal line seventy yards away he found himself running for his life with every player on the Garland team after him. Whatever successful strategy that Smithfield had was now totally obsolete by whatever the Garland team had figured out, and less than one minute into the game Smithfield was behind 7-0, Billy having fumbled the ball out of sheer panic.

Down on the field Smithfield's official head football coach, Mr. Cunningham had called a timeout, but from where they sat both Michelle and Joan could hear the unmistakable sound of Mr. Todd's voice from the middle of the huddle.

"WHAT THE BLUE BLAZES WERE YOU DOING OUT THERE?" Todd shrieked, waving his clipboard not four inches from Billy's face.

Billy knew enough to be silent, but was thinking I did exactly what you told me to do, but since you only did give us one play all season Garland has us all figured out.

"Coach Todd, I'd like to suggest..." started Mr. Cunningham but the referee blew the whistle and yelled, "KICK RETURN TEAM BACK ON THE FIELD."

By halftime, their instruments had grown cold and Michelle had gone to get some kettle corn for Brian. Here and there gaps started to appear in the stands as whole groups got up and left, unwilling to spend any more time on what was fast appearing to be an upset loss, and the Garland coach had wisely saved some of his best players for what was obviously going to be their extended season. It was with a sense of relief that first half ended, the teams ran to their locker rooms, and the band members went to share in the food offered by their counterparts across the field, picking up a dejected Ryan from beside his drum.

"I only got to play it three times," he said plaintively. "The biggest drum I ever saw and only three times."

George patted him on the shoulder. "Well, look at it this way, Ryan – at least everybody could hear you. All seven thousand five hundred and six of them. "

Ryan visibly brightened. "George, is there any way I could take that drum home?"

When some of the players were later asked about halftime, most of them blushed and immediately changed the subject. Whatever happened, however, the team that came out of the locker room for the second half was very different from the team that went in. By the beginning of the fourth quarter, Ryan was a lot busier and the team had narrowed the score from 49-6 to 63-48. The way the offense was clicking into gear, it looked like Smithfield might be able to pull it out of the fire after all.

The home stands had mostly filled back up and the band was starting to regret their half-time feast of barbecue, potato salad, corn on the cob, and lemonade. Down on the field, Mr. Cunningham was a lot more self-confident, while Todd, still wearing his official's headphones, positioned himself next to the line crew and kept his mouth shut. The team had apparently figured out whatever it was that Garland knew about them, so thanks to some wizardry by Jimmy the game was turning respectable again.

Except respectable wasn't going to cut it if Garland kept on this way. This was not only the Garland game anymore, it was the championship. By the fourth quarter, the score was Garland 77, Smithfield 63, and three of Smithfield's key players had been injured already, including one with a broken leg. Nobody was sitting down anymore, including the band, and for the first time that season Mrs. Coates had them playing the fight song over and over in the hope that the accumulated effect would carry over to the team.

Joan had great wind but this was more than she'd ever played before in her life and her stamina was starting to fade. Michelle, on the other hand, was great, as usual, as fresh as when they arrived and considerably more wound up. Smithfield got possession at 1:55, the cheerleaders were bouncing up and down, the band started up one more time and Jimmy took the hike, faded back, saw that Billy was open and launched an incredible pass forty-five yards downfield that Billy snagged out of the air. Even the band had stopped playing and was jumping up and down as Billy headed for the end zone but two Garland players were on a beeline to intercept him.

"Head for the sideline!" shouted Dwight, but he knew that Billy wanted to make up for that kickoff return in the first quarter and scoring this touchdown was going to be his only chance. One of the players moved ahead of Billy and five yards away from the goal they all collided like three runaway freight trains. Everyone was looking for the ball to squirt out into the open but it didn't happen, and when Billy got up he held up the ball. First down, five to go, we have the ball, instruments up everybody. What followed was not very musical but it was energetic…and then they noticed that the clock had run all the way down to 1:17, and Billy was being helped off the field with no timeouts left.

Joan

The roar was cranking up again from both sides as the teams lined up on the five-yard line. I wasn't exactly a football fan but the energy the crowd generated was something I had never experienced before, and it was neat knowing some of the people out on the field. Compared to the crowd at a Texas high school football game, the moms and dads at a fencing tournament aren't even from the same planet.

The ball was snapped, Jimmy faded back to pass and from out of nowhere two more Garland players were charging down on him, one from either side with no place to go but forward. The center of the line was now in a big pile right on the goal line so Jimmy simply ran right up and over the pile and dived forward into the end zone. The home crowd went berserk, Ryan started banging his drum, Mrs. Coates did one downbeat and we were off and running...except that five seconds later she is waving her baton for us to put our instruments down while the referee is making some announcement. Wouldn't you know it, there was holding and off sides in the same play, so the touchdown was canceled and we lost possession. There were some diehard fans yelling some not very nice things at the referees, but four out of the five referees had seen the exact same thing so the protests fizzled away and there we were, Garland's ball and the clock stopped at 0:34.

It was like somebody pulled the plug. Everybody either sat down or started packing their stuff to leave, and we didn't even watch as Garland made one halfhearted play and fell on the ball to run out the clock. Season over, see you later, no more kettle corn for a while, and I knew that I would miss it a lot.

Mrs. Coates had said something about a pep band for basketball games, but so far it hadn't materialized. Michelle got her Papa on the phone and he said that he'd managed to find a parking place up next to the high school, so instead of a nice fifteen-minute walk with Michelle, we walked out the stadium gate and around the corner to pile into the back seat of the car. Of course, by then it took half an hour to get out of the parking lot but Michelle fell asleep right away. I had learned that once she fell asleep you could practically play a pair of cymbals over her head without waking her up.

"Good game?" Mr. Dr. Han asked, moving up two more slots in the line.

"We lost," I replied, "but it was fun to watch in the second half."

Then I remembered the Volleyball tournament, did a quick look up on my phone and sure enough, they did it! Good for Christine...and Lisa. Although we were not great friends yet, there was at least peace between us that we could build upon and I found myself looking forward to hearing all about it when we all got back home. About then the combination of the warm car and the gentle rocking started to get the better of me, even with Michelle snoring gently in the seat across from me, so I'll close my eyes too, for a second, and...

III. Fencing
Michelle

I was lucky enough to be invited to Joan's first tournament and Coach Renoir agreed to take me along if I agreed to keep the official team records. Since there was only one person on the team it wasn't exactly the hardest job in the world, and believe me, I was excited! Joan's my best friend and this was a part of her life that I heard about but never seen before, but she did a good job of teaching me about some of the basics.

Every competitor wears a special suit that conducts electricity through it. When they get onto the competition runway they hook up a long wire that goes from their foil to the back end of their half of the runway, and when your opponent touches your suit with his/her foil an electrical circuit is completed and the point is registered. First one to five points is the winner, and that person moves on to the next round. There are some differences depending on the different types of weapons, but the basic idea is the same. Everybody wears a face mask so nobody is injured, and everything moves very quickly. My job was to keep track of Joan's individual matches and her overall scores for the day.

As we went into the gym I tapped Joan on the shoulder. "Break a leg, dork."

"Do my best," she answered, and I left her there to take my seat next to Coach Renoir. Joan had moved to where she could get a better view of the other matches, and after a minute I had to cover my mouth to keep from laughing out loud. She had what we called her "Border Collie" look, staring motionless at the upcoming competitors the same way out that Shadow, Ryan's Border collie, stared at the sheep he rounded up.

Three hours later Joan had made a clean sweep with five perfect scores in a row and the sheep were all herded together at one end of the bench not knowing what hit them. After a while, Joan came over looking tired and carrying a trophy about two feet tall. I never saw that trophy again, and when I asked about it later Joan told me she had put it in with a box of old clothes to take to the Goodwill store.

"It's not exactly something I'm proud of," she said.

I had a few of my own trophies from Chinese school and a chess trophy from when I was four and Mom and Dad treated them like prized family heirlooms, so this attitude didn't make any sense to me.

"Why do you go to tournaments at all if you're so good?" I asked.

"Because I love fencing," she said, "and the only decent way to do that is to face as many new opponents as I can. Someday, one of them is going to teach me something new."

That's how legends get started. Before today, Joan had been an unknown quantity, but afterwards her reputation preceded her into every subsequent match. She became the one they talked about, the one to beat, the one they climbed over each other to have the chance to face. Some of those who had faced her had very little enthusiasm for doing so again, however.

Joan had been fencing since she was three, so she had fully ten years of experience by age thirteen. Every bit of her accumulated training was in her hands, her fingers, the soles of her feet, and most of all in her bones. Once you do something that long, it becomes automatic, programmed into the muscle/brain connection so efficiently that the reflexes don't have to ask questions.

Half an hour later we're back in Coach Renoir's car on our way back home, and I'm dog tired and ready to sleep even though Joan was the one doing all the work at the tournament. Joan and I are snug in the back seat with Miss Renoir up front driving, and although I'm in the mood to talk I can tell something is on Joan's mind. The van is rocking gently and she's nestled in a corner looking out of the window into the darkness, the occasional light of a passing car shining on her face, her eyes glistening. She can be so goofy and sharp and here she is…crying, or doing her best not to. Her dad is in New York tonight but he's going to be home tomorrow and he called her before we got into the van. She won the tournament hands down undefeated and now…tears?

"Pretty dumb, huh," she says in a low, soft voice. "I should at least be – I don't know – happy?"

"You won, Joan," I reply.

"Guess so," and blows her nose.

"First official school tournament," I say, "and you won the whole thing. I mean, even after being away from it for such a long time."

"Yes," she answers after a pause. "Long time." She snuggles into the corner and leans her head on the window and I see another streak on her face.

And then I know, and it breaks my heart.

After a while, the van stops at a traffic light in the middle of nowhere. Miss Renoir turns from the driver's seat and ever so gently she reaches out and smooths Joan's hair. The light turns green again and the car moves forward but more slowly now. A very soft voice is coming from the front seat and I don't

know the words because it's in French, but there is something so unbelievably soothing and peaceful. Joan is asleep now, still rocking gently as the car heads toward home.

Joan's not so different from all the others but another, more fearsome dream comes to her. It's six hundred years ago, and her Fleur de Lys banner is a symbol for more than a thousand others who cheer her at the top of their lungs. She shouts at them to follow and climbs up, up and over rocks to and then up the ladder, rocks and arrows falling all around but none hitting her. Reaching the top, she leaps onto the parapet waving her sword, pulls her squire up beside her, and turns to acknowledge her soldiers. Suddenly, a lone swordsman crashes through her guard, sending her squire crashing to the parapet. His sword is on high, ready to strike but hers is faster and as she makes a single thrust the man screams and collapses in a pool of blood. Though her followers cheer, all she can see is fear, pain, and death.

Chapter Nineteen
Wreckage

It was the Monday morning after the big loss to Garland, and Rose was nervous. She had been downtown Saturday afternoon and already the football season posters were sticking out of the trash cans lined up along the street. It was too bad that everybody paid so much attention to football because the Volleyball girls did a fabulous job and deserved some recognition. In fact, Rose was waiting for Todd to come out of his office and approve the order for a new number for the sign outside, telling the world that yes, their Girls' Volleyball team was the 2015 State Champion. Coach Anita had already delivered the Volleyball trophy to the front office, and there it sat in the middle of the main reception desk.

With the new season starting this week everybody had their hopes set on the girls' basketball for another big tournament win. Christine had been voted Most Valuable Player by the Capitol sportswriters, and with practice getting underway this afternoon they should be just about unbeatable. Or at least that's the way it's supposed to be...unless something screws that up. Volleyball isn't the same as playing basketball, since basketball has a hundred times the running that Volleyball does, and with your opponents banging into you all the time your knees or head are always waiting for one bad fall.

Todd was sitting at his desk, banging a big pencil against the yellow pad he always had handy. He looked in his IN box, still piled with four inches of paperwork he'd put off doing last week as he worked with the football team. Might as well have gone to the movies on Friday night for all the good it did, although he was darn sure there would be a new football coach next season. He'd left work Friday afternoon expecting to have his two championships all wrapped up neat and tidy, but by Monday there was only one trophy out front and that wasn't enough to cut it.

When someone told him about Miss Renoir giving one of the students fencing lessons, his first reaction was to laugh. With the football loss, he'd thought about it some more, however, and there was something about this one made him rethink his original plan. Apparently, this new French-speaking kid was supposed to be some hot-shot fencing expert, and might even make it all the way to the top at the State Tournament. Todd liked having some extra insurance, especially since he already had a first-rate fencing coach right here in the school. He pushed the buzzer for Rose.

"Send for Miss Renware to come here for a few minutes."

The reply speaker crackled. "She's in class right now..."

"I KNOW THAT," he replied. "Go down and cover for her 'till I'm finished."
There was a new copy of Sports Today in the IN box about an inch down the
stack, so he slid it out and started to read.

A few minutes later there was a knock on the door and Miss Renoir came into
the office. Todd motioned to the chair in front of his desk and after he finished
reading the magazine page he stuck a note card on the top and tossed it back into
the box.

"You've had your first tournament?" he asked.

"Yes, sir, last Saturday," she answered.

He waited. And waited. "So?" he asked again, annoyed.

"So...Jeanne was the winner."

"What do you mean – the winner of exactly what?"

"The tournament has individual divisional winners, and then there is a
champion of the tournament. In that category, Jeanne was victorious."

Victorious. Todd liked the sound of that word. Victorious had wrapped up in
it the promise of putting all those years as someone else's flunky behind him,
moving to a big desk with a big sign saying SUPERINTENDENT in polished
brass and nobody else telling him what to do.

"Well, that's fine. Good to have people victorious around here." He reached
down and picked up the top paper from the IN box and held it up. "Got your
coaching contract right here," he said, waving it back and forth for emphasis.
"Time to get this all signed, sealed, and delivered."

But instead of a yes, sir she gave him a strange, quizzical look. "You said
contract, Sir, but that is a magazine, I believe."

Todd saw he was holding up the copy of Sports Today he had been reading.
He tossed it onto a pile and grabbed the next item in the box which thankfully
was the contract he was looking for. "We only need your signature to make it
official," as he handed it to her and held up a pen. Instead of saying Thank You,
however, the lady sat there reading.

"One moment," she said. "Regarding...payment. I see that is currently blank.
May I presume that there is no additional payment for this work?"

"Your agreement was to teach where assigned, Miss Renware," said Todd.
"For this next three months, this is your assignment."

Her eyes narrowed. "And who will teach the students?" she asked with a note
of anger in her voice. "We do not start students and then simply drop them like
they do not matter."

"Contract means that your Coaching duty is now part of your teaching. You
will teach your classes during the day, and then do your coaching after school or
evenings or whenever you have your games."

"Matches. Matches and then a Tournament," she said dryly. "Fencing is not
a game."

His normally bombastic voice grew icy. "Miss Renware, your agreement
with this school is that you will teach where assigned, and your residence in the
United States is contingent on that agreement. If you break this agreement or if
you are dismissed from teaching, you will have two days before you are..."

"Deported," she finished, and this time her voice was cold. "Yes, I know. That is the condition? I will teach AND coach fencing in order to stay at this school?"

Gotcha. "Correct."

Using her own pen Miss Renoir wrote her name on the signature line and dropped it onto the desk. "If we are finished here I wish to return to my class," she said frostily.

"Sure, go ahead," he said without even looking up, and a moment later the door closed behind her. He put the contract into the folder, dropped it into the OUT box, and as he was reaching for the magazine he noticed that his hands were shaking a bit. Stupid woman, he thought, we could have finished that in thirty seconds. He reached around to make sure the door was completely closed, then opened his center desk drawer and stuck in his hand all the way to the back. There was a soft 'clink' and a moment later he withdrew two small green bottles, each marked Mineral Supplement. He tore off the foil tops and gulped down both bottles, being careful to drop the empties into the side pocket of his coat. Within a few minutes, he could feel the energy so that once again he felt strong, in control, and ready to take on anything or anybody.

Time to get out of here, he thought, and looking down at the IN box he decided to put off the rest of the paperwork until...well, until I get to it. I'm the acting Superintendent here, after all. Only one problem: those two bottles of Mineral Supplement were the last of his supply, but his old buddy down the coast had twenty more boxes waiting for him. All he had to do was drive down there and pick it up. Yep, keys in my pocket, through the door and...

"Are you going out, Sir?" asked Rose but he ignored her and strode straight through the door to where his truck awaited him.

Chapter Twenty
The Best Laid Plans

It felt so good getting back home that Christine was as close to floating on air as she had ever been. After the game, she'd gotten some thumbs up from the people Coach Anita had pointed out as college recruiters, so she had her fingers crossed that with luck, there was a scholarship just around the corner.

Since it was Saturday morning she and Mama were sitting together sipping coffee before the little ones woke up.

"You'll be the first in our family to go to college, you know," said Mama warmly. "I was still in High School when your big sister was born, and well...there was no way after that. Your big sister came along and then you, and then your little sisters, and that's what my life is all about. We're lucky that things are finally settled down. They are very good to me at the College, I do a good job in the Art department, and we've got medical insurance now, thank God. I can even take a class for free if I want to. In three more weeks, I'll have my six-month anniversary, so the extra disability insurance will kick in and we'll be all set."

This was something out of the blue. "Is there something you're not telling me, Mama?"

"No, sweetheart, nothing I know of. Things have been good in that department."

Well that's something to be thankful for, thought Christine. "Coach said at least two college scouts were at the game."

"I'm so proud of you for your championship," Mama said as she poured some more milk into her cup. "Everything else going okay?"

Christine nodded. It was so rare that she and Mama had any time at all to talk, let alone first thing in the morning, but like it or not she still had work hours scheduled for today.

"I'll bring home dinner from the store, Mama, so you take it easy today. Let the little ones help out, they're always asking to do that," Christine said as she stood up from the table and pinned her employee badge on her shirt.

"I will, honey. See you at five."

The phone call came after two as Christine was restocking frozen dinners. Her hands were freezing but she had finished the last box when she heard herself called to the office on the store PA system. Folding the last empty box into the cart, she pushed it through the storage room doors before going up front to see what it was about.

"Sorry about this Christine, "said Mr. Jones, "but we got a call that they've taken your Mama to the hospital. Get your things and I'll drive you there right away. Hurry, now."

It was all Christine could do to stay calm until they got there. The nurses said that her Mama was semi-conscious but had quickly stabilized, so Christine tiptoed into the hospital room and made herself comfortable in the visitor's chair.

After a few minutes, her Mama stirred and Christine moved closer to the bed. "How you feeling?" she asked gently. "You gave me quite a spell, you know."

Mama smiled back, weak but with humor still there. "Never better. You know, I think this bed agrees with me. Almost as good as the food."

"What's the story? Is it the same as two years ago?"

Mama shook her head. "No, honey, they have me with something brand new this time. I'm anemic, I guess, and it's apparently been going on for a long time. It explains why I'm so tired." She was silent for a few minutes, her thumb gently stroking the back of Christine's hand. "Don't like having to pull you into this, but the full disability from the College doesn't take effect for three weeks. My job's secure and all, and the medical insurance is covering this, but there's only two hundred dollars a week disability until I get back on the job. Unless your Papa..."

"Mama, let's make an agreement right now that we don't talk about him, not now, not ever. As far as I'm concerned he doesn't exist." If it weren't for the hospital room Christine would be shouting this right now, or throwing something breakable out of sheer cussed frustration. Every time her father showed up at home with big promises he's back out on the street the next day after throwing something through a window and one more thing in the house would be missing, turning up later at the Pawn shop over in Garland. One time he'd brought some present for the twins, and....

"Mama!"

"Yes, Christine?"

"Who...who's staying with the twins?"

"A student is looking after them," she replied calmly. "One thing about Smithfield College is that folks look after each other. It's a high school girl, her father's one of the professors in our building, and as soon as they heard what happened she went right over. The twins are fine."

The hospital was two miles from home and Christine managed the run in twenty-three minutes, and as she saw her house up ahead she put on an extra spurt until she was up on the front porch. Sure enough, someone was in the kitchen cooking so she took a second to catch her breath before she opened the door.

The twins were on either side of the kitchen table, each with a bowl, a spoon, and a grin as their sister came through the door. Christine started to speak to whoever was cooking but to her surprise it was Joan, of all people, wearing Mama's apron and starting to ladle something into the matching bowls.

"Hi, Christine. You hungry?" Joan said as she put a bowl in front of each twin.

"How..."

"People call people. The secretary of the Archaeology department is the sister in law of the secretary of the Art department, and since they're in the same building and see me all the time. I borrowed a bike and here I am. Hope you don't mind that I made dinner."

"What is it?" Christine asked, not having any idea what else to say.

"It's a recipe I learned, called Crayfish Etou..."

"Etouffee," said Christine. "I thought it smelled familiar. I haven't had it for a long time."

"I put in shrimp instead. It's yummy."

As if on cue the twins were scraping the bottom of their bowls, something which jarred Christine back into reality. "Is there..."

"Plenty. Can I make a bowl for you, too?"

Christine nodded, and after bringing the pot and an empty bowl to the table Joan ladled it full and put another into each of the twin's bowls for good measure. It did smell good, heavenly in fact, and since she wasn't exactly thinking straight Christine decided that she'd sit and eat. Joan took a cloth to the sink, wrung it out, and proceeded to clean up the stove, humming a song that Christine remembered from somewhere. The soup was creamy and rich and there were little pieces of potato and the shrimp were a nice size and just chewy enough, and before Christine knew it her bowl was empty.

Joan sat down at the table still humming, and waited until the twins finished eating. "Okay you two, bowls to the sink, don't forget to run the water, do you take a bath or shower in the evening or the morning, where are your pajamas, would you like a bedtime story," all poured out, and happy chatter filled the kitchen. Yes, they took a shower in the morning, we are big now and the pajamas are in the bedroom and we brush our teeth and a bedtime story would be very nice thank you. Fifteen minutes later Joan was back in the kitchen, where Christine had finished what was left in the pot.

"They're asleep," Joan said and sat down.

"Why are you doing this?" asked Christine.

"Why shouldn't I be doing this?" replied Joan.

"Because."

"Because why?"

"Just because."

"Now it's sounding like we are in second grade."

"Are not."

"Are too."

The two girls looked at each other, each one waiting for the other to speak next, and then Christine started to laugh and Joan followed and anyone on the road outside would have thought the two people inside that kitchen must have heard the funniest joke in the world. There's a certain laughter when something is funny, and there's another laughter when you are doing it to keep from crying. Sometimes the difference between the two is as thin as a sheet of paper, and the strange thing with Joan and Christine is that it started out the first kind and ended up the second kind because of this thing called Reality that jumped up and bit you.

"What am I going to do?" asked Christine miserably. "I mean, with Mama in the hospital I'm going to have to work every minute I'm not in school to keep this roof over our heads. I'm not worried about going hungry, but someone has to take care of the twins, too."

Joan bowed her head for a second like she did to help sometimes to help her concentration, and after a minute she raised her head. "Got a proposal for you."

"Shoot."

"I will come here after school and take care of the twins until you come home or your Mama gets back. Would that help?"

Christine's eyes filled and she couldn't speak. Three months ago, Joan would not have been able to see behind these tears, but things happen and you start to know what things are like because they have happened to you. A moment later Joan's phone rang, giving Christine a minute to gather herself until Joan finished her call.

"That was Papa," Joan said. "He checked in at the hospital and your Mama's doing okay right now," said Joan. "She told him that they still didn't know why she's anemic, but sometime these things take some time to figure out."

Christine felt ashamed to be saying this, but Joan seemed like someone who wouldn't think badly of her, and might even understand. "There's basketball, too. It's my chance."

"For what?"

"A Scholarship. An athletic scholarship. If I don't play that goes out the window." She didn't say the rest of it: if Mama was seriously sick, then she'd quit the team, go to work at the Piggly Wiggly, and take care of the twins until they grew up. That's fourteen years away and I will never, ever get another chance.

Joan nodded and was silent. "Christine, I don't have an answer to that one, but if I take care of the twins after school for a while it will be one less thing for you to worry about. Would that be okay?"

Christine took a breath and the whole, stupid day caught up with her all at once and she was sobbing and then Joan was hugging her, a caring human to make her not feel so terribly, terribly alone in all of this. The bullying was there in the tears, too, the shame of it all and what am I compared to this saint with the black hair and fantastic soup?

"Never you mind," said Joan, ever so gently.

Chapter Twenty-One
Daddy's Back

Two days later Todd was at his desk having finished several long phone calls and a meeting with Coach Anita. Ever since he heard about Christine's Mama he had been in a panic, made a lot worse after hearing that Christine might have to leave the basketball team. If that happened, their chances for a State Championship were down the toilet.

Whenever there was a genuine emergency, his first response was to make sure he wasn't the one who was going to be blamed for anything. There had been some big questions raised after the Garland loss, but his contingency planning had been impeccable and Mr. Cunningham had conveniently taken the fall for that. Unfortunately, that didn't solve this situation: Mrs. Cooper was going to be in the hospital for at least two more weeks, and if Christine wasn't playing it would be way too late to make up for the losses they were sure to have.

That's when he got the idea. There was still some of that Special Education money left over, and all he needed was a way to direct some of that in Christine's direction so she'd be able to go back to the basketball team and keep things going through the end of the season. Whatever happened after that, well, Christine didn't play a spring sport so it was no longer his problem.

The door opened again and Rose appeared in the doorway. "Paul Cooper is here for his appointment," she said.

"Send him in," Todd replied.

When Paul Cooper came through the door his hair was combed and his shirt was buttoned but there wasn't much other evidence that he had done anything special before coming in. They had been classmates in high school, and although they'd had an unofficial rivalry to see who could be the biggest Jerk in the school, Paul Cooper would have won hands down if he hadn't been kicked out before graduation.

"Why am I here?" asked Paul, looking Todd straight in the eye. "My wife put you on to me?"

"Nope," answered Todd, taking a paper out of his desk drawer and tossing it across his desk. "Take a look at this."

Paul reached into his pocket and withdrew a metal box, opened it, took out one toothpick, closed the box, returned the box to his pocket, and put the toothpick into his mouth. He settled back into his chair, looked back at Todd for a second, then let out a big sigh and grabbed the paper.

"Says you're two years behind on your child support," Todd said, "and there's an open warrant out for you right now. I had a talk with the sheriff and he's letting us have this little chat to see if we can come up with some 'agreement'."

"What agreement?" Paul asked.

"Nothing too complicated," replied Todd. "With your ex-wife in the hospital and you not paying any child support, Christine will have to quit school and go to work. Well, I'm not about to let that happen. So, here's the deal: you get a job here at the school and report directly to me. We take three-fourths of your pay and put it directly into an account that Christine and only Christine has access to. You leave her and your kids alone and, well, you keep your nose clean and the sheriff won't act on this bench warrant. Everybody's happy. "

Paul looked sideways at Todd for a minute before speaking. It didn't take a genius to figure out that there was something else going on here. Todd doesn't give a darn about Christine or anybody else for that matter unless they have something he wants. What could Christine have that he....

"If Christine goes to work full time she quits the basketball team, right?" Paul asked. Todd nodded. "No Christine, no basketball team, and no what else? What's so special about basketball that makes you go to all this trouble?"

"The State Basketball Championship," said Todd. "We've got a good shot at it this season. Christine plays basketball, they win the championship, and scholarship offers will start to drop into her mailbox."

Paul laughed. "So out of the goodness of your heart and wanting poor little Christine to get her scholarship, you're playing Hero Rescuer of the Cooper family. And I'm Santa Claus except I ain't got a long beard this time of year."

"So, is it a deal?" asked Todd. "Not in an hour, not tomorrow, not next week, right now." Todd pressed the call button. "Sheriff out there, Rose?"

"Yes, Sir, do I send him in?"

"Not yet. Not quite done." Todd turned back to Paul. "There's a catch..."

"No surprise," interrupted Paul.

"...that will sweeten it up for you. Make you more willing, you might say. You do what I say, you show up to the school every day, you leave your family alone, and you don't actually have to do anything."

"Say which?" Paul heard that but he didn't believe it.

"You don't have to do any work. Get yourself a big old overstuffed chair in some empty classroom, watch TV, sleep, I don't care. You can even eat for free in the cafeteria and use the locker room for showers. All you have to do is show up here every day, leave your family alone, and don't bug me or anybody else at this school."

"How much are you talking about?"

"Four hundred dollars a week," replied Todd, "But you only get a hundred of that. The other three goes to Christine, remember?"

When he first got the message that Todd wanted to see him, Paul thought it was some parent-teacher thing because Christine was in some trouble and his ex-wife was in the hospital. Four hundred dollars a week for doing nothing? Might as well ask while the asking's good.

"Got three conditions," said Paul confidently. "One, I get an office, not some old classroom, with a name tag on the door and a fancy title. Two, I get a computer in that office like everybody else with the internet and everything. Three, I get a school car and school gas."

Todd laughed out loud. "You are one piece of work. Here I offer you the sweetest deal you will ever get your natural born life and you're making conditions." He abruptly leaned forward, all laughter gone.

"Okay, here's how it's going to be. Yes, to the computer, and we'll even give you a room with an outside door so you can get yourself a cot and have a cozy little apartment. No, not ever on the school car. So – we got a deal or not?"

Unlike Todd, Paul couldn't see a down side except, well, the money wasn't great, but he got free food and a free apartment even though it was at a school. If they let him stay all night, there are lots of things in the lockers that he could liberate if he felt like it.

"Deal," he said. "One hundred in advance."

"Fifty," replied Todd, and took out a $50 bill from his coat pocket and slapped it on the desk. "You get the rest at the end of the month." He opened his desk and took out an envelope, handing it to Paul. "To make it official I need a signature on this paper, and the key to the Maintenance Room is there too. You remember one thing – you may be at this school now but you leave that girl of yours alone. You don't talk to her, go down a hallway she is in, or mess with her or anyone else, or I swear the Sheriff will find a nice stash of something in that Maintenance Room." Todd didn't finish. He didn't have to.

Ten minutes later Todd had the signed contract nice and tidy in the OUT box and that was one more headache out of the way. We get Christine through the season and the tournament, and then, well, too bad but daddy's gone somewhere so the job is over, too. Works out neat and tidy, and it's going to be a great day all around.

Chapter Twenty-Two
Family Reunion
Joan

With everything going on in school and getting to know Michelle, Dwight, and all my new teachers, it was a busy time. Most of my teachers were wonderful, especially Miss Renoir, and I learned the trick of staying away from people like Mr. Todd. I went to every fencing meet, did my homework, helped out at Christine's house, did my fencing practice every day, and went to Toussaint's with Papa and Miss Renoir once a week. Mama always talked about doing your best but it's a lot easier when you have some complications in your life that make you work harder.

School had its own ups and downs what with Mr. Todd raging up and down the hallways and whenever I heard that bellowing I made sure I headed the other direction. But my life had its compensations, too, and I had lots of reasons to be thankful. One day I was sitting across the table from Michelle, listening and laughing, and suddenly I got all choked up. I guess my expression changed because Michelle stopped chewing and got a worried look on her face.

"You okay?" she asked.

"Just glad you're my friend," I replied..

Emotions in public always made Michelle uncomfortable, and she turned beet red and mumbled as she continued eating. She did manage to squeeze a smile and a tilt of her head so I knew she felt the same way. I also knew she was thinking of an irreverent zinger to throw back at me.

"Meeting you was like a box of chocolates," she said cryptically, and it took me a second to remember the rest of it.

"You never know what you're gonna get," we said in unison.

"Ain't that the truth," I said, at which she almost choked on her sandwich.

When we were at the Garland game Dwight, George, Ryan and I were taking our usual walk down to the popcorn wagon when Dwight stopped and lit up like he had remembered something important.

"Joan! I almost forgot. You're invited to come to our Family Reunion."

"What family reunion?" I asked.

Dwight looked like I asked him what color snow was. "OUR family reunion, the Kershaw family reunion, only the best party you'll ever go to in your whole life. Right, Ryan?"

"The BEST party ever," he replied, nodding enthusiastically.

"So, tell me more." I had been wondering exactly what we were going to do with this being the second Christmas without Mama. Last year I didn't even want to talk about.

"You know we have a big family?" said Dwight.

"A *Big* family," said George.

"Huge," said Ryan.

"Okay, okay, I get it," I responded with a laugh. "So, you have a big family, and....?"

"On the Saturday after Thanksgiving, we all get together over at Grandpa's house. We call it a family reunion except it's also an early Christmas party where we also invite our special friends. The Aunts and Uncles make family recipes, some of the Uncles break out a barrel or two of homemade wine, and anybody who plays an instrument brings it along. Everybody brings something – gumbo, an accordion, some dessert. It's great."

Even though I had known from the first day that Dwight was a good guy, it was great to see him super cheerful about something, but I had to get something cleared up first.

"You know, Dwight, you're a good friend and everything, and I truly would like to come to the party, but it's not a date."

"No, Joan, it's not a date," he said, still smiling, "but you're new around here and you're also a fun and interesting person. You're also one of the few people I know who'd actually enjoy our party, and it would give you a chance to meet Grandpa like you said."

"I'd be real pleased to come, Dwight, but let me ask Papa first."

George shook his head in mock disbelief. "Boy, you *are* new around here. When you get an invitation to a family party, it means to bring your whole family!"

When Papa came home that evening I had made a good dinner with fresh bread and everything, which was our signal that there was something I wanted to talk about. He understood right away and did have a good appetite, and I even opened a bottle of wine so he knew it was something big. Like we used to do in France, he let me have some wine mixed with milk, which was another part of the ritual since it calmed me down enough not to trip all over myself when I asked him.

When we finished eating I stacked the dishes in the sink and came back to the table. He had poured my glass of wine and milk and handed it to me with a flourish.

"Mademoiselle D'arcy?" he said.

"Merci, Monsieur le Docteur," I replied.

We both nodded and took a sip. It tasted sharp like always but I also knew that Papa was in a more relaxed mood after the dinner so I was in a good place to ask him.

"Papa, Dwight and George Kershaw have asked us to come to their family party, and I would like for us to go."

"Joan..." he started to say, but I drove right ahead.

"Don't come up with some other plans that we've made because I know we don't have any. Papa, I like it here and am glad we came. What's more, Dwight and George are Cajun so it's going to be a French party. It's not perfect but I've met some..."

"Whoa, Joan, slow down," Papa interrupted. "I was not going to say we are not going, I was going to ask you when it is. We are also invited to at least one party at Smithfield College, you know."

"What party?" I asked, already sure of the answer.

"Well, the Archaeology Department get together," he replied, with a deadpan expression. "You know, get a few old grave relics and play Jeopardy in Latin."

"Or Greek," I said. "Makes it much more entertaining."

"I can see the topic selection now," he said. "Sarcophagi for 500."

"Maybe a better topic for a Halloween Party," I replied, so I knew we were going. "The party is next Saturday at six o'clock, out at Dwight and George's grandpa's house."

"Put it on the calendar," he said. "Is there anything else we are supposed to do? I mean, besides bringing some food of our own and wearing our dancing shoes and take along a fiddle or guitar?"

He could have knocked me over with a stick until I saw him looking at me with a half serious, half comic expression.

"Joan, you may remember that I have lived in French communities before, and next time you forget that, look in a mirror and you will see one of the results." He then gave me a hug right out of the blue, and for a minute I nestled against his coat and buried my nose into his collar that always smelled of musty papers and a hint of his aftershave. This had been a good day, and he was starting to loosen up too. That was a good joke coming from him, and it calmed me down because maybe he and I were on the same page and that it was time to start moving ahead. For both of us.

I'm not half French and half American for nothing, and between Grandmother and Mama I had learned how to make a lot of basic French food and some specialties, too. Since Dwight said that everybody brought food, it probably didn't matter what I made as long as it tasted good and didn't kill anybody. I finally decided to make a traditional pastry called croquembouche, exactly the way we made them back in Domremy. Papa liked that idea, so the two of us banged some pots together for a few hours until we had about five dozen. Papa was an okay cook for things like chicken and soups, but this was something I was good at, and it tickled me when he got a nice dreamy expression after I popped the first one into his mouth. We both stopped for a second and knew that we had the same thought at the same time. Papa reached down and lifted one up like he was making a toast, so I picked up one too. Since neither of us could say anything, we popped them into our mouths as the memories flooded back of absent voices, past Christmases, and the little church at Domremy covered in snow.

"Bien?" I asked, after a minute.

"Tres fantastique," he answered.

The house where Dwight's Grandpa lived was four miles away from ours, back a long gravel road that turned to dirt at the end. As we got closer we knew we had a hike ahead of us, since before the dirt started there were already cars parked on both sides of the road. I carried the basket of croquembouche and Papa was carrying two bottles of wine along with a small black case I had not seen for a long time. It was still light outside and crisp like it is at the end of November, and both of us were wearing the closest to party formal that we had which was easier for Papa because he only had to put on a Professor suit.

"What's in the case?" I asked as we walked up the driveway where we could already hear the music and see the lights.

"Surprise," he replied.

96

Dwight had been looking out for us and came running down the driveway all excited. I was going to introduce him but he beat me to it. Grabbing Papa's free hand, he shook it and said, "Mr. D'arcy, I'm Dwight Kershaw and we are so happy you came to our reunion." He waved up toward where we could see a long porch strung with Christmas lights and loaded with people, all talking at the same time and carrying plates or drinks or both. Under some tiki torches in the front yard they had set up a big dance floor and about twenty people were busy at one end playing an assortment of fiddles and accordions of every size and shape imaginable. There were guitars, a big washtub with a rope coming out of it, a washboard, at least one flashy mandolin, some harmonicas, and a few instruments I had never seen before. Ryan was right in the middle of them, playing his mandolin, and the dance floor was packed.

You could feel the good time at this party, where people who care about each other get together, relax, recharge their batteries, and catch up on family gossip. In such a big family, there was bound to be lots of gossip and the guests were probably talking about anything you could imagine - and some things you couldn't.

We were standing there with Dwight and George introducing people by the dozen, and shaking hands with everybody one after the other and not remembering anybody's name. In the meantime, people were bringing us plates with food and Papa was handed a glass of homemade wine. He raised it to the giver who raised his own.

"Sante," he said.

"A Votre Sante," replied Papa.

The man put his arm around Papa's shoulder and they are walking away, speaking French a mile a minute. I didn't see Papa again until he came up for air about twenty minutes later by which time I had wandered over to watch the musicians. I had never been to a party where they had live music, and for this one, they even had microphones for the people up front. Most of the singing was in Cajun French, which my ear was getting used to by now so I understood most of it.

The first song ended so I clapped, meaning it, and then I got a tap on my shoulder. There was George, and at the same moment the music started, a bit faster this time.

"May I have this dance?" he asked, trying to be formal and light-hearted at the same time.

I made a little curtsy. "Enchante, mon Ami."

He took my right hand in his left hand, put his right hand gently on my waist while I gingerly took his shoulder, and away we went. He wasn't a great dancer but he also wasn't stepping on my toes, so I switched into a variation of my fencing stance. We were bouncing and twirling and bumping gently into other people, and in half a minute here comes Dwight and we switch over and he's about the same as George only faster, and I'm starting to get a bit dizzy but having the time of my life. I'm laughing and he's laughing and we start to sing along with the chorus. I turned around and there's Papa dancing with Dwight and George's Mama and they are laughing too and it's the first time in a long time I have seen Papa laugh like that, not the short "yes, I'm okay" laugh but one that comes right out of the heart. I also see that he's holding a glass and it's mostly empty, so I start to think about how we are going to get home.

I guess it showed on my face as Dwight spoke right up. "Joan, we have a whole fleet of taxis on duty for the night for those that aren't camping out in the house," he said, and I knew he's serious. "You let your Papa have a good time tonight without any fuss from you. We will take good care of him, I promise." He let go of my hand and looked me right in the eye. "Listen, Joan, we didn't ask you here because you're our friend, but because you need this, and what's more your Papa needs it too, maybe even more than you do."

Mama once told me that the difference between an acquaintance and a friend is that your friend isn't afraid to tell you the truth even when it hurts. It didn't make it any easier to hear, but it also showed me that there was more of my own story that needed to come out. Maybe Dwight was a good place to start.

"I miss her," I whispered. "We both do but I'm the one who has to keep it all together."

"Did you ever think that maybe he is doing the same thing for you?" replied Dwight as quietly. "But in the meantime – you're having a good time, aren't you?" I nodded. "Well then, the party is just getting started."

"This is just getting started?" I exclaimed, looking around at what seemed like hundreds of people, all talking, or drinking, or eating, or dancing, or all at the same time. Thinking back on this later, I had to laugh because yes, the party was just getting started, especially compared to what was coming. There was a sudden roar of welcome at the back of the crowd and I could see a man working his way forward slowed down by everybody along the way yelling a greeting or slapping his back. George had come up to join us by that time, and we had worked our way to the musician's side of the dance floor right next to Ryan. The new arrival finally emerged from the crowd, and I could see that it was a small man, not much bigger than me, dressed in a shiny suit and carrying a violin case. The band parted to make a space where he could play and he got out his violin and quickly tuned it before swinging it gracefully to...his left arm. I had never seen anyone hold a violin like that before, but what followed gave me an entirely new point of view on...well, a lot of things, including on how happy a group of people could get.

He nodded at the other musicians standing ready, put up his bow, and with a sharp down stroke launched into what was apparently the Cajun National Song. From the first note, everybody who could walk and some who couldn't were either singing at the tops of their voices or dancing enough to cause a ripple in the Smithfield College seismograph. I started to dance, the music the most completely infectious I had ever heard, and when it was all over I was flushed and happy, cheering and clapping along with everybody else.

I looked at Dwight breathlessly. "Is it started now?"

He grinned back at me, the old softie. "Oui."

98

All the dancing had made me hungry without realizing it, and as George came up I asked innocently where the food was. He acted shocked. "You mean you have been here all this time..." and looked reproachfully at his brother. "Follow me," he said, and we made our way through the crowd and up onto the huge porch that surrounded the house.

There were folding tables and card tables and planks on top of sawhorses and on top of it all the biggest spread of food I had ever seen. I have been to other parties since that one, but that feast still comes back to me in my dreams. There was roast beef, ducks, four enormous pots of gumbo, crawfish etouffee, oysters fried and on the half shell, venison, and at least six different kinds of fish. On the next table were cakes, pies, cream puffs, beignets still hot, Jell-O with mandarin oranges, four different kinds of chocolate tarts, and a whole extra bowl of fresh whipped cream. There was only one of my croquembouche left, which disappeared onto George's plate and as quickly into his mouth.

"I made that," I said.

"That is the best thing I ever ate in my whole life," he replied solemnly.

"Merci beaucoup, mon ami," I replied with a smile.

"Rien," he replied, bowing back, then he hit himself on the forehead like he'd forgotten something. "Joan, I promised I would bring you in and introduce you to Grandpa. Is now okay?" If you remember, Dwight had told me about his Grandpa being in Europe during World War II, and being half French meant that I owed those men a special debt of gratitude and a personal thank you.

"Lead the way!"

The house was very old, a traditional one story with a low slanted roof, a peak in the middle and a long line of bedrooms along the back. Inside the front door was a big combination kitchen and the living room full of comfortable furniture, the guests standing or sitting in small groups and talking quietly. It was half dark and cozy inside, and since George introduced me to everyone it took a while to make our way across the room where several people were waiting in line. Up ahead there was a very dignified looking older man patiently listening to a little boy, huddled with their heads close together, and after a minute the old man hugged the little boy, the boy bestowed a kiss, and went happily on his way. The old man chuckled as he watched the boy leave, and George found the right moment to speak up.

"Hey Grandpa," he said gently. "Joyeux Noel!"

"Joyeux Noel right back at you," said the old man, and there was a quick hug and kiss exchanged. "Did you bring someone with you?" and for the first time he looked up at me.

"Grandpa, this is my friend I told you about. She..." George froze. The old man was staring at me, his mouth open, seemingly unable to talk. George's breathing quickened and he was turning to go for help when Grandpa spoke up.

"I am sorry, young lady. Old people have...spells sometimes, you know. You are a friend of George, yes?" I nodded. "Well, well, that's fine. Joyeux Noel to you both."

"Mr. Kershaw?" I said, and as he turned his attention back to me something flashed over his face again before he recovered.

"I...my mother is...was French, and I want to thank you for what you did all those years ago. For helping to liberate my country." I had talked with George about this, and he said it was both okay and a nice thing to do, and that it didn't happen very often, either.

Mr. Kershaw nodded and I could see that he was getting dewy-eyed so I shook his hand one more time before George and I left.

When we got back outside it had started to get dark, but the night was still pleasant without any real cold starting to set in. I was getting mellow from the evening, helped along by the incredible food and...well, everything. George and Dwight had been especially nice, along with absolutely everybody else. I had met their Grandpa like I had wanted to, and Papa even came along with me.

Where was Papa? Oops, did I go away and neglect him, oh shoot, and as I turned to go looking for him, there he was in front of me, sitting over next to the band, listening to the music and swaying back and forth. He was still holding that little case on his lap and hugging it to himself when the song ended. There was a "Ta-da!" from the band, the talking stopped, and people started to move into a circle around the dance floor. The crowd parted and Father Martin walked out onto the floor. Dwight's dad went up to the microphone and tapped it twice, the thwang! getting our attention before the priest stepped forward.

Everybody with a hat swept it off and held it in both hands. It was completely quiet except for some soft sounds from the forest, and it made me appreciate how much nature was a part of this place.

"It's been a year since we have been together," said Father Martin in the most gentle, calming voice, "and our thoughts go back to all of the other Reunions we have known. So many memories for us, all the way back to when we were children, and our other memories of growing up, marrying, and having our own children with us. It's been a good year for all of us in some ways, a harder year for some of us. There are faces missing from our midst, those who have gone ahead of us. There are also new faces among us, new members of our family, and new friends who we welcome."

At this Father Martin smiled directly at me, and at the same time, George whispered in my ear. "Uh, Joan, I forgot to tell you something..." but I found out. Right there in front of everybody.

Father Martin continued. "It is another part of our tradition that our new friends share a bit of themselves. A poem perhaps, a short speech, something of who you are for us to remember." Father Martin continued looking right at me, and I was starting to panic but Papa stood up and took a step forward to the microphone.

"Good evening and Merry Christmas, everyone. I am Paul Darcy and my daughter Jeannette and I joined your community in August. We are very happy to be here." There was applause throughout the group, and Papa smiled until it grew quiet again.

I was used to hearing him speak so confidently in front of groups, whether reporting on his digs or simply teaching class. Even after Mama died some of his old confidence still held him in good stead. Tonight, his voice was different, softer and more vulnerable.

"My daughter and I are so very touched by your welcome. Like you, we have those we remember tonight." Two of us, not three, and my eyes were stinging. Papa turned and lifted something from his chair, and to my astonishment, I saw it was his oboe, silent for so long.

"I have been fortunate enough to have recently found this instrument that has been…well, quiet for too many years. I think it is time to bring it out again, with your permission." The applause returned as Papa wet the reed and played a note or two as a warm up.

This year there had been the bullying and Mr. Todd and the new school and being tired so much of the time and missing Mama, but there was also Michelle and Miss Renoir and George and Dwight, making peace with Christine and fencing tournaments and even playing in the Pep band. Lots of things had been trying to beat me down but more things had been there for me when I needed them. Yes, there was lots to be thankful for. Papa, dear old Papa, who had been so devastated by Mama's death that he had walked around in a fog for eighteen months, was with me at this wonderful party, and we had something of our own to offer.

The first notes of the oboe sounded and it was a visitor from the past, a beloved past coming to life again. He was playing the old carol gently and in the right tempo, the notes sounding clear and oh so sweet in the twilight. The circle of faces softened too, knowing and remembering at the same time, the words from childhood transported over the years, in my own memory the sound of Mama singing softly, her face lit by the lights on the tree:

> *Il est ne, Il est ne, le divin Enfant,*
> *Jouez, hautbois, resonnez, musettes;*
> *Il est ne, Il est ne, le divin Enfant;*
> *Chantons tous son avenement!*

It was a magical moment, old couples rocking gently with arms entwined, young mothers singing the words as a lullaby to infants half asleep. I had heard the song many times before on other Christmases, but never among so many who knew and loved it. From within the crowd, a woman's voice rose, caressing the words with such affection, people nearby turning, the crowd parting as she came closer. The second verse now, the words not quite as familiar but still humming, the last two people finally stepping aside.

Miss Renoir stood singing on the very edge of the crowd. I could hardly breathe as I saw her, wearing a simple red dress with a shawl over her shoulders, the very image of Mama, coming to stand next to me. She put her hands on my shoulders and I reached up to touch one hand, gaining confidence from the words and the wonderful voice. Papa saw us and almost stopped but miraculously kept playing, the crowd joining in each Chorus until the last line faded softly into the night.

On any other night, there would have been a surge of applause at the end of something so wonderful, but tonight was something different, when a treasured memory of an ancient homeland had embraced and blessed them all. Some came to shake his hand, or to make a quiet thank you, but most were so lost in their own thoughts that everyone let out a big collective sigh as Father Martin went back to the microphone.

"There are no words for what we have heard except...Thank you, my friend, for this gift you have shared. Welcome home." There was brief applause, but from the mischievous grin on Father Martin's face, there was something special about to happen. I don't know how you could beat what happened but...well, let's wait and see.

Behind me, Miss Renoir squeezed my shoulder and I squeezed back on her hand, and there was Papa. He looked...well, rested. Not worn out, not too much wine, just...like he too had been transported by what happened and the better for it.

"Joyeux Noel," he said, looking at her.

"Joyeux Noel," she replied, looking at him.

"Our musicians have been so generous tonight," said Father Martin at the microphone, "and we must make sure they have their share of our feast. For the next half hour, we will have some recorded music, and by special request, Ladies Choice." That brought applause from one-half of the crowd and at least a few stifled groans from the other half, but only from those who pretended they had too much to eat. I found myself off to one side of the floor but Papa and Miss Renoir were talking and oblivious to what was starting. There was a buzz from the speakers, and the music started.

You could have knocked me over with a twig. It was Celine Dion singing her song from Titanic but it's in French, and I'm overwhelmed by the old story that I'd heard a hundred times. When Papa and Mama were on their first date, they went to the Cinema in Neufchatel where Titanic had been playing every day for four years straight. Papa got so emotional during the film that Mama decided that a man who had such a kind heart was the one she was going to marry.

Miss Renoir was only two feet away and looking right into his face, and she's got the same hair as Mama and she's been singing so beautifully and I'm always going on and on about how terrific she is. The only thing missing is the mistletoe and that's not a French custom anyway, but Papa is also a gentleman and here is a beautiful and kind lady, they're both on a dance floor, and the memories are not only flooding back, we are completely submerged.

No words, only his left hand into hers and his right hand on her waist. A few other couples have taken the floor but here are Papa and Miss Renoir, the two most important people in the world to me, and I look in Papa's face and there's something in it I haven't seen in it for such a long time that it brings the tears back to my eyes. And I cannot help myself. I move up to them on the dance floor, Papa looks down at me, and Miss Renoir too, and without a word they fold me into their embrace.

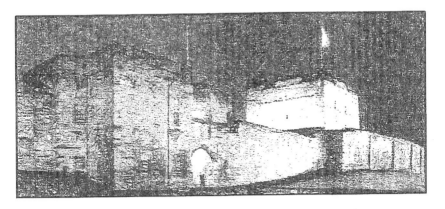

Rouen, France
The English Fortress
May 29 1431

There was only the fitful sleep every night given the moans echoing from the other cells, but most nights she was still able to gather back her strength for the next day's questioning. The rats often ran across her legs in their constant search for food, but she was lucky they never bit her or bothered her very much. They were God's creatures, after all, and France was their home, too. She did not hate the English, she truly hated no one, but the English claimed that France was theirs and they didn't care how many French or English had to die to make that happen.

The questioning had started two weeks ago, day after day and hour after hour, the same questions, she giving the same answers and never the ones that they truly wanted, for at bottom they wanted her to die. Unless she had broken canon law, there was no case against her except that she had come out of nowhere to lead an army and had three separate times defeated the English in the field of battle. When it came to her capture it was through trickery and bribery and by preying on the fears of her poor starving countrymen so that they finally delivered her up to this castle, but they had not yet succeeded in proving anything except that she was a good daughter of the church. They kept trying day after day, constantly urging her to change back into her battle dress. No matter how many times she refused, they kept at it, shouting in her face, denying her food, and wearing her down bit by bit until at last, they hoped, she would break. That was all they needed to condemn her, for they said that if she took back her military clothing she had relapsed and was truly a witch.

Last night they had been the worst yet, not shouting or pushing her down or trying to wear her out directly but stealthily, playing on her sense of duty. That was the hardest, for while she was inside the prison she was nothing more than a symbol, not of success on the field but of capture and eventual defeat. She had kept her vow and withstood all of it until they had finally gone, the bundle of her clothing left on the floor, not even as a pillow in this place with nothing else on which to rest her head.

Jeanne had her secrets too. She was not alone here, and they did not truly realize what that meant although they had thrown her own words back into her face as if some filthy thing instead of the source of her peace and comfort. For God and the Virgin were with her even here through her prayers and the memories of her visions, and France was all around her. If they released her tomorrow she would not even fight the English any longer if they would only go home and leave France in peace, but until they left she would not stop, not for one minute, even if they killed her.

Part Two
Chapter Twenty-Three
Victory

Fourth quarter and 56-52 with 49 seconds left, and Todd had to leave the gym to keep from losing it in front of the basketball crowd. In front of students it didn't matter, but parents...well, the last thing he needed was to rock the boat. They were playing Dale City tonight, and last year we beat them out of sight 49-6 so what is happening out there? His hands were shaking again and he still had one bottle of mineral supplement left in his pocket but so far, he had resisted ripping off the cap and drinking it. It didn't help that these games were so close, and in a league where there were only 24 games the whole season, one or two could make the difference between the State Final or...the alternative he didn't want to think about.

Out on the court Coach Anita had called a timeout and the players clustered around her. They had a decent size team with a full complement of eleven first-string players, but that didn't necessarily mean they were all good. She was usually able to rotate in every player for at least four or five minutes, but tonight was different. Dale City's girls must have been eating some fertilizer because every one of them was at least five feet ten inches tall, and her girls had to look up most of the time. Christine had been playing every minute of the game since the tip off, but Lisa had her usual temper problems and was now sitting with four fouls.

"We've got to keep possession as long as we can, or push them so hard they can't control their passing," said Coach Anita. "What do you think, Captain?"

Christine nodded. "Sounds good. Number 45 is so right handed that it's not even funny, but she also can't see anybody coming up on her left side. Number 37 is the opposite, except she can't see anyone behind her on the right. As far as Number 88 is concerned, she spooks if you move suddenly like you're going to grab the ball right out of her hands."

If Christine is seeing all that while still playing her heart out, then there's real hope for a scholarship after all. Colleges want smart players, not only tall ones who can't tell a basketball from a big grapefruit. Too bad Lisa can't keep her mouth shut, or at least her ears, because that's exactly what Dale City is doing: watching, listening, and then acting on it, baiting her over and over until she reacts.

"Okay – Bobbi, you do exactly what Christine says. Stay on 45 like glue but stick to her right side until she has the ball, then whip around her LEFT side low and grab the ball away from her. Stephanie, you do the same thing to 37 except on the opposite side. Christine..."

"I'll take care of 88," Christine said. "Got a good BOO in me tonight."

The girls laughed and Christine put her hands inside the circle, immediately joined by all the others. "TEAM!" As they ran back onto the court the Smithfield Pep Band began to play the Sponge Bob song and were immediately joined by the cheerleaders, the entire home team crowd, the team on the court, and hilariously a big bunch of middle school kids on the opposing team's side of the gym.

Joan and Michelle were happily playing along and relishing the humor of the moment, the Gym ringing with those words that had absolutely nothing to do with the game on the court but represented their team so perfectly. When the words "SQUARE PANTS!" finally echoed off the walls, Ryan beat his bass drum three times, five hundred people rose as one, and shouted "AYE AYE, CAPTAIN!" Down on the court, Christine turned to face the crowd and took a bow, which set off another demonstration that had to be shut down by a warning from the referee who was hard put not to let his smile show.

Sure enough, Christine was right. Dale City had possession and the very first player to get the ball was number 45, who planted herself and was looking to her right at Smithfield's Terri when slick as a whistle Bobbi's hand snaked in and deflected the ball so neatly that 45's hand went down to dribble and found that the ball wasn't there anymore. One quick recovery, a pass to Christine, and a perfect layup later the Pep Band starts back up and they're going into the Sponge Bob song again except Mrs. Coates shuts them down as Dale City's 46 passes to 37. Coach Anita wonders if there's some script that they're reading as Christine reaches out her arms and makes a big circle to 37's left, Stephanie runs past like she's on the track team, reaches out her hand and plucks it like a rose from 37's hand. Another pass to Christine who by this time is covered but she makes a quick pass to Terri who's right under the basket and never misses at this range, especially when there's nobody covering her.

Now it's 60-52, there are fourteen seconds left, and Dale City gives it right back to 46, who passes it to 88 who holds onto it like glue. Christine stands perfectly still for a second, which so surprises 88 that she also stands still for a second, then Christine jumps and yells "BOO" so loud that 88 hands her the ball. By this time there are four seconds left so Christine dribbles it down the court, three big, long bounces, then at mid-court launches herself off the ground right at the buzzer…and it swishes through the net without even touching the rim. The final score is 62-52, the pep band plays the whole Sponge Bob song, there's a big circle around Christine down on the court, and Coach Anita is beaming like a lighthouse, waiting for one of those scouts she saw up in the stands to come over and talk to her about Christine.

Joan

Dwight finished putting his trombone into its case about two seconds before George, and we all headed out to the parking lot where Brian's Mom is waiting with their big van that has all the special equipment and stuff for Brian's chair. It's nice that basketball games start at 6:00, so it's only 7:30 and lots of time left for the party at Ryan's house. The van is big and comfy and we are all feeling good after an exciting game, especially since we won. Five minutes later we're at Ryan's house, the van does its magic and deposits Brian neatly on the driveway, and we are all inside where it's toasty and warm. Another van has brought the girls' basketball team, all except Christine who sad to say is at home

106

tonight taking care of the twins. I still help now and then, but Christine said she wanted to take it easy tonight because she's worn out. We're all friends now and as Brian says, it's cool.

Ryan's Dad, who is also a Mr. Kershaw because he's Dwight and George's cousin, is real nice and knows everybody, so when he asks if anybody brought anything it's only Ryan who speaks up.

"I brought all these people." We all laugh, and his dad speaks up again and asks if anybody brought anything they shouldn't.

I now get it, that it's a traditional joke for Ryan, so I say I brought Michelle, Michelle says she brought Dwight, and it goes around the circle until everybody is covered.

"Well, okay then," says Ryan's father real seriously and everybody laughs, Ryan most of all.

It's a nice house, a bit smaller than some but nice and cozy, and I realize these are the first real friends I have ever had. I went to school in Williamsburg for five years, seven if you count preschool, but this is the first time I have ever been invited to a party at someone's house beyond Elementary School birthday parties where they make you invite everybody. Ryan's parents are Cajun like everybody else here except Michelle and me, but for the past few months we have become something like Honorary Cajuns because, well, I speak French and Michelle has learned how to cook a good Gumbo.

Every time when I am with a group of people, I slip back into my habit of watching how they do things and it's amazing how revealing it is. For example, even though Dwight and George are identical twins, Dwight sometimes reaches up with his left hand and pulls on his earlobe, but only when he's talking to a girl and especially when he's talking with Stephanie, who by the whole way she is standing obviously has a crush on him. Michelle is talking with Brian, her hand on her hip, so it looks like as usual, they are arguing about something.

Over in the kitchen, Ryan has opened the oven and the rich aroma of pulled pork fills the room. There's a pile of sliced rolls and a big bowl of fresh coleslaw on the table, a washtub on the porch full of melted ice and soft drinks, and an enormous freshly sliced watermelon on the table with wedges you can eat with your fingers. The talking slows down as people fill up their plates, some of the girls pretending to be fastidious and some of the boys changing into Gentleman mode as they find places for the girls to sit.

Someone says "Joan?" so I turn and there is Ryan, holding out a plate full of watermelon slices, piled high to the point it's hard to hold.

"I hope we're going to share this," I say, and he stares at me for a second before looking around to find a spot where there's enough room for two. It's one of the most comfortable chairs in the room, for which I thank him very much and we're on hold for a minute while I get situated, then we both start in on the watermelon. A moment later we hear a scratching at the door and a whine,

Ryan gets up and here comes Shadow over to the chair. He's wagging his tail and sniffing my hand, then Ryan comes back and Shadow lays his head on Ryan's knee while Ryan strokes and smooths the hair around his ears. It's truly touching to see someone so completely gentle with a dog, and it's equally obvious that the dog is totally dedicated to Ryan. If you want to see real adoration, watch a dog looking at his master, and I was starting to get misty eyed until I saw exactly where Shadow was looking.

Ryan had balanced the plate of watermelon on the edge of the chair, and one piece was starting to slide off. I rescued it in time and sure enough, Shadow was focused on that piece of watermelon like it was a sheep about to wander away from the flock.

"Go ahead," said Ryan. "He loves it."

I had heard about dogs loving hot dogs, peanut butter, even eggs – but watermelon?

"Are you sure?" I asked.

Ryan nodded. "He loves it, like I said. Go ahead."

I have got to see this for myself, so I hold out the watermelon. Shadow sniffed once then reached out and very, very gently bit off about an inch of the pointy end, chewed and swallowed it, then took another, larger bite and did the same. The piece was now small enough that he took the rest of it into his mouth like a giant black and white chipmunk, sat down and deposited it on his feet where over the next minute he reduced it to a thin piece of green skin. He looked up, licked his lips a few times, and I swear if he could talk he would say, 'That was very nice, thank you. One more, please.'

"Shadow saved my life," Ryan says quietly, while Shadow looked up at him with those beautiful brown eyes. "Yes, buddy, you sure did good boy."

"He's a great dog," I said quietly. "Can you tell me how?"

"How what?" replied Ryan, sounding confused.

"How he saved your life," I replied, "if you're okay to talk about it." By this time, Dwight and George had wandered over and were sitting on the floor in front of us.

"Go ahead, Ryan," said Dwight. "Joan's a friend and she doesn't know."

I remembered that sometimes if I don't look directly at people they relax better, so instead of looking at Ryan I just rubbed the back of Shadow's head. "I'd like to hear the story."

"I drowned," he said.

I wasn't sure I heard that correctly. "You drowned?"

He nodded. "I sure did. Six years ago today. But I didn't die."

Ryan

"When they pulled me out of that pond I was like some human Popsicle but I don't remember any of that. Different doctors have asked me if I have nightmares or something where it all comes back, but I say no and it's the truth.

The accident happened when I was in fourth grade. A winter storm had come to town and it was a real mess with about three inches of snow and lots of things getting frozen. On the way to school that morning, the bus started sliding all over the road so they turned around and took everybody back home. Since Daddy and Mama were still at work I thought I'd try and build a snowman or something, but I hadn't ever done it before and what I put together looked more like a big pile of snow instead of a man. We'd just gotten Shadow and he was following me everywhere.

We went for a walk down the road to the frog pond, and Shadow was snuffling through the snow next to the bench on the other side like he was looking for something. I started across the pond, and I remember seeing Shadow with his face covered with snow - it looked so funny, with him looking at me smiling like "look what I found, and then suddenly it was really, really cold."

By now a crowd had gathered and Ryan was talking in that calm, soft way of his, Shadow stretched out at his feet being petted and rubbed by about eight people at once.

"Mrs. Martin heard Shadow barking, and when she looked out and saw the hole in the middle of the pond she called the rescue squad. It's real lucky she mentioned the ice because the rescue squad had a special outfit. They dove right into that hole, but it took another minute to find me. Dwight's dad was on the truck that day, and he said that when they got me on shore I wasn't breathing and had already started to turn blue.

They got the respirator hooked up and slid me into the ambulance and were at the hospital in ten minutes, with Mrs. Martin riding right there in the back along with Shadow. The ambulance people weren't very happy about that but she put her foot down and said that any dog who helped rescue Ryan had as much a right to be there as anybody." There was some laughter at that, and about six more people started petting Shadow who by this time had already finished off three barbecue sandwiches."

"When I finally woke up it was February 9th," Ryan continued, "and I guess all that cold got together with my being underwater and part of my brain shut itself off. Reading is hard now, and I don't always know other words lots of times. I don't remember other things, either, but Mama says that for me, the time before the accident is now once upon a time."

When the story was finished, the room was real quiet, a lot of the kids were dabbing at their eyes, and Shadow was fast asleep.

"Well you don't have to worry about us, Cousin," said George. "As far as we are concerned you're the best guy in the world, and we're all real thankful that Shadow rescued you."

Joan couldn't help but feel a deep sense of humility. *I think I have problems, and here is Ryan with this terrible thing that happened to him. He can't do half of what he could do before the accident but he is still so nice and kind to everybody. What's best of all is that we moved here and these are my friends, and twenty and thirty or more years from now...*

There is something about loss that goes to sleep for a while, and then it comes back and clobbers you when you're least expecting it. You have someone in your life and then they leave on a trip and never come back, not even a piece of them, and it was in that moment that part of Joan's world, that carefully constructed world that she was making for herself, fell apart in the realization that it wasn't only the anniversary of Ryan's loss, but her own as well. She felt her face go numb, the sudden realization and guilt overwhelming her so much that she had to get up and go into the next room where she could be alone.

About ten minutes after she called Papa to pick her up, Joan forced herself to be nice to everyone and say thank you to Mr. and Mrs. Kershaw, and *no thanks, Papa's car is here in the driveway and I'm okay, thank you, only I've had a very long day and see you next week.*

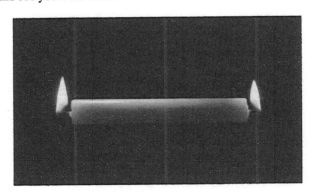

Chapter Twenty-Four
The Candle Burns at Both Ends

Christine couldn't quite get used to the fact that she could sleep until 8:00 on Saturday morning. She was sorry to miss the party but by the time she got home from the game the twins were already asleep and Mama insisted she go to bed and get at least one good night's sleep. Now that Mama was back home and the family had some extra money coming in, she also insisted that Christine cut back her hours and take care of herself for a change. Even though Daddy had by some miracle managed to get a job at the high school and three hundred extra dollars a week was coming in - a real Gift from God if there ever was one - the family had absolutely nothing left in savings and the twins hadn't gotten any new clothes for more than a year.

There wasn't any sense in staying in bed if she was wide awake, but that didn't mean she couldn't get up and make some coffee and a real breakfast. In fifteen minutes the kitchen was full of the heady aroma of brewing coffee, bacon, and eggs, and it was no surprise that the twins showed up a few minutes later. It was fun for Christine to arrange the two eggs and bacon into a big edible smiley face on the plate, something that Mama used to do for her when she was that age. It always took longer for the twins to finish eating, and when Christine took her own plate to the sink she noticed that the mail wasn't sitting in its usual place between the salt and pepper shakers in the middle of the kitchen table. Mama must have forgotten it, Christine thought, so she retrieved the mail out of the box and was back in the kitchen before she saw it.

Smithfield Hospital Accounts, it said, except that was what Mama's health insurance was supposed to be for? Isn't that the way it works, that we have insurance now and it's all covered except for $15 each time we go to the doctor? When she finally read it, she wished she hadn't, or even gotten out of bed for that matter. Yes, it was a bill, one with the word COPAY on it in big, black letters, their share for Mama's thirteen days in the hospital, and amounting to fifteen percent of fourteen thousand dollars. Two thousand one hundred dollars, please, the number sitting there on the paper and feeling like a lead sinker on their economic fishing line.

It could have been more, it could have been a lot worse, but the simple fact was they didn't have the money. Mama's pay was coming in again, but all of that was going to pay the bills that had piled up those weeks she was in the hospital. The money from Papa barely covered the rent, and the only money they had for food and absolute necessities was coming from Christine's work at the Piggly Wiggly. They were happy to have her work all the hours she wanted, but when that was added to the time it took for practice and attending school it came out to sixteen hours a day Monday thru Thursday, with another 20 hours on weekends.

When someone works that hard for so long, there's something they'll never dare tell you because they usually can't tell themselves. That's that point where they thought they had all the energy in the world and one morning it isn't there. The wake-up trumpet is missing, the energy machine is out of fuel, and the give a darn speech is all torn up and in the wastebasket. When you add an extra ten minutes here, a half an hour there, two hours spent studying for a test and everything else you don't even track, it adds up to more than you can take and the bill's coming due right now. But you can't quit, either, so you drag yourself out of bed and go through the motions so that nobody knows how tired you truly are.

Nobody at school knew anything about this, although Coach Anita probably had an idea. The catch was, their season had been fantastic with a 16-1 record so far, the players were happy, the engine was firing on all cylinders and Christine was in the driver's seat. Coach Anita was also changing her mind about Christine's plan to play on a college team – why not major in athletics and learn to coach? She mentioned it once to Christine and got her answer: thank you, coach, but not now, we're doing great so let me get back to work. There were only six games to go until the playoff, anyway.

When Todd returned from his trip down the Coast, he had enough of the Mineral Supplement to last at least another year. His contact said the recipe was changed, that there'd been too much heat about the steroids so they put in something else instead. Tired from his five-hour trip, Todd had sampled some of the new batch and within three minutes he felt like he could drive all the way back to Smithfield and then go an extra thousand miles for good measure.

It had been a near thing with the Garland game. Even though there was now an extra year posted on the Volleyball Champions sign, one championship wasn't going to cut it. It didn't help that he was getting tired of the paperwork, tired of complaining parents, and especially tired when midterm test scores were down fifteen percent from last year. When the time came for the tests in April he had a plan to make sure the scores would end up where they ought to be, but hoping for one more State Championship was leaving a lot to chance.

Two days ago, his personal soda machine went on the blink so he had to go to the teacher's lounge to use theirs. He was getting out his bottle when the room door opened and he heard Coach Anita talking with Mrs. Coates. Since the machine was tucked back in a corner, nobody knew he was there.

"I think we need to give Christine an enforced break," said Anita. "She's under a lot of pressure, and with her running herself ragged things will end up badly for her. I'm sure of it."

"She is stubborn," said Mrs. Coates, "but you're the coach, Anita, so she needs to do what you tell her." There was the sound of the refrigerator door opening, a pause, then closing again.

"She's the acting Assistant Coach now," said Anita, "and I'm telling you that's what she actually ought to do. Players come and go, but she's a natural leader. Even better, she also knows how to teach her players and that's why we're so close to the championship. I told her it's her decision: she's eighteen now, so she's the one who has to live with the consequences."

As the door clicked closed Todd stepped out into the room and it was all he could do to keep from throwing the bottle against the wall. No. No way. Not her, not now. Christine is going to keep playing until the State Championship is all wrapped up and in my pocket. If she's doesn't, then - a light bulb went on in his head and he saw what he needed to do. Poor kid, she's tired, run ragged the way Anita said. Well, Uncle Todd has the cure for that.

The new training room had opened the week before, the band risers gone and a new tile floor installed. Along with the weight machine, step machine, and making recommendations based on his advice. He had also made sure one of those extra video cameras was prominently displayed up in the corner, its little red light cheerfully reminding everyone there that yes, Big Brother was indeed watching.

The girls' basketball Team had come in for its first evaluation and the girls were scattered all over the room. Since everybody was supposed to be tested, they each went through the same routine: do a stress test on the treadmill, complete twenty stretches using the elastic bands, and then step into the office

112

for individual recommendations. Like a good leader, Christine had all the other girls go first so that by the time she got to the office the others were hanging around waiting. The trainer checked off a few boxes on her form then walked to the little refrigerator and took out a plastic bottle full of a creamy looking pink liquid. Handing it to her, she noticed her name was written on the label.

"What's this for?" she asked, the bottle cold in her hand.

"Some vitamins and stuff," he said.

"What's in it?" she said while turning it over.

"Listen, kid, "said the trainer, "the paper says you're deficient in Vitamins B12, E, Calcium, and Phosphorus. If you don't want this bottle, go to the drug store and get your own. Pay $20 out there or get it here for free. Make up your mind."

Twenty dollars was another shift from 10 p.m. to 1 a.m., Christine thought. "Okay," she said as she tore off the foil top, tossing it into the wastebasket as she drained the bottle. At least it didn't taste bad, she thought, and the cold charged her up. As she bounded back into the main room where the others were waiting, she yelled: "Okay, ladies, let's get outta here!"

"Aye Aye, Captain," they said, then jogged out of the room with the door slamming behind them.

Five minutes later the room was empty, the lights out and the door swinging closed as the last of the trainers went home. In the office, the little red light on the video camera reflected off the circle of foil lying in the wastebasket, a tiny wrinkle of foil showing where the syringe had entered.

Ryan

I miss band now it's over, but Mrs. Coates gives me things to do. I'm all over the school during the day, and two days ago, Mr. Todd saw me pushing a cart with some boxes of paper for the copy machines.

"You like to help, don't you?" he asked, nudging the cart with his foot.

"Yes, sir," I answered. I was nervous because he yelled all the time and that scared me. It didn't sound like he was going to yell right now.

"Would you like to work for me?" he asked.

Mama and Papa had talked to me about getting a job, so maybe they had talked with Mr. Todd and he's telling me all about that, but they also taught me how to ask good questions, too.

"What would you want me to do, Mr. Todd?" I asked, trying to be real polite.

"Work around the school, for the teachers and for the office now and then. We need help, especially in the afternoons when students are gone and it's easier to move things around the hallways." He patted the cart I was pushing. "We could make this your cart, for you to use, and you'll get paid for your work. Sometimes you could even help sort out papers in my office. Would you like that?"

Chapter Twenty-Five
Changes and Observations
Michelle

I don't know what happened with Joan over Christmas break but I don't like it. It seems like her sense of humor vanished, she's broody most of the time, and she doesn't want to talk to anybody. We still eat lunch together most days and some mornings she's relatively normal, but by the end of the school day she turns into an ogre if anybody asks her what's wrong. Worse, she's impatient, rude, and acts like a total jerk.

I tried to talk to her while we were going to the tournament last weekend, and she gave me a look that was supposed to say everything is fine, thank you, I just don't feel like talking now, except it actually meant leave me alone. There was nothing I could do except put up with her attitude the whole rest of the day. She swept that tournament, beating everyone who went against her. She's always focused during matches, but now she's not a laser beam, she's a death ray and there's a ferocious quality to her fencing that wasn't there before. She doesn't beat her opponents anymore, she slaughters them, and the kids who used to look forward to going up against her now actively avoid doing so. I even saw Miss Renoir try to speak with her afterwards, but Joan just said she was tired, so she slept the whole way home without talking to anyone.

Something's going on with her, and the way she acted last weekend was just wrong, pure and simple. By lunchtime, I was ticked off and I guess it showed.

"What's up, Michelle?" she asked.

"None of your business," I responded, not nicely. She gave me a quick, vulnerable look, and then the hard face returned.

"Don't be so sensitive, dork," she said, but this time dork sounded like she meant it.

"And you're the queen of sensitivity," I replied, not kindly. "Especially lately."

She lost her smile completely. "What do you mean, lately?"

"You've been a real jerk lately, that's what's lately. A number one, dyed in the wool jerk."

She got real quiet and she gave me the same look she'd been giving her fencing opponents. "Oh really? How?"

"For one thing, you missed two Friday Pep bands and we sounded thin and awful. You were also a complete tyrant at the tournament on Saturday. For another, you're walking around not talking to anybody. People pass you in the hallway and say hi and you don't even look in their direction." For a person as sensitive as Joan, accusing her of being insensitive was high on the forbidden topics list, and I could tell right away this one hurt. I didn't mean it to, but the shot hit home and she did not like it.

"I've got things on my mind, okay? Lots of stuff. Lots of stuff that's none of your business." She was raising her voice, which in the cafeteria means three things: one, everybody will stop talking so they can hear what's being said; two, whatever she said will soon be all over the school: three, it's going to attract the attention of a teacher who isn't happy about cafeteria duty and is waiting for some student to start something. Already there was whispering and the whole cafeteria was breathlessly waiting for Round Two of the Joan vs. Michelle Argument to begin.

I guess it's good to have a bad temper sometimes because it can keep other things from hurting so bad. Joan was my best friend, but here she was, telling the whole cafeteria that the stuff on her mind is none of my business. The flip side of having a bad temper is that you have grown up with everybody telling you to learn to keep a lid on it, so by the time you're my age the lid is mostly under control. It would have felt so good to let Joan have it for fifteen seconds, but I guess...I already had, and already that lid keeping was making me feel guilty. Darn it - I'm her best friend or thought I was, so what is her problem?

"None of my business? I hate to tell you this, Joan, but...."

I never got further because out of nowhere someone put his hand on Joan's left shoulder and her reflexes kicked in as she simultaneously pulled away, whirled to the left, and swung out her left elbow in defense. The owner of the hand crashed back against a cafeteria table but managed to grab the edge and struggle back upright as there was a collective gasp in the cafeteria.

It's Ryan. Good, kind, gentle Ryan who Joan almost knocked down and Joan is standing there unable to speak.

Ryan had gotten back to his feet, breathing fast and rubbing his shoulder. "I'm sorry, Joan, I'm so sorry, I heard you two arguing..."

I went over and led him a few steps away, rubbing his back like people do to help him calm down. Joan was still standing there numbly when a girl she didn't even know came up and said, "You should be ashamed of yourself, you jerk. Ryan never hurt anybody and you know it."

I looked at Joan and the old Joan had come back in a rush except it's the old Joan deflated, the fire sputtering. I was about to say something else when I saw it, like that night on the way home from the first tournament, a single glistening streak from the eye to the chin.

It's almost a whisper. "I'm sorry, Ryan. I...did not mean to, I really didn't," Joan said, but I heard it and Ryan heard it, too.

"It's okay, Joan. I know you didn't do it on purpose or anything, I guess I scared you."

I heard my own voice as I kept rubbing his shoulder. "That's right, Ryan. Joan would never hurt you. It was an accident." I looked at Joan and my own anger had deflated, too, but it was as if a light had dimmed in her eyes.

Joan

I can't believe what I did, or where I did it, or who I did it to. When I replay the whole thing in my head I don't know what was going on with me. Ever since the Christmas Party, I have felt like complete crap most of the time but it makes me mad at myself, too. Miss Renoir's class is the one place where I feel normal these days, but I figure it's because we speak in French the whole time and that feels more comfortable. Michelle and Dwight and Ryan and George have all asked me what's going on, and I know they want to help but if I can't figure it out myself, I don't know how they can.

After the thing in the cafeteria I didn't want to go to classes the rest of the day, but I did anyhow and developed a mantra that went like "I didn't mean to do it I'm sorry I didn't mean to do it I'm sorry" and repeated it enough times that by the end of the day people didn't ask me anymore.

I'm in the hallway after my last class when I see Ryan pushing his cart. He sees me, and comes up and gives me a hug instead of turning around and running the other direction. He's not aware that I have been getting grief the whole afternoon, but he does have nice hugs, so I hug him back as a big bunch of students come around the corner. One smart aleck says "Awwwww" in a syrupy voice and a lot of them laugh, but it's not a bad laugh and nobody is glaring at me anymore.

"What's up with the cart, Ryan?" I ask, grateful beyond words that he's such a decent guy.

"This is my cart," he said. "It's for me to use."

It is a good, solid cart and I make a fuss over it which of course makes Ryan happy. "Are you working for the school?"

"I'm working for the school," he said. "I'm putting things away and making money. It's a real job. Right now, I'm taking the paper to the copy machines."

"Wow, that's great, buddy," I say and pat him on the back. "They're lucky to have you."

Although I am sure Ryan forgave me for the accidental elbow thing I sure made it up to him with that comment. Like he does sometimes, his smile turned into a teary grin, the wet cheeks and here's a handkerchief kind.

"Nobody ever said that to me before," he said, sniffling.

"Well, it's true and don't let anybody tell you differently," I said. "Listen, Ryan – I have to go now but I'll talk to you tomorrow. Maybe – we can eat lunch together if that's okay?"

"Sure," he said. "I…I need to go too. See ya," and he rolls away down the hall.

Thank God for small favors, I thought, so at least I will sleep better tonight, but I dipped down so low today I'll have to get used to it for a while.

Straight Talk and Babysitting

At five o'clock Christine was waiting for Joan to arrive when she heard a knock at the door. It was nice that she was early today since Christine didn't have to leave for her evening shift until five thirty. To Christine's surprise, Joan walked up and gave her a hug. She'd never done this before, but Christine had already heard about what happened in the cafeteria she had figured that was the reason.

Smithfield High School wasn't very big but news traveled slightly less than the speed of light. Everybody knows everybody else's business whether they need to or not. Christine also knew that Joan apologized to Ryan and that they

116

were okay with each other, not that Ryan ever got mad at anybody, but good news never travels as fast as the bad kind.

"I have some coffee made and the twins are watching TV before bed," said Christine. "Mama's also gone to bed early so you'll have a quiet evening."

"Sounds nice," Joan said with a big sigh. "I guess you've heard?"

Christine nodded. "Since about one o'clock this afternoon."

Joan shook her head in dismay. "Christine, you know I didn't..."

"Of course you didn't mean to hurt him," Christine interrupted. "There are a few jerks who think you might actually do something like that but they would think the same thing about each other. Those people are never happy unless they have something to complain about."

"How do you keep it together, Christine?" asked Joan plaintively. "I'm so tired most of the time and everybody's always in my business..."

"Which is what, by the way?" Christine looked her right in the eyes. "Don't feed me any line, now."

Joan burst out laughing. "You sound like Mrs. T."

"Great lady," said Christine. "Stop changing the subject."

Joan hadn't talked about this to anybody, and if anyone had predicted a month before that she'd be having a talk like this with Christine, she would have thought they were totally out of their mind. Funny how things happen.

"I can't get it out of my mind," said Joan. "The Christmas Party."

"I heard it was a great party," said Christine. "Hadn't been for my having to work that weekend I'd have been there myself. So – what about the party can't you get out of your mind?"

"Only the fact that I was there," said Joan.

Christine sat there, puzzled. She'd heard all about the party, about how Ryan had told the story like he always did, and everybody had a great time and stayed past midnight. All except Joan, who left at least three hours before anyone else. "So why did you leave early?"

Joan looked at the floor. "It was the anniversary."

"Of what?"

Joan looked back up, her eyes stinging. "You know my Mama died, right?"

Christine nodded. "A while ago?"

Joan nodded slowly. "A year ago. December..."

"Oh," said Christine and nodded slowly. "You were at the party..."

"On the anniversary," they said in unison.

"So, what's the problem?" said Christine. "You were having a good time, right?"

Joan stood up, incensed. "On the anniversary of my mother's death, I go to a Christmas party? You don't see anything wrong with that?"

Christine shook her head. "No, I don't. Did she hate parties or something?"

If Joan hadn't been through what she had earlier that day with Ryan, she would have stomped out of the house, or worse, taken a swing at Christine.

"Why did you say something like that?" said Joan angrily. "You didn't know her or what she was like."

117

"And you haven't told me, either. Joan, until a minute ago, I didn't even know she was dead. I figured your parents were probably divorced and you were living with your dad. So now you think you were wrong to go to the party. Why? Why shouldn't you spend time with friends who care about you? Why shouldn't you make Ryan feel good the way you did?"

"Because it was the anniversary, for crying out loud!" said Joan.

"So, how's it been, then? Before this anniversary?" asked Christine, finding it hard to keep her voice down. "Or maybe I should ask, how was it before everything happened? You know, Joan, there are worse things than having someone die. I'm sure your Mom was a great person and that you had a good family life before she died. That's something you can carry inside without being ashamed to talk about it. Me, I don't have that. My Dad beat up my Mom even when she was pregnant, and when they got divorced he took everything he could carry and didn't give us a nickel, leaving Mama with four kids to raise. That's the memory I have about family life. Want to trade?"

Joan stared for a minute, then dropped her gaze and shook her head.

Christine glanced at the clock. "Anyhow, I have to get to work. You all set?"

Joan nodded. "Papa's coming for me at eleven. I have my phone and I'll camp out on the sofa and do my homework until he shows up."

Christine stood up and put her work coat on. "Don't worry, I'll be back before eleven."

"No sweat, Christine. Listen…we'll talk more about this later. You're right about a bunch of stuff. I just have to work things out."

Christine opened the door and looked back gratefully. "Thanks, Joan."

"Aye Aye, Captain," Joan replied. Christine grinned and the door closed behind her.

After she put the twins to bed, Joan settled herself in the big overstuffed sofa and opened the book that Miss Renoir had given her earlier that day. It was a nice change to be reading about that time in France where the sword was still important, and for the millionth time, Joan wondered about how it would feel if she had a real sword and had to use it.

A thought kept tugging at a corner of her mind until she turned away from the book for a minute and tried to figure it out. There was something about that conversation with Christine that didn't feel right. Joan's talent for observation filed away details that would be used once and probably never again, but unlike her fencing opponents Joan had seen Christine dozens of times after that first confrontation in the gym. While talking with Christine this evening, Joan was distracted by the way she was fiddling with her hands and feet, almost like she couldn't sit still. It was like she was wound up and unable to wind down, jumpy like there was a reservoir of overflowing energy inside that she couldn't control.

Joan also knew that watches can sometimes break from over winding, so she made a mental note to keep an eye on Christine. She owed it to Christine, not only because she had become a friend but because she hadn't been afraid to confront Joan with the truth.

I have a lot of things to make up to a lot of people, Joan thought, but maybe it was like this book here in her hand. Michelle and Christine and Ryan and Dwight and George and all the others are my real friends, and telling the truth is simply what real friends do for each other.

All for one, and one for all, as the book says.

Chapter Twenty-Six
It Makes a Lovely Light

There are few places where enthusiasm is as genuine as in a High School where a popular and successful team has qualified for a tournament. When a big school with a long history of successes does it year after year, the enthusiasm becomes ingrained in the whole school community, and this is the main reason it is so painful when a long winning streak comes to an end. Add another year to that losing streak, then another, and after a while losing becomes the new tradition, barbershops stop posting the football and basketball schedules, and the better players transfer to other schools.

When a newly successful team suddenly rebounds into having an actual chance at a title, it's like those dry ponds in the desert after a rainstorm. Fans pop out of the woodwork like the frogs pop out of the mud and "Our Team" reemerges as a major topic of conversation. The posters go back up, wagons and trucks are loaned out for pep rallies, and the members of the team bask in the spotlight.

To see Todd around town you'd think that the team's success was due to his enlightened administration and visionary coaching, and he was satisfied that the community saw it that way. Invitations went out for the team to have dinner with the Rotary Club, or do a hoop shoot with the Knights of Columbus, and Todd made sure he was there to introduce the team.

When a call came from the Sports Central Television network for a three-minute news story, Todd dipped into what was left of the Special Education money to buy dinner for the whole TV crew. When the finished product aired the following weekend, you'd have thought the story was all about a beleaguered High School Principal with limited resources who restores hope and prosperity to a desolate community through inspired, visionary leadership, and by the way, there are a few girls who shoot baskets now and then. When Coach Anita got a preview copy of the DVD and showed it to the team, she and Christine had to block the door to keep the rest of the team from storming down the hall to the Principal's office.

When Joan came to school the Monday before playoff weekend, she was greeted by the GOOD LUCK TEAM signs that plastered the hallways, along with one other sign posted outside the front office featuring, of all people, – herself.

> GOOD LUCK Joan Darcy
> First Ever SHS Finalest
> State Fencing Tornament

There was a photograph showing Joan in a particularly fierce pose, her foil bent into a nice arc against some hapless opponent. One thing about being the only one in the whole school doing a sport, they don't exactly give you a pep rally or send in the cheerleaders to buck you up. The picture was somewhat out of focus but what the heck – it was a nice thing to do. Joan didn't mind the picture or the spelling mistakes because she also recognized the handwriting: what she did wonder was who had helped Ryan with the poster.

She was still wondering when the first period was over and she made her way to Miss Renoir's classroom when she saw another poster on the wall outside Miss Renoir's door. Joan stood in the hallway looking at it when the door opened and Miss Renoir came out.

"This is…very nice," said Joan.

"Yes," said Miss Renoir. "I am surprised, Jeannette, that you say that it is nice. It is not like you, especially lately, to offer compliments. So – do you know about these? The who and the why?"

Joan realized Miss Renoir was speaking in English, which was not a good sign. "Ryan made the one in the front hall," Joan responded, uneasy from Miss Renoir's tone. "But I don't know where he got the picture from."

"I gave it to him," Miss Renoir said. "I received several photos with an email from one of the other coaches who had a student photographer at the match. He thought I would like to have them, especially since you won matches against all four of his students. He has become a fan of yours, you might say. He too was a champion fencer at one time, but was injured in Afghanistan and is now only able to coach and advise. In fencing, I am afraid having only one leg is something of a hindrance."

Joan remembered the coach, his prosthetic leg a great piece of engineering. She also remembered his team, starting the day with such enthusiasm and going down like bowling pins, four in a row, all shut out 5-0. By her.

"Am I supposed to lose on purpose or something?" Joan asked. "If I face them fair and square and win, that's all there is to it."

"True," said Miss Renoir. "And what did you teach them in the process?"

"What do you mean?" replied Joan, not expecting this.

"Just that. What did YOU teach them in the process? When the match was over, did you go to them and give any advice or tips on how or why you beat them? No. You were satisfied to knock them down 1, 2, 3, 4, without a word when it was over, no different than four paper towels you tear out of a dispenser, use once, then throw into a wastebasket."

Joan's face was burning and she was on the edge of walking away when Miss Renoir grasped her shoulder, pointed into the room, and ordered "Go sit. Now."

When the door closed, Miss Renoir stood and leaned against it while Joan sat in the chair, arms crossed, and with as intense an expression on her face as Miss Renoir had ever seen. Mon Dieu – in a match her opponent would see this, cross himself, and commend his soul to God…but these are High School students and they would simply pee themselves instead.

120

This mental picture was so ridiculous that despite her annoyance Miss Renoir cracked a smile, the opposite of what Joan expected. Miss Renoir immediately tried to look serious again but the mental picture got more real and more ridiculous that by now she was also holding back her laughter, then the strain made her need the toilet and the absurdity of it all finally burst so she stood against the door, shaking with silent laughter, tears streaming down her face.

At this point, Joan seriously considered calling the front office for an ambulance, but the dumb thing was that all her own anger had just evaporated. When someone is angry and enjoying it, they don't like it when someone succeeds in cheering them up because being that angry is truly refreshing and brings all of the poisons to the surface. Since you are now the other idiot in the room, the moment when you break through your own anger and laugh helps wash away the poisons from both of you.

It was fully three minutes until either of them could take a full breath without breaking into laughter again. Miss Renoir had sat down at the desk next to Joan, almost too weak to stand.

"May I ask a question?" said Joan, wiping her eyes.

"Certainly," responded Miss Renoir.

"What was so funny?" asked Joan.

Miss Renoir started to explain and got about fifteen seconds into the explanation before it set her off again, and Joan had heard enough to get an image in her head too, and the whole thing started all over again. It didn't last as long this time but wouldn't you know it, both now had to go and use the bathroom, but dignity took over and they both managed to hold it together.

Back in the classroom and feeling a whole lot better, Joan leaned back in the chair and looked at the ceiling. Miss Renoir had moved her desk chair to the front of the room and was sitting opposite, also relaxed now and looking at Joan. How you do fascinate and frustrate me, Jeannette, so much ability in one small package and yet so very unlike the others. You are the only one ever to live here, on this side of the Atlantic, and yet have so much heart and spirit within you.

"You should thank your friends," said Miss Renoir.

"I will," said Joan. "And I am sorry, too."

"For what?"

"For everything."

Miss Renoir shook her head. "No, Jeannette, not for everything. For being too much focused on yourself, perhaps. You may think you are focused on others, your opponents, by your analysis of their faults, but you equate their faults with who they are. That is unfair, wrong, and dangerous. Your opponents have only been children like yourself, open and revealing of everything."

"Someday, however, you will face an opponent who is a master at lying, at making everyone believe him and yet telling the truth to no one." She stood. "Our lesson here is finished for this morning, and there is no new French for tomorrow. You are to meet me at the College Athletics building at five o'clock this afternoon. You will inform your Papa and after we finish you and I will proceed to Toussaint's for supper at seven."

Joan had not heard this tone from her teacher before. From a stern reprimand to helpless laughter to the Commander in ten minutes was quite a journey, but Joan also recognized that it was time to get serious.

Later that evening when Joan got to the Athletics building, she carried her gear up the steps and went inside. She found the room at the end of a hallway on the first floor, the floorboards creaking as the first vestiges of spring had brought some moisture back into the air. She pulled the door open to reveal a medium size room with an old wooden floor and a high ceiling, two folding chairs and a pile of wrestling mats in one corner. Miss Renoir was in her gear already but to Joan's surprise, she was not wearing her mask. During her training, there had been a few times she had fenced against Miss Renoir, but her teacher had always worn her gear for every lesson, mask and all.

As Joan slipped into her own gear she noticed a long black case on top of the wrestling mats, its cover lightly scuffed and apparently, a part of tonight's lesson. Their routine this evening included a warm up, modified from the very first routine that Mama had taught her, but without her foil. This gave it a wider and sometimes slower scope, becoming more like the Tai Chi that Mr. Dr. Han had demonstrated. It was difficult at first, having to adjust her balance to the change in weight at the end of her arm, but the muscles adjusted on their own and she found herself flowing more easily.

"Very good, Jeannette. Now you must listen very clearly to what I am going to say. I saw that you changed your balance without the foil and with grace and confidence. This is very good and shows that your body is listening to you. I am now going to give you a weapon, and you must show it the very greatest respect. Do you understand me?"

Joan nodded.

"No, I must hear you say it. Do you understand me?"

"Je Comprende," Joan said, the French meaning adding gravity to her response.

Miss Renoir smiled slightly. "Wait here." She walked over to where the case lay on the pile of mats and reaching to the twin catches, unlocked both simultaneously. Very carefully, she opened the case and lifted aside a long, silk cloth, revealing something very long and glistening. She grasped it carefully, withdrew it from the case, and carried it over to Joan.

"Take this the way you always have. It will feel different in your hand." Miss Renoir took the blade in her left hand and withdrew her right from the hilt.

Nice gear, thought Joan and put her own hand on the hilt. Miss Renoir stepped away and Joan hefted the blade, grasping more tightly, her eyes taking in every detail, the grip thicker than her own, until...This is not a fencing weapon, this is the real thing!

"En garde!"

Half a second later Joan was in her defensive posture, feet just right, left hand tucked into her back, making the curve that Mama always said helped her right shoulder muscles, right arm gripping tightly and extended. Miss Renoir moved and Joan countered automatically, the two blades connecting but this time with a clash, not the metallic ripping sound they usually made. A step back and then another attack, lower this time, the clashing louder and much sharper, Joan still on the defensive but the panther starting to emerge, the muscles adjusting for the attack. when abruptly Miss Renoir took two steps back and spread her arms, her sword pointing away and defenseless, her eyes locked onto Joan's, no mask this time for either of them. Joan froze, her face pale, sword at the ready.

"What do you see?" said Miss Renoir. Joan hesitated.

"WHAT DO YOU SEE?" Miss Renoir shouted, her eyes still locked on Joan's

"I SEE YOUR EYES!!" said Joan, slowly lowering the sword which trembled slightly in her hand.

Miss Renoir grabbed one of the folding chairs, dragged it to where Joan was standing, and gently took the sword from her hand.

"Sit down, Jeannette. Now, please."

Joan sat, and Miss Renoir returned the two swords to the case.

"Now breathe more evenly, one, two as we have practiced. Match my pace."

Miss Renoir started to breathe in, out, in, out at the same pace as Joan, but after a few seconds began to slow the pace until they both were taking large, slow breaths together.

"Why did you do this?" asked Joan.

"To test if you were ready. You heard the words and were defending yourself before you realized exactly what was happening. What's more, you did not alter your technique except to compensate slightly for the heavier weapon. I am genuinely surprised and pleased, Jeannette, that you did not run or start to think too hard. I had no intention to proceed beyond the first clash, but you were ready to continue, were you not?"

Joan nodded, more slowly this time. "Yes, and it scares me."

"Now or then? Tell me – this is very important that you are honest."

"Now, of course."

"Why 'of course'? What does that say? Why not then?"

"Because it was…automatic, like you said. It's what I have trained for all these years. To be ready, to let the muscles react by themselves so I could…"

"You could look for a weakness, an opening to beat your opponent. In our fencing, however, there is something dishonest that is in no other sport, that you cannot see your opponent's eyes. You are standing and fighting against something that might as well be a machine. When one progresses to the degree that you have achieved, it becomes all about the opponent, the sword on the other side that you must meet, a collection of gear that you must touch first. In that moment, there is no human on the other side. This has become your greatest weakness."

"Now think about what I told you, and answer this question, but not until I tell you to speak. What is the real difference?"

Joan was staring into Miss Renoir's face as she was saying this, and an image from the past crowded into her mind and almost overwhelmed her. She had heard something like this before...somewhere long before, and it was like a film playing in her head of a tiny girl and a young woman under a tree, the woman asking and receiving a promise.

I will always protect the helpless, no matter what the risk.

"You may speak, Joan."

"Risk." Almost a whisper. "There is no risk. For me, anyway."

Miss Renoir felt an enormous surge of pride and at the same time a sorrow, like a parent who sees a child master a bicycle and at the same time knows that the bicycle will carry her away without you being along for the ride.

"It is a hard thing, Jeannette. To have this skill and then...to see it as something else, something incomplete, perhaps."

"Or dangerous," said Joan. "For everybody else. The ones I fight, especially. Maybe my friends, too."

"Like Ryan?"

Joan nodded. "Not exactly, because he knew it was an accident - but does he know any better?"

"He does. It so happens that Ryan is your friend because you are genuinely kind, and that you use kind words and actions. Unfortunately, that is his weakness because he trusts so easily. Since most people have been kind to him, he expects the best from people and almost all of them give that to him. The danger to him is from people who only want something from him and don't care how they get it. If someone uses the right words to Ryan, they are immediately trusted. He can't tell the difference and therefore he may be badly hurt someday because of it. Now how does this apply to you?"

"Maybe I'm not any different."

"How? You are on the right track but you must be specific."

"Ryan sees everyone as a friend or at least someone nice," said Joan. "I have friends, people like Michelle, Christine, and so on, but...not in fencing. When I am at a match I go against other people and beat them, and it's...sterile. Ryan sees friends, I see...a foil and a mask.... an opponent."

"Who is as human as you are," replied Miss Renoir, "who has practiced and struggled to get better, like you. Most of them, anyway. You have fought only with masks and guards at tournaments where everything is nice and clean and tidy and people are polite to each other. How would you face an opponent who ignores all the rules, someone who throws sand in your face or drugs your wine or attacks you with a real sword? What will you do when you see their eyes? Sometimes evil has the most human face you can imagine, and that is what makes it so dangerous."

124

I sat in the back seat on the ride to Toussaint's, wanting to hide in the darkness and think about what happened. Maybe I first thought tournaments were more fun when I was with Mama, but Miss Renoir is great. I'm getting a lot better, but it's not much fun anymore...no, that's not it either. I look forward to the tournaments and it's great to be with Michelle – at least when she's talking with me – but do I share it with her? What about that comment about evil having a human face?

In spite of myself, I felt a sense of foreboding, and something also made me decide I needed my friends around me when it happened, whatever it was.

By the time we had pulled into the parking lot at the restaurant I had made up her mind what to do, if Miss Renoir and Papa agreed.

"Miss Renoir?" I asked as the car was turned off.

"Oui, Jeannette?"

"I...hear you. I do. It's not going to sink in completely in one day but it's a start. Merci beaucoup."

"Rien, Jeannette. I'm hungry."

"Me, too."

Later, on my way home with Papa, I had figured out what I was going to do next week. We always took the school van to the matches anyway, so why not make a party of it? I'll bet Dwight and George would come if they're not booked up and I'm sure Ryan would get a big kick out of it. Don't know how we could get Brian's chair in the van but I'll ask him too. It's not like they've ever seen anything like this before and...it would be great to share it with them.

And maybe Michelle won't still be mad.

Chapter Twenty-Seven
Forgetting

For the past two months, Superintendent Joe had been spending literally all his work time inside his office, Gladys jealously guarding access by saying his calendar was full every time someone asked for a meeting. For those who tried to get around her by requesting a date still three weeks away, Gladys would respond that no appointments could be made that far ahead. For his part, Joe would sit at his desk impeccably dressed as always, everything on the desk neatly aligned, a yellow pad and pen at the ready. Whenever the door opened, he would rise to his feet wearing a big smile, his hand extended to greet whoever came in. The fact that Gladys was now the only person who ever did come in didn't seem to register, and for the last week she was getting the full treatment since Joe no longer even recognized her.

He had stopped taking his customary walks around the high school when one day Todd saw him heading into the girl's restroom. Intercepting him at the last second, Joe said that he smelled cigarette smoke, so Todd led him back to the

Superintendent's office and Gladys escorted Joe to his desk. Joe brushed off his suit as he always did, sat down and immediately began straightening up the items on the desk, the walk and Gladys forgotten.

"Can you handle this or not?" Todd growled. "That was too darn close for comfort. This gets out and the whole plan is shot." Gladys, always one for keeping family secrets close to the family, was of the unshakeable opinion that only a Martin was qualified to be superintendent and since Todd was the only Martin available she would do whatever it took to make sure he was the next one with the job.

The fact was, Todd was already doing a lot more than Gladys knew about. Since Old Mrs. Thibodaux had Joe in her very first elementary class back in the 1930's and Todd forty years later, both men had been taught handwriting that looked almost identical, making it easy for Todd to forge his Uncle's signature. Todd had also appropriated the combination to the safe where school board records, teacher credential records and state test forms were kept. He had already taken care of the whole band room renovation project, filing the signed copies directly into the safe where any future examination would show that yes, Superintendent Joe had indeed approved that purchase.

At 3:30 Gladys got the cash deposit bag out of her locked desk drawer, went into the Superintendent's office and emerged a minute later with Joe, who shook Todd's hand and asked him how his Daddy was. Todd's Daddy had in fact been dead for fifteen years but Todd said he was fine, thank you, and Joe would smile and follow Gladys out of the office. This was now a daily ritual since Todd insisted that Gladys leave at 3:30 so she could take Uncle Joe home at the same time she dropped off the daily deposit at the bank. This also gave Todd enough time to open the safe himself and make a few changes and additions to his own personnel folder while Gladys was gone.

Locking the office door, Todd took his briefcase and set it on the table next to the safe. The size of an old-fashioned wardrobe, the safe was a relic from the 1930's. It was divided into four large sections, including two file drawers and two large shelves where several large sealed packages were sitting, marked "Official Testing Documents" in large black letters. For Todd, it was like having the Crown Jewels within his grasp, except these jewels hadn't been opened yet and wouldn't be until testing started three days before the state basketball final. The packages had to be certified sealed until testing day when Gladys opened them in front of the Superintendent, but that's where the chain had a weak link.

After the students finished, the tests would be put into envelopes and brought back to this safe for verification before they were shipped. Todd had already convinced Gladys that Joe wasn't up to that job anymore, so he would take care of that himself, making sure to be late enough that Gladys would be out of the office when he started.

Problem was, there would be over a thousand test papers that he would have to go through to find the ones he had already identified as needing 'adjustment." These were the students who had failed tests the year before since the official school evaluation was based on improvement over a one-year period. What Todd had to do was to make sure that those students scored better than last year.

Unfortunately, the test papers he wanted were mixed up with all the others, and it would take a lot of time to go through all the envelopes and find them. If he was by himself, he would need a minimum of ten minutes to find one paper, take it out of the envelope, erase and change answers on the scan sheet and return it to the envelope, making it at least a ten-hour job. The original plan was to get some help from Christine's dad, but the guy had been gone since last week along with a car from the school's auto mechanics class, so Todd didn't think he would be coming back any time soon. The problem now was to find somebody who could both help and keep his mouth shut.

Todd took another look at the list and one name jumped out at him. Ryan. He was genuinely grateful to be working for the school, where the quiet rattle of his personal cart had become a regular sound around the hallways. He did a good job, delivering the paper to the copiers, and even sorting the mail. Despite his injury, Ryan could read names just fine, having the job of putting teacher's mail into the mail slots in the faculty workroom. Even better, he believed absolutely anything that was printed on a piece of paper. It didn't hurt that he was a student, and since he got his job – well, Mr. Todd was the greatest person ever. It would work.

Chapter Twenty-Eight
Regionals

The home crowd was practically breaking out the gymnasium windows with their shouting, and the bleachers were in danger of collapsing as the final quarter got under way with Smithfield 64, Garland 59. The game was the closest that most of the spectators had seen in years and the fact that eleven of Garland's points were from foul shots it seemed likely that some record was going to be broken. Lisa was on the bench with four fouls and three of the remaining players had three fouls each, but by some miracle Christine had managed to accumulate only one and that was more for giving the referee the evil eye than from anything serious.

Coach Anita stood back a foot or so while Christine was giving the final instructions, almost a recitation of their opponent's weaknesses that had become a team tradition. Usually, she only had to do it once at the beginning of the game, but the Garland coach was so frantic to find someone, anyone who could stop the Smithfield steamroller that she kept substituting players, trying to keep Smithfield off balance. The Smithfield girls had become minor experts at registering the tics and quirks and weak ankles of their opponents. Even Lisa was learning to focus her touchiness into something constructive, finally a real partner to her teammates who fed her setup after setup after they had snatched the ball from their opponents. It was unfortunate that Lisa also had a big mouth and the Garland game was her weak spot, so unless Coach Anita had an emergency Lisa would on the bench and keep her eyes open for those weaknesses Christine had taught her to spot.

As far as Christine's game performance went she had been brilliant, scoring 44 points of her own including four three-pointers, and to Coach Anita's amazement appeared as fresh at halftime as she had before the game started. This was not normal, however, and Coach Anita was strongly tempted to pull Christine out for at least a few minutes to give her a chance to rest. The problem with Christine being an acting assistant coach, however, is that for Anita to keep her promise about letting Christine be in charge she had to let Christine decide when to substitute herself.

The buzzer sounded and the teams ran back onto the floor. Garland put the ball into play and it was immediately apparent that a new strategy was in play. The girls were now spread out to the point that none was within twenty feet of any other. This meant of course that Smithfield had to change its own tactics to accommodate more of the court, and the constant movement of the Garland players prevented Smithfield from taking advantage of the tricks that had previously given them the lead. Two minutes into the fourth quarter Garland had pulled ahead 69-66 and Christine called a timeout.

Up in the bleachers, Joan was struggling up the steps carrying a tray full of drinks and two giant bags of popcorn, grateful that her legs were flexible enough to maintain her balance. It didn't help that the entire student section was going through its fortieth rendition of "We will Rock You", the whole structure shuddering with each WHOMP WHOMP of the song. Fencing is nothing if not about balance, fortunately, so by the time Joan made it up to where the pep band was sitting on the top row with its backs to the wall, most of what she was carrying was still intact.

Michelle was there, too, along with the rest of the Pep Band. Joan had approached her only that morning, giving her a few days to cool off and to see that Ryan was okay. They had sat on opposite sides of the room during English, and when the class was over Michelle left the classroom first. At lunch, Michelle had gotten to the cafeteria early and was sitting all alone at the big table where they usually sat together. Joan came up from behind, in part to make it harder for Michelle to simply stand up and move to another table.

She had stayed up late last evening making Croquembouche using Grandmother's recipe and had put the two largest into a clear plastic box which Joan now took out of her lunchbox and sat in the middle of the table. Joan started in on her own sandwich and made a point not to look directly at Michelle, but it didn't take long before Michelle was looking sideways at that box.

Without a word, Joan reached out and popped off the lid but didn't take one for herself. She had made one alteration to the recipe, adding little slivers of vanilla bean to the cream that she had whipped into a froth, and being inside the box overnight concentrated the aroma so that whole section of the cafeteria smelled like an ice cream parlor. By this point, Michelle couldn't keep her eyes off the box and had stopped eating the tofu and seaweed she usually brought for lunch.

"You're mean," said Michelle quietly.

"And stupid," replied Joan, still looking down at the table. "And apologetic."

"And you don't talk to me when you should."

"True. I'm sorry about that, Michelle. Really sorry."

Michelle was silent, but her eyes were still on the pastry. "So, what was the big deal?" she asked. "Something must have happened at the party but I couldn't figure out what."

Joan sighed. "It wasn't the party but...the date. Of the party." Joan looked right at Michelle. "I didn't remember until right after Ryan finished his story. It was the anniversary for my Mama. A year to the day since she died – and there I was at a party instead of being home with Papa."

Michelle got up and moved back halfway around the table next to Joan. "You were mad at yourself, right? Not at us?"

Joan nodded.

"Are you still mad? With yourself, I mean?"

Joan looked up, eyes honest and unprotected. "I'm not very good at being mad, Michelle. I don't handle it very well."

"Give you lessons if you want," replied Michelle, her eyes again glued on the pastry. "Want to know how much they cost?"

"One pastry per lesson?" replied Joan.

"Payable in advance," replied Michelle. "Like, right now."

"Agreed," said Joan.

In primitive cultures, the acceptance of a gift indicates peace between two disagreeing parties. This often includes food. As an American High School is a prime example of primitive culture, the two girls were headed in the right direction.

Joan had never been so thankful to make peace with anyone and was enormously relieved that they were at the game together. Finally reaching the top of the stairs, Joan said "Special Delivery," as the members of the Pep Band took their food and drinks, Joan making sure that Michelle got the one with the big M on the side. When she took her first sip, Michelle's eyes opened wide with appreciation.

"Thanks, dork," she said.

Well, hearing *dork* again was a step in the right direction, thought Joan. A package had arrived that afternoon from Grandmother containing a few books that Joan had requested along with a large box of something for Michelle.

"Little something for you, direct from France. Something of a peace gesture, I guess," said Joan as she pulled what looked like a candy bar out of her pocket and handed it to Michelle, whose eyes widened as she saw the label. It was a gourmet French candy bar called "Crispello", and its number one ingredient was Vanilla which happened to be Michelle's ultimate soul food.

"It's not sold over here," Joan said. "Hope you like it." Joan sat down, picked up her saxophone, and started to wet the reed while Michelle, unable to wait, tore off the end of the wrapper and took a bite. Merci Grandmere, Joan thought as she warmed up. If the way she ate that one is any indication, the box will be empty in about two days.

This was all brought to an abrupt halt, of course, when Mrs. Coates cued Ryan, who started beating his drum for the fight song. When Michelle, still chewing, grabbed her clarinet and began to play, there was a squawk from the clarinet and a tiny piece of white candy dropped out of the bell. Michelle recovered almost at once but not before giving Joan a glare, at which Joan laughed right into her saxophone, resulting in a much louder squawk than Michelle's. It was lucky that the crowd was on its feet screaming because the only people who heard it were the two girls who made it happen.

Down on the floor, there was a timeout and the Smithfield girls huddled around Coach Anita, but to Christine's surprise, Coach Anita looked at her. "Your call, Christine," she said, and mentally crossed her fingers. *If Christine's got what it takes to be a coach someday then here's the time to show it.*

Christine looked at the others who were looking back at her, fired up and eyes shining. "Chewing gum," she said.

"What flavor?" asked Lisa.

"Glue. 67 in for 81," said Christine, and sat down.

It was a tribute to how much she respected Christine that Lisa didn't blurt out 'you got to be kidding me!!!' but they had all been playing at a hundred and fifteen percent power the whole game and this was the first break Christine had taken since the opening buzzer. From her place on the bench, Christine put out her hands as Jolene tossed off the towel from around her neck and jumped into the circle.

"Team!" and the buzzer sounded.

Coach Anita had not been sure she was hearing correctly when Christine first described the chewing gum play to her. The strategy was to devote 100% of the game time to defense by shadowing every opposing player according to the catalog of weaknesses they had put together. They had tried it once before, two weeks ago, in a game against Arkana West, a school in the middle of the rankings, and were encouraged by the immediate chaos it caused. The name originated with Coach Anita, and when it worked the game slowed down to a crawl, with Smithfield never trying to steal the ball but shutting down every passing lane. As a result, their opponents went crazy trying to unload the ball. Since each Smithfield player was simultaneously targeting her opponent's jitters and blind spots and weak knees, after two minutes three Arkana West players asked to go back to the bench and Smithfield won the game in a walkover, 56-36.

Sitting behind the Smithfield bench were two tall, very athletic women in Smithfield College jackets, each holding a clipboard. They had managed to overhear Christine's instructions and were waiting to see what the results were going to be.

"81 on our radar?"

"She sure is now, except…she's the one who called this play! First time the whole game she hasn't been on the floor, she calls the play and takes a seat?"

"Anita knows what she's doing. Let's just see what happens."

After the buzzer, the Smithfield girls had taken their positions, each glued to a spot directly in front of a Garland player. The Garland defense had one player far up court meant to shut down any unexpected turnover, but the Smithfield player was someone they hadn't seen before. The problem was that once the ball was in play, the Smithfield player acted like she was attached to the hip of the Garland player, except for the Garland player it was more like a deer fly that she had to keep waving away from her face. The game went from a nonstop back and forth road race to a maddeningly slow pace, no action, no this way yes but no there she is again and got to pass but nothing open so I guess I stand here like half the players were glued to the floor. The clock was down to 0:45 when Bobbi accidentally hit her opponent on the shoulder, and the referee called a foul shot. Christine looked at Coach Anita, who nodded.

"Go get 'em, Captain," she said.

"81 for 67," shouted Christine, and ran out to the key.

The crowd on the home side started to yell and whistle and hoot as the Garland player stepped up to the line, aimed, and bounced one off the rim. The visitor's side let out a collective "Ohhhhh" as the Smithfield side cheered, the visiting team glared, and the referee returned the ball to the player at the line. The yelling and whistling and hooting rose again as the player shifted her weight and fired the ball up and......in, and as the buzzer sounded the scoreboard displayed 71-72.

Christine took her spot next to the tallest Garland player, and as Terri and Stephanie got ready to bring in the ball, she shouted "BUBBLE GUM!"

The other girls and the entire home stands rose and shouted "AYE AYE CAPTAIN" at which Terri fired the ball a whole two feet to Stephanie as the rest of the team crowded in, then Stephanie passed it to Bobbi who was dribbling further out, but more toward the Smithfield side which threw off the Garland players who started moving with them, the ball passing but longer each time, but Christine was the pendulum in the middle who abruptly ran up directly behind Bobbi who made a backwards dribble that turned into a short quick bounce pass immediately picked up by Christine, whose momentum had her twenty feet away before any Garland player could react, and as the final seconds 4, 3, 2, she was under the basket all alone, and made a ridiculous easy layup shot that would have done credit to a sixth grade player. Garland had possession at 0:01 and was behind 73-72, there was a desperation pass half the length of the court, then the final buzzer and pandemonium.

Five minutes later the girls had made it to the locker room all in one piece, some of them covered with Kettle Corn thrown by the fans when the game was over. Over by the door, a tall woman was talking to Bobbi, who nodded and went over to get Coach Anita.

"Hello, Coach, I'm Dr. Strong from the Smithfield College Athletic Department. We'd like to chat with you about that girl of yours."

"Christine Cooper?"

"Yes, that's the one. We couldn't help notice that she was helping to coach from the bench as well as playing one heck of a game!"

131

Finally, thought Coach Anita. Finally, finally, finally. "She does a lot more than that. I'd like you to know that she both developed and wrote up those last two plays, what we call our 'chewing gum' series. Got the idea from the movie "Hoosiers" and it seems to work."

The two coaches looked at each other. "Is she interested in..."

"I'm very sure of it," replied Coach Anita.

"Coach, the two of us are the mavericks in our department. We've made a proposal for an entirely different type of...opportunity. Tonight's not the time but let's make a tentative appointment for next Thursday."

"Well, since we won tonight we are now going to the State AA final game next Thursday, so perhaps Friday?"

They nodded. "Here at your school – say, ten o'clock?"

"That will be fine if you have something definite on the table by that time. I don't want Christine to get her hopes up and then for something not to pan out. You will never find a harder worker than that young lady."

Christine was the last person in the locker room that evening, Coach Anita asking her to lock up after she finished her game report, part of her ongoing job as team captain. The other girls were going to Bishop's, a local hangout three blocks from the school that specialized in onion rings, fried chicken, and other food guaranteed to replace some of the calories they had burned through. On game night, you were also sure to see about everybody who had been to the game. Mr. Bishop was a big sports booster, and since he had a policy that gave any winning team free food, lots of people came and everybody was happy.

Halfway through her typing, Christine paused to let more of the game's details filter down to her fingers. The chewing gum play had been a great success and Christine knew she should document how they did it. The problem was, though, that tonight her typing was becoming more and more difficult. Her hands were trembling, sometimes so strongly that Christine was hitting keys far away from the one she wanted. She sat back and gripped her hands together trying to settle herself down, but that only made it worse. It had been like this for a few weeks now, loaded with energy for practice and through a game, and then half an hour later she was like this.

She was now going to the training room three times a week, including this morning, and the vitamin milk was helping her energy level, at least on regular days. This night had been something different, however, a lot more intense, and she thought that maybe it was all the extra exertion that crashed her down this way. Her regular trainer had given her two extra bottles for the weekend and they were still both in her locker. Christine now remembered that unlike every other weekend for the past two months there wasn't a game or practice tomorrow since the regular season was over, so she didn't need to take a bottle tomorrow...except that now her hands were shaking so badly she couldn't type at all. Low blood sugar or something, Christine thought, so only half the bottle for right now. She took it out of her locker and shook it since it had sat there all day, and when she screwed off the top there were a few drops inside the cap that dribbled down over her hand and onto the floor. The silver sealed top was wet, but she was thirsty and paid no more mind to it as she peeled it off and tossed it into the trash. It tasted good, the slight tang along with the strawberry flavor, and what the heck just finish the thing there's always one extra.

Ten minutes later Christine had finished the report, attached and emailed it along to Coach Anita, and had closed and locked the door behind her. The night was crisp and there was a full moon, so she plugged in her earphones and started the jog over to Bishop's. As she ran around to the front of the school on her way to the road, she saw one light still burning in the Principal's office. Not like him to work this late, Christine thought, then put it out of her mind. The strawberry milk had done its work and now she felt like it was eight o'clock in the morning after a good night's sleep.

It's so close I can feel it, thought Todd as he sat at his desk and looked at the trophy Coach Anita had delivered. These girls are the best team the school has fielded in years and given the rest of the AA competition the tournament should be a shoo-in. Their opponent won't be decided until tomorrow but Garland had been rated higher than Smithfield and what do you know, it's my office with the trophy in it.

A half-liter bottle of apple juice sat open on the desk, the third one he'd had that evening. Apple juice seemed to add a zing to the mineral supplement, and he had to smile at himself as he took another large swallow. He had tried it in milk once like the dealer said and it almost made him gag. Of course, he had poured it in and drank before it got all mixed up properly, but he never was a big one for following directions and apple juice was working fine.

So, Christine pulled it off – or should I say, I pulled it off with help from Christine and a few bottles of that special strawberry milk. Testing is Monday and Tuesday next week, they get delivered to the State Capital Wednesday morning, and by Thursday our scores will be the most improved in the whole State thanks to some magic from me and my little buddy Ryan. All we have left is the basketball final on Thursday night and hello world, like to introduce you to Superintendent Todd, thank you very much.

While leaving the building, Todd passed the basketball posters and for the first time noticed the poster Ryan had made for Joan. Funny, I didn't know about this, he thought. Would be nice icing on the cake to bring home three State Championships in one year, so maybe I'll go to this thing and see what it's all about. Just in case.

Bishop's Drive-In was packed with cars, kids, and even some parents who could handle the noise. Mr. Bishop had to come on the PA every now and then asking kids to turn car stereos down, but business was booming and everybody was happy. The basketball players had arrived, and one of the cheerleaders had hooked up her iPhone to the stereo system so when the whole crowd yelled "HELLO CAPTAIN" the next thing out of the PA was the SpongeBob song played so loud it was stripping paint off cars across the street. If it wasn't sung exactly in tune, it at least had a lot of enthusiasm.

Joan and Michelle were in Papa's car, parked next to Brian's van with his Mom, Dad, Ryan, and the Kershaw twins. It's amazing how a few slivers of real vanilla can go a long way, and Joan was thankful beyond words that she and Michelle had made up.

"I have a whole case of the candy bars," Joan said. "Just in case, you know."

Before Michelle could think of anything particularly cutting in response, Miss Renoir opened the front passenger door and got inside.

"I have news," she said. "For Jeannette."

"State rankings?" asked Joan excitedly.

Miss Renoir nodded.

"So?" asked Joan.

"First in State," said Miss Renoir. "You are ranked #1 in the whole state."

"For age group? For girls?"

"Technically for High School girls, but three of the judges rank you as #1 for all high school including boys. You are therefore going directly to the State Finals next Saturday. Congratulations!"

The door slammed suddenly as Michelle leaped out of the car and bolted to the restaurant door where she ducked inside. Joan could see her talking excitedly with Mr. Bishop, and...please don't! but it was too late.

"May I have your attention ladies and gentlemen," boomed the loudspeakers mounted on the light poles all around the parking lot. "I am proud to announce that we have another champion with us tonight. Our very own Joan Darcy has been rated #1 high school fencer in the State, and will be competing at the State Final Tournament next Saturday!" The crowd was already pumped up from one win that evening, so it didn't take much for it to embrace one more reason to celebrate. For the next ten minutes, dozens of her fellow students came over to

134

her car and congratulated her face to face, not knowing exactly what it was but hey, a #1 rating is a #1 rating so it must be good, right? Good job, hope you win, we're proud you're one of us, go get 'em, can you give my little sister lessons – it all blurred together into Joan's memory. When it finally thinned out Joan was feeling dizzy.

"How does it feel, Joan?" asked Papa. "And don't say, 'how does what feel?'"

"I don't know yet, Papa," Joan replied. "I like it, but I don't know, maybe I don't deserve it."

"Why not?" said Miss Renoir. "What are you afraid of?"

For a second Joan was in the PE building again, the naked sword in her hand, the clash of contact with its twin, Miss Renoir's eyes boring into her own. "I'm not sure," was the best she could say right now. "But I want to win."

"For who?"

Finally, the big question, and Joan realized the answer was there ever since that first day of school. "For everybody out there and in this car. For all of us."

Bishop's had been a gathering place for so long that lots of the students had parents and grandparents who had lost count of how many bags of onion rings they had eaten over the years. Game night, Spring or Fall, you could always find one row of cars further back than the others, slightly gnarled hands on steering wheels and eyes moist as their owners watched the kids, lots of memories behind those eyes from when they were that age and celebrating some long-forgotten win. Onion rings always did go well with victory, and if you were flattened 65-10, well, they still tasted good and made everybody feel better.

Although Dwight and George had ridden in Brian's car, their dad and Grandpa were parked in the back along with the others. Both had been to the game, and although onion rings were not exactly on his diet, Grandpa was having a few to celebrate.

"It's a crying shame," said Grandpa from the passenger seat. "So many good kids out there and the whole school going to pot underneath them. Teachers are doing the best they can, but Todd's like a giant roadblock sitting in the middle of the highway. Only three years out of college, and he's already in line for the top job like some prince waiting for the king to hand him the crown."

Uncle Doug nodded. "Remember Jerry Boise? I hadn't seen him for years but he was there at the game tonight and we talked for a while. He's been living in Garland for the past twelve years, and they're going to add six extra classrooms to the high school to accommodate the move-ins. We have lots of kids who want to stay right here, but since we don't offer the courses they want, they end up transferring to Garland."

"I was against that training room from the start," said Grandpa, a trace of bitterness in his voice. "You want to add something like that you don't go tearing out a custom designed room to do it. Yes, the band was getting smaller like everything else but heck, if you eliminate the program completely you're going to make another bunch of kids want to go somewhere else."

"Jerry told me something else, too, and you're not going to like it," said Uncle Joe bitterly. "Garland is adding a new Assistant Superintendent position and you'll never guess who's gotten the job."

"Todd?" asked Grandpa hopefully.

Uncle Joe shook his head. "No such luck. Phyllis."

"It doesn't surprise me. She's a talented lady and she'll do a good job for them."

"And now she won't have to deal with Todd, and she also has a nice promotion with a forty percent raise."

"What are we going to do?" asked Uncle Doug. "Renee and James are in Joe's pocket and always have been, so with Joe on their side we're sunk."

"What if Joe's not part of it?" asked Grandpa quietly.

"What are you talking about? He's missed exactly one board meeting in eighteen years, and that happened to be when his grandbaby was born. He'd crawl out of his grave to be there."

"Have you seen him lately?"

"As a matter of fact, I haven't. Not for a while. Funny how I didn't notice until you brought it up right now. You think something's going on?"

"I tried two times to see him last week but Gladys will hardly let me through the door. The third time I sat in my car for more than an hour watching the door and nobody went in or out. I was at the barber shop two days ago, asking after him and Henry says that Joe hasn't been there for six weeks."

Grandpa smacked his fist into his hand. "That's got to be it. You know how Joe is, dressed up every day like he's having his picture made and down at the barber shop every Saturday morning. Then out of the blue, he just stops? There's got to be something wrong."

"When's the last time you read the School Board regulations?" asked Uncle Doug, a note of encouragement in his voice.

"You mean article ten?" asked Grandpa.

Uncle Doug nodded. "Exactly. 'In the event of a tie, the vote of the Board President shall count for two.' We have a meeting without Joe, then it's up to you and me." Uncle Doug pointed ahead. "Those kids up there deserve something a lot better than what they're getting."

"What if Gladys is right, that he's real busy and he comes to the board meeting?"

"Then we've got our work cut out for us. Let's have dinner next week at home and get both Renee and James there."

The car door opened and Dwight and George piled into the back. They were happy and flushed but their good mood lightened up the car as Uncle Doug pulled out onto the highway.

"Have a good time, boys?" asked Grandpa.

"Sure did, Grandpa. Great game, too."

"That it was," said Grandpa. "What was that announcement, by the way?"

"That was about Joan," replied Dwight. "She's rated number One in the whole state so she's going to be in the Championship Tournament next week."

136

"Number one in what?" asked Grandpa.

"Fencing. You know, swords and stuff."

"Is she that little thing you brought with you to the reunion?"

"That's the one, Grandpa. She thanked you for being a soldier and all."

"Yes, I remember now." There had been something about her, something that triggered some old memory, but he hadn't thought about it since that night.

"She said she was from France but I don't recall anything else." Grandpa turned his head so that he could see Dwight better. "Truth is, she is the spitting image of someone I ran into over there during the war, someone important. Couldn't be her, of course – Lord, that was seventy years ago – but there might be a connection we don't know about. Do you know exactly where she was from?"

"She said something about her birthplace; that she was born in the same village as some famous person. Want me to ask her?"

"Yes, and let me know."

"Sure, Grandpa," said Dwight. "Daddy, Joan asked George and me if we'd like to go see her at that tournament next week. Is that okay?"

"You know the rules so it's your decision, but it sounds like something different for you boys to see. If she's the only one on the team, she's going to need all the friends she can get."

Mid-year Report to the Attaché
MOST SECRET

Updated report as of March 10 on the progress of Jeanne Darcy. Jeanne continues as a student in the school where she began her studies on September 7 last after her father's acceptance of an academic position and subsequent relocation to this area. The overall adjustment has been excellent with the establishment of multiple personal friendships and, more importantly, a resumption of her fencing training under my supervision. Jeanne has also returned to tournament competition which has resulted in her undisputed domination of that sport in this region.

Her physical health is excellent but she continues to struggle with periodic emotional issues related to the events of last year. On the first anniversary of Chevaliere Catharine Darcy's death, Jeanne attended a Christmas Party but soon afterward realized what day it was and subsequently has demonstrated significant guilt as well as a period of depression and unexpressed grief.

Her intensity in fencing competition continues to be both a help and hindrance. She is the most brilliant student fencer I have ever seen, far beyond my own ability at her age. At present, she competes with a ferocity that sooner or later may become a weakness opponents will use against her, but she also is growing daily in dedication and compassion for those she considers friends and family. She continues to excel in her studies, especially French, and as we conduct her language classes only in French this appears to have a therapeutic effect.

There is a more significant environmental concern, however, over what appears to be the unstable behavior of the school's acting principal and the climate of fear that has developed at the school. Sport is now his defining focus and resources meant for academic development have been redirected to athletics with a total disregard for student needs. In addition, the direct family connection of the acting principal with the present Superintendent has caused a curtain to be drawn over internal practices and policies clearly not in the best interests of students. This individual is now the leading candidate to be named the next Superintendent if he meets three conditions: two State championships in Sport, and a minimum ten percent improvement in standardized test scores school-wide. One of these State championships has already been achieved and there is an estimated 80% probability of a second, thus completing two of the three conditions before the deadline of April 15.

However, the acting principal's redirection of State funds originally allocated for student improvement towards construction and expansion of a sports training facility. Given the circumstances under which these funds were misappropriated without outside protest, meaningful oversight of the school appears nonexistent. In addition, he means to subvert the testing system in order to submit scores significantly above those actually achieved by students.

If these three conditions are met by April 15 the acting principal will be promoted to Superintendent. If this happens then we must take urgent and immediate steps whereby Jeanne's training and education can continue elsewhere. If, however, she continues to progress at her current rate there is a strong possibility of completing all training before this becomes necessary.

Respectfully submitted
Catharine Renoir

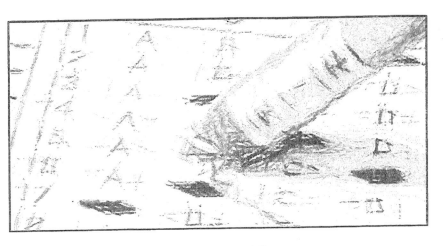

Chapter Twenty-Nine
I. Erasures

It was late Tuesday afternoon before the last testing envelopes were delivered, right as Gladys and Uncle Joe were leaving. Joe saw the envelopes and started to turn around but Gladys turned him right back around.

"There's a parent out here who wants to talk to you," she said, a surefire excuse and sure enough, Joe brightened up right away and brushed the imaginary dust off his lapel. "Always happy to talk to a parent," he said, so Gladys led him right through the door, into the parking lot, and into her car, the envelopes and parent already forgotten. Todd got out the sign he had already prepared and taped it to the door outside the Superintendent's office. He had already closed the blinds so with the door locked everything should be secure

About five minutes after the last of the buses was pulling away Ryan knocked at the office door and Todd let him in.

"Right on time, Ryan. Here are some cold sodas and a big bag of Fritos for you in case you get hungry," said Todd. "We'll get started in about five minutes."

"Thanks, Mr. Todd. Fritos are my favorite," said Ryan, and from the way the chips disappeared Todd was sure they'd be gone before the two of them were halfway finished with the papers.

The test had two hundred questions but it was the last fifty that were being missed most often. A quick scan of the first few papers resulted in scores of between forty and fifty percent, within a few points of the previous year. Todd found that if he started at question 150, erased every answer through question 190 and then bubbled in all the correct answers, the resulting score would come out somewhere between sixty and seventy percent for a sizable improvement.

Ryan's system soon resulted in a backlog of papers, but at the same time, Todd had started to memorize the list of answers so that by the end of the first hour they were keeping pace with each other. One thing about this batch of the mineral supplement is that a little went a long way, but Todd knew that to keep up this pace he needed more than usual. His daily dose had grown to two bottles, one at each end of the day, but today he added one more at lunch to be ready for this job.

Two hours later Ryan said "Here's the last one, Mr. Todd. That's all of them," as he checked off the last name on the list. They had been hard at it since a quarter to four, the work more than a bit tedious, the envelopes stuffed almost to overflowing and the scan sheets facing every which way. The tests were on paper, so each student had a test booklet and a scan sheet, and since everyone had been anxious to get it over with the papers were all mixed together. After sorting each envelope by putting the tests into one pile and the answer sheets into another, it was easier to go through the papers and figure out if that student's name was on the list. When he found one, Ryan put a checkmark next to the name and handed the paper to Todd, who was working behind a study carrel so that Ryan could not see exactly what he was doing.

The last paper was finished a minute later, and as soon as it was back in the envelope Todd sealed it with the special tape the State provided and signed Uncle Joe's name across the flap. Todd then inked the official district seal, stamped the envelope, and it was one down, twenty-four to go. The procedure was repeated for each, and the whole batch was sealed up and inside the safe by 7:05. It was as easy as pie, and Todd pulled a twenty-dollar bill from his pocket and handed it to Ryan.

"Ryan, I have to hand it to you. You did a great job of reading those names, and those students will now be in much better shape thanks to you. Now, remember your promise. I'm trusting you."

Ryan folded the money carefully and put it into his pocket. "Yes, Sir, I remember. I keep my promises."

"One more thing, Ryan. If you forget and break your promise, well, those students will feel ashamed and, well, you won't be allowed to work here anymore. What's more, that paper you signed at the beginning was your agreement to keep everything secret. If you do tell you could go to jail."

Ryan hadn't signed any such paper, but he would hear what Todd had said and consider it the truth. It was so easy to plant a memory in this kid that it wasn't funny, but it sure was useful.

Ryan's phone rang and the text message read

HI BUD IN FRONT OF THE SCHOOL LETS GO GET SOME DINNER PAPA

Todd opened the office door and took Ryan down to the front entrance where Mr. Kershaw was waiting, and he knew that he'd better provide some story in case Ryan forgot.

"Ryan's been doing a great job here at the school, Mr. Chenier. We were busy today but we got everything finished, thanks to Ryan. He also got his pay for the past week's work through tonight. He's developing some good job skills, aren't you Ryan?"

140

"I'm good at the tests," said Ryan, beaming at the compliment, and Todd almost lost it until he saw Mr. Chenier looking grateful.

"Well, Ryan sure loves working here, Mr. Todd," said Mr. Chenier. "We wish he still had a band to play in. He sure misses it and Mr. Landry."

"Yes, we all miss Mr. Landry," replied Todd, "but he insisted it was time to retire."

"Well, thanks a lot, Mr. Martin. Have a nice evening," said Mr. Chenier, and in a minute the red tail lights turned the corner onto the main road and were gone.

Two down and one to go, thought Todd as he climbed into the truck. Just so Christine pulls it off, and one more ace in the hole if she doesn't. Funny they would ask about Landry - as a matter of fact, after Mr. Landry's forced resignation nobody had seen him at all. Here one day, gone tomorrow, and now we have a nice big training room instead. Todd pulled out his phone and checked his calendar for Saturday. Rose had added the playoff game for Friday night, but so far Saturday was open. Maybe I'd better get to this state fencing tournament to make sure. Just in case.

II. Preparations
Basketball

When the girls' basketball Team arrived at their hotel in the State Capital, they had originally planned to take in a few of the sights before heading off to the University Gym for their designated practice time. When Coach Anita came back from registration, however, the sightseeing tour was canceled so that the girls could huddle in her hotel room and watch the few DVDs of their primary opponent. So many schools had closed and consolidated across the state that there was only a handful still rated AA, and their opponent was from a tiny town called Hamilton in the far north of the state that the girls had only read about in American History class as being in the center of the Dust Bowl. Their first reaction was predictable: little town equals little high school equals little team. It might have been funny it weren't for the fact that it also described Smithfield.

The shock came when they saw who their opponents were. Hamilton might be a town with a high school and a team, but one thing it was not anymore was little. A little high school maybe, but not a little team. Hamilton had recently developed a very diverse population due to the brand new FinnTech data center in a joint venture with Kenya Scientific. Forty-three families from Finland and Kenya had moved to the town to run the data center, and almost all their children were not only athletic but unusually tall. They totally transformed high school sports in that part of the state, and they were winning the championships to prove it. It was all so new and their league was so small that they were totally off everyone's radar until they popped up from out of nowhere to dominate athletics in their region. The selection process being what it was, based on a complicated system of points scored, individual player stats, and point spread per game, they were paired up against Smithfield for the championship.

141

Lisa had managed to get a copy of the program for that evening's game. Everybody's stats were there including their own, but what she read about the Hamilton team gave her the shivers.

"They average five feet eleven to our five feet six," she wailed, "and they've got one who's six feet five! How on earth are we going to deal with that? Four out of five of those people are going to be a full head taller than any of us!"

"We deal with it like we deal with everyone else," said Christine. "First thing we have to do is to see these girls face to face. During open practice this afternoon, I'll sit in the stands and get those ladies analyzed so we have something to work with. Meanwhile, I'm hungry."

Two hours later the two teams were in an arena bigger than either team had ever seen, and Christine was perched up in the twentieth row with her clipboard and binoculars. She had tried to make it through the day without any of the strawberry milk but the jitters were coming back worse than ever, especially since she had been sitting all day. It would have helped to get onto the floor and get her muscles moving but there wasn't time to do that and gather the information they needed if they were going to have a fighting chance. She glanced over to the bleachers above her own team where the only person sitting was Coach Anita. Guess we're not that scary, Christine thought. No need to check on little old Smithfield, since all that Hamilton needs to do is hold the ball up just a little higher.

Hold the ball up a little higher? Maybe *really* high, for longer than they're used to? Being tall isn't always an advantage. Christine had seen old College basketball movies on YouTube and one immediately came to mind. A player named Monte Towe had made first-string at NC State, probably the biggest basketball college in the country outside of Indiana, and he was all of five feet seven inches tall. The video showed him like a little dog barking at the feet of players more than a foot taller, which also meant that when he did have the ball his opponents were literally too far above him to work effectively. Maybe if she could combine her team' sizes to get the right proportion or even mix them up, Hamilton couldn't make the adjustments in time.

At the end of the practice, Christine had been able to draw up the rough outline of a strategy that at least would keep her team in the running. It was lucky that the girls had been used to her crazy ideas and had learned to give them a chance to see what happened, and it also didn't hurt that they had made it to the finals and no matter what happened they were behind her. As Christine trotted down the bleachers to join the team for dinner, the game due to get underway in two hours, she patted her pocket to make sure there was still one bottle of strawberry milk left, enough for tonight, then she could leave it alone whatever happened.

III. Fencing

Back in Smithfield Joan was in the fight of her life as Miss Renoir kept her on the defensive, relentlessly pushing her further and further back until some primal fury started to move her back the other direction. Except for wrestling, no other sport pits one athlete against another so relentlessly as fencing, and unlike wrestling, brute force doesn't help. When the tip of the foil is whipping at a couple hundred miles an hour past your face like an angry hornet trying to sting you right on the nose, your motivation for avoiding the sting becomes all mixed up with the fact that you are both trying to sting each other. This fight was different than anything Joan had experienced because Miss Renoir was not only in great shape but had a ridiculously efficient level of control. Joan simply could not read her the same way she had read all the others.

But she was getting steadily better. Miss Renoir insisted they keep score, the first time they had done so in all their practices together. For their first two matches, Joan had not scored a single point, something that had never happened to her before. Before the third match started, Miss Renoir had her stop, step off the runway, and the two of them go through Joan's warmup exercise again. Except for this time, Miss Renoir started out so slowly that despite herself Joan was reminded of the Banana Slugs she had seen in the bayou. At the time, she thought they were ridiculously slow until Miss Renoir showed her how exquisitely graceful they were. Joan slowed her breathing intentionally to match that of her teacher, and within a few seconds found that yes, she was moving more smoothly and the little tremors she usually had at this speed had disappeared entirely.

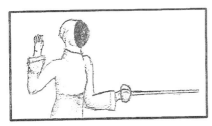 By the end of the exercise, something brand new had happened. Joan found herself much calmer during the match and there was also a liquid energy underneath all of it. She could pace her breathing, too, like a well-tuned sports car waiting for the driver to punch the gas pedal. As Miss Renoir was watching Joan adapt herself, she saw the Panther slowly emerge and takes its place behind Joan's eyes.

When they both stepped back onto the runway Miss Renoir could sense the difference. There was now a sinuousness to the way Joan moved, an economy of motion that belied the control that enabled it. This was going to be interesting, Miss Renoir thought.

"Prepare!" The two snapped their visors into place and took their positions, and then Joan did something completely unexpected. She nodded to Miss Renoir, steady, respectful, an acknowledgment. In all the matches in which her coach had seen Joan participate, she had never done this before. In a far corner of Miss Renoir's memory an old image appeared, something from a movie about the Roman Empire, gladiators lined up in the coliseum…

"En Garde," said Joan, and Miss Renoir launched into her main attack, except…it wasn't working. Joan was not responding the way she had five minutes before but was now using her torso and legs as much a weapon as her foil, the three in coordination so that the attack fell on empty air, but the motions faster than…is she watching me? thought Miss Renoir, and the tip of Joan's foil was bent against her shoulder. One zero. Joan has scored the first point like taking candy from a baby, and if I were to try and describe what happened I would not have the words.

Over the next three minutes, Miss Renoir had the fight of her life, trying every stratagem she had ever remembered or heard about and having about as much success as stirring an empty bowl. She did score one point on an abrupt lunge, but the next time she tried that Joan had not only anticipated the move but countered it exquisitely, scoring a touch without even moving her feet. By the time the match was over at 5-1, Miss Renoir was exhausted, but even more surprised when Joan came and wrapped her arms around her teacher.

"I'm sorry," said Joan. "Are you okay?"

Miss Renoir took hold of both Joan's shoulders and held her gently at arms' length. "You vanquish me like a professional, then apologize and ask if I am well." She suddenly leaned forward and kissed Joan on each check in the traditional French way after bestowing a medal.

"Oui, Jeannette, I am well. I am very, very well, and I am so proud of you."

"Do you think I'm ready?" asked Joan.

"Mais oui!" answered Miss Renoir.

On Thursday afternoon, immediately after school, two vans pulled up to the front of the school and the group of students who had been waiting inside the main entrance came out carrying suitcases and sleeping bags, followed by Brian in his wheelchair. Mr. Granger, Brian's dad, popped open the side of the van and in a minute Brian was all set.

"We sure wish Ryan could come along," said Dwight as he tossed his things into the back and climbed in, followed closely by George.

"We asked," said Brian, "but he's got some big thing at his church on Saturday." He looked over his shoulder into the back where the boys had gotten comfortable and Dwight had already opened a bag of Doritos. At the other van, Michelle and Joan had already loaded their things into the back and hopped in.

"If this is it, let's get the show on the road," said Papa, and Miss Renoir put the van in gear and headed down the driveway.

"About four hours, right?" asked Michelle.

Joan nodded. "Except for the game," answered Joan, looking at her phone. "It's three o'clock now and the girls' basketball tournament final starts at four thirty, so they'll be finishing up right about the time we arrive."

About an hour later Joan and Michelle had finished a game of cards and the last light of the day was fading. The road was straight and long and boring, the

144

van rocking gently, and the heater making everything cozy inside. Joan had tried to read but there was enough motion to the car that she started to feel carsick so she put it away and looked over at her friend. Michelle, unaffected by the motion, was deep into her own book so Joan decided to close her eyes for a few minutes. She had been practicing hard for the tournament and was thrilled that her friends were going to be there and finally see what all the fuss was about.

The motion of the car bumping gently against a parking divider caused it to rock enough that Joan woke up. She was feeling stiff from her position in the car seat, but a few stretches of her neck and walking would clear that up.

"How's the game?" she asked Miss Renoir as they emptied their suitcases from the van.

"We saw you were asleep so we never turned it on," she replied as the van belonging to Brian's father pulled into the empty parking spot beside them.

"I'm sure Brian will know," Joan said, and went over to the other van. The back door slid aside and Dwight hopped out.

"Just in ti..." Joan started to say but something about Dwight's expression stopped her in mid-sentence.

"You guys listen to the game?" asked Dwight, a grim look on his face. "There was an injury in the fourth quarter, a real bad one."

Joan felt her face go numb. "Who?"

"Christine," answered George. "Broken leg, probably a compound fracture. They took her to the hospital."

"And?" interjected Michelle.

"We lost," replied Brian bitterly, rolling up in his wheelchair. "56-51. We were ahead 51-44 until the accident, and then the other team ran away with the game."

"Is Christine going to be okay?" asked Joan.

"We don't know," replied Dwight.

Chapter Thirty
A String of Disasters

As Coach Anita sat on the long sofa in the hospital waiting room with the rest of the team, Christine had already been in surgery for an hour. Most of the girls had finally stopped crying except for Stephanie, whose face was still streaked by the occasional teardrop. Most of the team parents were there, too, forming small clusters and talking quietly or doing something on their phones. Christine's Mom had been listening to the game on the radio when the accident happened, and Coach Anita had promised to call with regular updates and the results of the surgery when it was all over.

When they took Christine into surgery the nurse had told Coach Anita that Christine had been stabilized, but that it was too soon to tell how well they were going to be able to piece everything back together. Anita had been through emergencies before, including getting a broken leg herself in high school soccer eighteen years before. The hard floor of a basketball court was more unforgiving than grass, however, and she knew she would never, ever forget the sound made by the bone as it broke.

The game had been going much better than expected, with the Smithfield girls adopting the approach that Christine worked out. Their strategy forced Hamilton to hold the ball far above their heads whenever they weren't dribbling, and although Hamilton had jumped out to an 18-9 lead by the end of the first quarter, Anita could tell that there were some sore arms on that team. The problem was that there were sore legs on the Smithfield team, too, and the simple fact that their opponent's legs were longer meant that her girls had to go three steps to their opponent's two.

All this takes a toll and by the half, the Smithfield girls were exhausted - which brought something back to mind that didn't make any sense. The Smithfield girls were exhausted, all right, all except Christine who was so full of energy that she was pacing up and down in the locker room while her teammates were stretched out on the changing benches. Some of the girls had even gotten annoyed to the point that they yelled at Christine to sit down, but even after that, she was still a bundle of nerves.

Or something else. Anita suddenly realized. During college, she had done some volunteer work at a local rehab center to get the experience, and Anita remembered seeing some high school girls in the emergency room who had too much energy to sit still and were pacing up and down like Christine. Those girls were all showing withdrawal symptoms and when they crashed, they crashed, hard, sometimes in mid-stride. Anita looked around the room at the other girls, sure that some of them had brought their team bags out of sheer habit.

"Did anyone bring Christine's bag?"

"I did!" called out Stephanie from the other side of the room, holding up a bag the same size and shape as the others except with a large picture of a Pirate on the side.

As she opened it, Anita saw the usual jumble of casual clothes along with two extra uniforms, a crumpled magazine, and a plastic bottle partially full of a pink liquid which she took out and held up to the light. There was a label on the side with no title but a checklist of vitamins and minerals. Anita screwed open the cap and sniffed. Smells like strawberry, sure enough, but there's something else there.

"Any of you know where this came from?" called Anita, holding out the bottle.

"Training room," said Bobbi. "The trainer said Christine needed some extra vitamins or something. Same thing every week."

The others came up and looked at the bottle. "Christine finished this off right before we left for breakfast this morning," Lisa said. "At least I thought she did. This must be another one."

"Anybody else get one of these?" Anita asked. Everyone on the team shook their heads. Anita opened the cap and sniffed again, more delicately this time. Something's not right. The waiting room door opened and the doctor came back in, her mask still in place.

146

"We finished the major part of the surgery," she said. "The femur is broken but not completely, but given the location of the injury, we had to put in a metal plate to make sure it holds together. The fall and impact on the floor did more damage to her knee, however. Not as dramatic looking at the crack but with the possibility of long term complication. Christine tore her anterior cruciate ligament – that's the one that helps your knee lock into place when you stand up. It will heal over time but chances are she'll always have some trouble with that knee."

"Long term?" asked Anita.

"Probably no more basketball," said the doctor. "At least not for a while. The good thing is that she's still growing. The biggest issue is that if she tears it again she'll have bigger problems. I've heard of basketball players who damaged their ACL once and went back onto the court six months later. I've also heard of basketball players who went back a year later and promptly tore it again. That ended their playing careers, period."

When the team had come back onto the court for the second half, there was an entirely new focus. Smithfield had modified its overall approach, keeping the ball much closer to the floor with very short, rapid dribbles and low, quick bounce passes. The Hamilton team was relying on its own strategy of holding onto the ball longer, but without much success since their possessions also dropped. The score seesawed back and forth until Smithfield was ahead 43-39 going into the final quarter. The game had gotten rougher as well: Lisa had fouled out and both Bobbi and Stephanie had two, including a rather nasty bump on Stephanie's head from an elbow hit that the referee claimed not to have seen.

Christine was everywhere at once, the squeak of her sneakers a constant sound as she grew more and more adept at steals, taking advantage of her ability to run low and hard far below the normal reach of her opponents. She scored twice and fired one to Lisa bringing the tally up to 51-42, but three seconds after Lisa scored a Hamilton girl made a nasty comment behind her back and Lisa's temper finally broke, pushing the Hamilton player and getting herself thrown out of the game. There was a lot of grief from the Hamilton bench during the timeout and the referees gave both teams a warning to tone it down, but the mood was getting increasingly ugly. During the timeout, Christine called for the chewing gum play to get a few more points on the board before Hamilton figured out their strategy. As they went back onto the floor two Hamilton players put their heads together for a few seconds, nodded, and got into formation on their side of the key.

The Hamilton player made both of her foul shots, and as the second came onto the floor Smithfield had the ball to bring in at mid-court. Stephanie was confronted by two of the Hamilton players waving their arms so that she couldn't find a spot to pass it in, but abruptly they stopped long enough to give her an opening, firing the ball directly at Christine but much lower than she was used to. Christine dashed forward to retrieve it, scooped up the ball, and had just turned to shoot when it happened. Two of the other Hamilton players had anticipated the pass to Christine and had positioned themselves so that when she turned to shoot they would be directly over her, their arms extended much higher than she could shoot. She was already in mid jump, however, that meant when she completed her twist she ran directly into a maze of arms blocking her way. Since the players were so close, Christine twisted away but still ran into the outstretched arms, changing her direction like a reverse ricochet. She slammed backward onto the floor, her legs both twisted under her and knocking over one of the Hamilton players, who then fell onto Christine's extended right leg.

There was a crack that could be heard across the court as the leg broke above the knee, along with a scream of agony from Christine that grew worse as the Hamilton player thrashed around in her own attempt to get up. Anita rushed out onto the floor along with Lisa, who took one look at Christine's leg.

"Fracture. Real bad one, too. Make sure the EMT's check for internal bleeding."

If it had been any other time Coach Anita would have given Lisa a hug or at least a pat on the back, but the sight of Christine writhing on the floor was enough for one day, or one coaching career for that matter. A week later when they were sitting in the ambulance with Christine on her way home, Anita asked Lisa how she knew what to do.

"Unlike some people, I am NOT a city girl," Lisa said. "Remember - I've lived on a ranch my whole life, a real one with cattle, Brahma bulls, and some real mean horses. I've seen my share of breaks, sprains, kicks, you name it – even saw one guy gored by a longhorn. The guy lived but, well, we had that longhorn for a barbecue the next week."

Christine laughed, but it was more groan than ha ha. It was almost the only sound she made the whole trip back home

Todd pushed the truck up to 85 miles an hour on Friday morning, every few minutes slamming his hands against the steering wheel in sheer frustration. He'd been there when Christine was hurt and knew there was no way for the girls to pull this one out of the fire. Christine was real popular, sure, but the Hamilton players were too big and the Smithfield girls too distracted to do anything more than a halfhearted defense. At the final buzzer, the score was 56-51, and half of the hometown crowd was already in their cars on their way home.

The irony of it was he'd gotten the preliminary test scores later that night, using the Superintendent's special access to the State Department of Education, and they were everything he dreamed of. Like he hoped, every one of those one hundred and sixty-seven students showed a significant improvement over the previous test, with two of them even getting perfect scores for good measure.

Except I'm the one with a problem right now, and I do not like it. One championship is still one championship, not two, and the deal was for better test scores and two championships. Everybody says this Joan kid is the greatest thing since sliced bread when it comes to fencing, and if she's already rated number one in the whole state the odds must be great.

148

As far as Christine goes, well with all I did for that kid by hiring her dad, just look what she did to me. The extra three hundred dollars a week just stopped, kiddo, and maybe I'll drop a hint like I did for Coach Reed and have them pay a visit to Anita's office for good measure.

Todd looked at the clock on the truck radio – 9:10 and a hundred forty more miles to go. Nice that there was a cozy room waiting for him at the other end, but he still didn't feel sleepy even though he'd been awake since 4:00 that morning. No appetite, either, but heck there's hardly any traffic and no need to stop for anything to eat. Todd reached into the cooler on the seat beside him where he had his own little stash of apple juice bottles that he'd specially prepared for the trip. A dozen more were in the bigger cooler in the back, and that should be enough to last until Sunday.

The two vans pulled into the big parking lot beside University Gymnasium and found parking without any problem. The school was out for Spring break, but there were at least three State finals going on, fencing enormously overshadowed by the State Wrestling Tournament on the lower level. As the group unloaded they could see other students walking toward the gym carrying fencing gear.

That morning's positive news about Christine's eventual recovery cheered them up enough so that everybody had a good breakfast at the Egg and I Restaurant across the street from the motel. Although Joan was worried about Christine, the fact that her friends came all this way in her support made her resolve to do her best. During breakfast, George said that one of his relatives talked about someone named Gipper that she was supposed to win one for, but he couldn't remember any of the little details like who Gipper was or even what sport he was talking about.

"Never heard of a fencer named Gipper," said Joan. "Is he from around here?"

"I think he died," said George. "The Coach talked all about him, though."

"What coach?" asked Michelle.

"Coach in the movie, I guess," replied George. "I didn't see the whole thing."

"Name of Rockne," said Dr. Darcy. "Ever heard of him?"

"Did he fence?" asked Miss Renoir.

"Sort of," replied Dr. Darcy, doing his best not to laugh. "I'll tell you about it on the way home."

The fencing tournament room was the same room the university used for big receptions and major events like Prom and Homecoming dances as well as sporting events. Four runways were in place, one at each corner of the room, each with its own group of spectator chairs, along with a small separate restricted area for participants and coaches. There was a concession stand with tables and chairs, and as they started to get their bearings Joan saw a table with a CHECK IN sign taped on the side.

"I guess you guys can wait here until we find out where to go," said Joan. "Guys, I appreciate you being here. It's the first time any of my friends ever came to one of these things."

"I beg your pardon?" exclaimed Michelle.

To Michelle's astonishment, Joan walked up and gave her a hug. "As far as I'm concerned, Michelle, your family."

As Joan and Miss Renoir made their way to the registration table, all over the room conversations ceased and heads turned. Some of the students already in fencing gear watched, and for fun Joan stared full bore at one small group that she recognized from three weeks before. Two of the kids turned white and another one ran for a trash can.

"Stop that," said Miss Renoir.

"Okay," said Joan, and grinned as they got to the table.

Fifteen minutes later the group was situated at Quad One, Joan and Miss Renoir off to the side, with Michelle, Brian, the twins in the front row of the spectator section and Joan's Papa one row behind. Joan's first opponent came up to the participant area, but before they could sit down Joan went over to shake hands and introduce herself, and the two competitors chatted for a moment.

"Good luck," she said and went back to her seat.

"Does it feel okay to do that?" whispered Miss Renoir.

"As a matter of fact, it does," replied Joan. "Name's Thomas Gooding. Went against him the first week of November, I think."

The referee stepped up to the runway, and Joan and Thomas went to their assigned spots and hooked up. Joan had a brand-new foil but was still using her favorite grip, so except for a slight difference in flexibility it still felt like an extension of her arm. Back at the bench, Brian was looking through the program that Michelle had picked up that listed everyone's ranking, wins, losses, and other vital information.

"This Thomas guy's season score is 185 to 44. What the heck does that mean?" asked Brian.

"He's made 185 points this season, losing 44 points to his opponents," replied Michelle. "Like a batting average." She pointed to the top. "While you're at it, take a good look at Joan's scores."

"Are you kidding me?" he said in wonder and held out the program to show the twins. "226 to 5. That's over...forty matches."

"Forty-eight, actually," said Michelle. "Now quiet down and watch."

The referee started the match and there was an immediate and violent clash as Thomas launched himself at Joan, who took one step back and then thrust herself forward, locking foils with Thomas, masks almost touching.

"How are you these days, Thomas?" she asked through the mask.

"Not bad," answered Thomas, gritting his teeth.

The two disengaged, stepped back and began again. This time Joan deliberately took two abrupt steps back as Thomas charged, throwing himself too far forward and losing his balance long enough for Joan to get a touch on his left shoulder. Thomas shook himself and stomped back to his position while

Joan slashed the air twice with her foil and stepped back into her own. She stretched her neck once, turned slowly, took a deep breath, and the panther emerged.

Dwight said something under his breath. "You'll have to confess that," said George.

Dwight nodded. "Remind me never to make her mad."

When the next round started, Thomas launched himself forward exactly like before, but Joan had taken one step back this time, her head lowered almost like she was bowing to her opponent, at which Thomas scored a ridiculously easy touch without even crossing foils. Joan stood up slowly, still staring at her opponent, then nodded slightly and returned to her place.

"I do not get this at all," said Brian. "First, she demolishes that guy in about two seconds, then she steps back and he gets his point without even trying. What is going on?"

Michelle grinned and hoped she was right. "She's reading him," Michelle said. "Watching how he moves, how his arms and legs work or don't work together. She's cataloging all of it in her head so she knows how to meet him."

As Brian watched what happened next, he not only knew Michelle was right but he saw some of what Joan saw. Like Joan, Brian had been an athlete starting as a kid and before the accident had nearly as many hours of practice as Joan. It was no surprise when the match was over about ninety seconds later with Joan on top 5-1. When she scored her final point, she took off her mask, went over to Thomas, and reached out her hand.

"Great match," she said. "You know, if you lift your left shoulder further back it should help you recover more easily."

"And why are you telling me this?" asked Thomas.

"Why not? No trick, only something I noticed," replied Joan. "Good luck with the rest of the tournament."

Wait a minute, Thomas thought. This is the female tiger, the predator half the people here are petrified of, the best fencer in the whole state. She beat me, so why should she lie?

"Thanks, Joan. Same to you. Go get that trophy!"

When Joan came back to her seat Miss Renoir was staring at her. "Now how hard was that?" she asked.

"Not hard," replied Joan. "Did you hear what he said?"

"'Go get that trophy'," replied Miss Renoir. "Any opponent ever say something like that before?"

"Never," replied Joan quietly. "I mean, I probably have more in common with these people than almost anybody else I know. They're not enemies."

"That doesn't mean you go into this halfway either," said Miss Renoir seriously. "That's not showing them respect. If you beat them and then give them some tips how to do better, they might turn around and beat you someday but they'll respect you a heck of a lot more."

Over the course of the next four hours Joan's friends followed her from grid to grid as participants were eliminated at the lower levels, so by the time she won

151

her 4th match there were only 8 competitors remaining. As the competition moved up the ladder, however, the experience of her opponents began to show as well as her fatigue. At this tournament, she was the one to beat, the only girl to be so highly rated and thus the target for everybody with dreams of fencing glory. She had won her last match by a score of 5-2, and after shaking hands with her opponent he was met by some of the other fencers coming up to congratulate him for the tremendous feat of scoring two touches against her, the first competitor all day to do so.

Since it was going to be at least another 45 minutes until she was up again, Joan and Michelle wandered over to the snack bar run by a campus group, where each purchased a muffin, an apple, and a small container of Greek yogurt for lunch. As they sat down at one of the tables in the food area, Michelle happened to glance over at the main doorway where a tall, florid man in a dark blue suit had entered.

"Don't look now and don't turn around," whispered Michelle.

Joan kept eating but followed her friend's advice. "Who is it?" she whispered.

"Wait." Michelle held up three fingers and began a countdown. "Three, two, one..."

"WHERE'S MY GIRL?" boomed out across the room, disrupting at least three matches and causing several coaches and two referees to have a mild hemorrhage? Michelle beamed at the others, who if they were holding anything at that moment they would have thrown it at her.

"Why is he here?" asked Joan. "It's not like he knows I exist or anything."

"If he said, 'where's my girl' I can't imagine he's looking for anybody but you," said Michelle. "Why else would he be here?"

The speaker came on to announce positions for the next round, and the two girls took a last quick bite and headed for the appointed quadrant. By this far into the tournament, there was a much larger group of spectators, many of them coaches and participants who had finished up earlier and were waiting to see Joan. She had become a minor celebrity but the unusually chivalrous way she talked with her opponents had brought more than a few to her side. There was some scattered applause as she came into the quadrant with Michelle, and both girls were relieved to see that Mr. Todd wasn't yet seated nearby.

Dwight called Michelle over to his seat. "Did you guys see who was here?" he asked, looking over his shoulder. "After making so much noise they almost kicked him out, but he showed his ID and I guess they let him stay."

Michelle nodded. "We heard him like everybody else in here," she said. "We don't have any idea why he's here, but I'm guessing he wants everybody to think he's Joan's number one fan."

"I guess I wasn't supposed to know about it," said George, "but there's something else going on. Last night we had Mr. Augustine and Mr. Austin over for dinner – they're the other members of the School Board along with Dad and Grandpa. I got hungry again about seven thirty and when I went back into the kitchen, the door to the dining room wasn't completely closed."

"They were having a big argument about Mr. Todd and whether he's qualified to be the next Superintendent. Apparently, Superintendent Joe is retiring or sick or something, and Mrs. Donner and Mr. Todd were the two candidates to replace him. Now that Mrs. Donner is going to be an Assistant Principal at Garland next year, Mr. Todd's the only candidate left."

"Why didn't they go out and advertise the job?" asked Michelle.

"That's the weird thing," George answered. "A Martin has been superintendent ever since 1925, and those two guys want to keep it that way. Got real pushy about it, too, like if they don't make Mr. Todd the Superintendent it will be the last straw and they'll shut us down for good and start sending everybody to Garland. Dad and Grandpa both argued that if they made Todd the superintendent he would screw things up so bad they'd shut us down for sure."

Michelle sensed that George knew something else. "So, what's this plan they were talking about? You're still not saying."

George sighed. "It's the weirdest thing I ever heard. Mrs. Donner and Mr. Todd were having a contest against each other, something to do with better test scores and all that, except Mr. Todd, who was told that if he had two State sports Championships and better test scores it would be enough to give him the job regardless. Mr. Augustine said they'd gotten in the test scores and they were the best Smithfield's ever had, and Mr. Austin said that Mr. Todd already got one championship with the Volleyball team. At that point, the basketball team looked like they were going to do it, too."

"Except they didn't," said Michelle. "We're safe, right?"

George shook his head and sighed. "All he needs is one more championship. Look where we are, and look who is sitting over there. Our buddy there is Mr. Todd's ticket to being the next Superintendent. All she has to do is win."

Joan had taken her place on the runway along with her opponent. While the referee was talking, Todd slipped into a chair in the back row of the quad, and a second later the match started. Joan was at the top of her game, the extra practice paying off in an iron-hard stamina. Her opponent lost three points in a row before showing a burst of energy to get one off Joan. It was his last one, and the match was over a minute later with Joan on top 5-1, her friends clapping and cheering along with the other spectators as they announced the results

After she had shaken her opponent's hand, Joan saw who was sitting in the back row.

"You must go and speak to him," said Miss Renoir. "He has come all this way to see you compete."

"He doesn't give a darn about me," replied Joan, gritting her teeth.

"Jeanne!" said Miss Renoir firmly. "Ten seconds, a hello and thank you for coming. That is all. You must do this as a gesture of respect." Jeanne, not Jeannette: that was a warning if there ever was one...but she could at least do this her own way.

Joan put on a bright smile and walked over to where Todd was sitting.

"Meester Todd, such pleasure zat you haf come to see me," she said in the same accent she used that first day in the hallway. "What a long drive you haf had."

"Thank you, little lady," Todd replied. "You win this thing, hear me?"

"Oh, I weel give it, how you say, ze old college try, yes?" said Joan. "Excuse moi, I must go. Again, merci. Merci beaucoup."

Joan ran back up to Miss Renoir. "Just like you said, I thanked him for coming and he told me to win this thing."

Miss Renoir looked closely at Joan, who wasn't exactly looking like she had done something distasteful, while two chairs away Michelle was holding her breath to keep from cracking up.

The referees called Joan and her opponent to the runway and the next match got under way. Unlike her previous opponent, this one was quite a bit taller and his longer reach made her work a great deal harder to keep out of his way. For the first time that day he scored the first touch, after which he made a YES pumping motion and bowed to the group of his fans who had gathered to watch the match.

Unfortunately, that proved to be his undoing as with those two simple gestures he revealed to Joan two distinct weaknesses. One, his right arm was somewhat muscle-bound to the degree that he had a limited range of motion toward the outside. Two, he was left-foot dominant which under the right conditions threw him enough off balance to expose him to an attack from his left side. Joan promptly took advantage of this to score three quick touches before he recovered enough to score one more time bringing the score to 3-2. He seemed to sense what Joan was doing so for the next round he changed his stance, slightly arching his back which threw off Joan's attack and allowed him to score one more touch on the rebound as his supporters applauded wildly.

The whole season nobody had ever tied Joan 3-3, and never had her strategies been so quickly unraveled by any of her opponents. This would not have been such a problem if her opponent were closer to her own size, but his advantage of eight inches in height also meant that his reach was a full six or seven inches longer than Joan's. If he simply stood and parried she would never be able to touch him at all. Joan remembered one lesson in which Miss Renoir had fenced on her knees, and what Joan had initially thought would be a pushover resulted in her being thoroughly trounced by her teacher, who could easily reach under Joan's attack.

That's it, thought Joan: use his height against him by getting closer and lower than he can reach. Joan had on occasion practiced running with her knees bent and found that with her slightly lower female center of gravity she maintained a good level of control from that height, a good six inches lower than normal, and with luck her opponent would not be able to compensate.

Sure enough, in the very next round he came at her from his usual height and was completely surprised when Joan suddenly got several inches shorter and neatly scored while his foil swished through empty air. Since she had also figured out that his strategy for the next move was based completely on what she

154

had done for the last round, Joan started the next round with a feint followed by straight in attack from his weaker right side, and the match was over 5-3.

"How the heck did you learn to do that?" he asked in a friendly way, shaking his head and laughing at himself.

"Helps to be short, I guess," she responded. "I thought you had me for a while, and this was the best match I've had all year. If you can strengthen that right arm extension you'll wipe the floor with me next time," said Joan, shaking his hand.

To her surprise, he reached out, took her right hand, and extended it upwards like she had won a boxing match, at which the whole group in the quad applauded. As she returned to her prep area Miss Renoir gave her a huge, warm hug followed by one from Papa.

"Jeannette, it is an honor to be with you here today," said Miss Renoir. "I say this in the best way: I wish I had been able to face you when I was your age, especially when you are acting the way you are today."

"Attention competitors," said the PA and the room grew quiet. "The final match for today's Championship tournament will take place in thirty minutes in the center runway, between Joan Darcy of Smithfield and Eric Larsson of Hamilton. In the meantime, please assist in moving the folding chairs to the center of the gymnasium. Thank you."

Dwight and George grabbed two folding chairs each and started to walk away when George had an idea. After a quick conversation with Brian, the twins folded up three chairs apiece and piled them neatly across the armrests of Brian's wheelchair, at which Brian rolled across to the center of the room where some of the other competitors unloaded and set them up again.

"Just goes to show you what I can do," said Brian, looking up at Michelle.

"Never doubted you," she replied, and surprised herself by leaning down and giving him a kiss on the top of his head, which she partially regretted immediately afterward when both Dwight and George started to say something but quickly stopped when she gave them a look that would have melted asphalt.

The whole group had set up headquarters in a small group of chairs two rows back and next to the aisle where Brian's wheelchair had easy access. Joan checked her equipment and sat down in the second row, stretching out to try and rest up a bit before the final. Todd had remained in the back rows, checking and rechecking his phone, every now and then taking a gulp from the apple juice bottle on the floor beside him.

"Hey, Michelle?" said George.

"Hey, what?"

"What did Joan talk to Mr. Todd about? I saw her go over to him about an hour ago."

"Just saying hi," Michelle replied, "and to thank him for coming today."

"What did he say?" asked George. "I mean, did he tell you anything?"

"He told Joan, 'you win now'. That's all."

"Yeah," replied George. "I'll bet he did."

Michelle was not getting this. "What's the point?"

"Well, Superintendent Joe Martin is going to resign, and, well, Mr. Todd is in line to be the next Superintendent...if certain things happen."

"Like what, for instance?"

"Like...all he needs is for Smithfield High School to have one more State Championship. He already got Volleyball and was expecting to get girls' basketball, but then Christine had her accident and that chance fell through."

"What's so bad about that?" asked Michelle.

"Where have you been this past year?" asked Brian bitterly. "How many times have you seen him out in the hallways, or coming into your classroom, or generally doing anything except staying in that big office of his or yelling at people? If you don't get the point, compare him to Mrs. Coates. Mrs. Coates, who loves kids, runs the best classes in the school, and would do about anything for anybody and at the same time keeps all of us in line without making us feel like complete idiots. You put a guy like him in charge, it goes right to his head. What qualifications does he have, anyhow?"

"His name," said Dwight, shaking his head.

"His what?" asked Michelle, still shaken.

"Martin," replied Dwight. "Joe Martin, Todd Martin, Grandpa Frank Martin, and a whole slew of Martins who have been principal or Superintendent here for the past seventy years," said Dwight. "My dad said Principal Joe was a great guy, out in the hallways all the time, knew everybody's name, even tutoring kids in his office sometimes! You have any idea how much loyalty that gets you?

Mr. Todd thinks he can let his Uncle Joe build all that up for him and then just slide into his shoes like they're his to begin with. Both Dad and Grandpa are against him being Superintendent, but the other two members of the school board think Joe Martin walks on water, and whatever Joe wants, he gets. Screwy rule of the School Board says that the Superintendent gets to vote on any promotion, so it's three to two and Mr. Todd's got what he wants."

The four friends were silent, each waiting for whoever was going to be the first to say the thing that was on everybody's mind.

"So, do we tell Joan?" asked Michelle. "I mean, this is her big chance."

"What would YOU do?" asked Brian. "To be the first in the whole state and only a freshman? Nobody's ever done that before!" He looked at Dwight and George. "You guys brought this whole thing up, so what's your take on it all?"

"Well, Dad and Grandpa are solid against it," said Dwight. "And supposedly Superintendent Joe is... over the edge. Alzheimer's, I guess."

"So maybe he doesn't vote and the whole thing's a wash anyhow and Joan gives up the championship for nothing," said Michelle. "This is her big chance and throwing the whole thing away on a maybe doesn't make sense."

At that moment, the announcer stepped to the microphone, and as Joan stepped out of the waiting area she got her first glimpse of her opponent and nearly stopped in her tracks. Eric Larsson was tall with a very athletic build, a great friendly smile, and an artificial leg. The way he stood and moved appeared perfectly natural, stepping and pivoting like anybody else except for a slight bounce whenever he stepped on his left foot. My God what it took to make it this far with that thing, Joan thought as she approached the referee, and here I am trying to beat him.

Chapter Thirty-One
The Final

Eric was long used to stares and it didn't bother him anymore. It also helped that he was also able to demolish most of his opponents, who very quickly forgot about his leg as they fought for their lives. It made him mad sometimes when it was suggested they were going to cut him some slack in their upcoming match. He had been fencing for three years when his leg started to act funny, and when the CT scan came back it was like a body blow: untreatable bone cancer of the fibula with associated lesions on the tibia, they called it. His parents had asked about radiation but the doctors had said unless they removed the leg right away there was an 80% probability of it spreading, so he had gone through the hell of walking on two legs to the hospital and coming out on crutches with one leg remaining.

For the first month of his initial recuperation, Eric searched online for the latest in athletic prosthetics and was amazed at both the variety and performance of the new designs. Based on use and movement instead of appearance, no one cared if it didn't look like a leg if it got you around as well. Within two months of coming home on crutches, he was taking his first tentative steps with his new leg. There was an exercise regimen he had worked out with both his physical therapist and his fencing coach, and as his balance and stamina came back he started to win matches again. That was two years ago, and by now the only thing his opponents thought about was how not to get beat.

So, this is Joan, Eric thought, the girl everybody was talking about, and he was surprised they had not crossed paths before.

"Pleased to meet you, Joan," said Eric as they shook hands. "Saw you looking at my leg, here."

Well, nothing like the direct approach, thought Joan. "It's neat. Does it work?"

"I'm here, so it must," replied Eric with a laugh. Well, part of what they say about her is true. Joan most definitely gets right to the point, whether with words or a foil. "Listen, because I have this thing I don't want you to try and do anything different. First, I don't need it because old Sparky here does me fine. Second, I fully intend to whip your butt so you'd better try to whip mine first. Got it?"

"Got it," said Joan, laughing, as they shook hands. This will definitely be one to remember.

From his seat at the back of the room Todd reached down to the floor for his bottle of apple juice. For several weeks he had been needing more and more of the Mineral Supplement and when he skipped a bottle he had tremors in both hands. Things hadn't quite reached that point yet today, but when he didn't find the bottle he turned to see if it had rolled under his chair. It hadn't, and he knew

157

that the missing bottle was the last one he had brought with him into the building. Up at the front of the room, the referee was ready to start the match, however, so with luck, the tournament would be over within a few minutes, the championship trophy in his hands, and he could renew his supply before heading home.

From the very first Joan knew that Eric was the best fencer she had ever faced except for Mama or Miss Renoir, and he had a much greater motivation for – in his words – kicking her butt. It felt very peculiar reacting to his stance, the spring of his foot giving extra speed to his lunges that at times she felt like she was going up against a very large jackrabbit.

After thirty seconds neither had scored and both were beginning to show signs of fatigue. Fencing matches are usually over quickly, and participants seldom need to significantly pace themselves to get through a match. Today, however, Joan's calf muscles were on the edge of locking up and at the first sign of hesitation Eric scored. Joan followed with a very aggressive attack and to her surprise, he appeared to have the same issues she did, where changing from forward to reverse altered balance and control. There was another intense exchange and Joan abruptly tried the "short" approach she had used in the quarter-finals, Eric overreached and she scored. The timer stood at 1:15 and the score was tied with both beginning to sweat.

"You're *good*, Eric!" panted Joan.

"Look who's talking," Eric responded.

The next exchange was measured more in miles traveled than in points scored, with both Joan and Eric making attacks and retreats without scoring. In a sport where both competitors were used to defeating opponents in thirty or forty seconds of actual contact, an exchange of this duration was unknown. With less than a minute to go sheer exhaustion was slowing their reaction time, so mistakes that otherwise would have spelled the end for one or the other became one more missed opportunity. At the three-minute buzzer, the score stood at 1-1, something that had never happened to either one of them before.

Both Eric and Joan went back to their respective coaches, took off their face guards and had a quick drink.

"He's *good*," said Joan, trying to catch her breath.

Miss Renoir nodded. "He earned every point, like you, and to do what he has done after what happened to him is nothing short of a miracle." She looked Joan right in the eye. "He had bone cancer. That's why the amputation. He fought his way back here with heart and hard work."

"Are you saying I should let him win?" asked Joan hesitantly. "I...he doesn't want that. He wants to do it fair and square. I owe him that."

Joan had never seen her teacher so radiantly proud, and strangely enough, it made her feel humble.

"This is your decision, Jeannette. I will honor whatever you decide."

The referees called both Joan and Eric back to the front and the room grew quiet.

"Ladies and gentlemen, the ending of a match with a tie of this kind has not happened before in the history of our tournament. We have found these two competitors so evenly matched that we are going to offer them two choices. The first, to declare the competition a draw and consider both to be co-champions. The second, to continue the competition and award the championship to whoever scores the next point. Competitors, please take a moment to consider your decision."

Despite everything, Joan knew what she wanted, and as she looked over at Eric knew that he didn't want to end it here, like this, with nothing actually decided.

"You thinking what I'm thinking?" asked Joan.

"It's like neither of us will ever know unless we do," said Eric. "Let's finish this."

Joan reached over and shook Eric's hand, then they both turned to the judges.

"One more point," said Eric, and Joan nodded in agreement.

They took their places and the entire room grew silent. Each nodded and snapped down their visors, and for many in the audience, it was for all the world like two knights about to begin a duel to the death. The referee took his place and the round began.

There was a fierce exchange from which many in the audience expected at least one of them to score but it was also like two slightly mismatched twins as they anticipated and countered each other's attacks, neither entirely on the offense from the need for on-again, off-again defensive moves. Joan's face was sweating and despite wiping it dry a minute before, she sensed more droplets of sweat gathering on her forehead above her eyes. In a heartbeat of a pause Joan snapped her head to toss the droplets back into her hair, and that's when it happened. Eric saw the head snap as an opportunity to attack, Joan responded, and then suddenly a pin came loose from Eric's artificial foot and it just folded up, collapsing on itself enough to push him right into the waiting tip of Joan's foil. Unable to recover his balance, Eric tottered forward and collapsed down onto the floor. There was a rush of people to the runway, where Joan had grasped Eric's shoulder and helped him to turn onto his side.

"Looks like I need a visit to the shop," said Eric. "Somebody help me up." With Joan and Eric's coach each supporting a side, Eric made his way back to his feet and holding out his suddenly shortened leg, Eric's dad found the wandering pin and locked everything back into place. Brian started to applaud and all at once the whole group in the Quad was on its feet, cheering so loudly that Joan could hardly hear herself think. There was suddenly a commotion off to the left, and Joan saw Mr. Todd had pushed his way up to the front.

"THAT'S MY GIRL!" he shouted.

Joan looked back at Eric, standing now and shaking his head ruefully, but with a grin that told her everything was okay. He stepped over to her, gingerly at first, and reached out for her hand.

She took a step back. "No way, Eric. Not like this."

He looked right into her eyes the way he had before. "You sure?" he asked,

159

Joan nodded. "I can't accept. I won't, not like this. "

"YOU WON"T ACCEPT WHAT?" Joan turned around to see Mr. Todd, breathing hard and with an unusually nasty look on his face.

There was a squeal and a thump as the judges tapped the microphone. "We are pleased to announce the results of the final for today's competition. This year's High School State Championship fencer is…"

"I DO NOT ACCEPT," shouted Joan.

The room suddenly silent, both judges looking completely surprised. "The rules are very clear, Miss Darcy - you scored the last touch and therefore you are the winner."

"But I do not accept," said Joan. "It's not Eric's fault that his leg had a problem, and as far as I am concerned he won. If that thing hadn't happened, he would have gotten the next point."

The judges hesitated. "Competitors may not refuse, Joan. If on the other hand, your sponsoring organization decides not to accept, that is another matter. What does your sponsor say?"

Joan looked at Miss Renoir, who looked back with the same radiant pride she had expressed a moment before. "I will concur with whatever Joan wishes," Miss Renoir said.

But by now Todd was in the front row again, standing between Joan and Miss Renoir. "Now you wait a minute. What do you mean 'you will concur'? You work for me, remember, and I say you will accept the championship. Got it?"

"No, I don't 'got it'," Miss Renoir replied, turning to face him directly. "This is Joan's decision. If she says…"

"I don't give a darn what Joan says," he hissed, "and if you value your job you will do what I say." He turned to the Judges. "The competitor's school is the sponsoring organization, correct?"

The chief judge took a deep breath and nodded. "That is what the rules say."

Todd turned back to Miss Renoir. "Last chance, lady. What's it to be?"

Joan took two steps to stand beside her teacher. "Eric won this thing, not me."

Todd nodded once and turned to the judges. "Smithfield High School, sponsoring organization for Joan Darcy, accepts the championship trophy and designation on her behalf." He turned back to Joan, his face livid. "So, you do speak real English after all. Well, you better keep your nose clean from here on out, you and your little college brat friend. As for you," turning to Miss Renoir, "I'll deal with you later.

He strode up to the championship trophy, and thrusting it under his arm he growled "this belongs to the school," and stalked out of the room.

Chapter Thirty-Two
Sunday Revelations

Ever since Ryan was born his family had a regular Sunday routine of Sunday school, services, and dinner at a restaurant. After his accident, it became a way for Ryan to get used to being around people he knew in an understanding, nurturing environment, and also help him rebuild his speech and memory as best he could. After any tough week, Sunday dinner was something the whole family could genuinely look forward to.

Schalmo's Chicken Deluxe was their weekly destination, an old established restaurant right next to the chicken and egg farm with the same family name. When they arrived, they were greeted by Mrs. Schalmo and shown to a table within easy reach of the salad bar. Some friends came over to their table to say hello, and Ryan was looking forward to seeing Brian who also came with his family most Sundays. Ryan was disappointed that he hadn't been able to go to the basketball game on Friday evening and he still hadn't talked to anyone who knew anything about Joan or her fencing tournament, but he was so hungry he was glad when the server finally took their order.

"Go get 'em, tiger," said Papa, so Ryan made his usual beeline for the salad bar, picking an ice-cold plate out of the special cooler and heading for his favorite jar of pickled eggs at the other end. When he got there, however, a customer right in front of him was taking out the last egg, so Ryan was still standing there when a man wearing a long apron came up to the table carrying a fresh jar.

"Here you go, Ryan," the man said, and to Ryan's surprise it was Mr. Landry, who could barely set down the jar before Ryan engulfed him in a bear hug.

"Whoa, Ryan," said Mr. Landry, disengaging himself. "It's good to see you, too."

When someone you see every day starts to age, you don't notice it because the change is so gradual. Mr. Landry had been gone for nine months, however, and the changes were obvious even to Ryan. Formerly gray, his hair was now snowy white, and he was walking a bit stiffly instead of with the bounce he had before. When he stopped by Ryan's table a few minutes later, Mr. Kershaw jumped up and motioned to an empty chair.

"Please, Mr. Landry – sit down with us a minute," said Mrs. Kershaw.

"Can't do it right now," he said. "I'm on duty until six this afternoon."

Ryan's parents looked at each other. "On duty – meaning you're working here? We thought you retired and went to Florida," said Mr. Kershaw, confused. "That's what Mr. Todd told us, anyway."

Mr. Landry's face flushed and he looked away for a minute, clearly upset. "Since last June I've been staying with our daughter over in Baton Rouge."

"But you are working here now?" said Mrs. Kershaw uncertainly. "You're back home, then?"

Mr. Landry nodded and reached up to wipe his eyes. "I guess so."

By now she was clearly upset. "Ryan has a right to know what happened, Mr. Landry. You did so much for him and he's been missing you so much."

Mr. Landry looked up at Ryan. "I've missed you too, Ryan. I never had a student who worked as hard as you did."

"What actually happened?" asked Mr. Kershaw.

There was no way Mr. Landry could tell Ryan what Todd had told him all those months ago, that there was money missing from the annual fundraiser.

The way it had been presented to him was so patently false that he was tempted to fight it out, but in a community like this, even the hint of a scandal was enough to ruin him. Loyalty only goes so far sometimes, and despite his years of service to the school, he was sure Todd wanted him out and wasn't very particular how it happened. The suggestion that funding was tight sounded plausible, anyway, so Mr. Landry grabbed it like a drowning man reaching for a lifeboat even though he had no idea what he would do next.

"I got a letter saying since we'd lost so many students there was no more money for the band anymore," said Mr. Landry, "and the position was being cut. Didn't have any choice so I put in my retirement papers. I was hoping to make it to ten years so I would get at least a decent pension, but the problem was, all those years I'd been part-time my pension hardly amounted to anything. I'd already been teaching four years past retirement age, so getting another job wasn't an option."

"So how many more years did you have to get the pension?"

Mr. Landry looked at his feet. "One. Only one more year. I got over to Baton Rouge and three months later read in the Smithfield paper that I'd quit." He looked over at Mrs. Schalmo who was gesturing impatiently to get back to work. "It's been nice to see you, Ryan, Mr. and Mrs. I...we'll talk another time."

Ryan watched as Mr. Landry went back to the kitchen door and disappeared inside, his expression stark. He didn't always have a good way to tell what he was thinking anymore, but some things made him happy and some things made him sad. Since most of the memories from before the accident were gone, his good memories of the accident were that much more important. There were lots of bad ones, like the nightmares he sometimes had where he was drowning all over again, and when people made fun of him or when his hands or feet didn't work quite right, but everything connected with Band made up for it.

Mr. Landry had been so patient from the beginning, welcoming him to the band even though he could hardly walk straight, let alone play an instrument. When Mr. Landry left, it wasn't just the band that had gone away – Mrs. Coates gave some of that back to him – but the way he ...well, disappeared, hurt way down deep. Nobody but Ryan knew how much Mr. Landry's confidence in him, in getting better, taking one step at a time, was the first thing that made him start to feel at least somewhat normal again.

"Why did Mr. Todd lie to us?" Ryan asked Mama when they were driving back home.

"I guess I don't know, Ryan," she said, "but it was wrong. Just plain wrong."

When they got home, Ryan got into his outdoor clothes and went into the back yard with Shadow, throwing an old plastic trash can lid that Shadow treated like some giant Frisbee, growling as he tried to grab it different ways until he got it right and carried it proudly up the stairs onto their deck to drop at Ryan's feet. Most days it never failed to cheer him up, but today there was too much on Ryan's mind. There was a big outdoor swing in the back yard where he could sit in the shade, and that's where Mr. Kershaw found them a couple hours later, Shadow's head in Ryan's lap and the two of them fast asleep.

"I don't like this one bit. Something's fishy about the whole business."

"Stinks is more like it," said Mrs. Kershaw. "I've been real glad Ryan's had a job up to now, but no way is he working for the Principal anymore. Any man lies through his teeth like that, who knows what other funny business he's been up to?"

Uncle Doug

Grandpa had been president of the school board for about a hundred years and he always said when Joe retired, he would too so that everybody would get a fresh start. With the news about Joe and the almost unbelievable story about what Mr. Todd did at the Fencing tournament, we agreed that we'd better do something right quick before Todd got away with it.

"What's the plan?" I asked as we rode along.

"There's a point at which any dynasty needs to step aside and let someone else take over. Joe loved every one of those kids like they were his own, but Todd's something else entirely."

"You know something I don't?" I asked. "Seriously. Don't be blowing smoke if there's no fire."

Grandpa shook his head and sighed. "Only a feeling I have. They used to say back in the War that the guys who survived developed a sixth sense to duck at the right time. They'd brag about it, and the next thing you know we'd be picking them up in pieces. Right now I have one of those feelings like we have to duck, but things are moving so fast that Todd is going to be Superintendent in spite of what we say. That's where we have our work cut out for us."

"Which is…"

Grandpa stopped and looked me right in the eye. "There's a point when they'll change their minds. We just have to get them there."

Joan

After the tournament, the trip back to Smithfield was something surreal. Nobody was talking, and Michelle fell asleep as soon as the van started to move. Every time Joan closed her eyes all she could see was the image of Mr. Todd snatching the trophy from the table and storming out of the building.

Miss Renoir had never been so quiet, other than to tell Joan that she had done exactly the right thing and not to worry about it. "I will contact the National Federation to see if the decision can be reversed," she said. "He had no right to do that – perhaps a legal right, but no moral right.

"What about you?" asked Joan. "Are you in trouble?"

"It is true that I did not follow his command, Jeannette, but because someone orders me it does not make it right. If there is the responsibility to be borne, then I shall bear it gladly. That is part of the pain of being right – there are times when you are the only one who is. You are still young and there are many things yet to learn, but tonight you showed everyone who you truly are. Who you can be – *who you will be*. Tonight, you truly became a Chevalière. Remember that."

"We are both proud of you, Joan," said Papa. "But something tells me this won't be the end of it. One of the problems with people like Mr. Todd is they can't handle it when someone disagrees with them, especially in front of other people, and even more so when they know they're in the wrong."

They had gotten home about midnight, and after they dropped off Michelle Papa said something surprising.

"Perhaps Toussaint's for a dessert or something?" he said.

"Yes!" said both Miss Renoir and Joan at the same time.

Chapter Thirty-Three
Dies Irae – Judgement Day

Joan

When Papa dropped me off at school on Monday morning, I didn't waste any time getting inside so I could hook up with Michelle. The entrance was getting crowded by that time with people arriving, so I hitched up my backpack and started toward the locker pod. The big screen TV with the daily announcements lit up and a big marquee-style scroll appeared:

...MONDAY APRIL 21ST....SPECIAL ASSEMBLY ... 11:00 AUDITORIUM.....

When I got to Mrs. Coates' class Michelle wasn't in her usual chair, but Mrs. Coates said that she was helping Brian get set up for the special assembly. It was

164

unusually quiet in the room, with several of the basketball players talking among themselves. I went up to the group and asked about Christine.

"She's going to be okay, more or less," said Lisa. "The surgery was able to piece everything back together but it's going to be a long time until she plays basketball again." She looked up at me in a friendlier way than I'd ever seen before. "We saw those flowers you sent, Joan. It was a nice thing for you to do."

"It's okay," I said, shrugging.

"I know I haven't exactly been…well, nice to you," said Lisa, "and I'm truly sorry. Anyone who's good to a member of my family is okay by my book. By the way, congratulations on that tournament thing."

"Thanks, Lisa. You heard what happened?"

Lisa nodded grimly. "Unbelievable, but I guess we shouldn't be surprised. For what it's worth, everybody says you were right to do what you did."

Brian had taken over running the school's entire AV system and computer network, and the school found it handy to have him around in case they wanted to do something special. Part of the deal was that he got to use the control room like a private office, and since the school still paid Ace Security the school got its own in-house systems manager and Brian got better and better at his job.

"See, Joan," he showed me one day, pointing to a garish bright red button on the computer screen marked MASTER TV CONTROL, "all I have to do is touch this and it turns on all of the televisions in the entire school." He pointed to another series of control icons that let him feed any video or computer signal from anywhere in the school to any other place in the school, even when the teacher wasn't aware of it.

Back in Mrs. Coates' room the morning announcements finally came on.

"Good morning Smithfield High School and here are the announcements for today. There will be a special assembly at the conclusion of the third period. All students should report back to their home rooms before coming to the auditorium.

Track and Field teams should meet at the stadium for practice immediately after school.

Reminder to all juniors to complete your online SAT registration by this Friday.

Lunch for today is hamburgers on bun, cheese sticks, vanilla pudding, and milk.

Freshmen are reminded to finish their course registration papers and turn them in to Mrs. T.

Congratulations to Joan Darcy on her victory at the State Fencing Tournament last Saturday.

This concludes the announcements."

The rest of English class went okay, but since the activity was another debate it didn't have nearly the energy it usually did when Michelle was there. Since I hadn't seen or talked to Miss Renoir since Saturday evening, I was anxious to see if she had been able to do anything about being able to reverse the results of the tournament. On the way home, she had suggested a petition, but I didn't think there was much chance of that.

Todd

It was 8:52 and by this time of the morning Rose was about a half an inch from getting up, walking to the office door, yanking it open, and telling him to please sit down and stop talking to yourself. Ever since she got to work this morning he was up and down and up and down and up and down and muttering and an occasional yell. Two different times she had opened the office door to see if he needed anything, but he yelled louder so she had to close the door and go back to her desk. She opened the second drawer on her left, took out a box labeled "Jackhammer Ear Plugs," inserted them into her ears, and started to relax as much as she dared. Maybe it would be better by the end of the morning when the assembly was finally over.

Inside the office, Todd was in his best suit, freshly laundered shirt, and new shoes which were already beginning to wear out from his incessant pacing. Yes, all of it had finally come together, what with that kid Joan pulling off a win in that tournament. It was the first time something like that happened at the tournament but rules were rules and I'm the principal and I can make myself into any job I want at any time I want, so now I'm the fencing coach and I accept the trophy for the school and you yell and scream all you want it's my decision.

He had arrived at school about 5:30, and let himself in through the door at the end of the languages hall. It had been a long time since he had been in that part of the school, but after he unlocked his old classroom it brought back memories from student teaching. There was now posters and other French language stuff on the walls but it still looked the same as it had four years before. Going over to the old built in cupboard, Todd removed the books from the bottom shelf and reached all the way into the back, sticking his little finger into a knothole hole on the bottom and pulling gently. The whole piece of wood popped out neatly, revealing an empty space about the size and depth of a shoe box. Reaching into his pocket, Todd took out a plastic bag containing ten of the mineral supplement bottles and put it into the cavity. It was a matter of a few seconds to replace the piece of wood, put the books back in place, and close the cabinet door.

Rose opened the door. "There are two gentlemen here, Mr. Martin."

"I'll be there in a second," he replied. Right on time.

Joan

When I entered her classroom Miss Renoir was busy writing in her planner so I sat down and took out our materials for the day.

"Une moment," she said, and after a final flourish, she replaced the giant paperclip she used to keep her place and put the planner on top of her desk. We were still reading Dumas so I turned to where we had left off the day before and began to read. Since I'd practiced some of the more archaic words it came easily to me today, the stylized language and situations the more enjoyable because of the story.

166

"What is the historical background as of this point?" she asked, but before I could answer the door opened and Mr. Todd came into the room along with two men dressed in dark suits. I've seen that smile on his face a thousand times in my sleep since that day, and the only time I've seen another smile like that was when I visited the hyena pen at the zoo.

One of the men took out a paper and began to read. "Catherine Renoir?"

"Oui. I am Catherine Renoir."

"I am Special Agent Donovan with the Bureau of Homeland Security and this is Agent Weckesser with the U.S. State Department. You are now out of compliance with the regulations regarding Foreign Nationals teaching in the United States," he read, "as you have been dismissed from your teaching position for insubordination. This classroom is also sealed as of now, pending an investigation into the distribution of controlled substances. We are placing you in custody pending the results of this investigation."

Miss Renoir stood, her face stark and furious, at which Mr. Todd took two steps forward and thrust his face two inches from hers.

"You've had your last day as a teacher in my school, lady," he said, then turned to me. "Show's over, kid. Touché." He pointed to the door. "Now get out of here."

Miss Renoir abruptly grabbed me by the arm and turned me to face her. "Don't," she hissed. "Just don't. I will be all right." She reached down, scooped up the books from her desk, and thrust them into my arms. "Now take your things and go!"

Two hours later and I'm still numb, not even going to the third period but sitting on a bench in the enclosed garden they had in the middle of the school. I wanted to stay with Miss Renoir but the Agent simply shoved me out into the hallway, closing the door behind him. No sirens, no police cars, and since there were no other classes in that wing nobody saw anything except me.

Over the years, I had read a lot of history and about how tyrants got started. Time after time people kept saying yes, give him that and he will stop, then well maybe just once more and he'll stop this time. There had to be a point where people finally said stop, enough, you shall not pass, you won't get away with it this time. Now that I knew what Mr. Todd was like, what could I do about it? Who was I, anyway? Only some stupid, naive kid who thought she could make a difference only to have it all blow up in her face.

I shook my head at how blind I was not to see it until Dwight told me. That's what I get for entering the tournament, for winning those matches, forever coming up with the idea for having a fencing team in the first place. Well, this is where it got me - he's going to be the Superintendent. It stinks, it all stinks, and the biggest stinker is me.

I can't sit here all day, and the whole schedule is screwed up with that big assembly at eleven. There's still somebody I can go see. Just maybe, Mrs. T will know what to do.

Todd

He looked at the clock on his desk and it was 10:45:30 and only fifteen or is it fourteen and a half minutes to the assembly. All the planning and all the work and all the stuff he had to do to get here but he did it and it was all going to come true in fourteen minutes and twenty-six seconds. He looked over at the door that connected the Principal's office with the Board room up on the Auditorium stage, and for the two-hundredth time that day he imagined himself going through the door with the whole school board sitting there and all of them standing up and applauding him, Uncle Joe coming to shake his hands and taking the crown from his head and putting on top of Todd's head. Even though it's only a job, I will be the Superintendent and nobody will shove me around anymore.

He yanked open the door to the outer office where Rose was standing at the copy machine.

"You got those programs printed yet?"

Rose turned her head and looked at him. "What did you say?"

"YOU GOT THOSE PROGRAMS PRINTED YET?"

"Almost done," replied Rose, "but we're running out of copy paper."

"WELL, GET RYAN TO GO FETCH SOME!" he shouted and went back into the office.

Todd sat down abruptly, his heart hammering and as he looked at his hands saw the sweat beginning to darken the ends of his cuffs. Abruptly he stood up and walked over to the board room and up to the tall locked cabinet attached to the wall marked Superintendent. He yanked his keys out of his pocket, jammed the right key into the lock and pulled the door open so hard the hinges buckled. On the top shelf, the open box was right on the top of a dozen more, left from when he had replenished the supply last weekend.

Thrusting his hand inside the box he could tell there were at least six more of the little bottle left. This should help, yes, this will be good so he pulled out two, broke off the seals, and downed them in one gulp, throwing the empties into the wastebasket. Sure enough, the warmth started to flow into his arms, he got all tingly and was finally awake and full of energy. He closed the door and pulled out his keys, the door closing but without noticing the hinges now partly askew, the latch not catching.

Todd strode back into the inner office, yanked open the door and stepped out into the reception area. It was too hot there, so he continued out through the door into the foyer and out to the open air of the canopy outside, his skin suddenly feeling chilled as the wind started to dry off the sweat now pouring from him. He was going so fast that he did not see Joan sitting in the reception area.

Michelle

I was walking down the hallway toward third period when I heard the PA came on calling Ryan, and a second later there he was hurrying toward the office. He looked so upset that I thought I'd better join him. Ryan was always such a sweet guy but today he wasn't meeting my eyes and kept clenching and unclenching his fists. As the two of us stepped into the office Rose glanced up.

"Just dropping off Ryan," I said.

Rose pointed over to the copy machine. "We're out of paper, Ryan. Mr. Todd says you're supposed to get a new box for the office."

At that moment, the door from the outside burst open and Todd came into the office, breathing hard and very wound up.

"Ryan – go get some more paper," he said and turned to go back inside.

"No," said Ryan.

Todd turned around and it didn't take a brain surgeon to see that this was not at all what he expected. "What did you say?"

"No, I won't get YOUR STUPID PAPER," replied Ryan.

Joan

I see Michelle and Ryan but they don't see me, and Rose says something about copier paper, then like a tornado bursting down the door, the office opens and Todd storms in. At that moment, Ryan says No, and I see the yell is coming.

"WHO DO YOU THINK YOU ARE TALKING TO?" Todd shouted, the abruptness of it making me drop my hall pass. He was beet red and swollen up like a frog. Mr. Todd took two steps forward and reached for Ryan's arm...and automatically I stood up and slipped between them like a letter into an envelope.

With my best On Guard stance, I braced my left foot behind me and thrust ahead with my right hand, pushing Mr. Todd straight back, shouting "GET YOUR HANDS OFF HIM!" and the voice is not my own but something primeval.

Michelle

Since that day, every time I have watched the Wizard of Oz I feel like I have a much better and deeper understanding of the movie. Not in any deep symbolic way about the meaning of friendship and the battle between good and evil, but the part where Dorothy is inside her house and the house is up inside the tornado, and there's all that danger and swirling outside but there is little Dorothy safe and sound, sitting on her bed.

That's what it was like at that moment. Ryan is totally petrified when the Principal storms into the office and yells, then the second he tries to grab Ryan, out of nowhere here comes Joan, little flyspeck of a Joan who could not possibly weigh more than 95 pounds, jumping in between Ryan and Mr. Todd and shoving Mr. Todd two feet straight backwards. Unlike the tornado in the movie, time stood still for about one second...and then the tornado returned, worse than ever, and this time it looks like Mr. Todd.

He stood real still for a second, then rushed forward and grabbed them by their collars. He yanked them through the door into his office where they fell flat on the floor as the door closed behind him. Even Rose was in shock and poor thing, I can see she's completely petrified and not going to do anything. I ran over and tried to wrench open the door but it's a big heavy thing and I can't make a dent in it, and what's worse I was hearing nothing from inside.

I'm not exactly what you would call a religious person, at least up to that time, but I swear as I am writing this some voice told me that I should go to Brian, my buddy Brian. The AV room is only about forty feet away through the office door so I was there in about six seconds. Motivation helps speed, you know. So does fear.

I burst in babbling about four hundred miles an hour and in a few seconds, he got the gist of it, reached over to the terminal and bing, bing, bing, punched three buttons. A second later the School Board room appeared on the big monitor.

Joan

Ryan and I saw that the door was open into the board meeting room so we managed to scramble to our feet as Mr. Todd was locking the door we just came through. But when we got into the board room I couldn't open the door onto the stage. Before we could do anything else the door behind us clicked shut. Ryan was so scared he could hardly move and it broke my heart to see it, so I turn around and faced Mr. Todd.

"You leave him alone."

"You have no idea how much trouble you are in," he replied. "You put your hands on me in the official performance of my duties, pushed me in fact. They expel kids for that, and I'm going to charge you with assault right along with it."

Even though his voice was calm on the surface there was a tremor in it, and I saw that his face was sweaty and there was an overall twitchiness in the way he was holding himself. My God, this guy is on something, I realized. All this time he was edging around the big conference table, step by step, while Ryan and I were edging around the other side trying to stay as far away from him as we could.

Mrs. Coates

We are still in Homeroom getting ready to go to the assembly when the classroom TV flickers into life. At first, it looks like some reality TV show, but we all recognize the actors and see that it's on live, right now, right here in our own school. Mr. Todd was on one side of a big table with Joan and Ryan on the other.

"You leave him alone," says Joan.

There is a collective gasp from the students, then they are on their feet, cheering, with more cheering echoing down the hallway.

"That's telling him, Joan!" shouts Dwight from the back of the room. A half second later there's a huge SHHHHHHHHH! from the students at the front as we struggle to hear.

"You have no idea how much trouble you are in," said the Mr. Todd on TV. Somebody BOOS at the back of the room, and I see that it is Lisa. Apparently, she likes this show.

170

Joan

What was it with this guy? Well – it's about time he got some of his own medicine. "You're the one in trouble," I said. "I know a secret about you."

"What are you talking about?" His voice wasn't confident anymore, it was shaky and he was doing that thing with his hands again like he couldn't keep them still.

Suddenly, Ryan woke up to what was going on. "You leave Joan alone."

"And what do you think you can do about it?" asked Mr. Todd.

"Lots, as a matter of fact," I said, and stepped in front of Ryan. "Remember how you framed Mr. Landry?"

Uncle Doug

We walked into the building, Grandpa moving more slowly because of his cane, and as we came through the front door the whole school seemed deserted, except for the sound of a voice echoing fainting through the hallways. I glanced through a classroom door and realized the girl on the TV was Joan, the one that Dwight brought to the Christmas Party, and the boy was Ryan, and the big guy on the other side of the table was...

"...framed Mr. Landry?" said the Joan on TV.

Grandpa gripped my arm so tightly I thought he was having a heart attack.

Joan

"What are you talking about?" Mr. Todd said, and stopped moving.

"Remember the band room?" I replied. "The old one with big closets? Big enough for two kids to duck into when you and some guy came inside? You told him you made up some story about some missing Band money so that you could get rid of the band director. *Remember?*" I was watching Mr. Todd very closely, and sure enough, he turned pale and his breathing slowed...

Without warning, Ryan screamed. "HOW COULD YOU DO THAT TO MR LANDRY?"

For someone so quiet, Ryan had a voice that could break glass, so I had to grab him hard to keep him from leaping across the table and Mr. Todd took a step backward.

"*I helped you every time you asked me, delivering those boxes, fixing all those test papers...*"

It was like Ryan had pushed some supercharge button inside Todd because he leapt forward far enough to grab Ryan's collar and drag him across the table. Ryan fought back, struggling to pull away, and when Mr. Todd gave him one more yank the table crashed onto the floor knocking us over. One chair tipped over and crashed into a big cabinet at the end of the room, while another slammed into the wall right under the plaque which teetered and fell on the edge of the table and snapped in two

171

Michelle

Life sometimes gives you such incredible coincidences that you'd think some slightly crazy author just made it all up, but what I'm going to tell you *actually happened.*

Smithfield's mascot is the Cavalier, an English guy from the 1600's who is always pictured carrying a sword, and the official logo for the school is a pair of crossed swords. Years before, some graduating class bought some real dueling swords, had them mounted on a plaque, and donated it to the school where it was put up in the school board meeting room.

So here was Joan, doing her best to protect Ryan from a Mr. Todd who apparently had gone completely out of his mind. Mr. Todd grabbed Ryan and tried to yank him across the table, but the table fell over and crashed into the wall. Since he weighed at least two hundred and fifty pounds he could crush them like bedbugs, but if Joan had a sword she could at least protect Ryan and defend herself.

That same Cavalier plaque I just told you about – the one that got knocked off that same wall – well, it, hit the edge of the table exactly right and snapped in two with the swords falling to the floor *right in front of Joan, the only person in the whole school who knew how to use one!*

If anybody dared to put something like that into a novel, nobody'd ever believe it.

In one smooth motion, Joan grabbed one of the swords and pointed it right at Mr. Todd's chest. "Let go of my friend. NOW!" The room became abruptly quiet, and Joan was totally, icily calm with the point of the sword never wavered a millimeter. Mr. Todd, who was on the floor all tangled up, slowly let go of Ryan, who scrambled to his feet and went to stand behind Joan. Joan took half a step back and the tip of the sword flicked up. "Get up. Come on, get to your feet," she said with that same half-whispered icy voice.

Mr. Todd put his right hand on the floor, still facing Joan, and slowly stood up as he took another step backward.

"Stay right there," said Joan. "We'll wait for the police and all this will be over..."

"*You fired Mr. Landry,*" Ryan said, dully. "And you're a big cheater!"

"Ryan, calm down," said Joan. "We'll find out about it later..."

"YOU FIRED MR LANDRY!" Ryan started to lunge forward, Joan trying to grab his arm, and there was a heavy banging at one of the doors like someone was trying to break it down.

That's when Mr. Todd made his move, grabbing a chair and sending it flying at Ryan. Joan saw it coming and pushed Ryan out of the way, but one of the chair legs grazed the side of her head and knocked her off balance. It crashed into the cabinet at the end of the room, shattering what was left of the door and sending a whole cascade of little bottles onto the floor.

172

Mr. Todd lunged forward and grabbed the other sword, losing his balance just long enough for Joan to grab Ryan by the shoulder and yank him back behind her. Mr. Todd regained his balance and with the sword made a vicious swipe towards Joan, who managed to parry it out and down so it stuck into the overturned table. Todd yanked it free but all of a sudden there's a pounding on the door like someone was trying to break it down. Todd let out a berserk roar and charged, sword held high, but Joan lunged forward, her sword piercing right into and completely through his left leg. He dropped his sword with a shriek and fell backward onto the wreckage of the table, the sword pulling free. At that moment, the door to the Superintendent's office clicked open and Mrs. T came into the room, the opposite door still shaking from the people on the other side trying to break it down.

"Joan?" said Mrs. T real gently, and Joan dazedly turned toward her, her hair disheveled and a bruise on her forehead starting to darken. Mrs. T reached out for the sword, and stepping over to the other door turned the bolt and opened it. Two police rushed into the room along with an EMT who went over to help Mr. Todd.

By this time, the school foyer was completely full of students, who moved out of the way to let the EMT and police into the building. Brian and I were still in the AV control room, Brian compulsively switching the video back and forth between the Board room and front office where EMT's have loaded Todd onto a gurney, a red-stained bandage on his leg and handcuffs on his wrist.

"Too late," he said bitterly.

"Too late for what?" I asked.

Brian started talking on and on and on about "It was Mr. Todd all the time," and "mineral supplement" and then back to Mr. Todd. He finally calmed down enough that I got to hear the whole story, and it made me sick to hear what that guy was doing. I looked back at the monitor and they're wheeling the gurney with Mr. Todd out the front door as one kid at the back starts to boo and within half a second the whole group was shouting. The gurney finally made it outside, and then Mrs. T appeared at the door holding Ryan's arm. A second later Joan appeared with a bandage on her head and holding the arm of another man in an EMT uniform who I recognized as Dwight's dad. Everybody in the hallway started cheering their lungs out, Joan gave a half smile and fainted dead away onto the floor.

Chapter Thirty-Four
The Hospital
Joan

It was a while before I came to, because after I got to the hospital the doctors put me under the way they do when they suspect a significant head injury. After the CT scan, they told Papa that I was going to be okay, but since I was probably going to have a whopper of a headache it would be a good idea to let me sleep for a while.

It's weird waking up in a hospital room when you don't remember how you got there. It's a nice comfortable bed but not your own, and despite general rules about noise, it is everywhere. There are little beeps from every direction, soft voices, and pencils on charts or computer keyboards clicking away, the rattle of little carts being pushed up and down hallways. There is a whole bunch of electronic spaghetti attached to you in all different places, and you might have a room to yourself or a temporary roommate with her own set of spaghetti.

My eyes opened and took all of this in, beeps and all, and I reached up and felt my head. There was a gauze bandage way up high on my forehead, and I pressed on it to see if it hurt. There was some pain when I pushed, but when I took my hand away most of the pain went away too. The monitor hanging from the ceiling above my head had little green lines going left to right in little blips up and down like they were supposed to and my blood pressure was 95/65, so I guess I'm going to live. At that moment some of the things that happened started coming back to me. An image of Ryan and how scared he was popped into my head, then the chair flying past my head, and all at once, the rest of it.

I stabbed Mr. Todd. Now I was awake for real, and I quickly lifted my left arm to see if there was a handcuff....no, and not on my right arm either. That means either that I'm not in trouble, or I managed to escape and Papa and I are on the lam in Canada or Mexico or something...

I looked at the wall and went down a mental checklist: 1) nothing is in Spanish so we're not in Mexico, and 2) nothing is in French either so we're not in Canada. Everything is in English and I am almost disappointed, then I see the sign that says Smithfield General Hospital and I know we are still at home. Then there was a small rustle over to my right and sure enough, there was Papa, stretching out his arms like he was just waking up.

"Good morning Squirt," he said. If he was worried he would say Joan, or if her was *really* worried he would say Jeannette, but Squirt is for when I'm okay and he's either in a good mood or proud of me about something, although right now I can't think of anything he would be proud of.

"So ...? I say and it's a real question, not a greeting, and I'm thankful nobody is turning up the lights because my headache is right there under the surface.

"Well, you're in the hospital and it's eight o'clock Wednesday evening," said Papa. His voice was warm and quiet and ever so gentle, and that also worried me because it makes me think that something is wrong before I remember he called me Squirt.

174

"Did you say Wednesday?"

Papa nodded. "That's a good size bump on your head and the neurologist wanted to make sure the swelling went down just to be sure. You're going to be okay but you might have a whopper of a headache for a few more days. How do you feel right now?"

"Okay," I replied. "Somewhat tired, though. Is Ryan okay?"

Papa nods. "Yes, Ryan is okay. He was real shaken up, of course, but he's not hurt, thanks to you. You...saved his life. If you hadn't..."

"If I hadn't what?" I ask, and try to sit up in the bed but it's too flat and my head starts to hurt until I lie back down again. Papa reached out to push a button and the top half of my bed started to come up so that I could lie back and still look at him.

"What do you remember about what happened?" he asks.

Papa is a great teacher and one of his rules is that he avoids giving a direct answer to a student, by always getting them to talk first, so I guess right now I am a student and just got called on.

"I remember being locked in the board room and Mr. Todd was yelling at Ryan, then Ryan said something about helping with tests, Mr. Todd went nuts and threw something which...." I reach up and touch the bandage on my head and it dawns on me that's where.... "...which hit me or grazed me, I guess, then I picked up one of the swords that fell off the wall, and then he picked up another sword and starts to come after us..." I start to slow down and although I know what is coming I don't want to say...but I am not a coward and out it comes. "I stabbed him, and he dropped it and fell down." There, I said it, and if the police aren't here yet they are probably waiting outside.

Papa nods. "That's the first part of the story, Joan. Everything you said is true but not exactly complete."

Now I'm getting impatient, like the teacher who says, 'yes, that's an interesting answer but would you elaborate please?' What else is there, I wonder, look Papa right in the eye, and at that point I apparently scrunched up my face the way I do when I'm trying to remember something.

"Let's try this, Squirt. You tell me what you remember, slowly, and I'll give you plenty of time. It's important that you remember what you saw and heard, not some fake memory somebody else gives you because then you won't be able to tell the difference between the two. Do you understand why that's important?" A touch of seriousness had crept back into his voice, and he was right, I needed to do this on my own as best I could.

"It was in the board room, and Mr. Todd was on the floor after he let go of Ryan. I...he got to his feet and I...told him to stay there, the police were on their way. He was moving away but I kept the...sword on him, pointed at him and we were standing there."

"And then out of nowhere Ryan started to yell, and..."

Ryan

Michelle said she needed to have me tell about this, so we got a digital recorder thing and I told her about it. She was real grateful and said it would be in the book like that other part, and she'd make sure I got a copy when it was all finished.

I was working for Mr. Todd when he asked me to come into the board office and help him with some of the tests that everybody took. He told me to get a whole bunch out of the envelopes, and then when I found the ones he wanted, he made a bunch of changes and I put them back into the envelopes like he told me. I thought I was doing something good but I guess I wasn't, but I didn't know it was bad or anything.

Then when I found out Mr. Todd got Mr. Landry fired it was the meanest thing in the world. Every time Mr. Todd was pretending to be nice to me, he was just a big fat mean liar. I don't like to get that way but he made me all mad and scared and I guess I said some things I shouldn't. He trapped me and Joan inside the board room, right where I helped him with the tests. I got so mad I yelled at him and told about the tests, and that made Mr. Todd mad because I broke my promise not to tell. Then he threw a chair at me but it hit Joan on the side of her head and crashed into that tall cabinet at the end of the room, the cabinet burst open and a whole bunch of bottles fell onto the floor. He grabbed a sword like Joan did and ran at me with it, but Joan stabbed him in the leg so he stopped. Then the door broke down, and Mrs. T and Uncle Doug came in with the police and Grandpa.

I sure hope Joan isn't in trouble.

Joan

"...and then it all went blank. The last thing I remember is leaving the office."

Papa nods and I lie back onto the bed, surprised my headache isn't getting any worse, but it hurts to concentrate. I had so many things on my mind for such a long time that I guess I shoveled in other things to think about, and now I'm here in this bed and don't know what is going to happen next. I close my eyes and it feels good to shut out the light for a while. Sometimes it's amazing how thin a line there is between being asleep and being awake, because I am sure I was asleep but also remember the door opening and a policeman coming in, talking with Papa in a real quiet voice.

"It's a real brave girl you've got there, Professor Darcy. One of the bravest things I've ever heard of, in fact," says the voice. "No doubt he would have killed them both if she hadn't done what she did. I've taken a lot of criminals to the hospital in my time, but never one who was stabbed by a sword."

I drifted back to sleep.

When I wake up again my head's feeling a lot better, it's four o'clock in the morning, and sure enough, Papa is asleep in the chair like before. The bed is still tilted up, my headache is gone, and I am hungry. There is a bag on that long table, and I reach out to find it's one of those little pouches of oyster crackers from Toussaint's, which reminds me of that heavenly soup, and that reminds my stomach how hungry it is.

I guess it was the crunching that woke up Papa again, but I'm still chewing and just say "Mpph," at him, keeping at it until I'm finished. He's looking more rested this time, and my stomach is a lot happier.

"Are you feeling better, Joan?" asks Papa.

I nod. "Is it Thursday today?"

Papa nodded. "You just slept sixteen hours. Feel better?"

I reached up and feel around my forehead where the bandage had been, and it's now about the size of a big Band-Aid instead of the way it was before.

"Joan, I don't know how much you heard because you were dozing in and out, but the police came and they're not pressing any charges against you for what happened," he said. "As a matter of fact, they think real highly of you for what you did for Ryan. Your friend at school with the AV thing...?"

"Brian."

"That's it. Brian had enough presence of mind to record the whole thing so it's all there, everything that went on in the boardroom. The prosecutor has a copy of the DVD so that's going to be some powerful evidence. Not only was it seen by nearly every student in the high school, it showed up on the local Cable Channel 21 and people all over town saw it, too. Of course, somebody in town recorded it so now it's gone viral."

"How many hits?" I asked.

He laughed out loud, "They're going to have a hard time getting a non-prejudiced jury around here for the trial, that's for sure."

"What trial?" I asked. Duh.

"Mr. Todd has been charged with a whole long list of things ranging from blackmail to falsifying State test scores to distributing drugs on school property. There are also two counts of assault with intent to commit bodily harm to you and Ryan. At this point, they're looking through papers in his office, and they have already discovered it's a huge mess along with other stuff that goes back years."

"Is he okay?" I ask.

"His leg is bandaged up but there's nothing serious. They took him over to the County Jail last night."

So, it's finally happened. I hurt someone, almost killed someone, and I feel sick. My headache sees that I'm awake and it rushes back so hard that I have to lean over the side of the bed and I'm sick into the wastebasket they put there for that reason. Papa jumps up and holds me until I'm finished, then he gives me a glass with a straw and some lemonade and my stomach settles right down.

Papa stays right there even after I'm finished but I'm still feeling tired, not tired like I've just run a race, but tired like I've been running one every day for months. He gets up and wets a washcloth in the sink, then comes back to the bed where he wipes my brow and my face, the cool feeling so good and the headache starting to go back under the surface. I look up into his face and it's peaceful, the way it's always been, and he's older than he used to be but his eyes are crinkled with the little crow's feet at the corners and I'm settling back and...

...and I slip under the surface but this time I'm a little girl back in France and Grandmother is serving me a big bowl of my favorite soup and the sun is shining outside, but this fades and I'm in Miss Renoir's classroom reading dialogue from Les Miserables and she's the crooked Innkeeper and I'm little Cosette. We're laughing and now we're at the fencing tournament, and I've won five matches in a row so my brow is sweating so that my eyes sting and somebody wipes them and it's...

Mama. Now she's the one with the washcloth and it's smooth and cool on my skin, and she's smiling too, the little crow's feet in the corners of her eyes and I open my eyes again but it's Papa, and he's there so gentle and...strong, and handling all of this like the great and good man he is, not all fallen apart with grief like I thought, just being a man and a Dad and doing his job, loving me and taking care of me like always, like he has every day since....Mama died. She's dead and not coming back. Ever. And I didn't even get to say goodbye.

But I don't know what happened. I don't know because nobody ever told me. I have to stop this, but I suddenly realize it's not because they never told me. I never asked. I am in this hospital bed and people are calling me brave for facing down Mr. Todd and saving Ryan, but if I am as brave as everybody says, then why didn't I ever have the courage to ask? Like I said, it's hard enough when you kiss your Mama goodbye for what is supposed to be a three-day trip and you find out the next day that she's dead. It's time.

I look at Papa and he knows what's coming, and I can't believe I'm this calm.

"Papa, please tell me what happened to Mama."

Mama

Joan is sleeping when the taxi arrives, so I lean over and give her a soft kiss right on her hair the way I did when she fell asleep in my arms. "Au revoir, Jeannette," I say, then give my husband a quick embrace and I'm outside and on my way.

The trip to Paris takes eight hours and I am reading the dossier the Ministry sent me, taking special care to memorize the different faces. The terror cell had apparently been discovered and the photos aren't very clear but the basic facts are there. Four of them, all brothers or cousins of each other, it's not very clear, so telling them apart will be a challenge especially if they have added or removed beards or mustaches, or simply grown their hair longer. I've always been very good at looking through the disguises and seeing the real face beneath, the face that tricks the facial recognition software that they had been using without success. It took an informant to work up enough nerve to reveal they were in Paris, and that some operation was imminent.

Unlike other groups this one was brand new, homegrown in fact, the third generation descended in ideology from the Algerian debacle of the 1960's, but with a new twist that wanted France clear of immigrants entirely. They had one failed bank robbery in Le Havre where an older brother had been killed, but the

178

other four escaped. These four were suspected of another robbery in Rouen, successful this time and getting away with half a million Euros in cash and an unmarked police car. The word was they were coming to Paris and that their operation, whatever it was, would take place there. This is the aspect that had the Ministry on high alert since one of the brothers was heard to swear revenge at the time the older brother was killed.

The ministry had a private room in the crypt of Notre Dame and after confessing and lighting a candle I slipped into the passageway and made my way downstairs. I used my right thumbprint to open the door, and slipped inside.

"Bonjour, Chevalière," said the Minister. "Please sit down and give us your evaluation."

I told them what I had learned, that there was a pattern to their changes in appearance that was almost comical if it were not so deadly at the same time. "When one adds a beard, they all add the same beard," I said. "The same with hairstyle, mustaches, everything. It is like they cannot think for themselves – if one changes, they all change together. "

"So?" he asked, faintly intrigued. "How will this help?"

"Again, they never work alone," I replied. "They may all have shaved, they may all look slightly like bears after a long winter. That is what we look for...except for one, the brother you mentioned. Another aspect of their pattern is that there is always one who deviates from the plan, who goes off on his own and this gets him into trouble. Like the one who was killed, he was the standout, the leader and he was on his own - but the rest are always nearby, always watching. "

The minister nodded. "I see," and at that moment the secure teletype printer chattered out a message. He stepped to the machine and tore it off, reading it as he took two steps and suddenly paled.

11:24 INTERPOL TOP SECRET URGENT CAR FROM ROUEN ROBBERY FOUND ABANDONED NEAR LUXEMBOURG GARDENS VEHICLE TESTS POSITIVE FOR EXPLOSIVE RESIDUE SUSPECTS HEAVILY ARMED OR EXPLOSIVE DEVICE IN CENTRAL CITY RECOMMEND IMMEDIATE EVACUATION.

"We have no time to lose," said the Minister. "GO. NOW. I hope we are not too late."

It was a matter of a few moments to be back up the stairs and onto the streets. Mon Dieu, but they could never complete an evacuation. Central Paris, right before Noon, the weather glorious and the streets full. The only thing I could do was to walk but watch, look at everyone, into and behind everything, for these people, and pray to God I see them before they see me. The right bank was in full flower, booksellers, and artists by the hundred, sightseers and young couples and old couples walking hand in hand, stopping here and there. This was good, no groups here, everybody with a partner but I cannot think that way since they do not think that way. These very booksellers and sightseers and old and young couples are not people, they are targets. It is part of their sick belief that to target the innocent will pay back some old disappointment from the time of their grandfathers, to remake the world the way it was before and avoid the future.

I passed the statue of Charlemagne, and thank heavens a cloud passed over the sun and a quick, unexpected shower made the people laugh and cover their heads or take a temporary shelter under a tree or canopy. I found myself walking by myself out in the open, the rain feeling good on my face, and turn to go onto the Petit Pont and cross onto the left bank. There was the sound of laughter behind me, and as I turned there was a pair of nuns leading a long line of small children in school uniforms, hurrying across the bridge to find a way out of the rain. A man in a heavy raincoat was right in front of me, looking from side to side, seeming uncomfortable until he saw the children...

And on the other end of the bridge there they were, three of them, looking like slightly mismatched triplets in long-sleeved striped shirts, long mustaches, and berets, and they were standing and watching. A few more steps and I am next to the man with the raincoat, and it is all wrong. The weather was warm and the lapel flops open enough to show the striped shirt, but there is something else under the shirt, belts and straps and red boxes, and I know. The nuns smile at us and some of the children say "Bonjour, Madame" with their best manners as I look the man in the face.

He knows. He turns to his brothers at the end of the bridge, his right arm reaching inside his coat but I lunge at him, grasping the arm and struggling but he is strong and I am losing, but here is the edge of the bridge so instead of struggling more I dig in my feet like one last fencing lunge, and he stumbles backwards while I push him backwards, ever faster backwards to the railing and up and over the railing and something pulls under me...

Papa

The story is finished and Joan is sitting there in front of me, her cheeks wet. She is silent for what seems like forever, and then three words. "Protect the helpless," she said.

I nodded. "Yes, that's what she did. There were fifty-seven children in that group along with the nuns, probably a couple hundred others crossing the bridge, and out of all that exactly one injury, a little boy who fell down while he was running and sprained his ankle. No more injuries."

"But one death," said Joan. "Two, actually."

180

I nodded quietly. "Yes, two deaths, but many more lives that now have a future because of your mother's bravery. I have to tell you, Joan, the blast was so powerful it knocked over people a hundred meters away."

"So, it was quick, anyway," said Joan, her voice dull. "You were right not to tell me right away, I think...but why now?"

"Because you finally asked, and because of what you did," I said. "And all the rest of it."

"The rest of what? Because I stabbed somebody I'm suddenly old enough to know how my mother died?" she responded angrily.

"No, because of all you have done. Not the fencing, not the tournament, but giving up the trophy for your beliefs, by holding it together after Miss Renoir left, by putting yourself on the line for Ryan, and lastly by looking death in the eye and not backing away."

"Funny how you refer to him like that," she said. "I guess some other kids saw him that way, too."

"Not like you did, Joan," I say gently.

And like a dam full to overflowing, her grief bursts and she is sobbing there in my arms, talking to Mama, me, her friends, Miss Renoir, to all those she has known and lost these past two years. Friends from past schools long behind her, fencing lessons under the tree, falling asleep in Mama's arms and getting that last gentle kiss on the forehead.

Chapter Thirty-Five
You'd Never Believe this, But...

Joan

I had to stay in the hospital for another day until the doctor cleared me to go home, and since I still had some headaches I went to school half days for a while. Some kids worry about going to school because of the way that other kids talk about them, but I don't think you can imagine how it was after the thing that happened. Talk about weird.

Things looked and felt differently to me since I made my own peace with what happened to Mama, and I slowly realized that I was becoming reconciled about what I did to Mr. Todd. I was sorry that I had to stab him to save Ryan and defend myself, but if the same thing happened I'd do it again. There's something about risking your life for a friend that changes how you think about a lot of things.

It was great being back with Mrs. Coates again, but the worst thing was second period since Miss Renoir was gone. I'd put everything from that last day of class into my locker, and when I went through it later I'd gotten hold of her planner. I looked through it week by week and found that the whole rest of the year was already planned. Papa made a few calls, and by the next day he'd worked it out so I could get the rest of the reading books from the college library, and starting next week I would start working with one of the French professors at Smithfield College. They say he's a real nice guy, but no matter what he's not Miss Renoir. I miss her so much there are no words for it.

Doc

I'm telling you, it was a shock what happened with Todd and it made me feel bad that I hadn't done something sooner. Doug and I got together with the other board members who by now were singing a different tune, and the four of us got into a car and went over to Joe's house. Gladys didn't want to let us inside, but Joe heard our voices and came over to the front door to say hello. He didn't know who we were and didn't remember a minute after we told him, but his manners weren't affected by the Alzheimer's and he was as friendly as ever. Since it didn't hurt anybody we let Gladys and Joe keep coming into the office, but we also had to make it real clear that Joe wasn't the Superintendent anymore.

Or at least that's what we thought we would do until a few things surfaced that settled things a lot sooner. In going through Todd's files, we found a whole big folder about the training room project and how he'd just thrown away the rest of the bids. We had a meeting with the contractor and came to an agreement that we wouldn't press charges if he returned half of the money he'd gotten for the renovation. He didn't like it but it kept him out of jail and just like that we had an extra $150,000 in the treasury.

We also didn't like what happened with Mr. Landry, and we discovered Todd had forged some of the fundraising receipts that he used to force Mr. Landry to quit. At the same time, Doug Junior remembered that Mrs. Coates had put together a pep band for the school year, which gave me a great idea.

"Does Mrs. Coates have an administrator's license?" I asked Gladys.

She didn't even have to look it up. "Of course, she does," Gladys replied. "She's been acting Assistant Principal for going on three years."

Well, that settled it as far as I was concerned. With that extra money, we could go a long way towards putting the spirit of the school back together if I could get the other Board members to agree. That part was both funny and sad, though. Renee and James had lots of egg on their faces after everything that happened, and they officially retired right along with Joe. First, however, we had a special board meeting where we appointed Mrs. Coates Acting Superintendent until the end of the school year, and Coach Anita principal. Mrs. Coates' only condition was that she could keep teaching her English 9-12 class, but we were sure she'd have plenty of time to think of some other ways to help undo some of the damage Todd had done.

When Todd was arraigned a week later the video from the board room was shown to the grand jury, and seeing Joan again finally made me realize why she'd looked so darn familiar. When you get to my age you don't always think in a straight line but my curiosity got the better of me. My old war buddy Crockett was in a nursing home, but his mind was as sharp as ever and he remembered enough for me to get started.

"That village was called Domremy la Pucelle," he said. "There are two other villages named Domremy in France but the one we liberated was the one where Joan of Arc was born."

The girl who warned us that day had come out of a house right across the street from the church, and using something called Google Earth Dwight managed to get me enough of a look at the house to come up with an exact address. It was strange, sitting next to him as he guided me through the town with his computer. It hadn't changed all that much, for one thing, and I could see as clear as day the building at the end of the street where that Tiger Tank had been waiting for us.

I was one of the lucky ones. I survived and had a chance at a wonderful life, with a family and a community to be a part of and to give something back. None of it would have happened were it not for a French girl who put her own life on the line long enough for us to get the tank out of the way, and Crockett, whose mechanical wizardry gave that old tank enough get up and go to jump forward out of the way. Sometimes I can still feel the shock of that projectile going by my head.

I used my old Army connections and my Legion of Honor to get in touch with the Military Attaché at the French Embassy, and of course like these things always work he knew somebody who knew somebody who came from that village, and in about three hours the whole thing is confirmed. I shared the news with the whole family, making Dwight and George promise to keep it quiet for the time being. Doug Junior whistled and said, "Are you sure?" so I got out that little picture of me and the girl, Dwight gets out one of the pictures he had taken at the fencing tournament, and when we put them side by side there was no question. Cut Joan's hair a bit differently and that's her right there in 1944.

"Joan's back at school, Grandpa," said Dwight. "She's okay, I guess, but…well, she's not the same."

"Things never are the same when something like that happens," I reply. "That's something I understand in spades. That girl had death staring her in the face and she didn't flinch. You get a whole different perspective on life when someone tries to kill you. Like everyone else in war, I've had people try to kill me, but you can also be darn sure it was never my school principal."

I picked up the phone and in an hour, it was all arranged.

Doc's Story
Michelle

Two days later I get in the car with Mama and Papa and Kevin, and we head out to this restaurant called Toussaint's that Joan had told me about. She had called the night before to invite us to a special meeting or something and wanted me to go along.

"I don't know why I'm still feeling spooked by these things, but I'd sure appreciate you being there," she said.

"Do I get to bring chopsticks?" I asked

"All you want," she replied.

We go into the restaurant and it's like Joan described, a big main room with a polished wood floor and the homey aroma of something fresh cooked. Joan waves to me from the other side of the room where they've put together four big tables, and I see Dwight and George and Ryan and all their Moms and Dads, everybody talking already. Dwight's Grandpa is at the head of the table with Joan and her Dad right next to him, and on the other side, I also see two wheelchairs. To my surprise, Brian is there, too, with Christine and her Mom sitting right beside him. They've left a place for us right next to Brian, so we get introduced to everybody and I finally sit down right next to Brian, but not before going up to Christine and giving her a hug. If anyone had told me eight months ago, well, things change, thank heavens.

Christine had a look on her face that reminded me of how Joan was looking these days, sharp but with a tinge of pain around the eyes like my cousin had after the diving accident. She had been back to school for a few days but it was a struggle getting around with the wheelchair, especially with the huge cast they had on her leg.

Dwight's Grandpa picked up a spoon, dinged it on the side of his wine glass, and we all got quiet.

"We are glad that all of you could be with us here tonight for this unusual special occasion, but before we get started we've asked Father Martin to say a few words."

The whole restaurant grew quiet, and the priest sitting next to Joan stood up.

"We are thankful for our friends and for their coming safely through their trials and returning to us. A bit more scarred, perhaps, but with the knowledge that – in the words Joan used so appropriately – we all have their backs."

"Amen," I said, and immediately blushed bright red before I noticed that everyone else at the table had said it, too, along with probably thirty other people at other tables in the restaurant. Across the table, Joan was stifling her laughter, and it saddened me that she was too far away to kick.

Two tall waiters looking like twins carried out huge bowls of soup, steaming and smelling heavenly. I could see that Joan was hungry too, and by this time I think I would have invaded the kitchen to get something to eat, so I was grateful when one of the bowls landed in front of me and annoyed when my Mom ladled the soup into it like she did when I was four. It helped that it was so delicious that I forgot all about anything else for a while, then when the sautéed crispy shrimp arrived I forgot even more, but when they brought the wild rice with tiny wild mushrooms there was nothing on my mind except the food. I looked across the table at Joan and to my astonishment, she was eating the rice with chopsticks like she'd been doing it all her life. She set down the bowl and reaching to her side brought up a pair and handed them across the table to me.

The food got the better of me and I had to admit that it was one of the best meals I'd ever had. Everybody at the table was in a great mood, and to my relief nobody was being squishy or overbearing to either Joan or Christine or making a big deal about anything except to offer more food all around. Finally, when I was convinced there was nothing more to eat and no room to put it if there were, the waiters brought out an enormous dessert tray, right as Dwight's Grandpa dinged his glass again.

"There aren't many times in life when we are genuinely surprised by something," he said, "but one of the reasons I have asked all of you here this evening is because recently this has happened to me. Some of you may know that I was privileged to serve in the U.S. Army during the Second World War, and it hasn't been a secret that I saw a lot of combat in France. What nobody here knew until recently is that something happened to me during the war that…well, let me tell you that story. First, please be so good to have a dessert so that I at least have the excuse of telling you the story while you eat."

There was a piece of Pecan Pie that caught my eye, even though I was bursting at the seams, which apparently was part of the plan because everybody was going to take a long time to finish. Dwight's Grandpa took a sip of wine and began his story.

ON THE NEUFCHATEAU ROAD
BORDER OF ALSACE, AUGUST 14, 1944

"Whoa," Doc called down from the turret. The Sherman ground to a halt, skidding a foot forward with the momentum. It had taken a while for the driver to get used to his commander's language, but having watched a few hundred cowboy movies as a kid he picked it up pretty quickly. It's one thing about telling a human to act like a horse, but another thing when you're driving something that weighs twenty tons.

Pulling a map out of his document case Doc scanned the roads around him, grateful to be up high enough off the ground that he could see a long way ahead. The road led into the little village exactly where the map said it was. Given the ground his division had gained over the past two weeks, there were times when they had driven off the map entirely and it was only by sheer chance that they hadn't ended up right in the middle of the German retreat. Yep, that crossroads in the middle of town was the only crossroads there was, and like three days ago, they were right up against the edge of the map again. He carefully scanned the horizon as far as he could see behind him, where thirty minutes before there was some dust being kicked up enough to show most of the division coming his way, but there wasn't any right now.

"Engine off," he yelled down to the driver, the tank sputtered once and was silent. Like he'd been taught as a boy, he opened his mouth and cupping his hands behind his ears he turned completely around. Nothing. Not a sound from any direction. Not a sound from ahead of him, which was good, and not a sound from behind him, which was not. No engines, no firing, nothing. His hearing was good enough to pick up the sound of a mosquito inside a frog, good even for the East Texas bayou country, and if there was one advantage of going up against German tanks, they were sure a lot easier to hear.

The edge of the village was about two hundred yards away, making the usual abrupt change from open fields to narrow streets, the wheat stubble somewhat obscured by the grass and wheel ruts left by the retreating Germans. This was the first day in two weeks that they had not been in combat although the increasing speed of the German retreat had made it more challenging to catch up. By some miracle, the bridge was still intact and untouched so they kept going forward at about six to eight miles an hour, taking almost five minutes to reach the edge of the village. The road made a gradual turn to the right past the village church, and some houses along the street showed a bit of smoke from their chimneys. Good sign, he thought, if they're cooking they're probably not hiding in their cellars. He heard some friendly artillery fire not too far behind and as the tank rolled forward he turned to see if the rest of his unit was catching up.

"Monsieur!"

A little girl had run out from behind the house on the right and was frantically waving at him and pointing down the street.

"Le Boche!"

At that moment, there was the roar of a motor down the street as the Panther left its hiding place and started to roll forward, its turret turning at the same time. Doc kicked Crockett hard on the left shoulder and reached down to the girl's outstretched hand, pulling her hard all the way up onto the pile of logs they had chained to the front for extra protection. In addition to his skill as a driver, Crockett was an inspired mechanic so the tank leaped forward right as the Panther fired. The projectile passed so close to the Sherman that Doc felt the shock wave before they were safely around the corner behind the church. He wasn't going to put it past the Germans to fire a round right through the church itself, so they kept going another fifty yards before pivoting around 180 degrees.

The girl was barely holding on as the tank rushed forward, and as they slowed, Doc took a closer look. About six or seven, Doc judged, her face framed with the short black hair and brown eyes that were so common in France, and, as it happened, right back in Doc's part of Texas.

"Merci, Monsieur," she said breathlessly.

"Merci beaucoup, Mademoiselle," he replied.

She smiled weakly, still barely managing to hold on to the grips on the side of the tank, but talking away about something that worried her. His Cajun French was good enough to get most of what she was saying, something about the Germans and sickness, but there were more pressing things on his mind right now, like whether that Panther was going to come down the street after them, and turn this into something very bloody.

He jumped out of the turret and pulled her up and inside, and in a moment, he was back in position and waiting. Doc shushed everyone, listening to a distant whine that got louder and louder, then turning into a screech as two P-51's zoomed by, strafing the German column and firing at the tanks retreating on the road ahead just as the first jeeps from his Division roared up the road followed by another line of trucks with more troops and supplies.

"Park her here," said Doc, the engine sputtered twice and was silent. The girl gingerly reached her hands up and through the hatch where Doc helped her out and onto the top of the turret. He jumped off the tank first, and as she tried to climb down he took her gently over his shoulder and set her feet first onto the ground. The other members of the crew piled out, coming over to the girl and thanking her in their best combination of Cajun French and English. As Doc watched, however, she began to wobble and as she took a step forward collapsed onto the ground.

Doc picked her up and after hailing a jeep drove to the aid station where Doc MacMillan did a quick checkup.

"Pneumonia," he said, shaking his head. "Temperature of 105 degrees combined with malnutrition and general debilitation."

"This kid saved our lives," said Doc. "Come on, there's something you can give her!"

Doc MacMillan reached up and scratched his head. "Well – we have a small case of this new drug called penicillin, and luckily we haven't had to use much of it yet. It's supposed to be just the ticket for pneumonia, deep infections, even syphilis. If you want, I can give it a try."

Three days later Doc and the crew went down to the girl's house, and to their joy she answered the door herself, her mother beaming behind her. She looked a heck of a lot better and invited everyone inside. Each man was carrying a duffel bag stuffed with canned corned beef, D bars, soap, and anything else they could find, which they carried into the back of the house and piled into a small bedroom. One of the correspondents heard the story about what the girl did, and on an impulse, he had Doc and the girl go outside and took a picture of the two of them in front of the house.

Half an hour later, Doc and the crew were back in their tank and barreling down the road on the way to Alsace, never coming back to the village for the rest of the war. A month later Doc ran into the correspondent who gave him a copy of the picture and was told he'd also given one to the girl before they too shipped out.

By this time most of the other restaurant guests were gathered around their table, the room quiet except for the sound of Grandpa's voice. As he finished, he reached into his shirt pocket and handed the picture to Joan.

"This is the picture that correspondent gave me," said Doc. "That good looking young soldier is me, and that's the girl who saved us."

The picture showed a small house built right up to the road, a low tiled roof, and a second story window box still full of flowers, the very same window box that Joan watered from the time she was big enough to carry a watering can. Papa was looking too, and Joan felt his arm around her shoulder holding her close. Grandmother was so young in the picture, her face thin as she recovered from pneumonia, saved by the penicillin that Doc had gotten for her.

"But you saved her," said Joan, her face wet.

187

"No, Joan – the doctor saved her, and I wasn't facing any danger taking her down the road to the aid station. Your Grandma's another story. If she hadn't risked her life to run out on that road right in front of the Germans, we would have been blown to smithereens before we drove another ten feet," said Doc. "Look in front of you. One little girl taking a chance – she saved our lives and then we saved hers. How many people at this table wouldn't be here except for that?

Chapter Thirty-Six
Candles
Joan

That dinner was a turning point for me because the nightmares I had been having off and on finally stopped. I was sleeping better, too, so the next weekend Papa and I decided to get out of town for a few days. The weather hadn't turned hot yet so we went down to New Orleans where we could eat French food, hear some jazz, and just talk. One of the nice things about the Café du Monde is that it's always crowded, and between the coffee, fresh beignets, and tourists it was easy to sit there and be anonymous. We'd talked about so many things on the way down that we were running out of topics, but there was still a giant thing on my mind that I had to talk about before I went crazy.

"How could I do that?" I asked.

"What do you mean, Squirt?"

"I mean, I understand that I saved Ryan and everything, but I still dream about the sword and…stabbing him like that. Like meat going onto a skewer. How could I do something like that and still be a decent person?"

188

"Do you remember what you were thinking when it happened?" asked Papa. "At that moment?"

Joan shook her head.

"I've watched that video maybe twenty times," said Papa. "And each time when he stands up and comes at you with his sword it's the same thing, but you don't notice something right away. He lunges and you parry, and at that moment your sword is pointed right at his belly - but instead of sticking him you change its direction and it goes into his leg instead." Papa shook his head in wonder. "I always knew you could think on your feet, Jeannette, but you had his life in your hands at that moment and you didn't take it away from him."

We walked out from the Café into Jackson Square, the evening sky is so clear it's practically sparkling, and I saw that the front door of Saint Louis Cathedral was standing open. It's like a magnet to both of us as we walk across the square, spring flowers in full bloom, and then through the door and inside. The light was muted and only the barest sound from Jackson Square could be heard behind us.

Six o'clock mass has started and I realize it's a Latin mass, the choir starting the Kyrie. Papa and I do our duty to the altar, but I see a row of red votive candles in front of the Blessed Virgin and for a moment I am a little girl back in Grandmother's house, we're in front of the statue on the mantle and she's helping me to light the candle...but it wasn't Grandmother this time, it's me. I'm kneeling in front of the candles and I look up at the Statue, and the question is there, and the only answer that comes to me is to drop three dollars into the box and light three candles – one for Mama, one for Miss Renoir, and I think I am about to light one for myself but I realize that's not the right answer. Who? Who is it for? It is suddenly clear, so with a trembling hand, I light one more – for Mr. Todd.

Mea culpa, mea culpa, mea maxima culpa.

Chapter Thirty-Seven
Remembrance

For someone who had crossed the Atlantic at least a dozen times, Joan was completely spoiled by sitting in First Class. The Embassy had been extremely generous, not only by the impeccable courtesy shown to Joan and her father, but also in the way arrangements had been made for picking up Joan, her Papa, and Michelle, and getting them to the airport.

Michelle was thrilled to pieces by the prospect of the trip ahead. No stranger to international flights herself, she nonetheless had never been to France and had spent so much time reading about Paris and its history that Joan felt somewhat dumb in comparison. Michelle was sleeping now, her first-class seat reclined so far back to become an unusually comfortable bed with its soft leather upholstery.

189

Joan was wide awake, however, having learned long before the value of sleeping before a flight. The attendant assigned to their part of the cabin was especially solicitous, treating her group almost like minor royalty. It was good to speak nothing but French again, but the central purpose of the trip took away most of the anticipation she usually felt.

Five days before, Papa had unexpectedly picked her up from school, saying there was going to be an important call from the French Embassy and that he wanted them to be together when it came. Usually, Joan would have been a nervous wreck, but with the events of the past month something had happened, and she even surprised herself at how calm she was. The person who put the call through first made sure that they were both present, and transferred the call to the Ambassador.

"Good evening Professor Darcy, and Jeanette. There has been a development regarding your late wife. During a recent police investigation in the area where the death occurred, human remains were found in the Seine that our laboratory has identified as belonging to Catharine Darcy. It is our hope that you will wish to come to Paris so that we may accord her proper burial with the recognition and honor she deserves. However, this is entirely your decision."

They had thanked the Ambassador and told him they would contact the Embassy by the end of the next day.

"What do you think, Joan?" asked Papa quietly. Not Squirt – not today.

"I'm still in school, Papa," answered Joan. "But...something tells me they'll give me an okay on this one. Things are a lot different these days."

"I'll bet," replied Papa. "Thanks to..."

"Thanks to Mrs. Coates," said Joan. "Not me. At school these days it's been a lot like opening windows on a spring day after a long, bleak winter. Can somebody cover your remaining classes?"

"Fred has been teaching the past month anyhow, so there wouldn't even be a ripple," replied Papa. "So, let's at least build in some down time. Say – three days in Paris, then a week at Domremy. That sound okay?"

"Papa – it sounds great, but do you think I could bring someone along?"

Papa nodded. "I thought you would ask that, and I presume you're talking about Michelle?"

Joan sighed. "I know I'm tougher than I used to be, but it would mean a lot if I could have my best friend with me."

"I think ten days in France under the official sponsorship of the French government would be acceptable to the Hans, Joan."

There was a gentle tap on her shoulder, and Joan looked up to see Jacques, the liaison that the Embassy had assigned to them for the trip. He had been a huge help already, from arranging for the limo back in Smithfield to checking their bags under diplomatic seal so they didn't even have to go through security.

"Are you awake, Jeanne?" he asked.

Joan nodded. "Awake enough. It's a smooth trip for a change."

"It is," he responded. "Jeanne, there is something we have brought to you, something you should see before we arrive in Paris. We discussed this with your Papa and he agrees. Is now a good time?"

For someone who had been through what Joan had been through over the past two weeks – winning a tournament, stabbing your principal, and now going to your mother's funeral - there wasn't much left that could be any worse.

"Yes. Can you tell me what it is?"

Jacques reached into his briefcase and removed a laptop that Joan recognized as the same type her Mama carried. As he handed it to her, Joan recognized the tiny French flag decal she herself had attached to the front cover.

"Do you recognize this?" asked Jacques.

Joan nodded, her finger gently stroking the smooth metal of the cover, the image of Mama always turning away from the keyboard to smile at her as she came into the room, sitting on her lap and being rocked gently to sleep with the up, down motion of Mama's arms as she typed. The sticker had come from a candy bar on their last trip together, purchased in a supermarket in Neufchatel on their way to DeGaulle Airport.

"Please open it, Jeanne, and turn it on," said Jacques. "We have unlocked it already, so you do not need to enter anything until it is fully started." As Joan watched, the startup screen appeared for a moment but then went directly to the desktop. Even though she knew what would be there, it still was a shock to see the desktop photo, a family picture of Grandmother, Papa and herself that Mama had taken in Domremy on their last trip together. Usually a tidy housekeeper, Mama had left several icons on the screen that seemed lost, perhaps looking for their folders.

Jacques pointed to a file labeled J in the lower right-hand corner. "That one," he said. "We have attempted to unlock it but the encryption is too complex. We ask that you open it if you can."

Joan double clicked on the icon and it opened into Word, but in the center of the screen was another dialogue box:

ENTER KEY CODE: _____

Joan sat back for a moment. If they have already unlocked the computer, then why are they asking me to do this...but a memory came to her of a birthday when she was five after they had started the fencing lessons. Mama loved to hide things, and she bought a whole sheet of tiny stickers all with the letter J that she would paste all over the house on things where she would hide a small toy or piece of candy. This is for me, Joan realized. It's not a State Secret, it's Mama's way of putting a sticker on a box for me to find. Her fingers struck the keys, entering her special code name a character at a time:

SquirT

A dialogue box appeared saying Decryption in progress, the screen blipped, and the document appeared, the three words in French at the top making her grip the sides of the computer.

Ma Chere Jeannette,

Jacques was still standing there but obviously wanted to see what she found, so Joan picked up the computer and turned it around. He took a glance and nodded. "This is what we expected," he said, "but we had to be sure. Do not hesitate to ask if you need anything."

"Don't worry, I won't erase it," said Joan, and Jacques was tuned in enough that he simply smiled and left. Joan pulled down the lid of the laptop so that she couldn't see the screen anymore, but not so far that she would have to restart the computer.

This is a message from Mama. She was probably writing it on the plane because she had about three hours to live after she landed. It's even possible that she was sitting right where I'm sitting, in about this place in the sky on her way to France, and there was probably some quiet music playing, maybe a glass of good French wine, and there was so much future ahead for the three of us. Or she knew how dangerous the trip could be and she was making sure....

Joan squeezed her eyes shut and gripped her hands together as tightly as she could, the only sure way she knew to keep from going down that spiral as she had several times before. Breathe, Joan, breathe as Mama taught you, evenly in, out, focus, focus, focus...

When Mama wrote this she was alive - that's the image I must keep in my head. She was alive and loved me and Papa and we loved her back and that's ours to keep forever.

Joan took a deep breath, opened the laptop, and began to read.

My dear Jeannette,

I am on the plane and the flight is smooth so far. I am sorry that this came up so suddenly, but if all goes well I will be finished tomorrow and on my way back to you. I have been excited about the tournament this weekend with much confidence that you will do well.

But I must tell you something because you are growing and we must not sugar coat things only to feel better. As you do not know if you will win your tournament, there is no guarantee that this trip will be safe or that my job in Paris will go well. Things happen to people, things they do not expect, things they do not deserve, and there is nothing left afterward but unanswered questions. For a long time, I have thought to write this letter so that if something happens to me you will know about who you are, and why. With

God's grace, I will see you again, but if not I will at least be assured you will know about the things I must now tell you.

In case you were expecting me to say that you are adopted, you may rest assured I am your real Mama and Papa is your real Papa, Grandmother is Grandmother, and you were born in Domremy la Pucelle in Grandmother's house. From the first moment your Papa and I saw you, we knew that an angel with a smile and a wisp of black hair had joined our lives. You were named Jeanne because it is a very old tradition in our family that from generation to generation first daughters are named Catharine and Jeanne in their turn. These traditions connect us to each other and to our common past, which for our family is very, very old indeed.

Catharine, Jeanne, Catharine, Jeanne. If you remember over the fireplace in your Grandmother's home there is a small painting with the word Catharine painted at the bottom, as on the wall of Grandmother's room there is a picture of St. Jeanne. If you recall your history of Domremy la Pucelle, Jeanne D'Arc was born in the village and lived there until the wars and her martyrdom in Rouen. Jeanne also had two older brothers and a younger sister named Catharine. The painting of Catharine over the fireplace is Catharine D'Arc, the younger sister of the peasant girl who became the Maid of France, and we are the direct descendants of that Catharine. Many years ago, when you were very small, I asked you which picture you liked, and instead of the Catharine over the fireplace, you preferred the painting of Jeanne D'Arc in Grandmother's bedroom because Jeanne was holding a flag and wearing a suit of armor and that the two of you shared the same name.

At the time, Jeanne became well known, the King of France had died but his son the Dauphin could not become King. Jeanne's appearance at court and the miracle of her identifying the Dauphin caused a great impression among certain members of the court, and when Jeanne succeeded in winning her very first battle against impossible odds, rallying thousands more to her banner, it gave the Dauphin enough courage to become crowned at Rheims with Jeanne present. To the English occupiers of western France, this made her a target to be eliminated.

Jeanne was later captured and sold to the English. The Dauphin, knowing that they intended to execute her, became convinced that his own lack of courage had resulted in this betrayal. Through a great act of courage, he disguised himself and in the company of a priest and young boy visited Jeanne in her cell, where he dubbed her a Knight of France. An event unique in all French history, the title was to be passed only through the female line to subsequent generations. Since Jeanne was martyred the next day, the title was passed to Jeanne's sister Catharine.

A young boy from Domremy who came with the priest became a hereditary squire to Jeanne's successors. This boy returned to Domremy and delivered the news to Catharine who assumed the knighthood in her turn. Catharine by this time had married and given birth to a daughter, named Jeanne after Catharine's martyred sister. Although Catharine later died in childbirth, this daughter Jeanne grew to adulthood, received instruction from the boy, and was knighted in her turn. The boy's son gave instruction to Jeanne's daughter, and so on through the centuries to your Grandmother and me. Someday, you will be the next, and with God's grace your daughter also, and so on into the future.

The boy's name was Paul Renoir, and Grandmother's lifelong friend Madame Renoir is a direct descendant. Her granddaughter Catherine...

Joan was so engrossed by what she was reading that at first, she did not at first feel the gentle hand on her shoulder, but when the touch registered she turned and looked up.

"May I sit, Jeannette?" said Miss Renoir.

"I thought you would be here," said Joan. "It took me a while to figure it out, but until about a minute ago, I thought I was crazy. Turns out I was right after all."

"About what?"

"About you. It was simply too much coincidence that someone like you – someone with your qualifications - would pop out of thin air and end up in a place like Smithfield right at the time Papa and I were moving there. Not that I wasn't lucky – but luck isn't the word. Is it?"

Miss Renoir shook her head. "Some people say the only luck we have is the luck we make for ourselves, but I have never believed that. You do not believe it, either, Jeannette, although right now you might think you do."

"I don't know what I believe right now, as a matter of fact," said Joan bitterly. "I'm on an airplane going to bury my mother. What luck did she have? Lucky enough to get herself blown up?"

"Yes, Jeannette, lucky enough to get herself blown up because by doing so she fulfilled the highest duty that all humans owe to each other – to love each other. You may call it by another name – duty, honor, protect the helpless, but it is still love at the end. To give someone else's life the chance to fulfill itself, perhaps. Was it luck that made you defend Michelle from bullying, or care for Christine's sisters, or step between Mr. Todd and Ryan?"

"That's different!"

"No, it isn't. Ask yourself this question – when you learned about what happened, about what your mother did, were you surprised? By the event itself, perhaps, but not why she did it. Am I correct?"

It was a hard thing to admit, but Miss Renoir was right. It was a scene Joan had replayed a thousand times in her head, the little girl who had built a church out of Legos, standing under a tree with her Mama on that day she started to fence.

"What does RISK mean, Mama,"

"It means fear and danger, Jeannette. It means facing both fear and danger if you are always to do the right thing, to protect people who cannot protect themselves."

"But that is a good thing, isn't it, Mama, to protect people?"

"Mais oui, Jeannette."

That was it after all. There comes a point when you must face the fear and the danger, and despite them do the right thing. Once long ago she had promised her Mama, and she had kept her vow.

Even though Joan wanted to bury her head in Mama's shoulder like on that day long ago, warm and safe, there was a promise made by a little girl under a tree on a beautiful spring day. The promise that Joan had kept all along, almost without realizing it because it was now such a part of her. The other, unspoken promises, kept to Mrs. T, and Mrs. Coates, and Christine – and to Michelle and Dwight and George and finally, to Ryan. And, in a way, to Mr. Todd, because he would have to get past her before he could hurt her friend.

Is this how it feels to be all grown up? When you know what to do next without having to ask anybody? Or is it when you finally take your medicine without someone waiting to give you a lollypop afterward? How do you feel at that moment when you know what your future is going to be? I guess it's when you don't ask those questions anymore, when you go ahead and do it, she decided. I told Michelle once, that you need to be able to look at yourself in the mirror. I now realize that finally, one day, you reach the point where you don't need to look anymore.

"What about you?" Joan asked tiredly, all anger gone. "What are you able to tell me?"

Miss Renoir could see the old, old pain in Joan's eyes. Some say it's a sin for a child to grow up so quickly, but sometimes life doesn't wait.

"I was born in Domremy la Pucelle like you, and my Grandmother is your old family friend Catharine Renoir, the great granddaughter 23 times over of the Paul Renoir who went to the dungeon where Jeanne D'Arc awaited her death. My parents both died in an automobile accident shortly after I was born so I lived with my Grandmother until I went to University."

"Did you ever see me, or did I ever see you? Before Smithfield, I mean?"

Miss Renoir smiled. "I attended your parents' wedding, and the day you were born I held you in my arms. I am only fifteen years older than you, Jeanne, and by the time you were five I had already started boarding school and then on to University. I saw you a few times over the years but with my special training summer holidays were few and far between."

"Special training?"

"My position – the hereditary position described by your Mama in that letter – is well known and respected by the Government of France. In certain circles I – we – are known as Persona Grata, and are therefore trusted completely. If we

195

pass certain qualification tests, then we receive the training. It is very rigorous and very demanding, but highly effective." She looked at Joan with a truly serious expression for the first time. "I must tell you this, Jeannette. It is my duty to tell you what you wish to know, but I must also have your word of honor. None of this to anyone without my express permission. Is that understood?

"You have my word," replied Joan. "But why now? Why especially today?"

"Because in our history going back to 1431, to the year of Jeanne D'Arc's martyrdom, you are the youngest to be ready."

"Ready for what?"

"Ready to become the next Chevalière, Jeanne. Your Mama was Chevalière Catharine. You, if you accept, will be Chevalière Jeanne."

Chevalière. That strange hybrid title someone had once called Mama during a visit to Paris long ago.

Then for some inexplicable reason, Joan had to do something to lighten up. There had been too much pain, sorrow, disappointment, and loss for the past week. Looking over at where her friend still slept, something popped into Joan's head. What would Michelle say to this question? In nine months of knowing Michelle, Joan had absorbed some of her friend's bizarre sense of humor, often saying something exactly wrong at exactly the wrong time, but on purpose and with such seriousness it defused a tense situation. Of course, sometimes it also was like throwing gasoline on a fire, but that's the chance you took.

"What's the catch?" asked Joan, with a twinkle in her eye. Miss Renoir's eyes widened but at the same time saw Joan's expression.

"How much time do you have?" replied Miss Renoir, and they laughed together.

"I do have a few more important questions first," said Joan. "What exactly did my Mother do? I know she was smart and bilingual and everything, but lots of people are like that. What did she do that was special?"

"Have you ever heard of an eidetic memory, Jeanne?"

"That's where you remember…well, everything. Faces and things like that?"

"Yes and no. Usually, an eidetic memory remains only during childhood, but for some people and in some families, it persists into and through adulthood. Your mother had a very rare eidetic memory where it was not that she could recall seeing something, she could also remember the most exacting details about it long afterward. For example, she had the ability to walk through an art gallery and weeks later remember every painting, every artist, the room it was in, and even the face of every person in each room. This meant that her skills were exceptionally valuable in locating and identifying persons who had altered their appearance since she could mentally alter the image to reveal the real face beneath."

"For you, this ability has taken a new and very interesting form. When you have a fencing opponent, you instantly register movement, mannerism, physical strengths and weaknesses – things that are impossible to hide. Another part is

196

your ability to instantly build a mental map of floor plans, city streets, and sequences of anything that moves."

"I presume this is a good thing?" asked Joan.

"It is, to put it mildly, immensely valuable to the right people."

"So, if I do this, if I accept, what happens to me?"

Miss Renoir grew serious again. "That is a complex question, Jeanne. As I said, nobody so young has ever been in this position. There is a ceremony, oaths to take. I have witnessed it only once, for your Mama, but I assure you it is a supremely solemn, beautiful thing."

"I'm not talking about the ceremony, I'm talking about afterward," said Joan impatiently. "Oaths to who? To what?"

"The oath is not to any country, but to your duty, Jeanne. This is no longer the Middle Ages and we no longer pledge fealty to a King. For one thing, I know you would refuse, but for another, I think I know you well enough that afterward, if you accept, you will greatly relish the challenges you will face. I know your Mother certainly did."

As the words registered within her Joan felt a growing sense of calm, like the feeling she would get after arriving at a much-anticipated destination. Many questions remained but very many had been answered as well, some she had long awaited finding the answer to. Something crept into her head, words she had learned long before, Papa or Mama repeating it when certain things happened:

> **It matters not how strait the gate,**
> **How charged with punishments the scroll,**
> **I am the master of my fate:**
> **I am the captain of my soul.**

Growing up in a family like hers, Joan was constantly nestled between two very smart people who used literature the way others use a knife and fork. Papa always had a choice quote for Joan when she complained about something, and as she grew older the quotes started to connect themselves to things in her daily life.

"How much does Papa know about this?"

"Everything," replied Miss Renoir, "from the day before he married your Mama. For a man with such an all-encompassing respect for the past, he understood the value of what your family was doing, and why. Oddly enough, the simple fact of your parent's getting together was almost ordained from the beginning. Look at your name, for example."

"Jeanne?"

"Think again. What do you think is the origin of Darcy?" Miss Renoir asked, grinning.

"You've got to be kidding!" said Joan after a moment. "Darcy comes from..."

"D'Arc," replied Miss Renoir. "Technically your father married his 24th cousin three times removed."

"If anyone's counting," replied Joan.

THE VISITORS
May 29 1431

There was a sound from outside, the rough voice of the jailer talking to someone with a calmer, deeper voice, and there was the sound of the bolt being drawn back. Jeanne was expecting her inquisitor, but was instead surprised to see a priest, tall and robust, accompanied by a cowled monk and young boy in brown robes. She rose and made her respect to the priest, who looked at her with a gentle expression and raised his hand in blessing. The cell door clanged shut behind him, and there was the echo of retreating footsteps.

"We are alone, my child," said the priest softly "but we have little time. Let me hear your confession."

Jeanne caught her breath. The English had sent in priests before, false priests who would hear a confession and then break its sanctity to lie about what she said. This priest was different, however, speaking with the accent of Domremy. She knelt, crossed herself, and poured out her confession, her fears and doubts so wretched with her fatigue, and lastly her fear of death although she was sure it was God's will that it be so.

She finished and waited to receive her absolution but the priest put his finger to his lips.

"The jailer has kept his word," he whispered "but time is short." He turned to the Monk and to Jeanne's surprise he bowed as the Monk stepped before Jeanne who was still kneeling on the floor. Reaching to his cowl, he dropped it back onto his shoulders and Jeanne's heart nearly stopped.

"Sire!" the whisper barely audible.

"Hush, Jeanne," he replied, and the words stopped in her throat. She looked at him in her confusion, the single question dominating her. WHY?

"It is a time for truth, Jeanne. They will never allow you to leave here alive, and if they simply lock the door and leave you our cause will die along with it." The King of France looked deeply into her eyes and Joan saw the pain that was still there, pain for a sundered kingdom and oppressed people. "You have a knight's duty, my child. You must defy them to the end, becoming a martyr whose sacrifice will be an inspiration for a thousand years."

Jeanne nodded, the import of the words what she had always known...but the King said something else. "Forgive me, Sire...a knight's duty?"

"Yes, Jeanne, a knight's duty. It is a wound in my heart that I have never truly shown my thanks..."

"Forgive me, Sire, but it was my duty...."

"Yes, Jeanne, and it is now our obligation to sanctify your courage for doing so." He rose back to his feet and put his hand gently on Jeanne's head.

"Father Gregory and this boy will bear witness. Jeanne, repeat after me. I will never traffic with traitors."

"I will never traffic with traitors."

"I will never give bad counsel and be truthful in all things."

198

"I will never give bad counsel and be truthful in all things."

"I will protect the helpless though it cost me my life."

"I will protect the helpless though it cost me my life."

"And this I swear to God, the Virgin, and all the Saints of Heaven."

"And this I swear to God, the Virgin, and all the Saints of Heaven."

The king took half a step back, and with the back of his hand gently slapped Jeanne on her cheeks three times as was the custom.

"I, Charles the Seventh, by the grace of God King of France, of Aquitaine, and Navarre, dub thee Chevalière Jeanne D'Arc and hereditary Count of Compiegne." He turned and motioned to the boy, who stepped forward and bowed before him.

"And you, Paul Renoir, I appoint you hereditary squire to the House of D'Arc, to protect and serve Jeanne and her successors. Do you accept this duty before God?"

"I accept this duty before God."

"Arise, Sir Jeanne," said the King softly. "Come, Father."

Jeanne again bowed her head, and in an even softer voice the Priest began to recite the words that Jeanne recognized as the Extreme Unction, and it was like a chill had entered her soul.

"Ego te absolvo in nomine Patriis, et Filiis, et Spiritu Sanctis. Amen."

"The cursed English would not even offer you this last consolation, my child," said the priest compassionately.

The King stood, but in the flicker of the torch Jeanne could see the tears on his face. "Jeanne, receive this from our hands. God be with you, and remember what a Knight of France would do."

There was the sound of a door creaking open nearby, and the boy tugged at the Priest's robe, whispering urgently. "Quickly, Father." The King, now cowled, stood behind the Priest with the boy behind him, as the jailer opened the door.

"Time's up."

The little group filed silently out of the cell, only the boy at the end quickly turning his head and giving her one last, fleeting, smile, then the door clanged shut and the bolt slid back into place.

A Knight? Me? A girl? It was impossible, but she had not imagined it. Now she knew she was going to die, and there was nothing she could do, except...

Except to show the English what a Knight of France would do.

When the jailer opened the cell door, the inquisitors entered to find the small shapeless mass of a dress neatly folded in the middle of the room, next to a girl, proudly dressed in military clothing, a studded leather jacket and spurs - A Knight of France.

Chapter Thirty-Eight
Paris

Although she had been born in France and spent a good part of her life there, Joan had never been in Paris more than to pass through on the way to the airport.

It didn't come as much of a surprise to find the weather beautiful, the streets bustling, and the air full of an amazing variety of scents ranging from fresh bread to bus exhaust. Walking with Michelle, Joan found herself envious of her friend's boundless energy, fueled no doubt by the fact that she slept the entire trip, but between reading Mama's letter and talking with Miss Renoir for most of the trip Joan's energy indicator was starting to blink on and off. Papa's idea to get a good cup of coffee helped somewhat, so Papa had let the two of them take off for a few hours after receiving their solemn promise to be back at the hotel no later than six o'clock.

The Seine was sparkling and crowded with sightseeing boats and other pleasure craft, everyone tooting their horns at everyone else. Michelle was in seventh heaven, everything new and interesting, especially the myriad of book stalls lining the river and the multitude of struggling artists trying to sell a dizzying variety of landscapes, building studies, and the occasional portrait. She and Joan had bought fried egg sandwiches at another stall, the egg still sizzling as it was scooped into the oven-fresh baguette with a sprinkling of fresh basil, and Michelle was trying to take a bite out of hers while she thumbed through a selection of books in one of the many bookstalls that lined the river.

 "This is so cool," she said, "and the last thing I ever expected to see here, of all places. I mean, The Three Musketeers in Mandarin?" Taking the book in her free hand, she managed to see the price, and through a series of complicated maneuvers held her sandwich in one hand while holding the book under her arm while she extracted her wallet with her other hand, opened it with a thumb, and complete the transaction while taking still another bite from her sandwich.

When Michelle was finished with the purchase and they had walked a bit further, Joan stopped and faced her friend. "You're never supposed to pay the price written inside, Michelle. It's not the actual price but more of a starting point for negotiation."

"You mean haggling?" said Michelle.

"Yes, as a matter of fact," Joan answered. "It's a tradition."

Ten minutes later, Joan was waiting as Michelle was arguing with another bookseller, the two of them throwing up their hands, crocodile tears rolling down their faces, the air full of French and Chinese, nobody listening to anybody. When the transaction was finally completed, Michelle emerged triumphantly with the book in her hand.

"Got it for half price!" she crowed. "Who says I can't find a bargain?"

"Next time I'll know better," replied Joan. "Looks like you were born to haggle, but a little bird tells me you didn't do quite as well as you think." As it happened another bookstall fifty feet away had a whole stack of the same book

Michelle had just bought, brand new and for half the price that she paid. Joan started to speak but Michelle put up her finger in warning.

"Don't," said Michelle. "Just don't."

Joan glanced at her watch and saw that they were due back at the hotel in thirty minutes. Her mental map of the city told her that they could either go back the way they had come or by crossing the river at the bridge ahead they could get there about ten minutes earlier

"Come on – this way," said Joan as she stepped out faster, leaving Michelle to hurriedly replace a book into the bin and run to catch up. The street was getting harder to navigate as it filled with Parisians leaving work and enjoying the perfect weather, so it took some squeezing to get through the crowd and onto the sidewalk that led across the bridge.

As she started across Joan saw a young woman with a child about five or six years old, standing about ten meters ahead and carefully leaning a bouquet of flowers against the railing. Both mother and daughter were wearing spring dresses, the first of the season, and as she and Michelle drew near the little girl looked up and smiled. Joan saw that the child had the same shining black hair framing her face as her mother, so very like Joan herself at that age. As Joan bent down to be at eye-level with the little girl, the mother put her hand on the child's shoulder in a gesture so reminiscent of her own mother that Joan caught her breath.

"My name is Jeanne," the little girl said. "Did you bring flowers?"

"No, little one, not today," Joan answered. "My name is Jeanne, too," and pointed at Michelle who stood impatiently to the side. "This is my friend Michelle."

After inspecting Michelle, the little Jeanne turned back to Joan and nodded solemnly.

"My best friend is named Michelle," she said.

Joan smiled warmly and turned to look at Michelle in her turn. "Mine too." Standing, Joan turned to continue down the bridge when another group of young women approached, each leading a small child carrying a bouquet. As Joan watched, the children stepped forward one by one and placed their bouquets against the railing, making it so crowded so that Joan had to move to make more space. The children all bowed their heads while one of the mothers recited a Hail Mary, while Joan, deeply moved, joined the chorus of tiny voices. At the end, all made the Sign of the Cross and the little group reorganized itself to continue across the bridge.

"What a beautiful gesture," said Joan. "May I ask, what was the remembrance?"

"For the one who gave all these children their lives," said one of the mothers. "This is where it happened."

Joan could hardly speak. "What is the name of this bridge?"

"This is the Petit Pont," the woman replied. "Bon Soir, Mademoiselle."

Something was going on here, thought Michelle, but Joan obviously wasn't in a talkative mood and I have no idea what they said. Mom has been trying to get some French into my head for this trip but I have a long way to go. Looking at Joan here on this bridge, it was like all of the events of the past month were written there on her face.

The children were acting as any children would on a spring day, unable to hold still but still too close to traffic to let go of their mother's hands. As Joan and Michelle watched, they formed into a straggly column toward the east, where the spires of Notre Dame softly glowed in the early evening light.

Fifty-seven, thought Joan, and how many Jeannes and Catharines and Pierres and Jacques among them, not lying in a lonely grave but alive, bouncing along with their mothers on a spring day with their whole lives ahead of them. She looked down at the pile of bouquets, the offerings of five children and who knows how many families spared unspeakable anguish. This is the culmination, this is the reality, the proof, the final commitment. Protect the helpless, an oath given and fulfilled honorably. Grandmother said it, Mama said it, and now it's my turn - but I'm not alone, either.

"We have a lot to talk about, Michelle. It's going to be a tough week ahead, and there are some things you should know." She looked at her friend, the wry humor, and yes, the strength. "I'm glad you're here."

Chapter Thirty-Nine
Homecoming

Over the next week, Joan often thought about those few hours, because once she and Michelle returned to the hotel everything got busy. Since Catharine Darcy was born in Domremy la Pucelle, she and Papa decided that was where they would lay her to rest. The government wasn't particularly happy but when

202

you put over six hundred years of loyal service on one side of the scale and a photo op for politicians on the other, there's not much of a contest.

It was with mixed emotions that they finally started on the drive to Domremy, the weather so beautiful they could travel at least part of the way with the windows down. The countryside was in full flush of spring with orchards in blossom and the sweet aroma permeating the air, and for Papa, Miss Renoir, Joan, and Michelle it brought back the sense of their many trips to fencing tournaments together.

"Now that I'm thinking about it, what happened after those FBI agents came to the classroom that day?" asked Joan.

"As you remember we returned from the tournament very late and went directly to Toussaint's. While we were there, your ...Mr. Todd went back to the school. He was very, very angry, Joan – not with you but with me. It was obvious from the beginning that he was under the influence of a drug of some kind, undoubtedly a stimulant as he seemed unable to calm himself. One of the great dangers of authority is that sometimes those at the top think of themselves as all powerful and immune, and although Mr. Todd had become quite a severe addict, he would never have admitted it.

"I had also heard about what happened with your friend Brian. After his injury, the police had received an anonymous tip about Coach Reed supplying his players with drugs, and when they arrived at the school the drugs were exactly where it was said they would be. In my case, there were indeed drugs found hidden inside my classroom, but it became obvious he was the one who had hidden them. Mr. Todd's fingerprints were all over both sets of bottles, the ones from my room and the ones that had been found in Mr. Reed's office."

"Why couldn't you let us know what happened?" Joan asked.

"For one thing, you were in the hospital, but it's not that simple. You see, my case is far more complicated than simply working for the school and being dismissed, or even being set up to make it look like I distributed drugs at your school," said Miss Renoir. "After the men who arrested me looked into my background, they discovered some things I would not explain. I was put under house arrest pending an investigation. I never suspected it would go this far, and in fact, it was only last week that I was released to our embassy, thanks in part to your Mr. Kershaw."

"Mr. Kershaw? Dwight's Grandpa? What did he do?"

"Quite a bit, in fact. Any man who has earned the Legion of Honor as well as your Medal of Honor has many, many friends on both sides of the Atlantic, and is a man those in authority will listen to. He made some calls on my behalf so that my case was immediately investigated at the highest levels. Subsequently, there were assurances made and agreed upon, so at last, I was free to go."

"So here we are," said Joan after a moment. She studied the face of her teacher for a moment, her eyes softening at the memories of all the laughter, the kindnesses, and most of all, the strength. Taking Miss Renoir's arm, Joan leaned gently against her shoulder and slept.

As they grew closer to Domremy and the countryside became more familiar, the mood in the car grew more poignant and tinged with melancholy. This was the first trip to Domremy Joan and her Papa had ever taken without Mama, but it helped enormously that Miss Renoir had accompanied them, not because of their fondness for her but to share her own poignant joy at coming home.

The village was expecting them, with hundreds of neighbors and townsfolk dressed in simple black and each carrying a freshly picked bouquet. Grandmother and Madame Renoir were waiting, too, and although Joan promised herself no tears there were more than a few as she held Grandmother close, her hair gently stroked as always. Joan introduced Michelle, who was immediately engulfed by Grandmother, simultaneously squeezing and murmuring Merci's and other things that Joan had to translate until Michelle was finally released.

"People are real friendly here," said Joan.

"No kidding," replied Michelle.

"It's time," said Papa.

As they entered the church Joan was transfixed by the sight of bouquets attached to every pew, the Chancel glorious, all the flowers from the gardens of the townspeople as a gesture of affection for one of their own. The coffin was placed a few meters in front of the altar where old Pere Bernard waited. Joan started to grit her teeth, the only way she had ever found to slow down her tears when she felt Papa's hand on hers. Looking up, she saw that tears were trickling down his cheek, his eyes shining.

"It is so like our wedding," he said. "The priest, the flowers, the townspeople, all the same."

They were seated at the front as was the custom, and for the occasion, there was a small choir made up of townspeople. Pere Bernard turned to the choir, who rose to their feet, one of their number stepping to the front. Joan felt her father's hand tighten on hers as the old, old words of the Requiem started to fill the church.

Requiem aeternam dona eis Domine
Et lux perpetua luceat eis.

Chapter Forty
Lady Knight

The day after the funeral Joan and Michelle were taking a walk around Domremy, stopping here and there to speak with old friends and neighbors who always invited them inside to offer their condolences as well as something to eat. By this time, Michelle was starting to say a few things in French other than Hello, Goodbye, My Name is Michelle, Thank you, I'm hungry, and Where is the toilet? Her Mandarin was a great help in fine tuning her ear for subtle details of pronunciation, but more than once Joan had to step in and help before Michelle said something like Thank you for the cow yesterday. It was helpful that when she got frustrated she could shift into Mandarin and vent, and when Joan once asked her what she had said Michelle just smiled.

During their walks, Michelle had asked a lot of questions so that she had a good idea of what was going to happen. As much as Michelle liked to talk, Joan knew that she was completely trustworthy in keeping secrets, not that anyone back in Smithfield would ever believe it anyway. Kids in high school come back from vacations with suntans and souvenirs all the time, but coming back with a knighthood is...well, different. What was making it more complicated was that Joan had asked if Michelle could be her Amicus, the special witness that every knight may request for the ceremony.

"It is highly unusual," said Miss Renoir, "but allowed. Does Michelle agree?"

"So far, so good," replied Joan, "if she knows what she is supposed to do. I trust her completely, and I'm going to need someone who has my back."

How exactly do you ask your best friend if she would like to be part of a six-hundred-year-old ceremony? Or maybe, how would you keep her away once she knew about it? Either way, it was a real stroke of luck that Michelle was Chinese and respected tradition so that she could appreciate this thing. It also didn't hurt that they were going to serve breakfast after the ceremony.

"Do you honestly think I'd turn this down?" Michelle asked. "I mean, I'll do it for you no matter what, you know that, but what do I tell my parents?"

"Papa talked to them and they said it was your decision," answered Joan. "He didn't exactly explain about the knighthood stuff, only that you were going to be a witness at a special religious ceremony."

"What about afterward?" asked Michelle. "I mean, do I have to bow to you or kneel or call you by some special name? I guess I could do that if I absolutely had to."

"There's only one thing you absolutely have to do, and it's something you do already," said Joan. "It's to be completely honest with me all the time."

"Like, to remind you not to take the last donut on the plate."

"Exactly."

"Or to tell you that you're not talking to me when you should."

"Exactly."

"Can you order me around?"

"No."

"Do you have to do everything I tell you?"

"No...Well, yes, as a matter of fact. If I know you're right, I have to listen."

Michelle beamed. "I'm in!"

When Joan had asked Miss Renoir how she was suddenly 'ready' for this thing, her answer helped it make more sense.

"There were three tests, Jeanne," said Miss Renoir. "The first test was to prove yourself truly unselfish and act in the interests of others. For you, this was the final championship bout with Eric where you still refused the trophy despite your being designated the official winner. The second test was to face real danger without backing down, which of course was your defense of Ryan. You have passed both tests, by far the youngest candidate to ever do so."

"You said three tests," Joan replied.

"The third was the truest indication of your readiness," said Miss Renoir. "In the heat of combat, you maintained enough presence of mind to show mercy."

Joan's face burned at the memory. "So, the thing is, I stabbed him but didn't stab him to death? Is that what you're talking about?"

"This is a hard thing, Jeanne, we know that," said Miss Renoir. "But let me ask you one question and you must promise me the truth, before God. Do you agree?" Joan nodded.

"After all of this happened, did you ever say a prayer for Mr. Todd?"

Joan bowed her head, remembering that afternoon in the Cathedral of Saint Louis with Papa. She put her hand up to her forehead and taking a deep breath, nodded.

Sir Joan

As was customary Joan spent the whole night in the Chapel, Michelle at her side, where they had talked until two o'clock. Knowing this was ahead of her, Joan had taken a long nap the afternoon before, so when Michelle finally fell asleep Joan was still alert and able to meditate on what was ahead. So many things went through her mind that night, from memories of Mama to the crowded five minutes in the Board Room, and it was infinitely comforting that she was in the church of her own baptism, where she could pray or light a candle or just sit and think.

The ceremony began at dawn. Joan was walking barefoot down the nave of the chapel, wearing a simple white robe and carrying a rosary in her hands. Michelle walked behind her, carrying a tall white candle and totally awestruck by the ceremony. Grandmother and Miss Renoir were standing in front of the altar, each holding a candle, and Madame Renoir, Papa, and Jacques were in the front pew. It was harder to see, but there were also two men in uniform standing in the shadows near the altar, their military decorations glinting in the candlelight.

As Joan and Michelle came to a stop, the Priest intoned a prayer, after which he stepped forward.

"Jeanne Darcy, do you make this commitment freely and without reservation?"

"I do," replied Joan.

Turning to Michelle, the Priest said: *"Will the Friend come forward?"* Joan had made sure to practice this with Michelle since the entire service was in French, so with a moment's hesitation, Michelle stepped forward to stand behind her as Joan knelt.

"In the Presence of God and these witnesses, repeat after me. I will never traffic with traitors."

"I will never traffic with traitors," replied Joan.

"I will never give bad counsel and be truthful in all things."

"I will never give bad counsel and be truthful in all things."

"I will protect the helpless though it cost me my life."

"I will protect the helpless though it cost me my life."

"And this I swear before God, the Virgin, and all the Saints of Heaven."

"And this I swear before God, the Virgin, and all the Saints of Heaven."

At this point, one of the uniformed men came forward, and Michelle saw that it was Grandpa Kershaw. His face was old but he was tall and imposing in his full-dress uniform with the twin decorations of the Congressional Medal of Honor and the Legion of Honor gleaming on his chest. The other uniformed man reached out to the altar, gently picked up a sword, and handed it to Grandpa Kershaw.

Turning to Joan, he lifted the sword and gently touched it to Joan's right shoulder, then lifted it over her head to touch her left shoulder in turn, then back to the right shoulder as he intoned the words, his Cajun French sibilant in the Chapel.

"I dub thee Knight in the name of the Father, the Son, and the Holy Ghost." He replaced the sword into its scabbard, and with two hands gave the sword to Joan who took it and kissed the hilt. "Go forth and do justice. Rise, Chevalière Jeanne."

Half an hour later they were in the grassy field outside the church where a large round table had been prepared, the aroma of fresh croissant, cheese, coffee, and raspberry preserves combining with the scent of apple blossoms to give everyone a good appetite. Joan was seated between Papa and Michelle, with Dwight and George next to Grandpa Kershaw at Grandmother's side and Papa sitting with Miss Renoir. When everyone finally sat down Miss Renoir introduced the other uniformed man who had been at the ceremony.

"Jeanne, this is Louis Alphonse, the Duke of Anjou," she said. "If France were still a monarchy, he would be the King and you would have been dubbed by him. Since France isn't a monarchy anymore, he's just plain Louis, an economist working for a bank."

"Congratulations, Jeanne," he said with a smile. "Oh, for the good old days."

"Times change, I guess," said Joan with a glint in her eye. "Very nice to meet you, Mr. Alphonse. Thanks for coming."

Although she was glad to see them, at first Joan was surprised that both Dwight and George were there with their Grandfather. Earlier that day he had taken her aside to assure her they knew nothing about that morning's ceremony.

"It's just that I've been telling that old war story of mine so many times since that dinner of ours, that these boys simply wore me out begging to show them where it all happened," said Grandpa. "As it is, we're sitting right on the spot where our tank stopped after that dash across the road." He turned to Joan's Grandmother who sat beaming next to him and leaned over to give her a gentle kiss on the cheek. "Thanks to this teenager, here."

"Got some news for you, Joan," said Dwight after they shared a hug. "Lots of things going on at home, and for a change, it's all good news, too."

"It's about time," said Joan with a sigh of relief. It would be nice to have one day – just one! – Where all the news was good. "What's happening?"

"Looks like Christine got her scholarship after all – well, not exactly a scholarship, but she's going to be an assistant volleyball and basketball coach at Smithfield College. Seems like they're excited that Christine will be able to show them all about that analysis stuff she was doing before her accident. She may even write a book or something about it, too."

Joan felt a surge of joy for Christine. Not only would she have a real career doing something she loved, but she would finally be able to get the college education she longed for.

"Brian texted me this morning that they released Coach Reed from prison yesterday," said George excitedly. "And Mrs. Coates rehired Mr. Landry so there will be a real band next year. On our way to the airport, we stopped by the school and saw that Ryan was helping to unload a truck full of brand new band uniforms. He already has his picked out – and you'll never guess what his job is going to be."

Michelle and Joan looked at each other, then back at George. "Drum Major?" they said in unison.

"You're no fun," replied George.

An hour later the brunch was over, the table and chairs put away, Grandpa Kershaw had gone off with Dwight and George on a day trip to Bastogne while Joan and the rest of the group went back into the church. After they removed the flowers from the pews, they were carried over to Mama's grave and in a few minutes the mound of earth was covered in flowers, white petals fluttering in the midday breeze.

After leaving the cemetery Joan led the group down to the banks of the Meuse River where an old, old path meandered along the pastures and little clumps of

ancient willows, the rustling of their long, slender branches blending with the cheerful gurgling of the river. As usual Grandmother and Madame Renoir had their heads together, and Michelle was up ahead walking, smiling and swinging her arms. Papa was walking further ahead, and to Joan's surprise he caught up with Miss Renoir and was walking hand in hand with her. About time, thought Joan with a smile, surprised it hadn't happened sooner.

As always, many others were also out walking on that spectacular day - teenagers holding hands, cheerful old men escorting cheerful old ladies, and especially young mothers trying to keep restless children in tow. Under one particularly large willow, a tiny girl with black hair had snapped off one of the branches and was chasing her mother who ran laughing ahead. Joan stopped to watch for a moment, the child's laughter infectious as the mother finally caught up with her.

"Can I ride?" asked the little girl, whereupon the mother lifted her neatly, turned her around, and plopped her onto her shoulders, the girl giggling with pleasure the whole time.

"Can I ride up here the whole way home?"

"Yes, Cherie.'

"Promise?"

"I promise," replied the mother.

And with those simple words Joan remembered another spring day not that long ago, under a graceful old willow where another young mother had taken her daughter, a green branch waving in the dappled sunlight, a promise asked and given.

The End

Afterword

The story is set on the Texas/Louisiana border, an area in which numerous French-Canadian immigrants settled after being expelled from British Canada at the time of the French and Indian war. Known as Cajuns, the majority settled in the area immediately around New Orleans but many also pressed further west and beyond the border into Texas where their communities continue to this day.

Domremy la Pucelle is a real village on the border of Alsace next to the Meuse River. This area was a scene of the rapid advance of American forces in the late summer of 1944, with the Germans stiffening their resistance through a combination of retreat and rear guard action. Numerous Americans were awarded the Legion of Honor, including the actor Charles Durning, Audie Murphy, and singer Marlene Dietrich. The character of Grandpa Kershaw is a composite of French-speaking Cajun soldiers serving in France during the liberation of 1944-45.

High School fencing exists within the United States primarily among private schools or in much larger schools able to support a team. It is rare but not unheard of for boys and girls to compete against each other, but there is no current official tournament system that would have a boy pitted against a girl. This is wishful thinking on my part, although there are many girl champions who would win if given the opportunity.

Invictus
By Williams Earnest Henley

Out of the night that covers me,
Black as the pit from pole to pole,
I thank whatever gods may be
For my unconquerable soul.

In the fell clutch of circumstance
I have not winced nor cried aloud.
Under the bludgeoning of chance
My head is bloody, but unbowed.

Beyond this place of wrath and tears
Looms but the Horror of the shade,
And yet the menace of the years
Finds, and shall find me, unafraid.

It matters not how strait the gate,
How charged with punishments the scroll,
I am the master of my fate:
I am the captain of my soul.